SPANISH ROCK

By the same author

ANOTHER DAY, ANOTHER JACKAL

END AS AN ASSASSIN
– Andre Warner, Manhunter Vol I

I KILL
– Andre Warner, Manhunter Vol II

THE MAN WHO HUNTED HIMSELF
– Andre Warner, Manhunter Vol III

REACTION OF THE TIGER
– Andre Warner, Manhunter Vol IV

SHE KILLS
– Lisa Power, Vigilante

SPANISH ROCK

ANDRÉ WARNER, MANHUNTER – Volume V

LEX LANDER

Kaybec Publishing

Published in 2019 by Kaybec Publishing
441 Avenue President Kennedy
Suite 1003
Montreal
Québec
H3A 0A4

www.kaybecpublishing.com

ISBN: 978-1-989030-06-6 (Paperback)
ISBN: 978-1-989030-08-0 (mobi)
ISBN: 978-1-989030-07-3 (epub)

Printed and bound by Createspace

I

ENGLAND HATH NEED OF THEE …

Chapter One

Cassandra screamed.

The oncoming headlights flared across the windshield, brighter than the sun, whitewashing the interior of the Aston and erasing the night. At a closing speed of 100mph or more we were only seconds from impact.

Noise hammered at me: Cassandra squealing, the bellow of the oncoming car's horn, the wailing protest of the tyres as I instinctively trod brake, making the car judder as if it were travelling on a badly-maintained cobbled street.

Then the glare was gone, wiped away, the lights ripping past on our left as the other driver took to the wrong side of the road to avoid a head-on smash and its probably fatal outcome. The Aston crunched onto the shoulder and came to a stop, canted over like a beached ship, offside wheels in a shallow ditch. In the rear-view mirror, twin pinpoints of red oscillated crazily, then stabilised before dwindling finally to nothingness.

Cassandra's scream tapered to a whimper and the music from the CD player became audible once more – a piece from Chopin by the New York Philharmonic. Bizarre what trivia lodges in your mind after a near-death experience.

I sucked oxygen into deflated lungs. It was heady stuff. Cassandra sat limp as a discarded rag doll, her face skeletal in the dashboard lights. I killed the CD; I was a classical *aficionado* but I hadn't been able to appreciate it anyhow, not with the vocal competition from Cassandra.

I wasn't drunk, or even near it. Two glasses of a dry and too-long-in-the-bottle white wine were all my stomach contained. No, the cause of my being where I had no right to be lay not in alcohol, nor even in my forgetting I wasn't in a country where driving on the right held sway, but in the heated exchange between Cassandra and me. Verbal abuse, distracting enough on its own, had degenerated into assault; Cassandra lashing out with her bag, causing me to jerk sideways to avoid it, inadvertently wrenching the steering wheel over, losing control …

Strands of mist writhed in the headlight beams. The engine throbbed, a mechanical heartbeat. For safety's sake I should be making haste back to my own side of the road, but traffic was sparse on this little-used shortcut between Beaconsfield and Cassandra's house, and I needed a moratorium, needed to regroup my wits.

The after-effects of shock might have been expected to put a stop to the slanging, even flung us into a reconciliatory embrace. But no such romantic notions for Cassandra this night. Our three-month diversion had run into a cul-de-sac. She was too spoiled, too rich, too used to getting her own way. The bedtime romps didn't quite compensate for the daytime brawls.

She stirred. Without looking at me she said slowly, every syllable precisely pronounced, 'It's over, André. Sincere apologies and all that. I've met someone else more to my taste.' More accommodating of her brattishness, was my guess. 'So let's stop pretending there's a core of goodwill to rebuild on. It's an illusion.' Her eyes swivelled towards me, glinting with tears. 'What I need you can't provide, and vice-versa. Okay?'

It was more or less okay. It had never been love between us, just a physical pull of the kind that usually burns itself out once the novelty has ceased to be novel.

'Sure,' I said, forcing off-handedness into my voice. Or maybe I didn't have to force it. 'You're right, honey. You go your sweet way, I'll go mine. Just like it was before we met.'

I gunned the engine and, offside wheels skidding a little in the ditch, gingerly guided my precious heap of metal back onto the road.

* * * * *

The Giovanni Paolo Hospital in Venice had done a fine job of digging the two bullets – 9mm calibre – out of my tender flesh and patching me up inside and out. Damage to my left lung had been superficial and would cause no long term issues, I was assured in halting English.

The surgeon had been skilful and careful, the nurses caring and attentive, and the bill astronomical. They restored me to my former functionality and got me fit again. Liza came to visit at least once a day, and sat with me for hours. Through the open window came the sounds of birds chirping and vaporetti chugging. If Liza had been the love of my life, it would have been near-perfect.

'*Now* will you retire?' she demanded, the afternoon of the monthly anniversary of my admission to the hospital.

'I keep trying,' I countered. 'But the dark forces won't let me.'

That didn't spook her at all. Not much did.

'Simple solution.'

I regarded her with a degree of circumspection. This girl, who had risked so much to track me down to proclaim her love. This girl, who had become a woman too quickly and been spoiled in the process. Not physically – her loveliness, though superficially marred, was intact, the rest of her blooming as ever. It was inside her head where the damage had been done. Where the sickness still festered. Not in an obvious way: she talked and behaved much as any girl not yet twenty-one would talk. But her outlook on the world was warped by the hurt and degradation she had endured at too-tender an age.

'A simple solution, eh?' I said.

'Sure. Eliminate the dark forces.'

* * * * *

In the end I persuaded her by subterfuge that she should take off and visit her mother in Massachusetts. It was on the day they told me I could check out next morning. When Liza showed up at about eleven, I pretended to her that I would be kept in hospital for another week at least.

'A week! Is there something wrong you're not telling me?'

I gave her hand a reassuring squeeze. 'Nothing like that. The doc said there would be risk of complications if I left prematurely, is all.'

She didn't argue. She most likely figured that any objection on her part would make it sound as if my health didn't matter. Accepting the bogus ruling with an ill grace, she was still resistant to my suggestion that she drop in on her ma. Any separation from me was as welcome to her as the curse. But she had a sense of duty, and conceded that she would have to go sooner or later, and that it might as well be now, while I was confined to a bed.

Because it was our last meet-up, and maybe destined to be a permanent farewell, I remember with the clarity of crystal how she looked that morning. Her tawny hair was long and loose, almost down to her waist. Her grey eyes, devoid of enhancement, her mouth a perfect combo of lips and teeth, her body exquisite in the dark blue crop top and white shorts; skimpy but not brazen. Just right for the climate. She would have been easy to love as a lover. Instead I loved her mostly as a daughter. Couldn't help it. Our history, back when she was in my care, when we lived together in my house in Andorra, was too rooted in my memory. It couldn't be dislodged. Not that I hadn't tried.

'I'll skype every day,' she promised. 'Make sure you're available.'

'You bet.' I hoped my enthusiasm didn't sound as fake as my excuses.

We kissed. Lips to lips, with her trying to make it a full-on job, and me trying to respond with restraint. I felt bad about the deception.

Next morning, as I dressed, still a bit shaky, she called me on WhatsApp video, with Venice airport bustling in the background. She looked happy enough, which I was glad about. We would be parting on a high. It would only last on her side for as long as it took to find me out in my lies. Forgiveness was likely to be slow in coming.

A flight was announced over the speaker system. It was hers. We exchanged multiple goodbyes and blown kisses, then the screen went abruptly blank.

Within the hour I was in a cab, en route to Mestre collect a Hertz rental. From Mestre it would be a fast haul on the *autostrada* across the Po Plain to Ventimiglia and France. Alone again, but at least alive. For the present.

* * * * *

Now here I was, back to being alone unless you counted the staff in Cassandra's stately home, Waverley Hall. Big enough to house a jumbo jet. It had been my home too, since I moved in at the peak of the rutting season, a couple of months back. The squatter's rights granted by Cassandra had now been foreclosed. It wasn't in writing; it didn't need to be.

My relationship with her had been what is known as "open". If either of us felt inclined to wander, we were allowed a slack rein. No deception, no apologies. Uncommonly, I hadn't once felt the urge. She, on the other hand, was on permanent heat. Her sexual demands exceeded the capacity of mine, leaving nothing in reserve for chasing other opportunities.

When it began to go bad on us, easy-come easy-go degenerated into bickering which led to flaming rows and slammed doors and abuse and deadening recriminations. Culminating in that first show of violence between us in the car, marking the end of the sham our co-habitation of convenience had become.

Something soft and warm brushed against my leg, mewing imperatively. I reached down absently and tickled the receptive chin of Simba, Cassandra's Burmese cat, all the while staring out through the tall window at the line of elms, unscathed by the disease that had all but obliterated the species from the land. Long denuded of foliage, they did nothing to relieve the dreary skies of December in England.

In some respects I would miss Waverley. It had been a short stay, but fun while it lasted, and being waited on by the staff had not been a disagreeable experience. To them, no doubt, I was just a grubby freeloader.

Over the great Regency fireplace with its marble surround was a study in oils of Cassandra, commissioned, so she told me, on her thirty-third birthday. It depicted her at her magnificent best, in an eighteenth century ball gown, a style that might well have been created for her figure – low cut at the front, a hint of shadow between her well-defined breasts, nipped-in at the waist, flaring at the hips in an exaggeration of Cassandra's own rounded form. Her skin was pale, her hair naturally ash blond, sweeping her bare shoulders. Her blue eyes were haughty, in keeping with the manner she was prone to adopt with anyone she perceived as her social inferior. To describe her as beautiful, even sensational, was to miss the point. Cassandra was a woman on whom superlatives were wasted.

I lifted my glass to her. It was empty but that was somehow apt.

'Here's to you, bedmate.'

The arched eyebrows seemed to mock me, the eyes to glint with scorn. I weighed the chunky glass in my hand, debated whether to let her have it full in her luscious kisser.

Then the telephone rang and I shrugged off such pettiness. The library extension was on a pert little accent table by my elbow, which enabled me to lift the receiver ahead of the butler.

It was Tobias Wyatt, older brother of Cassandra by twelve years, known to family and friend alike as Toby. For me, the name Toby always evoked visions of jolly little fat men in tricorn hats. Not so this Toby, who was uber-tall and built to last.

'Hello there, old bean.' He really did talk exactly like that. To my surprise, considering my socialist-inclined views on inherited wealth, he and I had hit it off from the get-go.

'Hi, Toby,' I said flatly.

'Hoped I'd catch you in. Fact is, we're throwing a binge on Saturday and thought you might care to grace it with your ungraceful presence.'

'How could I refuse such a flattering invitation. Who thought – you or Sam?'

An impatient snort. 'Does it matter?' Pause. 'Sam, as it happens. She's developed rather a soft spot for you.'

Tall, svelte, energetic Samantha had once demonstrated how soft was that spot by dragging me down onto a bedful of coats – mostly fur, of course – at some West End shindig a few weeks ago. It was her long legs I remembered best of all, and the white self-support stockings that set them, and me, off. Since then, whenever her name came up, I had this vision of elasticised stocking tops and twin pillars of pale thigh emerging from them. We didn't consummate the act, mostly because she was too smashed and I had too much liking and respect for Toby.

'It's mutual.'

'Saturday then?' Toby prompted.

'Are you sure you really want me there? You do realise Cassandra and I are no longer an item.'

Toby sighed. He could sigh very forcefully.

'André, don't be so damned tiresome. We enjoy your company with or without Cassie. We might even be able to sneak away for a game. You owe me a chance to get even.'

He was talking about chess. We had played a couple of games, and I had beaten him twice.

'Is Cassandra on the guest list?'

'You need not fear. She was, but declined. So we can count on you?'

I grunted an affirmative.

'Any time after eight,' he said briskly. 'Dress informal.' Which meant lounge suits, not jeans and a Stuff-the-World T-shirt. 'There'll be a running buffet, so come hungry.'

'I'll look forward to it.'

'Good.' No gush, just warmth. Just pleasure. In time, Toby could probably become a true friend if I kept the contact going post-Cassandra.

From the telephone I turned back to her portrait.

'You see,' I jeered at it. 'Somebody in your lousy family still loves me. How does that grab you?'

The eyebrows remained as aloof as ever and the derisive glint was undimmed. If anything it glowed brighter, as if she were saying, 'So what? Toby was always a poor judge of character.'

Against Cassandra I don't think I would ever have been able to win. Except by walking out on her, and she had even denied me that small triumph by doing the walking herself. Leaving me in possession of Waverley – a transitory monarch under notice to quit. Three days' notice, to be precise.

I collected my parka from the stand in the hall and went outside. I strolled down the gravel path, past the stone arch where Cassandra and I had made drunken love one evening the day I moved in. The halcyon days.

Whatever there had once been here for me at Waverley was no more. It had fled with my paramour, beyond recall or rekindling. The house was just a house, the garden just a garden, and my life once more stretched ahead, barren and pointless.

* * * * *

My only sister, Julia, was in town with her Scots husband, Willie, CEO of the London division of a US computer outfit. Julia was very blonde like me, blue-eyed like me, and inclined to mother me, though she was a couple of years younger. Willie was of medium build, very fit, and prone to beat me at squash, snooker, and chess.

Since Cassandra entered my life we had made up a few foursomes, usually dining at the Travellers Club, in Pall Mall. This occasion we were down to a threesome. They were sympathetic, supportive.

'Maybe you can still patch it up,' Julia said, in her rather drawly home counties voice.

'Not a hope.' I was trying to stay upbeat so as not to spoil the evening.

'So live a little,' pragmatic Willie said. 'Go back to playing the field.'

Julia swirled cognac around her balloon glass. 'Maybe André doesn't want to. Maybe he's still in love with Cassandra.'

Willie grimaced. 'Are ye?'

'Uh-uh. I was never in love in the first place. It was a collision of over-active hormones.'

He tittered into his wine glass; Julia clucked reproof. She could be maiden-auntish about topics scabrous.

'He's in love with Maura,' she said primly, then as an afterthought, 'or Liza.'

'The former,' I confirmed. 'But it's not getting me anywhere.'

'Cannae think why,' Willie said.

Because she doesn't agree with my killing people for a living, was the explanation that dared not speak its name.

'The trouble with you, André,' Julia said, in the kind of tone that warned me a sisterly lecture was due to be delivered, 'is that women come too easy to you. You have the looks of a movie star and that attracts women, I'm sorry to say, because they ought to be more interested in what's behind those looks. In my experience, men who are really good looking are vain, spoiled, and self-centred, not to mention sexual predators.'

Was that me she was describing? Once upon a time, maybe. Nowadays less so.

'Until you know a person, looks are the only thing on show.'

'How true, brother dear. But the type of man I've just described almost always come across as vain, spoiled, etcetera from the get-go. That's the time to pull back, take stock and, in most cases, get the hell out.'

'Same goes for women,' Willie said, grinning so as to take the sting out of it. 'The vain spoiled part, I mean.'

Julia had been his wife too long to be offended. 'That's true too, darling, but women are generally *expected* to be more shallow and self-obsessed, so it's not such a huge issue.'

Willie guffawed, turning heads in the vicinity. 'Guid job *I* didn't say that. I'd be lynched by the MeToo crowd.'

Julia's homily had me pondering. My looks had indeed served me well in the female attraction department. Too well on occasion. Women I met often hung a 'very good looking' tag on me unasked and unwanted. Having heard it so often and *ad nauseum*, at least it had convinced me I wasn't repulsive.

'Speaking of Liza,' I said, to steer the subject away from me and my looks, 'did she phone again?'

'And again, and again. And came in person last week, to see if I was lying about your not staying with us.'

My guilt about taking off and leaving no contact details plagued me still. I had sent a goodbye text but declined to read, let alone answer, her increasingly frustrated texts and emails to me. The calls I just muted.

'Sorry about that.'

'No need to be. I like her. *We* like her...' Willie's head bobbed assent '... but there's something not quite ... right with her, isn't there?'

I grunted. 'That's a diplomatic way of putting it.'

I didn't elaborate and she let it drop, moved on to a subject that had long been dear to her heart, namely settling me down with a respectable woman, preferably of my own age.

'Come and stay with us for Christmas?' was her next suggestion. 'There's a very nice widow living next door. We could introduce you.'

Some introduction. This is my brother. He's free of baggage. Just fifty-odd corpses that would be walking around today if it weren't for him.

'I'll think about it. I'm staying at the Connaught at the moment. I'll probably spend Christmas in Spain.' Conscious of sounding churlish, I touched her forearm. 'Thanks for the offer.'

Julia was getting restive. I recognised the signs – she needed a smoke. I signalled a waiter to bring the check.

Julia and Willie started to speak together. Ever the gentleman, Willie backed off and left the floor to her.

'Why not go on a cruise, Drew?' she said.

'Give me a break. A little while ago you suggested I fall out of love. Exactly how do you do that?'

'How do you fall out of love?' Julia checked them off on her fingers: 'There's no magic potion. You just fill every waking hour with activity. You impose on your friends and family to the point of pissing them off. You never sleep alone. You find a good cause to get involved in.' She paused, threw me an engaging grin. 'That do, darling?'

'Yeah, for starters.' I leaned across the table and kissed her cheek. She smelled of lilac. 'It's a pity you're my sister, otherwise Willie and I might fall out over who takes you home tonight.'

She pretended shock, smacked the back of my hand. 'You're a *bad* boy to have such evil thoughts.'

'Any port in a storm,' was Willie's airy contribution, which earned him a glare that would have burned a hole in sheet metal.

* * * * *

The door of Toby's Belgrave Square flat had grown a peephole since my last visit. A concession no doubt to the increasing number of break-ins in the district, often accompanied by acts of violence towards the occupant. Toby, mildly complacent, had at last conceded that if his home was to remain his castle it needed to be done up like a fortress.

Music – a plodding piano – wafted out past me with the opening of the door. Toby's live-in maid, a pretty thing with a vacant expression that belied a sharp wit, let me in.

'Oh, it's you, Mr Warner,' she cooed in an Eliza Doolittle take-off, making humming bird's wings of her eyelashes. ''Ow nice to see you, I'm sure.'

'And you … er …' What was the girl's goddam name?

'Victoria. Fancy you remembering. I *am* flattered.'

I grinned crookedly and proceeded down the narrow hallway into the vast sitting room, source of the festivities.

'André – *darling*!' Sam, always an exemplary hostess on the alert for newcomers, lunged towards me through the islands of threes and fours that people invariably form at these events.

'How lovely to see you!' She pressed her warm cheek to mine – in heels she was almost my height, so I wasn't required to stoop. Her auburn hair was prickly, like wire wool.

'You're looking marvellous!' I said, and in her case it wasn't just flattery. Her dress was full length and glossy as polished armour, a blend of colours that swam together like oil on water. It was loose, disguising her shape, which was a shame. For her fortyish years she was well-preserved.

'You can pour your smooth-tongued balm over me later, if you must. In fact, I insist. But first a drink for the poor homeless, abandoned waif.'

A gin and tonic was summoned, a little too heavy on the hard stuff for drink and drive laws. I resolved to sip rather than gulp.

Sam, catching and interpreting my frown, said, 'Stay the night if you're troubled by plastic bags and green crystals and all that nonsense.'

'They don't have those anymore,' I said absently. 'It's a little computer gadget now. But I might take you up on the invite anyway – get rid of Toby and let's make a proper night of it.'

'Naughty, naughty,' she said, adept at fielding risqué quips. 'Now ...' She jutted her chin, a bird-like movement that exposed some unflattering creases under her jaw, and cast about the room. 'Where's Toby got to?'

A good forty souls were gathered about us, mostly middle-aged and rising. My own younger set – forties, ha-ha – was not well represented. Toby's parties were a far cry from the frenzied splurges of his Belgravia contemporaries, affairs that were calculated to kill, cure, or infect, depending on your chosen pleasure. The music was low-key and high-brow, a background to sober discourse. Later, it would be pepped up.

The room was long and L-shaped and normally cluttered with restored Regency furniture and knick-knacks. Much of the former had been shunted aside to create an area in which people might congregate into their inevitable cliques and name-drop, name-swap, and dissect Brexit and Donald Trump's suitability as leader of the free world.

Sam had spotted her husband, not too difficult since he stood half-a-head taller than the others in his immediate circle. She lugged me off his-away, weaving skilfully through the clearings.

'Aren't you going to introduce me to anyone?' I said, feeling like a railway carriage hooked up to a runaway locomotive. Some of the faces were familiar, most were not. Toby tended to rub shoulders with a different stratum of society from Cassandra – staider, more sober society. He was a career diplomat with the Home Office, quite high level according to hearsay, though he pretended otherwise. Cassandra cultivated the young and hip, though her qualifications for membership of that cult were becoming marginal.

'Toby will take care of all that,' Sam said, half-turning and promptly running into a tippling male guest, slopping his drink. 'Oh, Charles, how clumsy of me ...' And 'Charles', roly-poly, florid complexion, replying with a chortle, 'Think nothing of it, m'dear. Any excuse for a refill, what?' He patted her behind as she charged on, her grip on me as tight as ever. Then we came to our terminus, and Toby was towering over me, reducing my six feet one to the comparative stature of a circus midget. He drew me inside the exclusively male congregation he had assembled. Sam melted away behind a spate of blown kisses. She knew her place. Or acted as if she did.

'André, so good to see you. How are you? Have you met the Hon. James Pelligrew? James ... André Warner, a friend of Cassandra's. Ex-friend, I should say.' A ripple of amusement. 'André ... Robert Ludlow ... Lord Swanley ... Trevor Robinson ...' Nods, handshakes, the usual murmured bromides. All were strangers to me, although Robinson I knew by sight and repute as a self-made plutocrat, risen from the unswept gutters of Bermondsey. The sort of go-getting, wealth-generating IT baron that Toby was mixing with of late. Seeing the breed perhaps as the backbone of Britain in an EU-free zone, powers-to-be in the land.

When I next glanced at my watch it was already after eleven. Apart from Sam I hadn't conversed with a single female the whole evening, possibly a personal record. I decided to circulate. Toby was lecturing the shifty-looking Editor of the *Guardian* about the need for more restraint in reporting on people's private lives (a subject dear to him), and I was able to slip away unnoticed. Except by the woman into whom I reversed.

'Excuse me,' she said, in a Transatlantic twang as alien in this gathering as a dog's bark in a home for stray cats. It made me feel a little less lonesome.

'Entirely my fault.'

As women go she was far removed from my type: a plumage of brassy blonde that could only be fake, a good fifteen years my senior, buxom and broad of hip. But she was new company.

'You're American?' I said, for something to say.

'In one. Don't exactly sound like a Brit yourself.'

'Transatlantic. Anglo-Canadian, to be specific. You live here?'

'For the time being.' She held out her hand to be shaken. Her nails were silver-painted and too long for natural growth. Her grip was as firm as a man's. 'Rosalie Pridham.'

I winced inwardly at the 'Rosalie'.

'Warner. André Warner.'

'Like the movie company, eh.'

I nodded.

'Well, it's a pleasure to make your acquaintance. And what's a tall, blue eyed, blond haired, handsome Transatlantic male doing here all on his ownsome? If I wasn't burdened with my other half … ah, God dammit, here he is in the flesh. Allow me to present my incredibly boring husband.'

A lofty, spare, bespectacled man – the physical flip-side of his wife – eased into the gap between us. Unsmiling, though there was humour in the hazel eyes with crow's feet at their extremities, magnified by horn-rim glasses. His grey hair was cut *en brosse*.

Rosalie did the introductions.

'Hi, André,' her husband said laconically, instantly informal in true North American tradition.

'Hi, Dave. Are you a friend of the family?'

'Professional acquaintance.' He sipped from the glass of wine in his fist. 'You?'

'The same. How long have you lived in the UK?'

'For the last four years.' This from Rosalie. 'My husband is something at the Embassy. Not sure what.'

The music, some dreamy sonata, was abruptly cut off. I exchanged enquiring eyebrows with my companions. Conversation around us dried up as if in expectation of some announcement along the lines of 'We interrupt this programme ...' Then a thudding beat boomed from the speakers, grossly over-amplified, was hastily lowered. A space opened up in the centre of the block floor and some of the less geriatric couples began to gyrate.

'About time too,' Rosalie Pridham grumbled. 'I've been dying for a jive all evening. C'mon, André.'

She whisked me away before I could dig in my heels, her complaisant spouse taking charge of our drinks.

She had a sight more energy than women her age and shape usually generate. After three hectic numbers I was starting to feel all my forty-plus years while she, barefooted, having kicked her shoes into orbit, was still full of bounce.

'Once more then,' I agreed, 'then I'm done.'

We whirled off to the metallic outpourings of Beyoncé.

Dave Pridham was tucking into a plateful of calorie-loaded pastries when we rejoined him. He commiserated.

'Sure am grateful, André. My wife can go on like that all night long and if there's no other willing sucker within grabbing range, I get to do the partnering.'

'You poor decrepit thing!' Rosalie extracted a cigarette from a hammer-finish case on the buffet table. Dave lit it for her from a book of matches bearing the "Annabel's" logo.

'Another of my vices,' she said dismissively, funnelling smoke at me. 'Helps pass the boring time. Tell me, André, do you find time boring?'

'From time to time,' I punned.

She snorted and smoke puffed from her nostrils. It stank like a joint.

'You married?' she said.

'Not right now.'

'So you were once?'

Dave Pridham didn't seem disturbed by his wife's nosiness. Developed an immunity to it, I expect.

'Way back when.'

'You'd make a great spy judging by how much you don't give away,' Rosalie said with a yelping laugh. She flicked ash indiscriminately. Some of it landed on the broad lapels of her husband's immaculate lightweight suit. He made a hole in the corner of his mouth and blew it off.

'Any kids?'

'Nope. Someday maybe.'

She glanced at her husband. 'Talk about economy of speech. Maybe you should give this guy a job. You could lay off a coupla dozen of those nattering old women you keep in idle luxury at the Embassy.'

He expressed faint mirth.

Her brusque, outspoken style didn't put me off, though it's a North American trait some Brits can't abide. For me, being a half-breed, it was close to home.

'Do you have any children?' I asked, just making polite conversation.

It was Dave who answered. 'We have a daughter – Linda. Or we *think* we have.'

I said nothing. Simply left a conversational void in which he could elaborate or change the subject as he saw fit.

'She went to live in Spain two years ago,' Rosalie said, no longer bantering.

'She's … er … grown-up then.'

'Sure.' Dave again. 'Twenty-eight, rising twenty-nine. And verrry independent.'

Some semi-drunk reeled into our midst – slack-jawed, hiccuping, tie askew.

'Saw you dancing just now,' he burped at Rosalie. 'Terr .. hic.. ific. Want some more?'

Rosalie smiled brightly into the drunken face. Diplomatic responses were second nature to a diplomat's wife.

'Sure, Bozo, why not?' She donated her lipstick-tipped cigarette to Dave and hauled the semi-drunk away to the dancing zone, now the most popular part of the room. While Dave was disposing of the cigarette, I looked around for Toby, sighted the back of his well-groomed head chairing another debating society. Talking was his favourite pursuit.

'What does your daughter do in Spain?' I asked Dave. 'Work for the Embassy?'

'Worked, past tense. I fixed her up with a job there, but she quit after a year and moved down to Malaga to join some travel outfit. Then she left that job, oh, three months back. Since then …' A spread-hands gesture, a mix of bafflement and frustration. 'Not a word. She doesn't answer her cell. No texts, no emails. We have an address for her, even wrote a letter. Never heard back. We've made enquiries, informed the police, hired a private dick. She moved out, no forwarding address.' He shrugged again, his distress all too apparent. 'Get the picture?'

I clicked my tongue in sympathy and made ready to move on to subjects new.

'She's our only daughter,' he said, forestalling me. 'Naturally we're worrying ourselves crazy about her.'

It's said that the Devil makes work for idle hands. Right then he was busy making some for me.

'I keep a boat at Sitges. Been thinking of cruising down the coast to Gib, probably over Christmas. If you like, I'll stop off at Malaga and check out her address. At the very least, I could stir the police up a bit.'

It was the sort of gesture you make just to be friendly, on the same level as inviting people you dislike to come to dinner 'sometime'. You don't expect to be held to account over it. A miscalculation in this case, as he almost pounced on me, his hand gripping my arm, fingers pinching the flesh.

'Would you do that, André?' He blinked behind his horn rims. 'Truly?'

'Be a pleasure.' His eager, even desperate acceptance of my offer caught me wrong-footed. Backing out wasn't an option, so I took out my cell phone. 'Linda Pridham – right?' I entered the name on the contacts page. 'What's the address?'

Reading from a pocket diary with the US Great Seal embossed on the front, he spelled it out – Calle Hinojo, 14B, Fuengirola. South of Malaga. I tapped it out dutifully, plus her cell phone number and email address. For good measure we exchanged our own cell numbers too.

'We've a good likeness of her at home, a studio portrait, taken just before she left for Spain. I'll mail it to you tomorrow.'

'Great idea.' Much relieved, I stowed the diary away. By morning he would have forgotten he ever met me.

'Give me your address, will you, André?'

Then again, maybe he wouldn't.

* * * * *

He didn't, God-damn it.

A postcard-size colour print turned up in my letter slot at the Connaught two mornings later, together with a short covering letter which read:

Dear André,

Rosie and I were glad to meet you at Toby Wyatt's the other night. I enclose the most recent likeness we have of Linda.

We would like to take you up on your generous offer to enquire after her whilst you're in Spain.

Meanwhile, we're giving a cocktail party Thursday next, 11am. Come along if you can.

Yours in gratitude

Dave and Rosalie Pridham.

The address was W1, same as the Connaught. Walking distance.

The "likeness" was a professional job and top quality. Even allowing for the certainty that it had been selected as the most flattering of a bunch of similar studies, Linda Pridham was worth an enquiry or two. Dark brown hair, bit of a kink, and on the short side, like the man said. Pronounced cheekbones underscored eyes that would always laugh no matter what the mouth was doing. Colouring pale, verging on pallid, but it suited her the way it suited Cassandra, darkening her hair and the eyebrows that kinked like a dog's hind leg, and reddening her lips. She looked happy, vivid, full of spirit. Wilful.

I slid the print inside my wallet. The letter I shoved in a pocket inside the lid of one of my suitcases. The invitation to cocktails I forgot.

Two days later the Aston and I were on a ferry to Spain.

Chapter Two

'Is this a buying expedition or a bar crawl?' I grunted as we exchanged the heat of a noisy, smelly, overcrowded bar for the heat of a noisy, smelly, overcrowded street.

Baynes raised his limp, wide-brimmed hat and mopped at the hairless dome beneath with a sodden handkerchief.

'Just combining business with pleasure.'

Shielding my eyes from the burning sun, I peered at the surrounding buildings. This was not the most salubrious part of the resort of Fuengirola. The sea was less than a half a kilometre away, but might as well have been on the far side of the planet: high-rise blocks segregated it from this part of town as effectively as a prison wall. Nor was the concrete outlook uplifted by the graffiti that scarred much of it. Between second and third floor windows of a building opposite a message in faded red letters half a metre tall eclipsed all others:

JUAN CARLOS – EL JEFÉ DE LOS PUTAÑEROS!

'Juan Carlos?' I glanced at Baynes. 'Is that the ex-king?'

'I can't think of another one famous enough to get his name in graffiti.'

'What's the accolade? Looks like chief of something.'

His lips gave a risible twitch.

'The chief of the pimps.'

'Not very complimentary. Why so?'

'Somebody didn't like him?' Baynes postulated, fanning his red face with the hat. 'Anyhow, he's gone and now we have King Felipe.'

We were finely balanced on the edge of the curb, swaying a little like a pair of drunks undecided which way to fall. Traffic, mostly with non-Spanish plates, chugged past in a haze of poisonous fumes. Even in January with Christmas gone and the Spanish Three Kings Day to come, tourists were as numerous as ants in a colony. Spain was enjoying its hottest start to the year in living memory.

'Where next?' I said wearily.

Baynes belched discreetly, consequence of too many gassy Spanish beers.

'Well, there's the Alcazar. But that's even more wrong side of the tracks, I'm afraid.'

I plucked my sweat-damp shorts free of my crotch. 'I'm not exactly impressed so far, you know, Colin.'

'I don't dictate the market prices. If you could go to a million, say ...'

'I could, but I won't.' Half-a-million euros was plenty for a wild, ill-thought-out scheme to put down roots by buying a bar.

He shrugged unhappily. Like all his breed he was anxious to make a deal, preferably a lucrative one, but any deal beat none at all. The way things were shaping up though, no deal was the increasingly probable outcome of this fiasco.

To give Colin Baynes his due, he had put a lot of effort into our bar hunt. We had inspected fourteen in two days. None had appealed to me, mostly on account of their downscale locations. Some were clearly not well-patronised. If the best a Spanish bar in a tourist resort can muster mid-evening is a trio of gnarled cardsharps, it's a sure sign of some underlying malady. Baynes tended to be dismissive of empty bars, pointing out that we were in the low season.

As we stood by the roadside he unfolded a much-folded list and studied it. I waved away fumes from a leaky exhaust. Passers-by jostled us good-naturedly and the list fluttered to earth, became impaled on the spiky heel of an African girl with braided hair. Baynes rushed after her.

'For God's sake ...' I growled, the combination of heat and bar-hunt fatigue straining my temper.

The list now had a tear in it and a footprint across the top half.

'We could try the Corregidor,' Baynes said doubtfully.

'I've a better idea – let's call it a day.'

His relief was as naked as the sun worshippers on the naturist beach on the south side of town.

'A beer before you go?' he proposed.

'Haven't you had enough? My bladder is stocked up until the end of next week.' I patted his shoulder. His shirt was damp, the original dark patches under the armpits having spread like fungus over the back of the garment. 'We'll meet up tomorrow. Ten o'clock suit you?'

'Whenever you say, Mr Warner.'

The rented BMW was parked about a kilometre away. I sauntered back, window-shopping as I went, keeping to the shady side of the street. What am I doing here? I asked myself in between distractions. Buying a bar? Lunacy! It wasn't as if I liked Spain all that much. And this was supposed to be a vacation.

It was the Irish owner of the Dubliner Bar on the Paseo Maritimo who had sowed the seeds – Cathal O'Rourke, married to a Spaniard 'these twenty-foive years an' all'. A great life, he had enthused, over generous drops of some seriously hard stuff. Make a good living, meet lots of interesting people, live in the sun. It was an easy sell. It sounded as if it could be fun. Being in a personal and professional limbo had put me in a receptive frame of mind. So the next day, on O'Rourke's recommendation, I tracked down expat estate agent Colin Baynes, late of Southend.

Salesman though he was, Baynes had not gilded the lily. The problem, he explained over beers in his front line office with its wall-to-wall colour prints of this, that, and the other desirable property, was that the bars in the "better" areas commanded a higher price than my stated €500,000 ceiling. Hence I would have to lower my sights. A beachside location was still possible, but not in the most fashionable strips to the south. Baynes proposed I junk the idea of buying an apartment nearby, and the money saved added to my stake.

'Most bars have living accommodation,' he asserted. 'Be more secure too, living on the premises.'

At a practical level he was right. I just hadn't figured on living over a bar, even my own bar.

Lack of progress and looming complications were waning my enthusiasm. I would give it two more days then, if I didn't find a suitable place, I would call off the search. Dream up some other lifechanging gimmick.

My next assignment was unrelated to my bar search. The previous evening I had received a call on my cell from Dave Pridham, anxious for news of his missing daughter. Fact was, I had forgotten my promise to check out her address. He was polite about my feeble excuses and even apologised for the 'imposition'. Quite right too. After all, I was doing him a favour.

So, post-Barnes, I set off in the Beamer in search of Calle Hinojo. The GPS guided me there through lookalike back streets to the suburbs, far away from the beach. No.14B was in an apartment block, four floors high, with what looked like a penthouse with a balcony on the fourth level. Brown awnings screened all the windows. The entrance door was in a porch accessed via an archway. To the right, a garage door occupied the rest of the front of the building.

I had purposely left it until after five, in case the present occupant was at work. Beside the entrance door which, as expected, was locked, was a rank of buzzers. 14B was occupied by "IANCU". I thumbed the button, held it down.

An eventual curt '*Sí*?' was my reward. Definitely not Linda Pridham.

'*Disculpe las molestias*,' I said. 'I'm a friend of Linda Pridham.'

'She go away.' His Spanish was if anything worse than mine.

'I know, but I need to contact her.'

'Wait there.' Surly, grudging. Not happy to be of service.

When he came, he closed the door behind him and talked to me in the porch. He was thin as a reed with unSpanish features and fair hair done up in a cute ponytail. From his name I took him to be of East European origin.

'Who are you?' he snapped, like a small dog trying to be big. 'Are you police?'

'A friend of Linda's,' I said, keeping a grip on my civility. 'Her parents are trying to find her.'

'I tell you,' he said, reverting to English. 'She go.'

'I got that. Do you have her cell phone number?'

'She change. I not know new number.' Then the tension went out of him, and a weak smile emerged. 'But you lucky. She coming back.'

'To live?'

'No, no.' His headshake made the ponytail sway becomingly. 'She leave things, clothes, CDs, tennis bat … stuff like that. She fetch.'

Which was a break for me in my unsought after quest.

'When is she coming?'

'Saturday. She say *cuatro* … four in afternoon. You can come speak with her.'

That I could do. Saturday was two days hence. I thanked him.

'You use anything?' he said to me as I turned to leave.

'Use anything?'

'You know …' He glanced up and down the empty street: 'Skunk, dust, applejack, I got all kind.'

As always when a drug pusher intersected my path, my thoughts went straight to Liza, remembering how her abductors had drugged her into submission and abused her, and the battle to get her off dependency when I finally brought her home.

I stuck a finger under his nose and, speaking slowly and distinctly so he would get the message, said, 'Don't say another word. Just turn around and go back inside and I'll forget all the lives you're ruining.'

Quick on the uptake, he backed away, entered a code on the lock pad and was gone without so much as a puff of smoke.

When I reported my progress to Dave Pridham later that evening I didn't mention that his daughter had been shacked up in a part of Fuengirola where drug merchants operated. It wouldn't have done much for his peace of mind.

* * * * *

On Friday, I took a break from viewing bars and went sailing. *Seamist* was a handful for a crew of one, but manageable. It was a balmy day, with only a flutter of wind from down south, so even with a full complement of sails, I barely made headway. I even read most of a book while cruising down the coast to the small town of Benalmadina, where I grabbed a visitors' berth and lunched on shellfish *paella* at a restaurant on the marina.

A restful day. No special worries, just a lingering niggle about whether *Il Sindicato*, my regular employers whom I had displeased, would come calling anytime soon. Their silence was more unnerving than their threats.

Saturday afternoon I returned to the apartment on Calle Hinojo. I left the Fuengirola marina at three, so as to be sure to be there ahead of Linda Pridham. Being the weekend, and more people presumably at home, parking space on the street was all taken up, so I left the car in adjacent Avenida de los Lirios.

Jingling the car keys in my pocket, I rounded the corner into Hinojo. A woman was emerging from the doorway of no.14. Young, well put together in sawn-off denim shorts and a yellow top; brown hair secured with a yellow and blue headscarf. Maybe she had her stuff run up from second-hand Swedish flags. She had an armful of dresses and other garments on hangers, some of which were not yellow and blue. It was only when she showed me her profile while chucking the clothes on the back seat of an open top electric-blue Mustang, that I made the connection. It was the Pridham girl, a half-hour ahead of schedule.

I hailed her as she slid behind the wheel. When she didn't react, I broke into a trot and called again, but by now she was gunning the engine and the noise drowned me out. Either that or she took me for a stalker.

'Linda!' Louder now, but too late. She was already moving away from the curb while I still had twenty metres to cover.

To the crackle of its twin mufflers, the Mustang accelerated down the narrow street. I waved my arms frantically, hoping she would spot me in the rearview mirror. If she did, she wasn't curious enough to delay her departure.

An obscenity or few escaped my lips as I backtracked at sprint speed to the Beamer. Luck was with me: she was held up by traffic at the far end of Calle Hinojo. As I fed gas to the engine, she moved off, swinging left. At that point, I came close to quitting. Then, some vague noble impulse took over, urging me to restore the missing miss to her anxious parents. I gave the Beamer the gun.

By ignoring the speed limit I still had her in sight when I made the left turn at the Stop sign. She was just taking another left, two streets along. Traffic was light, so I was able to stay with her as she proceeded towards the ramp that led to the *autopista*. By the time she hit it I was snuggled up behind her, separated only by a decrepit pick-up truck.

The Mustang's left indicator was winking as she infiltrated the four-track freeway, easing into a gap in the traffic stream. The pick-up followed through; two passing cars held me back, then I too was on the freeway, looking for an opening to shorten the gap between the Mustang and me.

Signs and the sun told me we were heading south-west on the A7. A Lidl supermarket on the right came and went as we hit the 100kph mark, the legal limit on this stretch. The road veered right, crossed a river. Up ahead, on a hill, was a Moorish castle with grey walls and a single turreted tower.

Not knowing her destination, I settled down for what might be a long haul. She was three vehicles ahead. I passed two of them, then drifted back into the inside lane behind a Fiat 500.

My expectation that it would be easy to keep track was blown away when she started passing every vehicle. Eventually she lost a duel with a Porsche, conceding *force majeure* with a resentful honk. Miss Linda was not to be messed with.

I allowed her to pull away a few cars' lengths again, chiefly because I didn't want her to catch sight of me and drive even more recklessly in a bid to shake me off. I wasn't about to risk my life doing Dave Pridham a favour. Her Swedish-flag scarf was fluttering wildly in the airstream, like a ship's pennant. She had a cell phone pressed to her ear, flouting the law that specified hands-free only when driving.

As Fuengirola receded in my mirror a new urban area began to spread across the windshield. On this section of the *autovia* the scenery was mostly solid concrete, relieved only by the glitter of the Mediterranean between the tower blocks. Out of season holidaymakers trudged the sidewalks and promenades. Over-commercialised as it was, Spain still had plenty to offer: endless sun, endless beaches, great food, passable wines. If it was to become my adopted country, I could do worse.

Mounted on a rise beside the *autovia* a line of large white lettering, not unlike the famous Hollywood sign. LA CALA DE MIJAS it spelled out. Abruptly, without signalling her intention, Linda swerved from the left-hand lane into the right, and from there onto an exit ramp. She almost threw me off her trail. I braked hard, triggering the ABS, and earned a bleat of protest from the Fiat as I cut in front of it to merge onto the ramp. The exit sign, white lettering on blue, read La Cala de

Mijas, Cambio de Sentido. The ramp led down to a traffic circle. Linda took this too fast, tyres whimpering, leaving the circle at the second exit with me leeching on to her rear bumper.

Back under the freeway, the shade as dark as night, momentarily blinding. Now the sea was ahead of us, that azure blue that hurts to look at. Lights, intersection, left turn, into a street of front-line row houses. Palm trees bordered the street, some of them dead, victims of a disease that was rampaging across Spain, decimating the species. To the right was a parking lot that appeared to serve an apartment block with the vertical inscription EL OCEANO down one side. Linda whipped the Mustang off the road and into the lot too quickly for me to stay with her. I found a space between a couple of cars parked on the street and tucked the BMW in there.

On foot I hustled back to the parking lot. The Mustang was there, but empty of its driver. That didn't worry me. Nobody would leave an open top car full of clothing in a Spanish street for more than a few minutes.

Across the road was a restaurant – El Oceano, like the apartments. With the sun now slipping towards the saw-toothed palisade of mountains to the west I was on the hot side of the street, so I stationed myself under the roofed entrance of the restaurant to wait. It wasn't a long wait. A slim, hawk-featured man in army uniform – slacks, short-sleeved shirt with officers' epaulettes – ambled up to me. He was bareheaded, his hair black and smooth as an otter's pelt.

'*Buenos tardes, señor*,' he said, smiling in a relaxed, friendly fashion.

I nodded politely, wondering if I was about to be subjected to a random identity check. Normally a function of the police rather than the military, but in a come-lately democracy like Spain I wouldn't have ruled it out.

His next utterance was longer and interrogatory. My understanding of Spanish being limited to what I had picked up during my infrequent sojourns here, I shrugged my incomprehension.

'I don't understand,' I said in English.

He took that in his stride. 'I ask if you are waiting for someone.'

I stared. I was tempted to tell him to mind his own business. Before I could reply though, Linda Pridham reappeared around the side of the restaurant. She strode mannishly towards the Mustang, her cut-off denim shorts tight across her behind, her legs long and smooth and tanned, just how I like them.

'Linda!' I called, starting forward. There was no break in her stride, and I was immediately blocked by the army officer. He was slight of build and quite a bit shorter than me. I could have slapped him aside without flexing a muscle but discretion got the better of doing the Pridhams a favour.

'Stay where you are – please.' His eyes flicked leftwards and I followed them. Two unusually large species of homo sapiens gazed bovinely back at me, near identical in their olive green shorts and T-shirts, and cropped hair-dos.

The penny dropped. These three were protecting Linda Pridham! But how come the military, and how had she magicked them to her aid?

The Mustang bumbled off. No glances for Warner. Linda Pridham had set her dogs on me and wasn't sticking around to witness the savaging.

The officer took my arm. His grip was slack yet confident.

'You will come with me.'

'Now wait a second, pal ...' I said, disquiet giving way to outrage.

'No talking, please.'

The two big fellows were closing in. I might outpace them in a hundred metre dash and then what? If the army wanted me, they would have me sooner or later, hard or soft. Still opting for discretion, I let the officer lead me to the door used by Linda Pridham. Shoppers were milling all around me. None of them showed interest in my plight. Again I considered making a run for it and trusting that they wouldn't gun me down. After all people don't get gunned down in broad daylight in a busy street.

Do they?

Behind the door lay a long corridor with stairs branching off and another door at the far end. With the officer leading and the junior ranks stepping on my heels, we went out through this second door which opened onto a parking and loading area for the hotel. It was deserted apart from a few cars. I was bundled into the back seat of an olive-green overheated Seat sedan. The officer slid in after me, nudging me along. I tested the door on my side; no joy there, the safety lock had been set.

'Thank you for being so sensible,' the officer said as the door on his side slammed shut.

'I don't know what your game is,' I said, trying not to splutter, 'but you'd better have a fucking good explanation for it.'

'So,' he returned quietly, eyes glinting like wet pebbles, 'had you.'

The heavy platoon piled into the front seats causing the car's suspension to sink noticeably. The engine rumbled into life and we reversed in a series of jerks. The officer rattled off a command, the cropped head in front of me bobbed, and we edged out into the street, opposite the parking lot where I had left the BMW.

'My car …' I started to say, then realised how fatuous it would sound. Whatever trouble I was in had to be lot bigger than an abandoned rental.

The officer's lip twitched as if he read my mind. He had a slender moustache, the sort of embellishment that died in America with Errol Flynn. Maybe it was meant to age him. If so, it didn't work. He still looked like a teenager playing at being grown up.

We were on the ramp back up to the A7, tagging on behind a garbage truck. The driver kept his speed down, taking no chances and making no attempt to overtake. Cars flipped past, some going at well over the 100kph limit, those bearing British and German plates being the most inveterate sinners. Whenever this happened the officer clucked and shook his head. Finally he said, 'You foreigners. No wonder so many of you die on this road.'

'I haven't noticed your lot winning any prizes for skill and courtesy,' I retaliated, adding, when he made no comment, 'And would you mind explaining what this is all about?'

'Yes,' he said evenly. 'I would mind.'

After that I shut up. Why give him the satisfaction of putting me in my place. If only I knew what my place was.

At an intersection in the middle of nowhere we left the freeway onto a single track road. No signpost. The position of the sun, reddening now, told me we were headed approximately north-west. The knowledge was not a lot of use to me.

The cell phone in my hip pocket vibrated. I didn't pick up in case my captor decided to confiscate it. It was probably Liza, so I wouldn't have answered it anyway.

The road snaked through cultivated fields and the occasional avocado or citrus plantation. Once, we bisected an abandoned vineyard. As we came to the foothills, the twists in the road became more frequent and more severe. The terrain changed from bleached green to dead-looking ochre. To our right the whole coastal plain was spread out as on a map, with Fuengirola a smudge under the faint evening haze away to the east. The sea was that rich ultramarine that comes with the approach of night.

We came up behind a tractor and were slowed to a crawl until we reached a village – no more than a huddle of shacks under the shadow of an escarpment – where we made another turn, to the left now, immediately descending via a spiralling road, skirting the escarpment and crossing a high plain, a step in the mountainside. The road was rough and dusty and we trailed a brown pennant that must have been visible from a satellite.

Dusk fell. I was hot, tired, and in need of a leak. If I could persuade them to stop I might yet make a break for it.

'Look, I need … er … *toiletto*,' I hazarded to the officer.

The soldier in the front passenger seat sniggered. The officer gave a sympathetic nod.

'*Servicios*,' he corrected. 'No problem, *señor* – we are almost there.'

I faced frontwards. Coming at us, straddling the road, was an archway not unlike the giant Dunlop half-tyre replica that used to be a feature of the Le Mans racetrack. Except that this archway was stone and decorated with massive seashells that spelled a name I failed to decipher before we passed beneath it. About a hundred metres beyond the arch we came to a halt alongside the inevitable gatehouse, a prefabricated building the size of a large shed. A soldier came hurrying out, stiffened to attention, saluted.

'*Comandante*!'

The officer returned the salute with a languid pivot of his forearm. The Seat moved on and I screwed round to look through the rear window, noting the high mesh fence topped by coils of barbed wire that ran from either side of the arch towards the horizon, to be swallowed up in the fading light. This was one big hunk of real estate we were driving through. The road was vastly superior to the dirt track we had just left: full width and a proper paved surface. Serious money had been spent here.

Journey's end came five minutes later when a pyramid rising out of the sunset-splashed plain turned into a roof, then expanded into a great sprawl of buildings, most notably a house with a balcony at first floor level that extended the full frontage of the building and around both sides. A number of vehicles, including two jeeps, were drawn up before it in an open asphalted area, seriously floodlit, though it was not yet dark. Beyond, a military helicopter was parked inside a white landing circle, its rotor throwing a long shadow shaped like a crucifix. We stopped next to the jeeps. Acting in concert, the two heavies vacated the car and released the "Comandante" and me. I climbed stiffly out, flexed the cramp from my legs.

On this, the sunless side of the building, the windows were black, like empty eye sockets. As if to welcome me, as I stood there flexing, wrought iron lamp standards spaced along the front of the house and around the parking area came on.

What struck me most about the place was the stillness. No movement, no sound other than the hum of what was probably a generator in some outbuilding. The sky behind was lurid, like a frozen explosion, the sun lost behind purple clouds that hugged the horizon. The setting was almost eerie.

A hand pressed between my shoulder blades, propelling me forward. Again I contemplated escape. If only there was somewhere to escape to. The terrain offered no cover for any creature bigger than a field mouse.

The Comandante walked me to the house, more in the manner of a genial host than a jailer. The junior ranks again brought up a discreet rear, well-schooled in how to behave in the presence of a prisoner and equally, I didn't doubt, in half-a-dozen ways of killing a man with their bare hands. My SIS training had left me well-supplied with unarmed combat skills, I just wasn't quite ready to take on odds of three-to-one against. Not to mention the weaponry they were wearing.

We followed a footpath around the side of the house, coming upon another asphalted area, big enough to serve as a parade ground. A single-storey building with heavy-gauge wire mesh over the windows awaited us. Lights blazed from all corners. My stride slackened. Once inside there I was finished. Military prisons are hard to break out of.

'Follow me,' the Comandante said briskly. The terrible twins had closed in, ready to foil any escape intentions on my part.

If it hadn't been for the guns I might have chanced it. But where would I run to, even if they didn't put a bullet in me? I settled for the line of least resistance, in other words no resistance at all, and mounted the two concrete steps. Inside, a vestibule, not quite square, furnished only with a steel desk, a plastic chair, and a sweaty NCO who erupted to attention when the Comandante entered ahead of me.

I was checked in and marched to a bare, windowless room in a basement. The two goons, plus two more, awaited me. The Comandante joined us, standing to one side, and ordered to me strip. I refused. I was grabbed from behind. I struck out at the soldier standing in front of me, rammed an elbow into yielding flesh behind me. Impact negligible. They didn't hit back, just forced me to the floor by weight of numbers. I was forcibly stripped, the ultimate humiliation. Another officer, older than the Comandante, entered and examined every cavity of my body for concealed machine guns and mortars, his only utterances grunts and nods. Examination complete, he withdrew. My clothes, the worse for their enforced removal, were emptied of belongings, including Canadian passport, cell phone, credit cards, and a few hundred euros, then returned to me. My belt, watch and wallet were withheld. Nobody spoke. Except me.

'I'll get you for this,' I said to the Comandante as I pulled my torn T-shirt over my head, my voice shaky and off-key.

'I doubt it,' was his bland response. He was thumbing through my passport, his brows contracted in a frown. Maybe he was having trouble with the long words.

My bladder was close to bursting by now. Swallowing my humiliation, I told the Comandante. He made some remark from the corner of his mouth to his underlings, who chuckled and marched me to a modern flush toilet and watched over me while I discharged the afternoon's beer intake. I had barely zipped up my shorts when I was towed away to another room, grey-painted and as cosy as a derelict igloo. From the nature and positioning of the furnishings – a small table with a chair on either side – I recognised it as an interrogation cell. It wasn't the first I had been in over the years.

I sat meekly as ordered, on the interviewee's side of the table, my back to the door. A lot of stuffing had been knocked out of me by that forced strip-search. André Warner, hit man, former SIS operative, was temporarily *hors de combat.*

'I want a drink,' I said.

'Later.'

The Comandante departed leaving the two goons to watch over me. It was quieter than a tomb and almost as cold. Even this far south the nights can be chilly in the January. I tried not to shiver, failed. Behind me, my two guards sniggered. To while away the minutes I studied my surroundings. A piece of grey plaster had broken away from the ceiling, next to the light globe, leaving a white patch the shape of a short fat fish. Otherwise the grey was uniform. No bloodstains, which I suppose was something. Unless they were painted over after every session.

Distant footsteps intruded on the stillness. Two sets, one very brisk and decisive, soles and heels snapping on bare concrete. Coming closer.

The door flung open. I rotated in my seat. A man stood in the doorway. He wore a uniform, the upper parts of which were heavily braided and blazing with badges of rank and a double row of medal ribbons. Lower down, jodhpurs and brown riding boots, the latter polished to a dazzling gloss.

'Good evening, Mr Warner,' he said, in a voice that managed to combine civility with menace. 'I am General Julio Irazola ...'

Chapter Three

In my borrowed cashmere suit I descended the sweep of the staircase to the entrance hall, passing under a chandelier which for sheer tinsel extravagance rivalled those in the Hall of Mirrors in the Palace of Versailles. A servant of some kind, wearing white gloves, inclined a wrinkled, lizard-like head towards a set of double doors with painted panels that depicted some biblical scene. I fumbled briefly for my shirt cuffs before I remembered the shirt, also borrowed, was short-sleeved.

'*El Señor* Warner,' the manservant intoned through the double doors. I strode in as if I were there by birthright, and never mind that the suit, which belonged to the General's son, was too tight all around and made me look like a once-fit man gone to seed.

'Ah, good evening, Mr Warner,' General Irazola trumpeted, taking my arm almost possessively and tugging me into the drawing room. The grey-brown uniform was gone, replaced by a pale grey lounge suit of immaculate cut. 'Come and meet my children.'

Far removed from his attitude of two hours earlier, when we had glowered at each other across the steel table, like stags with antlers locked. Then, when he had said 'Good evening, Mr Warner,' it had had the ring of a threat. 'You are Mr Warner, are you not? It says so in your passport.' His English was near-flawless.

'Then that's who I am,' I had growled, refusing to be intimidated.

'It will, in any case, do for the time being.' He had settled his medium-sized frame in the chair opposite me and laid, very precisely on the table between us, my passport and the photograph of Linda Pridham, the latter now looking a little tired from too long in my wallet. He studied me through a swirl of acrid smoke from his large cigar, from which he had not removed the gold band.

'I believe in coming straight to the point, Mr Warner.' He sucked gently at the cigar, simultaneously tapping the photograph. 'Please explain to me why you were pursuing Miss Pridham?'

At least we were now getting to the substance of the matter, progress of sorts.

'Only if you first explain to me what the hell it has to do with you.'

He frowned. His was a handsome face: on the long side with a firm jaw, lightly tanned. His hair was that rather attractive tawny colour you occasionally find among Latins. Age, somewhere between forty-five and fifty.

'Do not make your situation more difficult than it already is. Let there be no misunderstanding, Mr Warner. I shall have answers to my questions or you will not leave here alive.'

This had to be some kind of sick joke.

'I thought the days of Franco were long gone,' I protested. 'Isn't Spain a democracy, with human rights and all that?'

General Irazola exchanged a glance with the Comandante that I can only describe as pitying.

'There are democracies and there are democracies. Some live, some die, some are transient, some are merely surface dressing. Here in this room, on this estate, there is no democracy. There is only me. And I have the power of life and death.'

'Like being God, is it?'

Irazola sighed. He stood up and did a couple of circuits of the little grey room, his head shrouded in a swirl of cigar smoke like the top of a skyscraper obscured by low cloud. Whenever he disappeared from my line of vision I tensed, expecting a chop to the back of the neck, or hands at my throat. Eventually though, he resumed his seat. Laid the cigar very precisely on the edge of the table. Stared at me broodingly.

'I am making allowances for your English sense of bravado.'

'Half-English' I wasn't trying to be funny. It was a reflex, product of years correcting impressions.

'It's the same. I spent six years in England and two in America when I was a young man.' This would account for his command of the language. 'It would not be truthful of me to say I have much … ah … affection for the Anglo-Saxon race. We have warred too bitterly in the past, and many English and Americans fought for the Government forces during our Civil War. At heart we are neither friends nor allies. We will cross swords again someday, you will see. Spain has a *casus belli* in Gibraltar…' He frowned again, the dark eyebrows almost meeting across the bridge of his nose.

I didn't automatically spring to Britain's defence. Keeping things friendly between me and the man who had the power of life and death over me was first priority. Supporting the wrong side in the Gibraltar imbroglio was guaranteed to make an enemy of him.

'If I had my way, if I were making the policies, we would drive your pathetic British forces out tomorrow!' The cigar found its way back into his mouth. 'Regrettably Spain is run by old women. Even King Felipe speaks less of our claim to Gibraltar than his father used to, and curries favour with your Royal Family.' The thin-lips twisted with distaste. He jabbed with the cigar in the direction of the Comandante. 'Ask Navarro here. Ask the younger generation what they think.' Comandante Navarro coughed in a slightly embarrassed way, and Irazola grimaced self-depreciatingly. 'You have brought out the political beast in me, Mr Warner. Let us leave the subject of Gibraltar. You and I alone will not remove that thorn from the side of Spain. You will please now answer my question or I will extract the information forcibly from you. Do you understand?'

All too well. I had been down a similar route years before, in Afghanistan. It would be senseless to antagonise him further, so I nodded. As far as I was aware there was no reason – and certainly no security reason – why I should not tell General Irazola the truth. Only the Warner creed of old that resented giving something for nothing drove me to barter.

'If I tell you,' I said, trying to sound as if it was still remotely possible that I wouldn't, 'will you tell me what your interest is in the girl?'

'Afterwards? I might. If I judge you harmless.'

I hugged myself to contain what little body heat was left. Irazola didn't seem to notice my discomfort. But then he wouldn't; he was dressed for the conditions.

Accepting that my bargaining power was nil, I proceeded to tell him the whole story, and even managed to stick to the truth. Nobody interrupted. One of the gorillas cleared his throat now and again, otherwise my voice, hollow in that underground chamber, had the floor to itself. Even when I had finished, General Irazola did not immediately speak, tapping an index finger on his philtrum, eyes only for the thumb of ash at the tip of his cigar. It was Navarro who broke the silence.

'For this … work you make for the father of Miss Pridham. How much have he pay you?'

'Not a dime.'

'Please?'

Irazola intervened. 'He means he was not paid.' The ash toppled from the cigar onto the table. He shifted his gaze to me. 'You agreed to look for this girl without payment?' His tone was incredulous.

'All I said was that I would keep an eye open for her. You understand the expression?'

'Yes. And the distinction,' he added, just to show how extensive was his knowledge of English semantics. 'I could believe this if you had not followed … not *pursued* Miss Pridham from Fuengirola to Cala de Mijas at great speed.' He paused, then rattled off some Spanish at Navarro. The latter puffed out his cheeks like a glass blower.

'*Cientocinquenta kilmetros por hora*?' Navarro hazarded. A hundred and fifty kph. That much even I could savvy.

'Just so.' Irazola tilted back on his chair, fixed me with a sceptical gaze. 'A dangerous speed. Just for the purpose of telling her to contact her parents. Miss Pridham is a … free agent, is the correct expression, I think. An adult. Responsible only to herself.'

'It wasn't a hundred and fifty. She kept to the limit, so did I. I did it for her parents. They're worried about her, and I promised to look out for her.' I gave a shrug, or maybe it was a shiver. 'I had nothing else to do.'

Irazola dipped his handsome head. A near-smile played across his features.

'You are some kind of playboy? Is that what you would have me believe, Mr Warner?'

'Well …' I hesitated, unsure of the nature of his relationship with Linda Pridham.

'Go on. You may speak frankly.'

I blew into my cupped hands. My fingers were numb.

'I was only going to say … I might not have bothered if she was ugly.'

Feet shuffled behind me. Navarro stared fixedly at some invisible point on the far wall. Had I spoken out of turn? Irazola himself was impassive. Maybe the firm, aggressive jaw had tightened a shade, the hazel eyes narrowed marginally. Or maybe I was imagining these subtle shifts in his composure. I was so cold I scarcely cared any more.

'Mr Warner … I am going to give you the benefit of the doubt. I am going to believe your pathetic little story.' He rocked back on two legs of his chair, eyebrows hoisted as if awaiting a gush of gratitude.

I managed a frozen grin. 'It may be pathetic but it's the truth.'

He wasn't sure how to take that, but smiled back readily enough.

'You've gotten what you want, General,' I said, flapping smoke from the space between us. 'Now, how about that explanation?'

The smile stayed put but became fixed.

'What explanation?'

'The reason why you illegally abducted me because I followed an American girl, a foreigner, who can't possibly be of any interest to the Spanish military.'

Behind me, in the quiet that followed, a discreet cough from Navarro. In an apparently fossilised state, he was still studying the wall. Irazola contributed more smoke to the already dense atmosphere. My eyes were beginning to water. I was thirsty. I was cold. I was thoroughly pissed off.

'*Comandante*,' he said, his voice soft and level. Navarro stiffened to attention. There followed a stream of Spanish.

'*Si, mi general*.' Navarro barked a command and behind me the two guards stamped their feet in perfect harmony, and did a quick-march exit. Navarro pivoted on one foot, stamped the other and went out without a sidelong glance. The door closed leaving me alone with Irazola. He wasn't armed, so if I was going to make a break, it had to be now or not at all.

He rose. I massaged some feeling into my chilled forearms and watched him pace. For his age he looked to be in good physical shape: slim of waist, no flab above or below the belt, a solid-looking chest. Slightly shorter than me, say five-ten, but height has never been a prerequisite for military advancement. Look at Napoleon, look at

Montgomery.

Irazola dropped the remains of his cigar on the floor, ground it to powder with the heel of an elegant riding boot.

'I suppose,' he said, turning to look at me, hands behind his back, 'you do merit some sort of explanation.'

'At least.'

He ignored that.

'Can I rely upon your absolute discretion?'

'Sure,' I said unhesitatingly. 'If that's what it takes.'

'Very well.' He threw his shoulders back as if to brace himself. 'Miss Pridham is my mistress.'

* * * * *

There was no Señora Irazola. She was gone these fifteen years. Sensationally beautiful, I was told, she had dumped her general – then a mere half-colonel – leaving their two children in his care, to take up with a flamenco dancer. A year later the dancer turned nasty and knifed her to death.

Irazola related this poignant little tale over the dessert – some sort of fruit pie, syrupy, on a thin crumbly pastry that truly did melt on the tongue. I had never been much of a devotee of Spanish cooking but this evening's spread had me revising my opinion.

'You never married again?' I asked.

'We wouldn't let him,' his daughter, Elena, said in English that was the equal of her father's.

Irazola rumbled under his breath.

'How's that?' I asked Elena.

'Luis and I were seven when Mama went,' Elena explained. 'Not quite old enough to understand why. We thought it was because Papa had been cruel to her. We often heard them screaming at each other when we were in bed – our house was not so grand in those days. For a time after she left, Papa wasn't interested in ladies. When he finally brought one home we played a trick on her ...' She snickered behind her hand.

'It was so funny,' her brother, Luis, chimed in. 'We made a mixture of oil and soot and fixed it on the door so it would fall on her when she came in …'

'Only Papa came in first …' Elena chuckled.

'Of course we were severely punished …'

'But that didn't matter because we succeeded the second time …'

'And she never came again.'

General Irazola glowered indulgently at the memory.

Elena was still chuckling. 'Then there was the night we put a dead rat in the soup tureen.'

Luis shared her merriment. 'And fleas in the bed of that horrible woman from Cadiz – the one with the hairy mole on her nose. I never understood why you liked her so much, Papa. She had the face of a pig.'

'A very ugly pig,' Elena emphasised.

Irazola grunted. 'She was rich, and in those days we were poor, well, fairly poor. The pay of a *coronel-teniente* did not go far, not with you two gobbling up so much of it.'

I sipped neutrally at my champagne and stayed on the sidelines of this family banter. It was odd, but running through it I sensed a thread of enmity. It was as if the repartee was staged, a cover-up for some deep mutual dislike. Most likely it was no more than my imagination working overtime.

The Irazola children were twins, in their early twenties, I gauged. Not much physical likeness except about the eyes and the skin colouring, though having said that, all Spaniards of my acquaintance are sallow complexioned. One feature Elena and Luis had in common was their striking good looks. If anything, Luis, was the more perfect – slim, athletic, with regular features that toned with the physique. He had the air of a cut-throat razor: touch him in the wrong place and you'd open up your skin. Elena was of average height with a tendency to buxomness that was exaggerated by a tiny waist. Her legs, I had earlier noted, were long and well-shaped and topped by a compact pair of buttocks. Her face was a smidgen too round for classic beauty, even redeemed by hooded brown eyes and a soft, expressive mouth, which in turn was marred by the smudge of a moustache. She wore a fringe, straight and over-long and was constantly flicking it aside.

She caught me out in my scrutiny and stopped in mid-sentence. A flush spread over her face, unnoticed by father and brother, who had taken up where Elena left off, with an account of the downfall of yet another of the General's hapless paramours. I smiled at her noncommittally, which flustered her even more, so that she looked away.

'You haven't yet told us who Mr Warner is, Papa,' she said, stammering a little in her discomfiture, as a breach opened up in the reminiscing. 'I mean, we know he's English, wishing to buy a property in Fuengirola, but that's all. How did you meet? Are you doing some business together?' She gave me a long look that was meant, I guessed, to be intriguing. She just didn't have the panache to pull it off. So as not to disappoint her I did my best to look intrigued.

Irazola spooned up the last morsel of tart and held it suspended, a spoon's length short of his mouth. 'Mr Warner and I met as a result of a misunderstanding.' Then, facing me, 'For the treatment you received at the hands of my men, I apologise most sincerely. I hope it will not prevent us from establishing, ah … cordial relations.' He glanced at me, an unspoken enquiry pulling his eyebrows up at the edges.

'On the contrary,' I said in my smoothest, most sycophantic manner. 'I hope we'll meet again some sunny day.'

These words of smarm came not from a forgiving nature but out of self-interest. You never knew when you might need friends in exalted places. As an SIS operative in my twenties, I had schooled myself to avoid antagonising power wielders out of pique. My success rate was lower than I would have liked.

Neither of the twins attempted to draw Irazola out further on the subject of their guest, and the talk slid into a debate on the Catalonian independence movement and its chances of breaking away from the rest of Spain. Every once in a while, I caught Elena, and less often, Luis, directing a look almost of hostility at their father whenever his attention was elsewhere. It was puzzling.

A female servant came to clear away the dishes and serve coffee and liqueurs. I contributed desultorily to the debate, which was carried out in English out of courtesy to me. As it began to dry up, Irazola suddenly said, 'Play something for us, Elena.'

Elena nodded, looking pleased. She wandered over to a far corner of the room where a grand piano stood, partially obscured by a screen. On the curved side of the case the words, picked out in gold, Steinway and Son.

Elena sat on the bench. The music rack was empty so I figured she was good enough to do without.

A short pause to compose herself then she launched into a piece that I didn't recognise at once. A few bars along it hit me. It was the Funeral March, but in a faster tempo than intended by Chopin. General Irazola was frowning, perhaps at her choice of music. She didn't notice. Her back was to him and she was absorbed in the piece, her body swaying in time, her fingers flowing over the keys like poured oil, the light of the chandelier skipping over highlights in her raven hair.

The clock with the octagonal dial set into an immense rococo dresser opposite me struck eleven-thirty. I was tired. There was nothing to keep me here, now that the General and I had 'established cordial relations'. The BMW had been collected and was parked outside the main entrance. If they had discovered the secret compartment with its lethal occupant, I guessed I would have known before now. I ran the linen napkin over my lips.

Elena wound up the March with its simplified and, in my opinion, too-abrupt coda, and crossed the room amid appreciative applause from we three males.

She curtseyed with a flourish and resumed her seat.

'I am a bit out of practice,' she said modestly.

'Nonsense, my dear,' Irazola demurred. 'But next time you play the March please stick to lento. In largo it is too frivolous.'

I tendered my congratulations to Elena on her piano playing, omitting her father's qualifier. To Irazola I said, 'General, I must ask you to excuse me. It's a long drive to Fuengirola.'

He stared, as if I had let go a loud and noxious fart. 'Don't be ridiculous, Mr Warner. What kind of host would I be to turn out a guest at this hour of the night? The least we can do is offer you a room for tonight.' He raised a peremptory hand, as if to forestall my objections, though I had none. A soft bed a mere staircase away had the ring of something close to paradise.

'Of course you must stay,' Luis said, his smile quick and warm. He had an attractive personality that went well with his appearance.

Elena just looked at me with smouldering eyes. There was a lot of pent-up passion stored away there, waiting for the right combination to release it. Not that, with her looks, she should be short of applicants for her favours. Maybe she fancied a bit of Anglo-Saxon stud as a change from the Latin variety. I pretended not to notice.

* * * * *

I was sliding into a cocoon of crisp white linen when I remembered I hadn't visited the bathroom. The need was not pressing but to ignore it was to risk being forced out from between my warm sheets in the small hours, to trek down fifty metres of corridor to the elderly and unheated bathroom I had used earlier.

So I wrapped Luis' spare bathrobe around my naked body, and peeked out. My room was close to the head of the stairs. Here at first-floor level all was quiet; only the faintest mutter of voices below hinted at continuing table talk in the dining room. I was stepping out onto the narrow strip of red and gold scrolled carpet that ran the length of the corridor when a telephone rang down below, at the foot of the stairs. I trekked on towards the bathroom. When I was about halfway there the ringing stopped.

'*Quién habla*?' I heard someone say faintly.

The toilet had a noisy flush that followed me back down the corridor and not until I came up to my door did I hear General Irazola delivering a blistering harangue in Spanish. Though most of the words meant nothing to me the tenor was unmistakeable. As I crossed the threshold he switched abruptly to English and, without thinking, I slowed to eavesdrop. My espionage breeding has been known to get the better of my good manners.

'I beg your pardon,' were Irazola's first words in my native tongue. 'You made me angry and I curse better in my own language. I will say it for you in plain English: I cannot begin preparations for moving my troops until the date for the talks has been fixed. It is not even certain yet that either the Spanish Government or the British will agree to talks. If they do not, we must think again. In any case, de Cadalso has the Prime Minister's ear, he will keep me fully informed. It is the King who will be the stumbling block.' A short break for his caller to have his say, then, 'What do you think?'

I edged towards the balcony. Irazola's tan-coloured crown came into view above the landing floor. He had his back to me. He was silent, head nodding, as the other party rambled at length.

'Gibraltar is not the priority it once was, my good Ricardo. The King and many in the Government consider it irrelevant. They are too wrapped up in the problems of the European Union, terrorism, immigration and water shortages. However, do not be despondent. I have de Cadalso's personal assurance that he and Querol will raise the matter at the next sitting and force the issue.'

More nodding while the 'good Ricardo' discoursed anew.

'Promises have been made,' Irazola said, with a touch of irritation. 'You know this.'

A second or two later, a snort from Irazola.

'You know very well to whom. To Lavrov for one. I meet with him in St Petersburg on Saturday. He is not a patient man and Vladimir the Great even less so. They demand …'

I never got to hear about the demands of Lavrov, whoever he might be, and the even-less-impatient Vladimir (could this conceivably be *Putin*?) because Luis emerged from the dining room at that point, called out '*Buenos noches, Papa*,' and began to ascend the stairs at a run.

From inside my room, my back pressed against the door and my heart bumping, I heard him walk down the corridor whistling. I allowed him a full sixty seconds before opening the door a crack. The ping of a telephone receiver being replaced reached me, followed by the general's brisk tread on the tiled hall floor. I had learned as much as there was to be learned.

The sheets had chilled thanks to my prolonged absence. I lay between them, shivering a little, wondering why I had listened in on my host's private conversation. I had no cause to spy on him.

Wondered too, who was Ricardo and what he and possibly the Russians had to do with de Cadalso who had the Prime Minister's ear, and Gibraltar. My dormant MI6 instincts were awake and baying for enlightenment.

I fell asleep, none the wiser.

* * * * *

'A small favour, General,' I said next morning as I took my leave on the doorstep.

'If I possibly can.'

'Ask Linda … Miss Pridham, to make contact with her parents. Let them know she's okay. Send an email or something. I could do it, but it would come better from her.'

'It does not seem a lot to ask.' He was less formally dressed this morning in a beige short-sleeved shirt that clung to every bulge and hollow of his impressive torso, and matching pants with a crease that was painful in its precision. Not a wrinkle in sight. A contrast to my freshly-laundered and mended but decidedly battle-scarred vacation garb.

We shook hands. He had a mean grip. Luis came forward. His grip was a fraction easier on the knuckles though by no means soft, while Elena left her hand in mine just long enough to reinforce last night's unstated messages.

'We'll see you again, I hope,' she murmured.

'I'll look forward to it.' That was as much encouragement as I dared give her in front of her old man.

General Irazola said, 'I almost forgot – leave me the number of your *movil*, will you, Mr Warner.'

'My cell? Sure.'

It seemed a reasonable enough request. I jotted the number of the cell phone I used for harmless personal chats on the back of a double-glazing representative's card I found in my wallet.

'And your address,' he said smoothly, his face blank.

Always security-minded, my first instinct was to refuse. My second instinct was to invent. My final instinct was to play it straight. After all, I wouldn't be in my rented villa for long.

So I added the address to the cell number, and hoped it would be enough for him. It was.

All three of them waved me goodbye as I piloted the Aston around the fountain and across the sunny courtyard. But only Elena stayed on the doorstep until I passed between the gates and we were lost from sight to each other.

Chapter Four

The bar was in Malaga, south-west of the city centre, on the N340 Carretera de Cadiz. It was named La Palma de Oro – The Golden Palm, more suggestive of a ritzy night-club than a humble roadhouse. A shade noisy, and more than a shade run down. The owner's accommodation was on the floor above, with an expanse of balcony and a die-for view of the Med, the whole caboodle badly in need of some TLC. But, Colin Baynes enthused, it had simply enormous potential. All the holiday traffic passed its front door, and it was already well-patronized by truckers of every nationality. Clean it up, put in some new furniture, paint it gaudy, and you wouldn't recognise the place. To complete the transformation, erect some billboards on the N340, a kilometre in both directions to alert all and sundry travellers to its existence.

It was big, that much you could say for it. Baynes came up with the idea of dividing in two the present bar/café set up, to create a family restaurant in one half, and generate more revenue.

The owner of The Golden Palm, a Catalonian of sixty-odd who wanted to spend the sunset of his life in his home town of Tarragona, was prepared to 'sacrifice the fruits of thirty years' toil' and accept a mere 300,000 euros, say US$270,000 for the freehold and the business combined. I said I would think about it, which visibly disappointed him, not to mention Baynes.

Two afternoons later, I was still thinking about it. On the terrace of my rented villa, lulled by the crash of the waves against the rocks below the palm-lined garden. With my feet up on a sun lounger, my body cooled on the outside by an awning of many colours and holes, and on the inside by a steady supply of beers from the refrigerator. Was this truly the life I craved? Year-round sun, daily siestas, and the essence of ozone wafting over me. Perhaps the appeal lay only in its contrast to the years of violence and killing and being suspicious of anyone who showed too much interest in me.

On the other side of the coin, I needed purpose, I needed contact with humans who weren't either running from me or running after me. To vacillate too long would be to end up doing nothing. My old métier was defunct beyond revival and, in any case, had long held no appeal. Lacking other skills, I either bought a business or I drifted on a voyage to nowhere.

I raised my glass and slowly drained it. As the last dregs trickled the length of the glass towards my mouth a blurred figure materialised in the round base. I lowered the glass and gaped. Then I removed my sunglasses and gaped harder.

'*Hola de neuvo*, Señor Warner,' my visitor said. Adding, in English, 'I knocked but nobody came.'

I backhanded a dribble of beer from the corner of my mouth and got to my feet.

'*Señorita* … Irazola,' I said. 'What a pleasant surprise. I didn't hear your car.'

'I rode,' she said succinctly. She gestured with a riding crop towards a tall bay horse quietly grazing beyond my garden hedge.

'All the way from your home?'

She giggled becomingly. 'I am visiting with friends near here.'

'Well, er … it's good to see you again. Can I get you some refreshment?'

She was hot, her face flushed and sweaty, her red shirt dark under the armpits. Jodhpurs suited her, emphasised her tiny waist and the bulge of her hips.

'You are drinking beer, I see. Beer will be fine. '

Still too bemused to ponder what had prompted her visit and how she had tracked me here, I fetched a couple of cans of Kronenberg and a glass from the kitchen. When I returned she was standing gazing into the pool, slapping an elegant boot with her riding crop.

'Your pool needs cleaning,' she remarked; seeing that I was about to fill her glass, she said, 'I will drink it from the can.'

'Be my guest.' Like a true gentleman, I popped the can for her.

'*Salud*!' She lifted the can and drank in little gulps that made her throat ripple.

Lowering the can, she smiled at me. Her teeth were good – even and strong looking, if on the large side, and when she smiled she was almost radiant. The incipient moustache was still an asset she would have been better off without.

'You are asking yourself why I am here.'

'Am I? Actually, I was wondering how you found me.'

'You gave this address to my father, don't you remember?'

'I *did*?' Then it came back to me. 'You're right, I did.'

My thoughts were distracting me from intelligent conversation. Here I was with the loveliest girl I had met in many a month, behaving like a eunuch. Next thing we would be talking about the weather.

'As you do not ask, I will tell you. I am here,' she spoke very slowly as to a backward child, 'because I wanted to see you again.' She flicked her long fringe aside, grinned nervously. 'Alone.'

I nodded as if I had known all along. Which I had, I suppose.

'I'll drink to that,' I said, and slurped from my can. This seemed to relax her. She imbibed along with me, moved closer.

'Let's sit down,' I said, extending a hand towards the seats on the terrace.

She shrugged. I had the idea that lying down was more her style. But she condescended to accept my invitation and we took a seat apiece, side by side, facing the dunes, the sea, and the darting sailboats that even in January were a daily presence.

'It is very hot,' she grumbled. It wasn't, but I suspected her boiling point was lower than mine.

To emphasise just how very hot it was, she unbuttoned the red shirt, peeled it off and tossed it away from her in a ball. Underneath she was wearing a black bra of some silky material trimmed with lace. She was in good shape to go with her nice shape. No midriff ripples of fat. Arms toned, and just the right amount of muscle and sinew. I speculated on how long before the bra joined the shirt.

Pretending to take her brazen behaviour in my stride, as if it were routine for girls to start stripping off after five minutes in my presence, I asked if she fancied a swim. To cool off.

She glanced at the pool. 'Later perhaps. I didn't bring a swimsuit.'

'Is that a problem?' I said, just to prove I wasn't averse to a bit of skinny dipping.

'Not for me.' The look she gave me was direct and full of Spanish promise. 'Perhaps though you do not feel it is quite … hmm, proper?'

'Your daddy might not approve.'

A toss of her lovely head dealt with daddy's approval.

She picked up the riding crop from the floor beside her chair. She used it to smack the palm of her hand.

'How would you like to use this on me?'

If the mini-striptease had caught me on the hop, the invitation to a spot of SM left me momentarily stuck for a response. Not that she didn't deserve a good spanking.

The faint brown stripes across her exposed rib cage that I had noticed when she unloaded the shirt now told a story.

'Is that what made these marks?'

She nodded enthusiastically.

'Did you enjoy it?' I asked, genuinely curious.

Her breathing quickened and she nodded.

'It was *fan*-tastic.'

'Spoken like a true masochist.'

'Masochist?' She sat upright, frowning. 'Ah, *si* … *masoquista*. Yes, that is what I am.'

Sadism in general and flagellation in particular had never attracted me as an adjunct to sexual pleasure. But, ever anxious to please, I was willing to let her persuade me.

'Didn't it hurt?' I was still curious. From a purely technical aspect.

She slid lower in the seat, stretching her arms. I noted that she didn't shave her armpits either and the hair in that quarter stood out in damp spikes.

'Of course it hurt. That's not the point. No, I mean, that *is* the point. I like to be …' Her near-black eyes fixed on mine. 'We say *dominado*.'

I thought back over the years of lovemaking with the few women I loved and the many women I merely used. Some had been inventive and uninhibited, others more restrained. Now and again I had seduced a woman with a penchant for bondage, but nothing wilder than that. Maybe, as Liza had once complained, I really was a bit of a dinosaur.

'Is that what you're … er, inviting me to do?' I asked. 'Dominate you? Punish you?'

'Yes.' The simplicity, the lack of emotion in that response took me aback. This girl was as far from being a shrinking violet as you could get. She pouted at me, eyes sparkling, breasts suddenly heaving. She was hot for it all right. She leaned forward so that her breasts swung salaciously against their silky restraint. The restraint survived to live another day, but I didn't give much for its chances of a long life. 'It is not for you, hey? You like your sex straight. No violence.'

'Maybe I'm outmoded. I never thought so until now. Maybe I should read some books …'

'Try the Internet. It's full of ideas.'

'I've tried it. I wasn't impressed.' I stood up. 'Let me get you another beer. Help you cool off.'

Chirpy one minute, sullen the next. She flopped back in the seat, giving the bra some relief from the stresses and strains imposed on it.

'All right.'

I brought the beer, popped it. Her thanks were grudging. She hadn't liked being sidetracked from the purpose of her visit.

'It's getting dark,' I pointed out. 'Will your horse be all right?'

'He's used to waiting for me, don't worry. Look, André, are we going to do it or not?'

'Sure.'

'We *are*?'

'Sure we are. Just not today.'

Her face had lit up; now it reverted to mean and moody.

Rejecting what was on offer was alien to my character. Age wasn't a factor, and never had been. Could be she was simply too blatant. I prefer to make the running.

'All right,' she said, capitulating. 'Some other time.'

But she didn't put the shirt back on. Still hopeful, then.

She gave me maybe ten seconds respite before she asked, 'Are you married?'

'Was. A long time ago.'

Somehow we progressed from sex to politics, a subject that she professed fascinated her. In particular the present unrest, with regions agitating for more autonomy. As we talked the glow of sunset faded from the walls, the light degenerated into gloom. I switched on the terrace lamps and heater. If Elena felt the drop in temperature it wasn't enough to make her cover up.

As she discoursed on Spanish history, economics, and literature, I began to develop a grudging respect for her intellect. She was well-informed on the ongoing Catalan rebellion, the wish of the province to gain autonomy if not actual independence.

'They will succeed,' she stated, with total certainty. 'It's just a matter of time.'

'If they can do it without violence, it would be some achievement. Not like the Basques.'

She frowned at that, but made no comment.

Talking politics had brought back memories of her father's late night telephone conversation with a certain 'Ricardo'.

'Does your father have connections in Russia?' I asked. I was still only making small talk; still merely curious.

'Not as far as I know. What makes you ask?'

'Nothing much.' I kept it casual. 'When I was staying with you I had to go to the john and overheard him talking on the phone.'

She didn't speak, just treated me to a puzzled look.

I elaborated. 'He mentioned Vladimir the Great. I wondered if he was referring to Putin.'

'Putin!' The puzzlement was replaced by consternation. 'You mean the Russian president?'

'That's just it, I've no idea. Vladimir is a common enough name. He also mentioned someone called de Cadalso – I think that was it.'

Now she sat upright and really paid attention.

'That's our new Foreign Minister! He was at our house last week. You say my father was talking about him in connection with Putin?'

'If it was Putin,' I said hurriedly.

'That's really strange. Papa isn't into politics at all. In fact he despises politicians.'

I gnawed at this but extracted no goodness from it. Irazola, army general, non-political, plus Foreign Minister, plus maybe Putin and another Russian called Lavov or Lavrov. My old MI6 instincts were titillated, no more than that.

'Why are you interested in these people?' Elena wanted to know. Before I could answer she stood up. 'I want a cigarette.'

'Sorry, honey, can't help you.'

'I have some in my shirt pocket.'

She found her shirt crumpled up behind the chair. The packet of Marlboro in the breast pocket was equally crumpled but contained one last cigarette. She lit up with a slim lighter from the same source. Smoke drifted away towards the dunes. I drained the last dregs from my can.

'What is your interest in these men?' she asked again.

'No interest at all,' I answered glibly.

Elena abruptly left off probing and returned to the subject that was so dear to her heart.

'We don't have to wait for another day, do we?' It was a plea straight from the erogenous zones. 'Let's go to bed. You don't need to whip me, just *fuck* me.' Her breasts gave a little quiver to provide encouragement.

I felt myself weakening. I was only flesh, blood, and testosterone. Where was the harm? She was a consenting adult. Neither of us were committed elsewhere. Me, especially. Since Cassandra dumped me I had been living in no woman's land.

The buzz of a car engine in my driveway registered only on the fringes of my hearing. I didn't connect it with a visitor to my house.

Elena was standing over me now, still brandishing the riding crop.

'Well?'

That was as close as we came to carnal knowledge that day. From somewhere in the house, a voice, female and American by accent, enquired, 'Is anybody home?'

* * * * *

In real life and close up Linda Pridham did full justice to her studio portrait. Not ravishing to the same extent as my Spanish visitor, but with the kind of understated good looks that endure, something that's hard to capture in a still photo. Tallish, say five-six, her curves more subtle than Elena's. Hair much as in the photo: dark brown, bobbed, slight kink, an unsensational frame for a classic oval face. Lavender-coloured eyes, deep-set, and surmounted by those eyebrows that zigzagged like a dog's hind leg. One of them was raised inquisitorially.

'Excuse me for just barging in,' she said. 'But it's been a long drive and it was obvious somebody was home. Maybe you should check your cell phone sometimes if you don't go for surprise visits?'

'Maybe you have a point. I just have a rule not to answer calls when I see an "unknown number" message.'

'I'll try and remember. Not interrupting anything, I hope.'

We were in my living room, and Elena was out of sight on the terrace, but Linda couldn't have failed to notice the horse tethered by the hedge alongside the driveway.

'Nothing that won't keep,' I said, throwing gallantry to the winds.

She wasn't sure what to make of that. 'I guess we don't need any introductions, but, anyway, I'm Linda Pridham.' She stuck out a hand. No rings on the fingers, and no paint on the nails. She wasn't wearing ear-rings either. A no-frills gal.

'André Warner. Nice to meet up without your bodyguards present.'

She laughed. 'Isn't it?'

She was dressed in loose white slacks, the bottoms rolled up to calf height, and a sleeveless white blouse of some thin, opaque material. A striped sweatshirt was knotted about her neck. Casual but chic, with the self-assurance to carry it off.

'Sit down, won't you?' I indicated a chair.

'No, I can't stay long. Besides ...' The lavender eyes twinkled, '... one girl at a time is enough, surely.'

'If the girl looked like you, I'd agree.'

Now both eyebrows ascended. 'You don't waste time, do you? Hitting on me only two minutes after we meet.'

'Forgive me. It was only meant as a compliment. No hidden agenda.'

I crossed the kitchen and took a pack of coffee beans from the cupboard. A silence descended, as I dumped beans in the coffee mill.

She ended it with an embarrassed cough.

'To get to the reason for coming,' she said, a defensive note creeping in. 'I wanted to, like, apologise, I guess.'

'Another apology? You don't owe me one as far as I know.' I started up the mill, let it grind away for the recommended thirty seconds.

Linda Pridham looked exasperated. 'What is it with you?'

I switched off the mill. 'Coffee?'

'I came to apologise, not to socialise. Well, I apologise, formally and herewith for my part in the treatment you received at the hands of Julio … General Irazola. Accepted or not?'

'It wasn't your fault. He –'

'Shit!' she hissed though gritted teeth. 'Don't be so goddam forgiving.'

She mooched about the corner that she had made her territory. I got on with making the coffee. Miss Pridham was as prickly as a prickly pear.

'Julio told me,' she said at last, 'his goons gave you a hard time after they picked you up on account of me.' She gave me a very direct look that also contained an appeal. 'It was *my* goddam fault they did what they did. When you were chasing me, I used my cell phone to yell for Julio.'

'Can't blame you for that.' I leaned against the worktop and folded my arms. I was content to just to look at her, as she paced to and fro about my kitchen. She had the kind of figure that grows on you. Not sensational like Elena's, just generally well put together.

'Yesterday Julio told me the reason why you were on my tail. I felt so mean I made him give me your address so I could come and apologise in person.'

'Well, I appreciate you making the effort.'

Movements on the other side of the kitchen door caused a break in the conversation. A door slammed with such force it shook the wall behind me. Elena was advertising her displeasure at my truancy.

'Your friend seems kind of sore,' Linda remarked, not noticeably put out by the thought.

'She's a fast recoverer.' The percolator was beginning to boil. I hunted around for a cup. 'Sure you won't have some? I make the best coffee in the house.'

She shook her head.

'Your loss,' I said. 'Anyhow, you've done your duty. Consider your apology accepted. Are you going to contact your parents? I wouldn't like to think I got roughed up for nothing.'

'I did already, on WhatsApp. They're cool with things.' She shuffled her feet. 'Seems like I'm having to apologise to everybody.'

'They were worried about you,' I said. 'What you did, just dropping them, was pretty shitty.'

Her jaw sagged. 'Do you have to punch so low? How the hell'd you get involved in the first place? There's a lot of stuff you don't know ... we weren't exactly the best of buddies, me and my dad.' An agitated flick of the wrist. 'Ah, it's a long story.'

'Tell it. I've got time.' The toilet flushing on the other side of the wall reminded me that perhaps I didn't have all that much time.

'You reckon?'

Elena came in, glowering, red shirt back in place. She barely acknowledged Linda.

'Are you coming back?' she demanded sulkily.

In the presence of Linda Pridham's more toned-down good looks the appeal of Elena's voluptuous figure and dark beauty was less irresistible.

'Linda meet Elena,' I said, with a lightness I didn't feel. Elena glowered some more. Linda smiled and said, 'Hi.'

'Want coffee, Elena?' Without waiting for her answer I rustled up another cup and poured for both of us.

'I know you,' Elena said to Linda, and it was close to a snarl. 'You're my father's secret mistress.' She laughed without humour. 'He thinks we don't know about you, Luis and me.'

Linda bit her lip and was silent.

'Break it up, girls. Let's keep it convivial.'

Elena shook her fringe aside, scorning the proffered coffee.

Then, before I could restrain her, before I even realised what she intended, she walked up to Linda and slapped her twice across the face, forehand, backhand. They were hard slaps and they rocked Linda's head. She yelped and staggered against the wall. Elena stepped back, aimed a gloating glance at me, and stalked out through the door to the terrace, statement made.

I crossed the room to Linda's side in a few strides. 'You all right?' I asked, taking her arm.

She pushed me away. 'Oh, piss off, I'm not delicate. I've been slapped around by experts.' Her cheeks were flaring. At least they matched.

'I'm sorry ...'

'Don't *you* start apologising. Though you might have warned me it was Julio's daughter you were screwing.' She straightened up, pride intact. 'I'll leave you to her, Warner. You probably deserve each other.'

'Hey, simmer down. For your information, I wasn't screwing her.'

Not quite. We just hadn't gotten around to it.

'No? You surprise me. You look the type, and so does she.'

Her exit was dignified. I didn't try and dissuade her. I drank my coffee and listened to her over-revving her car engine, messing up her gear change, and spraying gravel on the window.

The coffee was not one of my better efforts. Too many distractions. I drank it just the same. I was rinsing out the cup when Elena reappeared, slashing at the air with her riding crop. Maybe she was tempted to use it on me. The red shirt was still in place, making a statement. No sex today, thank you. Her mouth set in a lipless line, she stormed through the kitchen and out into the dusk. Equine noises ensued. You can't over-rev a horse, or crunch its gears, but she certainly made the beast feel the sharp edge of her displeasure. Its whinnies of protest died away. Hooves thudded on sunbaked earth, faded rapidly.

As rapidly as my fortunes, I reflected sourly. Two women guests one minute, none the next. As lost opportunities go it would take some licking.

Chapter Five

The thickset, bearded Spanish trucker had been spoiling for trouble from the moment he and his three buddies swaggered though the door. He had dominated the conversation, demanded constant service from Gustavo, my willing little waiter, and every intervening sentence was to the detriment of the Anglo-Saxon race. Intentionally loud. Make a great stage actor. He even chose a position at the table where the watery February sunshine cast a spotlight on him.

This was the slack season and demands on my services behind the bar at The Golden Palm negligible. I had resolved to use my free hours to improve my Spanish language skills. Thanks to French being one of my two native languages, it had come easier than I expected, and my fluency was now such that I could hold my own in most conversations. The downside of this newfound skill was that I could understand the insulting remarks that the bearded trucker was trumpeting around the bar, to the accompaniment of gratuitous laughter from his trio of cronies.

Gustavo came away from the table with an order for four beers. He was trembling. I operated the pump mechanically, filled the glasses to the brim with frothing golden liquid.

'He is going to make trouble,' Gustavo said to me in an aside. 'It is better you call the *policia* now.'

'Forget it, Gustavo. I don't need any help from the police.' I wasn't worried. Admittedly bar-room brawls were outside my experience but I had had plenty of training during my service with MI6 in how to disable my opponents. Otherwise known as fighting dirty. Plus, I was back to peak fitness, thanks to my daily sessions in the gym I had installed in the basement.

I pulled the last half-litre and sent Gustavo on this way. The bearded trucker was in the act of lighting a cheroot when Gustavo came alongside; in tossing the dead match aside the trucker caught the edge of the tray and beer slopped on his shirt sleeve. It was thanks to Gustavo's balancing act that the whole trayload didn't land in his lap. That didn't stop him lashing out at the poor guy.

Although the blow was poorly-directed it had a lot of power behind it. Gustavo and the tray were separated, and sent skittling in different directions. Glasses shattered on the floor, spraying beer and slivers of glass to all corners of the bar. My only other customers, a pair of regulars playing crib in the sunniest alcove, reared up in alarm. Too old and decrepit to make a dash for it, they took shelter under their table, scattering playing cards asunder. It was like a scene from a Western B-movie.

A show of authority was now obligatory. If I turned the other cheek the word might spread and every trouble-seeking truck driver from Malaga to Madrid would be dropping in to show the boss who's boss.

A baseball bat was slung below the counter for such occasions. Two feet of hardwood, as yet unblooded. I unhitched it and moved in on the foursome with the bat behind my back. The bearded one was facing away from me and unaware of my approach. His nearest companion tugged his sleeve in warning a second before I laid the bat gently but firmly on his shoulder.

'*Basta,*' I said in Spanish. 'That's enough.' I pitched my voice low and reasonable. I wasn't out to provoke him. 'Pay for your drinks and go. I'll overlook the damage.'

His whole frame tensed, the tendons of his neck above the greasy shirt collar tautening perceptibly. I stepped away from him, creating space to manoeuvre.

The squat head rotated slowly, showing its profile.

'Pay up,' I repeated, 'and get out.'

One of his sidekicks tossed a handful of euro coins on the table. All three pushed back their chairs, looking nervous. Unlike their belligerent colleague they weren't in the market for a serious roughhouse.

The troublemaker grinned sideways at me. It was a broad grin, wolfish, and exposed the many gaps in his teeth. Legacies, no doubt, of other days such as this.

The chair he was sitting on went flying, kicked away as he rose. He moved fast, but was at a disadvantage in having to twist round to get at me. I sideswiped with the bat, connecting with flesh and bone just above the left elbow. It produced a yelp of surprise which changed to wariness when he realised what he was up against. Then the wolfish grin returned and a knife jumped into his fist: a slender switchblade, a weapon long since banned in most of Europe but available over the counter in Spain. It sparkled prettily as the sunlight caught it.

He lunged. Clumsily, in the manner of a man who expects no opposition, and easy to avoid. I lunged back at him with the bat at head height, its bulbous tip driving in on the bridge of his nose. I put all my strength behind the blow and he went over backwards with a grunt that came all the way up from his gut. His cronies by now had seen the light. The retreat was disorderly and noisy. It was down to me and the bearded one, now sitting on the floor.

He tried to rise and failed, shaking his head, making the corrugations of fat on his neck wobble. His nose was bleeding. The knife was away across the other side of the room. I closed in, hefting the bat. If he wanted to go the whole route I was ready to accommodate him.

But the belligerence had drained out of him. Blood was running over his chin now, and dripping onto his faded jeans. The skin between his eyes was split. It wasn't serious, though his nose was probably broken. He just wasn't used to being on the receiving end. Tough as he was, he had won too often and too easily, and his victories had made him overconfident.

Dazed, he tried again to haul himself up using the nearest table. The table toppled on him and he subsided, moaning. His mates, in a twittering huddle by the door, finally plucked up the nerve to return and help him. Between them they got him to his feet, still only semi-conscious and totally unaware of what was taking place around him.

'Keep him away from here,' I said, holding the bat across the front of my thighs. 'If he ever comes back, I'll give him more than a bloody nose.'

'*Si … si, señor,*' one of them muttered.

In a compact body they shuffled towards the open door. Gustavo saw them off the premises like a sheepdog herding its flock. Emboldened by our victory, he added a few farewell expletives to my caveat.

I righted the overturned table, leaving Gustavo to clear up the rest of the mess, and was returning to the counter when someone hailed me.

'You certainly have a persuasive way with you, André.'

I turned slowly in disbelief. The figure in the sunlit rectangle of the doorway was tall and wide at the shoulders. His features were in shadow, only the hair, a smooth brown cap, not a strand out of place, was highlighted by the sun.

'Toby?' I said, scarcely able to believe it was my lost love's brother.

'The same.' He came towards me under Gustavo's enquiring stare.

'Well, I'm godamned!' I grasped the extended hand and squeezed it. 'What a coincidence!'

A sardonic smile played across his bland countenance.

'As you say, dear boy. And how are you? I heard you'd bought a bar – is business booming?' He surveyed the room, empty of paying customers but for the two ancients, now back in their seats, sorting out their cards.

'This is the quiet season. Is Sam with you?'

'Inspecting the delights of Malaga. Quiet season, you say? It didn't look quiet to me.'

'Oh, that?' I said dismissively. 'That was just a work out. Come and park your butt and let's chew the fat.'

'Yes. Let's do.'

We took up positions on opposite sides of the bar counter, he on a stool, me standing; dry martini for him, draught beer for me.

He was his usual immaculate self: dark blue blazer with the Royal Lancers skull-and-crossbones regimental crest on the pocket, tie to match, made-to-measure cream silk shirt. Every inch the blue blood, that was Toby, the only discordant note struck by the lantern jaw, the chin to end all chins. He put Punch in the shade and no mistake.

'What's the idea of the vegetation?' he asked, stabbing a finger at my newly-acquired face fungus, symbolic of the new anti-establishment Warner.

'It arose out of lethargy. Now I've quite taken to it.'

'Can't say I'm at one with you there, old chap. Still, they're your looks, I suppose.' He drummed fingers on the bar top. 'It'll have to come off, of course.'

I gaped. 'Will it?'

'Mmm. Tell me, old boy – seriously – are you making a decent living out of this, er … enterprise?' He scanned the room, his gaze lingering on the ceiling, stained khaki by tobacco smoke and variegated with cracks. I had spent a fair sum equipping the restaurant and replacing the furniture and some of the fixtures, intending to tart up the decor out of the profits rather than capital. All very fine if the profits had been up to the task.

When I didn't answer he made his own assessment.

'Why not?' he said.

I sighed. 'It's almost wholly reliant on passing truck drivers to cover the overheads. The cream comes from the tourist trade, the bulk of which happens between June and September. What I didn't appreciate was that Malaga is quite industrial. There are plenty of tourists out of season but they usually eat in town or down on the beach.'

Toby fiddled with the stem of his glass. 'Er … didn't you do your due diligence before you parted with your cash?'

'Don't be smart, Toby,' I said, and my voice had a sting in it. 'The place was relatively cheap and I wasn't looking to make a living out of it. I don't need the income. So I didn't dig all that deeply. It was a bar, it was trading, it was by the sea …' I shrugged. 'It's not a career, just a change of pace.'

'No complaints then.'

I picked at a crack in the laminate surface of the counter. 'No complaints. Though I could do without big mouth truckers, like the one I just had to deal with. When I get bored and need new challenges, I'll get rid of it, or put it under management.'

'It's about new challenges I want to talk to you.'

'Some other time. It's too soon to be getting itchy feet.' I knocked back my beer, stood aside to let Gustavo through with a shovelful of broken glass. 'Putting aside my problems, what's the news from London? You're still with the Home Office, I suppose?'

'Well, no, actually, I've moved sideways. To the Foreign Office.'

'Really? How is it there? Good? Bad?'

'Indifferent, I'd say.' A wry smile to go with the pun. 'That's the Civil

Service for you, especially for we minions.'

Toby was no more a minion than I was Spiderman. Quintessential man behind the scenes was Toby. Manipulator of politicians, one of an exclusive band of bearers of a passe-partout to all reaches of the Whitehall warren. His official status as Deputy Under Secretary was a fraud, once exposed by Cassandra under the influence of too many gins and tonic, yet still fatuously maintained.

'Seen Cassandra lately?' I asked next. 'How is she? Alive and well and living in sin, I suppose.'

'Actually, no … not well, I mean. In fact, she's been quite ill.'

'Oh?' Concern prickled. The ties that had bound us weren't completely frayed away. 'What's up?'

'Some woman's thing. Can't quite get to the bottom of it, she won't even admit to a cold. You know Cassie.'

Yes, I knew Cassie.

'I'll phone her.'

'Jolly good idea. Or better still, go and see her.'

I massaged my chin beneath the foliage. 'See her? I can't leave this place to run itself. Gustavo is fine as a waiter, but he'd be hopeless as a manager.'

A male blond head peeped around the doorway, muttered in what sounded like German. Withdrew. A client that never was.

Toby grimaced. 'Like that, is it?'

'Ah, it's just the time of year. I don't sweat the footfall. The place needs a lot more TLC. I'll get around to it soon. Put in a few slot machines too, though there's a lot of official red tape bound up in that.' I made a gesture at Toby's empty glass. 'Another of those?'

'This round's on me.'

Behind us, the crib game was degenerating into a squabble, too heated for me to follow, culminating in one of the players storming out. The other, grousing to himself, began to gather up the cards.

'And then there was one.' Toby grinned lopsidedly.

'I told you, I the footfall doesn't bug me. It's a past-time, not a job. I never expected it to make me want to spring out of bed every morning.'

'How's your Spanish?'

'Improving. I can hold my own in a conversation.'

'That'll be useful.'

I narrowed my eyes at him. 'Are you hinting at something? What was that about new challenges?'

'Not exactly hinting, old boy,' he said, putting on that well-practised hurt look that was his trade mark.

'So you're not hinting. Why are you here then? There I was thinking you found me by accident, that it was just a coincidence.' Then it came back to me. I had texted Cassandra and mentioned the name and location of the bar.

'Cassie, I suppose,' I said, my voice accusing.

'You suppose correctly. Was it meant to be a secret?'

I sighed. 'I guess not. It didn't occur to me any of her family and friends would care one way or the other.'

'Well, it's always good to see you. But … let's put it this way: you've heard what's going on between Britain and Spain, haven't you? You haven't become a complete hermit.'

'No, much as I'm tempted.'

Outside the sun had gone in. An omen? Was my new life about to be prematurely foreclosed? I had no desire to return to my former trade. My Spanish was ever more fluent, I was gaining a small circle of acquaintances, both indigenous and expatriate. In effect, I was discovering what the normal life I had craved so long was like, and was even beginning to hope that Maura could be persuaded to share it with me. The other hope was that *Il Sindicato* had forgotten I existed.

In the midst of this, Britain's squabble with Spain was of less significance than a fleabite to me.

'Well?' Toby was still waiting for a proper answer.

'You mean Gibraltar?' I said, reluctant to admit I was even aware of the recent news of moves towards a conference on the status of the ex-colony.

'Yes, I mean Gibraltar.' Toby's face was stern, as if deploring my insouciance. 'And I'm sure you don't need me to explain the strategic importance of that hunk of rock.'

I sneaked a glance at my watch: it was five minutes after noon. Smells of cooking were drifting through from my restaurant, titillating the taste buds. I was bored with this talk of politics. Strictly apolitical, even when

I worked for the British Government I had kept my views to myself. It was of the past, dead and buried, never to be exhumed.

Toby pressed on. 'You'll have heard about the ... unrest in Gibraltar, about this new political faction who want to break away from the UK, become independent.'

'Vaguely. Is Sam coming here to meet you? Why not stay for lunch? I can't offer you anything exotic but ...'

'André!' Toby was a man with a slow burning fuse, slower even than me to rouse to wrath. My prevarication had brought him up to flashpoint. 'Over the weekend there was a riot on the Rock,' he told me, 'stirred up by these GIBESTÁ people as they style themselves. You must have heard about it. A number of people were injured, property damaged.'

I stared at him. Not out of sympathy for the injured, nor out of surprise that such a peaceful community could be stirred to violence. I stared in accusation.

'You want to drag me into it, don't you, you *bastard*?'

He blinked.

'It's not that ...'

'Yes, it fucking is that. What makes you think I'd be willing to get involved in a load of political shit?'

'Your history. You worked for the Firm, for a start.'

I waved that aside. 'That was a lot of years ago. I've grown up since then.'

Now he fixed me with a flinty stare. 'Not so long ago as that. If I mentioned Finland, would that mean anything?'

I let my disgust show loud and clear.

'It would mean that somebody's got a big mouth.' I swirled my glass in aimless circles on the table, thinking hard. Finally, when the thinking had gotten me nowhere, I gave it up and said, 'Who do you want killed this time?'

'Killed?' He started to laugh then saw my expression and sobered up fast. 'You are joking, aren't you?'

I slapped him across the shoulders. 'Sure I'm joking. I only wish *you* were.'

* * * * *

It was six months since I had used a gun in anger or for profit. Work had been offered, I had passed on it. More crucially, *Il Sindicato* had left me in peace, either resigned to my retirement or reluctant to start a war. They never said. I never asked. It might have been expecting too much that they really were going to let me resume the life I once had, before Marion was murdered and the tectonic plates of my world had slid sideways, tipping me off into a dark chasm, where good was indistinguishable from bad, and right from wrong, and the moral compass that had always guided me to the side of the angels swung in the opposite direction.

My new life as a bar owner had given me hope anew. Hope that I could finally break free of the chains that had bound me to my deadly profession. My thoughts wandered into the past, to the three women in my life, any one of whom could have transformed it. Marion was the first and most lasting. My only wife so far, who died because I worked for the British Secret Intelligence Service, otherwise known as MI6.

In the wake of Marion many, many women entered and left before Liza, who wasn't my lover, though I had loved her in another way, and still did. Liza who called me at regular intervals, and whom I had shut out, for no reason than that I was afraid that the purity of my feelings for her would be corrupted by the primeval pull of the flesh.

Finally, Maura. Not a replacement for Marion, but a new, real love who found that, though prepared to overlook my past, she couldn't tolerate a future in like vein. So we had parted, then reunited, then parted again. We could take up where we had left off, whenever I wished. Provided I left off killing people.

Now here I was, proving to myself that killing had been banished from my daily cycle. And when I had finally proved it to my own satisfaction, I would present myself to Maura and we would go forward together, with her daughter Belinda, and become the family that I had hungered for ever since I stepped outside the law all those corpses ago.

* * * * *

The three of us – Sam had checked in with us – lunched in my adjoining restaurant. Carlos, the chef, did us proud with a *paella de mariscos* to start and chicken cooked in pineapple rings to follow. Simple Andalucia grub, but so tasty. Washed down with a bottle of Condado Viejo, a dry "oloroso" style white wine from the Huelva region, on the Atlantic coast.

We talked mostly of niceties and Brexit. The subject of Gibraltar and its troubles was avoided. Afterwards we parted, they to visit the *alcazaba* – the fortress – obligatory for tourists, I to return to the bar. Customers were still at a premium. Gustavo would have no difficulty coping at least until the evening "rush" began. So I took off for a drive along the coast road, south towards Torremolinos. The earlier sunshine had been superseded by grey clouds, their bellies swollen with rain, and as I pulled off the road into a turnout overlooking a bay, the mutter of thunder reached me from out at sea. Rain began to spot the windshield.

I cut the engine and lowered the window to let the ozone in. As always at times of stress I sought solace in the balm of music, feeding the slot with a CD of Brahms' Fourth Symphony conducted by Bernstein. The low-key start with its sweeping violins quickly leads to a sense of conflict with unexpected interruptions by other instruments. It was not really soothing music. It was in keeping with my mood.

'You *bastard*, Toby,' I growled over the swirl of the cellos. 'You goddam, scheming bastard.'

It was not a serious slander, though it was certainly heartfelt. His proposition was not welcome. The side of me that yearned for normality told me to reject it flat. If owning a bar in Malaga was no cakewalk and less than lucrative, I was at least answerable only to myself. I was in a legal business. The demands on me were slight, the lifestyle easy-going. Meeting new people of all backgrounds and nationalities every day brought out an affable, sociable side of me that I hadn't been aware existed. Even the occasional troublemaker didn't ruin my day – they kept me on my toes.

The clouds towards the horizon were darkening. Brahms' pounding climax was accompanied by visual effects – sheet lightning flashing on-off, no sooner seen than gone. The splashes on the windshield grew in size and density, merging to become rivers.

Toby had painted me a lurid picture. Street violence in Gibraltar was unheard of under British governance, the only incident there since World War II being the shooting of an IRA bomb squad by British undercover agents. Yet since the date for the Madrid conference had been set – 8th May – there had been a series of demonstrations by this GIBESTÁ crowd. Until the weekend, the violence had gone no further than the odd scuffle, some juvenile stone-throwing, and scattering the contents of litter bins in the streets. Hardly the stuff revolutions are made of. All this had changed last night.

GIBESTÁ – a contraction of "Gibraltar está", meaning simply Gibraltar is – had been formed only recently, as far as was known, before the Madrid conference was mooted. My knowledge of it, before Toby had enlightened me, was confined to a mention in *El Correo Español* sometime last week: an adherent had thrown rotten tomatoes at the front door of the Governor's residence. Mild crowing from the Spanish press, though GIBESTÁ, so Toby told me, wanted no more truck with Spain than they did with the UK. They represented Gibraltar for the Gibraltarians, a great number of whom, in any case, have Genoese not Spanish forbears.

And what was Toby now proposing I should do? Get in amongst them, for Christ's sake. Infiltrate and report in order to sow the seeds of their downfall from within. Admittedly, in my period as a lackey of the Secret Intelligence Service, I had often operated under cover. My talent for subterfuge was less likely to be the reason for my selection than my outsider status. The British Government would go to any lengths to keep its hands officially clean. By using me they could deny complicity if it all went pear-shaped on them. It had been done before. It had been done by them to *me* before, not very long ago at that. I had fallen for it then. To fall for it again would, I was convinced, be a colossal error of judgment on my part.

'Can't afford to have the Rock opting out of the jolly old club, can we, dear boy?' Toby had said breezily, puffing away at his cigar as if it were the last he would ever smoke.

'This call for independence is just a spontaneous reaction. They're running nervous. Afraid your masters are going to hand them over to Spain, and I can't say I blame them for that.'

Toby had looked exasperated. 'But it's simply not true. We've reassured the Gibraltar Government that under no circumstances will we relinquish sovereignty.'

'Like in Northern Ireland, you mean?' I scoffed. 'No wonder they're not buying it. But if that's really your position, why hold the talks? What will you talk about if not a handover?'

'Oh …' He gestured vaguely. 'We'll offer some concessions … placebos, bear a few gifts to soothe their Iberian sensibilities. Agreeing to the Madrid venue was itself a major concession, you know.'

'If that's the attitude the negotiators start out with the whole exercise will be a fraud.' I gave him a suspicious glance. '*Will* it be a fraud, Toby?'

Toby flared his nostrils and hid behind cigar smoke.

'Toby isn't like you, André,' Sam, looking younger than her forty-five years in a cashmere sweater and tight pants, observed. 'For him the Government can do no wrong. Unquestioning obedience is his battle cry.'

So it might have been for him. But my world did not begin and end with Queen and Country. For me, there was life on other planets, other causes to espouse, other circles to circulate in, and none of them touched on Government or politics. God forbid that they should.

'Anyway, why me, Toby?'

He sucked his teeth.

'You're here, for a start. You speak Spanish, you know explosives, you're for hire. That enough for you?'

'Explosives? Jesus, Toby, that was nearly fifteen years ago. And it was a one off.'

'No matter, dear boy,' he said airily. 'We'll give you a refresher course. Oh, and you're a freelancer. We, I mean they, like freelancers. If anything goes tits up the Government can feign innocence.'

The explosives bothered me. I couldn't see the relevance, unless he was expecting me to blow up the Rock from within so they could blame it on the Spanish.

Toby rested his elbows on the table, fixed me with an earnest look. 'Between you and me, you can write your own cheque for this one, André. You're in good odour with Sir Peter, thanks to that business in Finland, on top of which they're pretty desperate. Let me put it like this – England hath need of thee.'

'Is that a fact?' I stifled a laugh. 'England hath need of me. Is that a quote, or a Toby original?"

'No good asking him,' Sam said with a snort. Of the two she was by far the more erudite. 'He's the most unliterary man in the Civil Service. Actually, it was Wordsworth, in an invocation to Milton. It's incomplete though – shall I finish it off for you, dear?' She smiled sickly-sweetly, portending mischief. '"England hath need of thee: she is a fen of stagnant waters."'

I roared with laughter. Toby did not share my amusement.

* * * * *

Some heavy vehicle ground past the turnout, brakes squealing as it entered the poorly cambered bend just beyond. The charcoal-coloured cloud was sitting overhead now, darkening land and sea. Wind beat at the car in gusts that grew stronger by the minute. The windshield blurred over with rain; I started the wipers. The horizon had been gobbled up by the advancing storm, and only a narrow band of water, white in its turbulence, remained. I stared gloomily into the greyness of it all.

Gloomily, not on account of the weather, but because, for all the plethora of good and valid reasons why not, I was sorely tempted to do as Toby asked. Go to London. Talk to the Foreign Office. Suit up for the occasion, shave off my beard (no, screw that for an idea. Let them learn to love it), put on a dedicated face. Be sucked into a world of red tape, rubber stamps, and inter-departmental memoranda. Become one of *them*. I must have been mad to even contemplate it.

One saving grace, and it was a big one: they weren't asking me to kill anybody.

Good news awaited my return to The Golden Palm. My good and faithful friend, Colin Baynes, had phoned to say he had found me a caretaker manager. I interviewed the man that same evening at Baynes's office overlooking the Rio Guadalmedina. His name was Fernando de Valasco Ruiz and he struck me as unambitious and colourless. On the credit side he wasn't demanding an extortionate salary and had a commendation from his previous employer who had sold his restaurant to some property developers.

Baynes undertook – for a fee, naturally – to keep a watching brief, and this, coupled with my impatience to absent myself for a few days, clinched the deal. I just hoped Fernando's fingers wouldn't stray into the till too often. He would start the following morning, receive a day's tuition in how to pull pints and balance the books, leaving me free to make an unscheduled trip to the Rock on Thursday morning.

* * * * *

'Come on over, old top,' Toby said when I phoned my decision to him. He was staying at the Miramar, 5-star luxury funded by the British taxpayer. 'We'll open a bottle of something to celebrate.'

'Celebrate? Is that what I should be doing? A wake would be more appropriate. You celebrate, Toby. Mug recruited, mission accomplished. The PM is bound to make room for you in the end of term Honours List.'

He began to protest his purity of soul.

'Forget it, *amigo*. I'm only pulling your leg. Say g'night to Sam for me.'

I hung up, wishing he'd stayed in England. Wishing I wasn't so readily seduced. Yet, perversely, as excited as a kid contemplating a trip to the seaside.

Now why was that?

Chapter Six

Toby returned to London later in the day. I was to report to him the following week for more briefing and to sign the Official Secrets Act, though they had had my signature on that dusty scroll for years. In between times I was looking forward to my jaunt to Gibraltar. It was a private project, which, out of my innate distrust of people in the pay of the British Government, I did not disclose to Toby. First-hand knowledge of the Rock would be a card up my sleeve, to be produced if ever I needed to bolster my position.

My farewell shot to Fernando and Gustavo was designed to motivate them with the twin incentives of profit and loss: a bonus if they did well, the boot if they screwed up. They waved me off, insisting on jointly transferring my overnight bag to the trunk, and minutes later I was rolling along the highway, known otherwise as the *autopista* A7.

On a clear day the Rock of Gibraltar becomes visible about five kilometres north of Marbella, heaving up from the flat skyline where the shore joins the sea. Gibraltar, from Gebel Tarik – Tarik's Hill – after Tarik-Ibn-Zeyad, commander of the Berber armies who landed there in 771AD. Bi-lingual Spanish-English. The last British garrison left in 1991 and the Royal Gibraltar Regiment was now the sole arbiter of keeping the Spanish out. No combat aircraft were stationed there on a permanent basis. What else had my Google trawl thrown up? As a British Overseas Territory it was still under the overlordship of a Military Governor – Sir Gilbert Dover was the newly-appointed incumbent. However, it had its own civilian rulers: the moderate Fabian Picardo and his Socialist Labour Party had seized power from the even more moderate Social Democrats in the 2011 election and held on to it in a subsequent election. The GSLP's policies were uncontroversial, their stance on the whole pro-British. They could be relied on to back any moves to break up the GIBESTÁ outfit as a bunch of renegades. So sayeth Toby.

I left the *autopista* at San Roque, where it bears away westward to skirt the Bay of Algeciras, and headed into La Línea, the last outpost of Spain. From here the Rock appeared as if detached from the sterile foreground of undulating hills of scrub, haphazard electric pylons, and plumes of ochre-hued smoke marking the position of some chemicals plant in La Línea. A cloud crouched over the Rock itself, as it often does, according to my Google search. It was ragged-edged, in constant flux like smoke trailing from a steamship's funnel. The summit, twelve hundred feet or so at its highest point, was lost in it. Now, too, across the Strait of Gibraltar, the rampart of the coast of Morocco, blurred by haze, joined the backdrop.

Finally the sea hove into sight. I turned left onto a road running alongside a shingle beach. It was early afternoon and at this southerly latitude the siesta is observed by many throughout the year. Consequently the traffic was light, and the frontier quiet. Spanish customs, notorious here for their delaying tactics, checked the trunk and waved me through. The British, ever respectful of upmarket wheels, gave my British passport a perfunctory flick-through. Anyone who drives an Aston with a personalised licence plate is respectable by association.

Just goes to show the power of appearances to deceive.

* * * * *

In Gibraltar's Main Street I window-shopped, soaking up the ambience.

At a superficial level it was just another town, Main Street much as Main Streets and High Streets all over the Anglophone world. Yet it was like no town I had ever known, Moorish architecture rubbing walls with European. There was a timbre of Englishness – a Marks & Spencer store, policemen in English-style uniforms without guns, pubs by the dozen, red telephone kiosks. The people generally were a mixed bag of fair-skinned Anglo-Saxon and typical Latino, with a proliferation of Asian traders, and the occasional caftan-clad Arab hawking dubious wares. Most curious of all were the ones who looked English yet spoke Spanish and to a lesser extent vice-versa.

But what struck me above all else in this somehow scaled-down toytown was the hush that hung over it. A good part of Main Street was closed to through traffic and this had to be a contributing factor, but it was the looming massif of the Rock most of all that created this peculiar acoustic effect. It was like being in a church with no roof.

Like all towns it had its downside: it was grubby in places though litter was not an obvious problem, kept at bay by numerous garbage bins, interestingly sponsored by businesses, and the exhortations to KEEP GIBRALTAR TIDY that leapt at you from billboards. Street acts added colour or lowered the tone, depending on your point of view. Jugglers mostly, a girl in a bowler hat balancing on the shoulders of a guitar playing man was the best of the bunch, if only because she had a good body and was dressed to exploit it.

The sun wasn't shining. The cloud clinging to the Rock saw to that. Yet it was warm and humid and many people sported light summer clothes. Some of the bars towards the end of Main Street, where it expands to become Cathedral Square, had tables outside, and I sat down opposite a couple of shaven-scalped skinhead youths, who gaped at me as if I had green skin and a TV antenna sprouting from my skull. By the standards of nowadays, maybe my conventional grey chinos and striped polo shirt marked me out as the oddity, not them.

I settled for a Kronenberg from the wide selection of beers proposed by the waiter. It was a while coming. The skinheads conversed intermittently in cockney English, remarking on this or that 'nice bit o' cunt', an observation that was followed by some lewd speculation on how the object of their admiration might 'perform', given the opportunity.

After a second beer and some limp, gladwrapped sandwiches, I drifted off towards the dock area. This lay beyond the battlements that extend the length of the town, facing out across the bay towards Algeciras. Towards the old enemy.

The docks side of the portal through which I passed was painted in black and bore the curious legend RAGGED STAFF GATES. As I wandered along a road named Queensway, more of these captions appeared at intervals along the walls, interspersing the gun embrasures: KING'S BASTION, ZOCA FLANK BATTERY, PRINCE ALBERT'S

FRONT, WATERPORT CASEMATES. My cell phone's Google explained that they were the names given to different gun batteries when Empire was at its zenith. They invoked the noise and the heat of battle, the stink of gunpowder, and the ripple of cannonballs and chain shot cleaving the air. And the cries of the mutilated and the dying. And, yes, the silence of the dead.

I shook off my macabre mood and walked on past these relics of past glory. Despite an affinity for most things British, the nation's warlike history was not in my blood.

The cloud moved off the Rock mid-afternoon and at about the same time I took a taxi tour round the island. We drove past the vast disused rainwater catchment area, on the eastern slope of the Rock, now known as the Great Dune. Water is ever in short supply in Gibraltar, the taxi driver told me, and the reservoirs fed by the catchments used to provide a large part of the community's needs. Now it mostly comes from a desalination plant.

On the catchment side of the Rock was Catalan Bay Village, a tiny community dominated by the Caleta Hotel, a multi-storey edifice perched on some rocks at the southern end of the bay.

'You want a room for tonight?' my taxi driver asked as I disembarked on the Catalan Bay sea front.

'Maybe.' I crossed his palm with euros. 'Do you recommend that one?'

'Very nice hotel. Not too expensive, very friendly.' He made to count out my change; I waved it away. 'You want me to fix a room for you?'

I looked across at the hotel and figured it would do.

'Why not? Warner is the name. Tell them I'll be along about six. And if you'd like to collect me here at, say, five thirty, to take me to my car, I'll make it worth your while.'

Contract sealed, he roared off in his rusty Nissan. By chance he had deposited me outside a little bar called The Village Inn. Customers, most of them patently tourists, sat at dilapidated tables by the sea wall. I plonked down next to some locals – three youngish men, very Spanish looking, and one much older with more folds in his brown face than a scrotum. They were debating, in oddly-accented Spanish, the boom in property development on the Rock in recent years. They were not in favour.

'I cannot afford anything more than a studio,' one lamented. This sparked off a chorus of agreement.

'But there is more money to be made nowadays,' the old man said shrewdly; he had tiny eyes that glinted moistly as if filled with tears. Before him was a glass of pale liquid, probably some local firewater.

'What money? Have I ever seen any of this money? Why am I broke if there is so much money here?'

'Peter is not broke.'

Peter – the name sat awkwardly with his swarthy features – made a throwaway gesture.

'Business is better this year than last, it is true, but the profits are not so good as they once were. There is more competition now, too many new shops. The Indians are the new rich.'

The third of the younger trinity looked glum as he said, nodding, 'If I had my way we would close the border and keep it closed. We do not need the tourists, especially not Spanish tourists. We are better off without them.'

I signalled a waiter who had just emerged from the bar and ordered a Kronenberg beer in Spanish. This brought me to the attention of the man Peter, who was nearest to me. He stared, but out of curiosity not rudeness, and I twitched the corners of my mouth at him to show I wasn't hostile.

'You are English, *señor*?' Before I could reply he went on to say: 'You speak Spanish well.'

'Thanks for the compliment. I live in Malaga.'

The other three heads were tugged in my direction.

'I hope you won't hold that against me,' I said, adding, 'I couldn't help overhearing your comments just now.'

The old man studied me, shielding his eyes against the sun, now dipping behind the Rock.

'You like the Spanish?'

'As much as I like any other race. There's good and bad in all of them.'

'Hmm.' The old man fingered the lapels of his black waistcoat, a venerable garment, much frayed around the pockets. A fob watch chain was looped across his chest.

'It is the thin end of the wedge,' Peter grumbled. 'I remember when we had a guard on the frontier, now he is long since gone. The Spanish Government makes more and more demands. Soon they will be given unrestricted access to our airport. Also, they insist that their people should not have to pass through immigration and passport controls. What do you think of that? Why should they have such special treatment? Even the British are not exempted from normal immigration procedures. It is bad enough that we must let in their tourists and their workers –'

'To steal our jobs,' the man who had bemoaned his lack of funds chipped in.

'Right, Louis, right. They take the food from the mouths of our babies.'

'Don't you think you're exaggerating their impact?' I said mildly, risking an uproar.

Peter swung round on me, his black eyebrows drawn together to meet across the bridge of his nose, his Latin temperament surfacing.

'I mean to say,' I went on, smiling so as to keep the temperature low, 'there's not much sign of poverty here. The beggars you were talking about just now are from across the border, aren't they?'

'What can you know about our country?' the fourth man sneered. 'A foreigner!'

'You're right, I don't know much. But I've got eyes. Britain has brought a lot of prosperity to this place.'

'Not for much longer,' Louis said, tapping the side of his nose. 'Changes are afoot.'

'Independence?' I said, and the three younger ones nodded. The old man hooded his eyes.

'It might be the answer. Then again you might be too weak to survive without British money and a British presence. It's a tough world out there. You need a patron.'

'Britain will still be our patron,' Peter said loftily, 'even when we are independent.'

It sounded smug but he was probably right. Untying the strings was one thing, discarding the apron altogether was an altogether greater risk.

It occurred to me that I could easily be in the company of paid-up members of this GIBESTÁ organisation, or at least sympathisers. It might be smart not to appear anti at this stage.

'Can I get you a drink?' I said, to give emotions a chance to cool and to consolidate the opportunity created.

The old man put away what remained of his in a single hurried swallow. Louis called the waiter and orders flew across the table.

Even with the sun now sunk behind the upper rock it remained warm. The breeze that scoured the side of the Rock from north to south was benign. I stripped off my windbreaker and hung it over the back of the chair. Peter, Louis, and their colleague, introduced to me as John, wore only cotton shirts and shorts.

'What is your name?' Peter demanded.

It might have been wiser to use my alternative identity of John Henley, but I didn't have long enough to figure out the implications, so I stayed true to my real self.

'André.'

'This is your first name?'

'Yes.' I didn't volunteer my last name.

'André?' He hesitated, gently massaging the point of his chin between thumb and forefinger. 'It is a French name, is it not? And you speak English with a bit of an American accent.'

'I was raised in Canada. My mother was a Quebecer.'

'Ah.' John frowned, maybe unsure whether that made me friendly or not.

'Anyway, we accept you as an honorary Englishman,' Louis said magnanimously.

I thanked him tongue in cheek and turned my head towards the old man. 'You have not been introduced, *señor*. Do you wish to remain anonymous?'

He gave another of his cackles. 'No, no. My name is Eduardo. They call me El Jefe. I am their unofficial counsellor – though they rarely take my counsel.'

El Jefe, meaning the chief. 'It's an honour to meet you, Jefe.'

He tendered a magisterial bow of the head, acknowledging my words of respect.

'Do you think the frontier should be closed again?' I asked El Jefe, so far reticent on the subject of the Spanish incursion.

'Closed or open, it makes no difference. If the Spanish decide they must have Gibraltar at all costs they will simply walk in and take it.'

A minor furore broke out among the younger men. They all started talking at once. I kept out of it. This was a debate I wanted to hear run its natural course.

'We will never let them walk in!' Fair-haired John, the quietest of the three, spat, with the vehemence of a zealot. 'They walk in here over my dead body; yes, and the body of my wife and my unborn child. What do you say, Peter? And you, Louis? Where do you stand in this?

'Alongside you,' Peter said with such quiet simplicity that I knew instinctively that he was sincere. Louis murmured agreement, then said, 'I have no wife and children to offer as sacrifices, but if I had, and it must be, then I would offer them. I would defend Gibraltar to the end.'

El Jefe was unmoved by these fiery declarations. His old head wagged in gentle dissent. He wouldn't see seventy again, yet his faculties had not conspicuously dimmed with age. His hair was thin, lying in wisps along his scalp, the skin underneath mottled and dead-looking. The eyes, those tiny chips set wide apart over an eagle's beak of a nose, blazed with the fires of nihilism. Here was a sometime fighter who was still, I sensed, for all his calmness and air of acceptance, a fighter.

'It will not happen though,' Louis said, sounding resigned, even disappointed. 'The days of Franco are no more, and the mentality of Spain's leaders owes nothing to him. Look at Sanchez. Can you see him leading Spain into a war? Hah! They are trade unionists. Spain is a member of NATO and of the European Union. They bang their drums but it is all bluster. They have enough problems with Catalonia.'

El Jefe had listened in pursed-lips silence to the boastful rhetoric and the reasoning of Louis.

'Maybe,' he said, his voice pitched low, his lower lip trembling a little. 'I hope you are right, but I am not so sure.'

Chapter Seven

The boom-boom-boom of the drums was reminiscent of a Loyalist march I had once witnessed during a stopover in Belfast. A slow-time percussion, rising and falling, coming unstoppably nearer. The stride of passers-by checked and their ears cocked in the direction of the sound. Then, for the most part, they moved on, went about their business. Only a very few stayed where they were, to await developments. Two men standing close to me jabbered at each other in fast Spanish, punctuating each remark with a nervous snigger. From them I learned that the drums portended a demonstration staged by GIBESTÁ to present a petition to the Governor against Gibraltar accepting Spanish rule.

'On a Sunday they should be in church, not clogging up the streets,' the man nearest to me said to his neighbour, and they both chortled, as if at a smutty joke.

I had found myself in a square called Convent Place, sharing with a dozen or so others an oblong of shade thrown by the Gothic-style porch over the entrance to the Governor's residence – known as The Convent from its monastic origins. It was only a few minutes before noon and warm with it. The sentry standing under the porch, rifle at the slope, gave no sign of having heard the approach of the marchers. He was as solid as the pillars supporting the porch. The rifle would not, of course, be loaded. Neither were the two naval cannon flanking the entrance to the building. They were symbolic. Brits set a lot of store by symbolism. As if it were bullet-proof.

Crowds were forming on all sides of the square, jostling for vantage points. A throb of excitement was in the air and a strange quiet had fallen, belying the increase in numbers. Now the drums had entered the street; the steady, controlled *boom* .... *boom* ... *boom* drowned all other noise.

Several more policemen had congregated under the porch. None of them carried guns, but riot sticks dangled from their belts for all to see and be afraid.

The advance guard of the procession consisted of three policemen: an officer between two constables, marching out of step, an emaciated blue line. The officer had an Alsatian on a chain leash. As they passed, a small dog popped out from between the forest of legs at the roadside and scampered across to the Alsatian, yapping deliriously. The Alsatian, displaying a natural canine interest, slowed. A jerk on the leash reminded it of its duty and, casting a last wistful glance at the other dog, it fell back in step.

The front ranks of the marchers themselves were coming into sight around the corner to enter Main Street. Necks craned, mine included.

'That man's got a sword,' said a little girl sitting astride her father's shoulders, pointing at a man walking alone, dressed in a ceremonial uniform of pale grey, not dissimilar from the old Confederate Army livery, except that the piping was dark blue, not gold. On his head was a dark blue beret. No insignia or badges of rank, just the sword, a sabre of some description, in an ornately-wrought scabbard.

The man was big and wide of shoulder, and conveyed an instant sense of presence. The hair below the beret was all silver, and his moustache was in perfect harmony, though his features in contrast were almost unlined. He passed by at a funereal pace, and the first rank of his followers, twelve drummers in three rows, drew level with my section of the crowd. Apart from the lack of sword they were identically attired to their leader. Their faces like stone, they beat the drums with strap pads, twirling the pads in between strokes. Visually too, they harked back strongly to the Belfast Protestant parades. Behind the drummers came two men bearing a banner, unsurprisingly emblazoned with the GIBESTÁ motif which consisted of indigo lettering forming the shape of the Rock, on grey. They were followed by a woman – young, black hair falling to her waist, her uniform making no concessions to her sex. She carried the movement's standard, also grey, hanging slackly in the still air.

A gap of some twenty metres separated the flag carriers from the next section of marchers, a hundred or so uniformed men and women, in ragged order but exuding a proud defiance. There was no segregation of male from female; the ratio was about three to one, and the average age looked to be in the twenty-five to thirty-five range, though I spotted a couple of grey heads and at the opposite end of the scale a boy who couldn't have been more than twelve.

Last of all came the civilians, the less-committed supporters. A dense phalanx of humanity, several hundred strong for sure. The majority were young. I thought I spotted Peter, my new acquaintance from yesterday, but a head bobbed in front of me and blocked my view at a crucial moment.

From the authorities' angle it was a sobering show of solidarity in favour of an independent Gibraltar. That so many out of a civilian population of some thirty thousand were prepared to declare publicly for independence was some achievement for such a newly-created movement. Powerful political factions have arisen out of humbler beginnings.

'Where are they going, daddy?' the little girl on her father's shoulders asked.

'To church,' her father replied shortly and facetiously.

'Which church? Is it St. Mary's? Can we go too?'

'No. Be quiet.'

As the tail of the column plodded by under the harsh sun a wiry spectator beside me muttered 'Bravo,' and elbowed through the fringes of the spectators to tag on to the column, a volunteer off to fight in the trenches. Somebody cheered, sporadic clapping broke out.

As the drums tailed off to a mutter the crowd began to break up, chattering excitedly. I forced a passage through to the Convent porch. The policemen were still in evidence, at ease now that the potential threat to Crown property had receded.

I singled out a young police sergeant, whose swarthy features were out of place under his bobby's helmet.

'Somebody told me they were going to present a petition,' I said. 'What happened to it?'

He looked me up and down, frowning, but his reply when it came was respectful enough.

'They will be presenting it at the end of the march, sir.' His English was precisely enunciated, almost accent-free.

'So they're coming back here.'

'Yes. They will walk down Main Street as far as Cooperage Lane and back here via Irish Town. The Governor has agreed to receive the petition at one o'clock.' His expression became searching. 'You're a visitor to Gibraltar?'

'Just a day tripper,' I said with a grin and moved away. I didn't want to become familiar with or to the Law. Not until my exact function here was spelled out.

Those among the crowd who were in the know were still hanging around. They had formed little knots and were engaged in quiet discussion. The drumbeat floated over the rooftops, a reminder that normality was not yet restored. Within a minute it began to swell again and now, though the tempo had not obviously quickened, it seemed somehow more ebullient, more defiant. As if the final run-up to the delivery of the petition had injected new vigour into the drummers.

As if they were expecting something to happen.

Or planning to make something happen.

Without conscious effort on my part my feet were on the move, transporting me towards the throbbing drums. Beginning with a walk, becoming a trot, building to a lope. I came to a square, remembered from my yesterday's saunter.

'Which way to Irish Town?' I demanded breathlessly of a young guy, propped against the wall of the Tourist Information Office, nursing a beer glass.

In wordless reply he indicated the next turn left. I rushed off through the animated throngs, performing bodily contortions to avoid collision.

Irish Town was not a town but a street. A police constable on the corner bestowed a baleful stare on me. I had arrived alone in the middle of the road; the sidewalks on both sides were packed with folk. The drums were louder here, booming down between the buildings, the procession less than a hundred metres away and heading straight for me.

'Get off the road, sir,' the constable ordered, stepping off the curb in case I needed encouragement.

'Sorry, officer,' I nipped past him and burrowed into a section of spectators lining the front of a synagogue. Opposite was a police station, fronted by a row of arches. As you'd expect, the law had concentrated its strength here. Policemen were also spaced along the marchers' route. Not nearly enough of them if things turned nasty.

As before, the various factions trooped past: the three policemen, the big man with the sword, the drummers... The main body of uniformed GIBESTÁ supporters was just coming into sight between the bobbing heads on my right when the stone was thrown.

It might have come from the crowd, it might equally have been projected from an open window overlooking the road. It struck the black-haired girl, the standard bearer, a glancing blow on the cheek and was deflected on to land in the gutter, causing some people there to leap back in alarm.

The girl herself had given a short, sharp cry at the moment of impact. Letting the standard fall she clutched at the injured spot. Her hand came away, smeared scarlet. Yet anger, not hysteria was in her stance. She was shaken but not intimidated.

'Cowards!' she railed at the silent ranks. 'If you want to fight, come and do it in the open!'

The rest of the procession had stopped. Several of them were running toward the girl. Another stone flew, knocking the beret from the first GIBESTÁ marcher to arrive at the girl's side. He stumbled, more in surprise than through injury. Shouts were exchanged. Up ahead the drumming lost cohesion. The front rank of drummers had reached the next corner and were halted there, turning rearwards awkwardly, restricted by their ungainly instruments.

From within the main mass of the uniformed GIBESTÁ-ites came a ripple of movement. A section of the crowd had broken away and was in amongst them. Berets flew. I heard breaking glass, a fusion of shouting and cheering. The police went into action, converging on the mêlée, some with riot sticks already drawn. Now there was a flurry of missiles, including what looked like half-bricks. A half-brick struck the gutsy black-haired girl as she stooped in the road to recover her fallen standard. It caught her at the back of the skull, just above the neck, and the impact sounded like a sledge hammer hitting concrete. She didn't cry out. One second she was crouching in the road, the next she was spread-eagled face down. If anyone else in the vicinity noticed, they were either too preoccupied with their own problems or too shit-scared to care. The girl lay motionless, stepped over, walked around, ignored by police and protagonists alike. Her hair was a black glossy fantail, her beret lay just beyond the reach of one outstretched hand, was trampled on even as I watched. A scarlet tentacle pushed out from under the splay of hair, formed a ribbon that wound lazily towards the roadside. And still she lay unattended.

The last thing I needed was the glare of publicity. I was about to be sent here on Her Majesty's Government's Business – *undercover* business. To play the Samaritan was to put my secret status in jeopardy. Toby had drilled into me the need for discretion, to the extent that I almost turned my back, almost left her there. Then, in a rush of shame, instincts deeper rooted than devotion to Queen and Country and wallet, took over. Pushing aside a pair of nattering, excitable women, I plunged into the fray. A GIBESTÁ drummer swiped at me in passing but while he was off-balance I shoved him backwards and he was absorbed into the crowd. Then a policeman's riot stick, flailing indiscriminately, thumped into my kidneys and propelled me forwards so that I tripped over the fallen girl's spread legs.

No flicker of life issued from her. I pressed my ear to her back, strained for a heartbeat, but if it was there, it was drowned by the pandemonium all around.

The medical profession wouldn't have approved, but I rolled her onto her back. Her body was a dead weight, her limbs slack and floppy like a marionette's. Blood from the wound at the back of her skull soaked into my sleeve, dark as a Bordeaux red. She was very young – seventeen, eighteen maybe. Quite plain, except for her eyes: they were huge, incredibly dark, with long eyelashes. They seemed to be staring into mine; staring in surprise and fear of the unknown. I cradled her, held her to me to protect her from the many feet that scurried here and there, miraculously missing us.

But there was really nothing to protect. She was somewhere else, not here in my arms. Somewhere far away, in a place from which there was no coming back.

It was in this eye of calm in the hurricane of violence that the big man, the GIBESTÁ leader, came and knelt beside me. He bore the scars of battle: a button torn from his tunic, his head now bare and his silver hair in disarray. A gash just below the hairline was weeping blood.

His hand rested on my shoulder. His grip was hard, conveying his apprehension, his dread.

'My name is Michael Vella,' he said, quite calmly, as if we were meeting at a cocktail party. 'This is my daughter, Adriana. Is she … badly hurt?'

I looked at him and felt the prickle of tears glazing my vision.

He seemed to deflate, as if an essential part of him had been excised. His arms reached out, as if in supplication, to take his dead girl from me. A wandering knee jarred my shoulder. I scarcely felt it. Dumbly, I loosened my hold. The man called Vella drew his daughter from me so gently I was hardly aware of the transfer. A uniformed GIBESTÁ-ite came blundering up, chest heaving, sweat glossing his face.

'Michael!' he gasped. 'Michael! Is she all right?'

No answer was forthcoming, nor needed. The GIBESTÁ leader cradled his daughter to him. Her hair swung, a broken black wing, covering his knee.

A passing policeman witnessed the little drama, pivoted on his heel.

'*Señor* …!' He sheathed his riot stick and bent to look closely at the girl. 'I will send for an ambulance,' he announced, and was gone. Nobody told him not to hurry.

The commotion was dying around me as the police gained the upper hand. My place was elsewhere, far from the demand for witnesses and statements that would inevitably ensue. The GIBESTÁ-ite was already puzzling over my presence. It showed in his questioning glances, from me to the dead girl and back.

I squeezed Michael Vella's shoulder in sympathy but failed to penetrate his grief. So I left him with it and melted away into the dispersing crowds.

* * * * *

It was as though I had been living a dream for the last thirty hours. Only when I pulled up before the dusty forecourt of The Golden Palm did I waken, to look back and marvel the tragic event that had marred my brief stay in Gibraltar.

The death of the girl had made a deep impression on me. She was a stranger, meant zilch to me, and death itself was commonplace in my world of violence. Yet, I had been touched by this particular death, maybe because it had been so unnecessary, so sudden. Or maybe because of her youth, her defiant courage, her pouring of scorn on hostility.

During my absence The Golden Palm had continued to function as normal, i.e. at negligible profit level. No matter, I wasn't in it for the money I kept reminding myself. The good news was that, based on the experience of the last few days, the business wouldn't fall apart when I wasn't around. This left me free to wing north on Thursday morning.

Back to dreary, over-populated London. Back to breathe a million exhaust emissions. Back, well and truly, in the yoke.

Chapter Eight

From where I sprawled in an over-stuffed ministry chair, the vista through Toby's office windows was of sky – a blue, crisp, early March sky. The sunshine had helped compensate for the relocation to northerly latitudes and so far the VIP treatment the Government was meting out – a plush room at the Park Lane Hotel, chauffeur driven transportation – was keeping me sweet. Unlikely it would continue after I had signed on the dotted line.

'Well,' Toby said, speaking from his desk. 'You're here and I'm now authorised to tell you what's going on and where you fit in.'

I fingered the knot of the tie I was unaccustomed to wearing. It was warm in Toby's office and the sun, encouraged by the high windows that were the kind that don't open, was slowly roasting me.

'Not before time.'

'Hmm. Be that as it may, talks between the governments of the UK and Spain on the future of Gibraltar will begin on 8th May in Madrid.' He paused, perhaps expecting me to react with awe and reverence. When I didn't oblige, he resumed sniffily, 'Our position has always been that no transfer or sharing of sovereignty will be entertained until and unless a majority of the people of Gibraltar expresses a desire by plebiscite in favour of such a transfer.'

'In plain English, that means they have to vote for it, right?'

Like Queen Victoria, he was not amused.

'Keep your sarcasm to yourself, André.'

'That wasn't sarcasm, it was plain English.'

'We don't expect such a plebiscite to produce such a result, therefore the chief purpose of the talks will be to keep faith with certain interested parties, notably the United States, NATO, United Nations, and the EU.'

'Not Spain, then.'

'Ostensibly, yes.' Even that was said reluctantly.

He sipped from his dainty cup – Royal Doulton bone china or of that ilk, nothing less would suffice.

'A secondary purpose will be to leave Spain in no doubt as to the prerequisites for a transfer of sovereignty –'

'But you said transfer of sovereignty isn't going to happen.'

'Don't interrupt,' he said, severe as a schoolmaster. 'It is to be made clear that those prerequisites are non-negotiable.'

He was losing me. 'What fucking prerequisites?'

He expelled an exasperated sigh. 'That information is privileged. You don't need to know.' Again the glower, before continuing. 'A further secondary purpose will be to reinforce our commitment in the eyes of the world to the continuation of Gibraltar's present status. In other words, to preserve the status quo.'

'Congratulations,' I murmured. 'Is that all the purposes?'

'The final purpose is to maintain equable relations with Spain, as fellow members of NATO.'

A silence fell upon us. Toby sipped more tea. I had never liked the stuff so I left mine alone.

'Any questions?' he asked.

'If it's all a big, fat sham, no, I have no questions.'

He stood up and paced the obviously expensive carpet as far as the window and back, to loom over me.

'Some sops will be offered to Spain, such as adjustments to rates of duty inside and outside Gibraltar, investment facilities, easing of conditions for Spanish workers, and so on.'

'I guess that'll satisfy them. Thank God I won't be on our negotiating team. They could get lynched.'

Toby lit a cigar and to hell with the no smoking rules.

'Any questions, dear boy?'

'Only a million or so.' I gave him a disarming grin. 'But you wouldn't answer a one of 'em.'

He effected affront. 'Try me.'

I regarded him, trying to penetrate the bland exterior. And failing.

'If you insist,' I said, and threw in a yawn just to show I was convinced it was a waste of effort. 'Just between us friends, is the

Government prepared to make any concessions at all on sovereignty?'

'Trust you,' he said tetchily, 'to ask the wrong question.' A pause for puffing. 'Pass.'

'You don't say.'

'Officially,' Toby did say, a furtive note creeping into his voice, 'I shouldn't have told you as much as I have. You're still officially an outsider.'

'Thank Christ for that. I still don't quite see what the talks have to do with my particular project.'

'Directly, nothing. I've taken the liberty of giving you an insight into the likely course the talks will take, to illustrate how the rise of this independence movement will weaken the position of our negotiators.'

'You said that without pausing for breath. What about the need to know? I don't actually need to know, do I? Just wind me up and give me a push in the right direction.'

Toby gave an impatient grunt. 'We can do without your flashes of so-called humour,' he said stiffly.

I tugged the carefully arranged damask handkerchief from my breast pocket and patted my forehead with it.

'Is the aircon broken?'

'It's centrally controlled and not switched on until May.'

'The Government being frugal with taxpayers' money for once. I approve, but how about something cool to drink before I sweat right through my suit.'

He looked pained. 'Must you? Oh, all right, but only mineral water.'

He organised it by telephone.

'You're so kind,' I said, picking up a folder from a pile on his desk and fanning myself with it. He snatched it back with a glare. 'Returning to your point about GIBESTÁ, I don't agree that they'll weaken our position with the Spanish. The whole movement's an irrelevancy.'

'Now you're being obtuse. If the Spanish perceive a crack in the colonial fortress they'll move heaven and the Iberian peninsula to exploit it. It matters not a whit that these GIBESTÁ people are more anti-Spain than they are anti-UK. With the right kind of hype and a dash of distortion the Spanish press will have us Brits looking like a bunch of Nazi bully boys and the Gibraltarians like a poverty-stricken slave race before you can say "front page story."'

'If that's what you really think you must be paranoid.'

Toby's expression hardened.

'Not you personally,' I said, making soothing motions with my hand. 'I was speaking collectively.'

He subsided somewhat, sucked genteelly at his cigar. Said nothing.

'But paranoid or not …' A tap at the door had Toby silencing me with a finger over his lips. Two bottles of Perrier on a tray entered, conveyed by a sturdy middle-aged woman, drably dressed, and with one of those permed hair-dos that became extinct along with *Picture Post* magazine.

'Don't you even trust your own people?' I said when we were on our own again. 'You take it too seriously, Toby. It's just a great big game, you should know that better than I.'

I unscrewed the cap from one of the bottles, poured into the Government crystal.

Toby laid his cigar in an ashtray made from the base of a shell case and followed my example with the other bottle.

'Let's come to your specific role, shall we?'

'Let's. Put an end to the suspense.'

He sniffed. 'The Government feels that the existence of GIBESTÁ is prejudicial to stability within Gibraltar, and even more so to the outcome of the Madrid talks. Consequently, we aim to curtail their activities and bring about the dissolution of the movement. A meeting is to be held later today, in these very premises, to settle on the methods.' His gaze centred on me. 'You are required to attend. In fact, in some ways, you'll be the guest of honour.'

It sounded mildly threatening. As if 'guest of honour' were synonymous with facing a firing squad.

'My, oh my. Guest of honour. Don't you think we should agree terms first?'

'No,' he said sharply. 'Let's hear what the policy wonks have to say and your views too – your constructive views, I mean – before we talk contracts.'

'Right, teacher. Can I go now?'

'No, you cannot. You and I are having a working lunch together.

While you're here and as long as we're paying your expenses, you're going to put in a full day's work every day.'

I looked wistfully at the square of blue sky. I'd been looking forward to shopping at Harrods.

'You lot in the Civil Service wouldn't recognise a full day's work if it sank its teeth in your throat,' I said spitefully.

If looks could speak volumes I would have been deafened.

* * * * *

After that tedious 'working lunch' I was allowed off the leash for a couple of hours. I used this free period to call on Cassandra who coincidentally was in town, staying at her Chelsea mews cottage. I had visited the place only once previously. It was no different from others of its genre all over the capital except that it was two cottages made into one, to create, by mews' standards, a palatial dwelling place.

Unthinkingly I parted with the cab before establishing that my wandering ex-paramour was at home. She wasn't. A rueful expletive was dying on my lips when a car turned into the courtyard – a sleek red Ferrari with dark tinted windows that reduced the occupants to obscurity. I guessed at once this was Cassandra's latest extravagance and I was not wrong.

She got out, elegant and ravishing in her furs, her wax effigy-like beauty exactly as I remembered it. Straightening up, she stared at me over the roof of the Ferrari as if I were the last person she expected to come calling.

'André,' she said, no warmth at all.

The nearside door opened and from it, predictably, emerged a man. A tall, very good-looking man of twenty or so. Blond hair done up in soft waves that bounced when he tossed his head. Which he was doing now, piqued, as if he suspected Cassandra of double-booking her dates.

'Still cradle-snatching, eh, Cassandra?' I said, deliberately *sotto voce.*

'What's that?' she snapped, and slammed the door on that costly piece of machinery with enough violence to make me wince. 'What do you want, André?'

She talked more like the Queen than the Queen herself. Expletives aside.

'A welcome back?' I suggested.

The blond man jutted his jaw at me and clenched his fists.

'Who the fuck are you?' he demanded, his accent betraying his East London origins. Cassandra's spare studs were seldom culled from the aristocracy.

She came round the front of the car, gave her boyfriend's forearm a soothing squeeze.

'This,' she said with the longest of long-suffering sighs, 'is my ex-bosom companion André. André, meet Clive.'

'What you after, mate?' Clive said, his tone suggesting he wasn't delighted to make my acquaintance.

'Never mind me. What's this I hear about you, Cassie? Not well, Toby tells me.'

'Toby's an old woman and a gossipmonger.'

'Agreed. But even he wouldn't dream up an imaginary illness.'

Cassandra made a wearily dismissive gesture. 'Let's just say he's exaggerating. I'm fine … fine.'

Clive, feeling neglected, asserted himself. 'Look, sunshine –'

'Hey,' I said, raising a warning finger. 'Butt out. I'm talking to Cassandra, not you.'

While he was getting used to being relegated to the sidelines, I said to Cassandra. 'You look lovely, really lovely. But you don't look fine. What's wrong?'

Cassandra, hummed and hawed and finally said, 'I'm seeing a specialist on Tuesday next. Let's leave it at that.'

'Is it … serious. Can I do anything?'

'I said let's leave it at that. Now be a darling and fuck off out of my life, will you?'

'You close-mouthed bitch!' I snarled, the last thread of my compassion snapping. 'Can't you see I … I …'

'Care?' She smiled, a symmetrical curving of her starkly red lips; but there was no joy in it. 'Thank you then for caring, my dear one-time lover boy. Anything else on your mind? Do you need money?'

'Money?' I almost choked. 'When did I ever ask you for money? You must be confusing me with this cretin.' I nodded towards the simmering Clive.

'Who the fuck are you callin' a cretin?' he blustered.

'Oh, you know what it means, do you?'

He bunched his fists and got ready to prove his manliness.

'Right, that's it,' he growled. 'On yer fucking bike before I make yer lick me boots.'

'I'm almost curious enough to see how you'd make me do that, you lowlife peasant.'

His eyes bulged. His body stiffened, the fists got ready for launch.

'Clive – no!' Cassandra cried, seeming concerned that I might get hurt. She tried to force herself between us, but Clive showed his true breeding by shoving her aside.

While he was momentarily distracted from the main objective – putting me in hospital – I planted a knee in his balls, putting so much effort behind it that I lost my balance and fell to the cobbles with him. I left him thrashing about down there, squealing the way a pig squeals when they winch it up by its hind legs prior to cutting its throat. Master Clive wouldn't be doing stud duty on Cassandra this afternoon or any other afternoon this side of a long period of celibacy.

Chapter Nine

The table was oval, its surface sheathed in red leather. The ten chairs were made to match. Not antique, not modern, just top quality. According to Toby, most inner sancti of the more prestigious government departments are furnished without regard as to cost. If the taxpayers realised how large chunks of their contributions were put to use there would be a second civil war.

And yet I sat down in and amongst the red leather and the panelling and the carpet of rich interwoven patterns that was surely never made anywhere so lowly as Axminster, willing enough to wallow with the plutocracy when it suited my best interests.

Toby was acting as Secretary. As such he was neutral, immune to controversy.

'I'm merely a taker of notes, dear boy,' he had explained, before we went in. 'Just as an accountant will merely do the sums yet have no interest in their interpretation, so I must have no bias towards what's proposed or rejected at these meetings. I observe, I record, I do not take sides.'

So far though, I was still pretty much in the dark as to which side I would be on.

Toby introduced me to the committee and vice-versa. In the chair was the Minister of Foreign Affairs, the Foreign Secretary's number two: the Rt Hon Malcolm Crabbe, MP. About forty, a shade overweight with pouches under his eyes and the beginnings of jowls. An honest face, a valuable asset in a politician.

Also present was the Prime Minister's personal snoop, Richard Kirkland, a tall slender man, also about forty, with silver blond hair cut short and flat to his scalp. Azure blue eyes that crinkled at the corner were contradicted by thin lips – lips so red they might have been lipsticked. It was a cruel mouth, yet softened somehow by the pronounced dimple in his chin. According to Toby, Kirkland was a newcomer to the PM's stable of advisers, spin doctors, and miscellaneous cronies, and too implacable, too ambitious to be popular, even by the hatchet-wielding standards of the political spectrum.

The other two present and correct were the obese and gravy-stained Stanley Smilley, a panjandrum of a politician, representing the MoD, and a wide-shouldered individual with the lumpy features of a pugilist who was introduced to me simply as Abercrombie. MI6 was my guess, though not from my era.

I shook hands with them all, even Abercrombie. His battered face bothered me, a reminder of what could happen to you in the sort of games MI6 played. And I was about to play again.

I indicated the two empty chairs. 'Is this all of us?' I asked Toby. 'Or are bigger guns expected.'

Toby's smile was both amused and cynical.

'My dear André, this is about Gibraltar. You don't expect Secretaries of State to concern themselves personally with the doings of a mere overseas territory, do you?'

Actually, I did. Especially since I had been seduced here at great expense and grovelling, to perform certain irregular duties in respect of that mere overseas territory.

'I thought Gib was of strategic importance.'

Here Abercrombie chipped in with, 'Let us worry about strategy, Warner. All you'll have to do is wriggle your way into the nest of these GIBESTÁ vipers.' His lip curled. 'A very insignificant part of the grand scenario, I can assure you.'

'Thanks for putting me in my shabby little place.'

'Now then, children,' from Smilley. He had the aura of a benevolent uncle, so playing the part must have come natural to him.

'Order, gentlemen, please,' Crabbe called from the end of the table. The tip of his neat little nose had acquired a pair of lozenge-shaped, half-frame spectacles. Now he looked intelligent as well as honest. 'Mr Secretary –' to Toby, '– are you quite ready?'

Toby nodded. 'Minister.'

So far Kirkland, apart from a mechanical response when we were introduced, had not spoken. Now he said: 'For the record, the PM has instructed me to report back in person on this meeting.' He bestowed a passing glance on me, the red lips twitching. 'Is that a big enough gun, for you?'

'It'll do. But just so we're clear, I couldn't care less about politics and politicians. I'm doing this – assuming I do it – because I'm in between jobs and for old time's sake.'

'Thank you for putting it so succinctly,' Kirkland said. His mouth formed what was meant to be a smile, I think, but it ascended no further than his nostrils.

The meeting proper began with Crabbe stating the terms of reference in Toby-speak.

'We are not concerned here with the wider issue of Spain's claim to Gibraltar and the talks to be held in Madrid in May. Nor indeed are we concerned with the future of the territory of Gibraltar itself, although the decisions we make and the actions we take ...' He paused, half-smiling '... Poetry unintended, gentlemen. Our decisions and actions will assuredly influence that future.' He leaned forward, an earnest, sincere man, doing what he had been told to do. Like all of us. 'What concerns our modest caucus is this GIBESTÁ movement. They are, as you are all aware, a growing force. They make a lot of noise and noise carries a long way. Spain sees GIBESTÁ as a fissure in the Rock. They fancy that if they shove a crowbar in there and throw enough muscle behind it they will cause confusion and dissent, leading to a gross weakening of our hold on Gibraltar.' He looked around the table, slowly, catching the eyes of all of us in turn. 'Does anybody here not fully understand, or disagree with the picture I have painted?'

I refrained from repeating my 'paranoid' jibe. Put like that, in what, for a politician, were fairly bald terms, it sounded eminently possible that Gib could be lost to Britain.

Smilley, who was Crabbe's counterpart at the MoD, bristled at the implication behind the Foreign Minister's last question.

'We're not schoolboys, Malcolm,' he said testily, 'and you're only sitting in that chair as a convenience.'

The double-entendre was not lost on the assembly. Even Crabbe grinned, brown eyes twinkling, shaking his head.

'GIBESTÁ is led by a man called Michael Vella.' His eyes scoured the table again. 'Fifty-two years old, a widower, one child – a daughter, who, tragically and coincidentally, was killed during a demonstration by the movement on Sunday last.'

'Bloody good show,' Abercrombie muttered.

Anger surged inside me at his callousness. I could still the feel the girl in my arms, still warm with life yet organically dead; still youthful and innocent, yet doomed to decay before her due. No one here knew that I had witnessed the demonstration and the killing, of which they spoke so clinically.

'The death itself is unimportant,' Smilley observed. 'It's the implied escalation that worries me. The last two demos by this crowd have ended in violence resulting in injury, damage to property, now this first fatality. How many next time?'

Crabbe brushed aside Smilley's rhetorical question. 'Let's not digress, Stanley. I wanted to give everyone such background information on GIBESTÁ as appears relevant.' Smilley scowled, acknowledged Crabbe's supremacy by interlacing his fingers over his considerable midriff and subsiding into his chair.

'Michael Vella,' Crabbe went on, 'was born in Gibraltar of Gibraltarian parents. His pedigree is therefore impeccable. He owns a travel agency and an estate agency in Gib and has business interests in both Spain and the UK. He's tolerably well off. Prior to forming GIBESTÁ he had no active involvement in politics, although he apparently subscribes generously to the coffers of the GSD party. Sir Peter Caruana, who was the leader of the party and Chief Minister of Gib until 2011, is, or used to be, a close friend. There is no evidence that Vella is similarly chummy with the present Chief Minister, Picardy.'

'Picardo,' Toby corrected gently.

'I do beg your pardon … Picardo.'

'Do you think, Minister, that the loss of his daughter will discourage Vella?' Kirkland tapped a pen absently on the table top as he spoke. His gaze was thoughtful and fixed on the high window. The pale gold light of the setting sun struck his face but it didn't seem to bother him; he didn't even squint.

Crabbe reached for a glass tumbler, one of eight forming a laager around a water jug.

'Impossible to predict at this stage. His daughter was only buried today. His record suggests not. As a matter of fact, he appears to be a man of some mettle. Served in the police when he was young. Awarded the George Medal for rescuing somebody from a blazing car.' Crabbe shuffled some notes around. 'He left the force when he came into money from a deceased relative. Considered a man of integrity and a great espouser of causes.'

'The kind we all love to hate,' Smilley said. He seemed to speak for the most part simply to remind us of his presence and ministerial parity with Crabbe.

'Just so, Stanley,' Crabbe said indulgently. 'A list of other leading GIBESTÁ lights is available and will be distributed after the meeting.'

'Homework,' Smilley grunted.

Crabbe sipped water before saying: 'I'm sure you've done yours already, Stanley.'

'Who – me? Not bloody likely. I'm here on sufferance. This GIBESTÁ business is political not military. You don't need my department.'

Crabbe didn't demur.

'Moving on then to GIBESTÁ itself. We estimate its official membership at one hundred and eighty and rising. It has a further estimated one thousand five hundred or so active supporters, and perhaps two or three thousand sympathisers. Say a minimum of 15% of the permanent adult population of the Rock.'

'Up from zero four months ago,' Kirkland pointed out.

'A rapid rise of fortunes by any benchmark,' Crabbe conceded.

'At that rate they'll have the support of a majority by the end of the year,' I said, to prove I was on the same page as the rest of them.

Toby bestowed a warning frown on me. Perhaps he thought I was being facetious.

'Happily,' Crabbe said, 'political parties don't achieve straight line growth of support. Our projections suggest they'll top out somewhere between twenty and twenty-five percent. Which is worrying enough, I might add.' He rustled more papers, peered down his nose at them. 'You'll find all you need on GIBESTÁ in the dossiers to be distributed after the meeting. Now …unless there are any pertinent questions on the organisation I would prefer to move straight on to the proposed action and the part to be played in it by Mr Warner here.'

There were no dissenters and Crabbe, after gulping down more water, proceeded.

'Six weeks plus one day from today the Madrid conference on Gibraltar will open. By D-DAY minus seven of the conference, at the latest, GIBESTÁ must no longer be an active force.' He beamed around the five faces, favouring me with an extra long, extra bright beam.

'Sounds simple,' Smilley grunted from the depths of his chair.

'Oh, it is, Stanley, it is. I'm sure when Mr Warner brings his undoubted skills to bear on it, it's days will be numbered. Thirty-six, to be precise.'

'Simple but not easy,' I demurred. 'Do I get any guidelines, any advice as to the means to be employed?'

'Not from me, though please feel free to consult with Mr Abercrombie and Mr Kirkland outside of this meeting, if you wish. Tobias will of course settle all the contractual details with you and will act as your controller throughout.'

Toby was wearing a downtrodden expression. He ran a finger along the inside of his collar, a sign he wasn't totally at ease with the commission.

'What I would like to know,' from Kirkland to me, 'is what qualifies you so uniquely for this task?'

'That's irrelevant,' Toby said shortly. 'It's all been settled.'

Kirkland's air of sleepy condescension was no more. As for Toby's comment, it might as well never have been made.

'Warner?' Kirkland said, and his look was direct and unblinking.

'Search me. I used to be with MI6, as I'm sure you know. I have experience in undercover work. I speak Spanish.'

'Ah, yes, so I heard. *Donde vives en España*?'

I grinned. 'In Malaga.'

'*Como se dice esto en español*?' His Spanish was faster and more fluent than mine.

'*Vivo en* Malaga,' I expanded obligingly.

'Congratulations,' Smilley grunted. 'You've established that he understands Spanish.'

'I assume you're available immediately?' Kirkland said, as if bent of finding some flaw in my suitability.

'Affirmative.'

'And what contacts do you have in Gibraltar? Do you know – personally know – anyone influential?'

'I personally know Michael Vella.'

Which stopped him as effectively as buffers stop a train.

Nobody asked me to elaborate. And after that there were no more questions of any kind.

'If we're all agreed on what's to be done I think we can up stumps, gentlemen?' Crabbe obviously considered his job well done, his chairmanship properly discharged. He dispensed with the lozenge-shaped spectacles. 'All clear, Mr Warner?'

'I expected a more precise brief and the timescale's a bit short for undermining a political party, especially one with such popular appeal.'

'Tobias will brief you in greater detail, be assured.'

'Then I guess I'll manage.'

'Then I can take it …' A frowning glance at the now silent Kirkland, still basking in the glow of sunset, 'and the Prime Minister can take it that thirty-six days from now, or sooner, GIBESTÁ will have ceased to exist.'

I sat up straight. 'Ceased to exist? That's putting it a bit strong. That wasn't the brief I was given by Toby.'

'Really? Well, I think you'll find the pay will compensate you for the enormity of the challenge.' Crabbe dealt pale blue folders to each of us in the manner of a casino croupier; red MOST SECRET stickers blazed out from them. 'Thirty-six days, Mr Warner. Agreed?'

'And you'd better deliver,' Kirkland said, in measured tones.

'Or else?' I snapped back, resentful.

'Ex-actly.'

If ever somebody put out a contract on Kirkland, I hoped they'd give me first refusal.

* * * * *

Toby reined in his horse, a big black stallion with a mind of its own. His halt was unexpected, and I cantered on a good thirty metres before realising I was alone.

'Whoa, girl,' I said to my borrowed mount, a five-year old sorrel mare. A light tug at the bit and she decelerated to a walk.

Toby was, or appeared to be, admiring the view. 'If only I were an artist,' he said as I reined in alongside him.

The hill whose crest we were riding overlooked the Thames Valley, a gentle incline down which mist rolled to the silver snake of the river. Beyond, woodland clung to the far slope, dead-looking, awaiting the first kiss of spring.

I patted my mare's damp neck. She waggled her head in acknowledgement. Though I hadn't ridden in months, a rapport had quickly been established between us.

'What's on your mind, Toby?' Not in a million years had he really stopped for an eyeful of scenery.

'You saw Cassandra,' he said, which wasn't really any kind of answer. Nor was it an enquiry.

'You know everything. Everything connected with the family, at any rate.'

'We've always been close, she and I. As you know.' He gave me a doleful look, as if being close to Cassandra was a penance.

'If you're so bloody close then you must know what's the matter with her. You don't have to be a medical wizard to see she's not good.'

Toby twiddled his riding crop. His horse, sixteen hands or more, grazed contentedly on a stubble of coarse grass.

'I wish I could tell you, dear boy. I'm … well, to be candid, I'm worried about her.'

'Good. So we're both worried about her. Presumably that makes it all right.'

'Changing the subject,' Toby said, so abruptly it was almost an interruption. 'Does the name Irazola mean anything to you?'

'It might. But then there might be thousands of Irazolas in Spain.'

'Who said he was Spanish?'

Clever Toby. Canny, shrewd, astute Toby.

'All right, yes – if you mean the Spanish Army General Julio Irazola, it so happens I have met him. Socially.'

It took a lot to shake Toby from of his bland insouciance. But my casual announcement did the trick.

'You've *met* Irazola?'

'I spent a night at his house in Andalucía,' I explained. 'He impressed me. Intelligent, forceful, and ruthless in my judgement. Travelling in a straight line towards some goal or other and prepared to flatten anyone who stands in his way.'

'First Vella, then Irazola,' he murmured, in a far-off voice. 'My choice was better than I knew.'

Having exhausted all vegetation within full neck-stretching range his horse sauntered towards a virgin patch. My mare drifted in his wake, maintaining station.

'I'll treat that as a compliment,' I said.

'It was meant as one, dear boy.' Toby tapped his lips with his riding crop. 'Your assessment is interesting too. Our sources have it that General Irazola was instrumental in agitating for talks to be reopened on Gibraltar. Not directly, you understand, but through the media of two Government Ministers, Foreign and Defence. Now why would a Spanish general want talks on Gib?'

'Don't be fatuous. They want it back.'

Toby eased his backside in the saddle, shook his head. 'Now who's being fatuous. The military want Gib restored to Spain, yes, but not through negotiation. They would prefer to provoke a showdown. Generals thrive on conflict. Talks are for diplomats.'

'So maybe Irazola is pitching for diplomacy. Maybe he wants to stand at the next election.'

'*Does* he?' Toby asked. 'Is that the goal you were speaking of?'

'Keep me out of it, Toby. Don't use me as aspirin to cure your headaches. And whatever I've said on the subject of Irazola is strictly not for quoting. I've been hired to do a job and it doesn't extend to playing the part of adviser on Anglo-Spanish relations.'

'Nevertheless, old boy, your terms of reference have just been extended. I want you to cultivate Irazola. Keep an eye on him and report back, the sooner the better.'

If only I had kept my mouth shut. Tangling with the likes of Julio

Irazola was not part of the programme. Any man with an army corps at his disposal has to merit serious respect. The memory of my first confrontation with him, before we became buddies, had not dimmed with the passing months.

'Have you given any thought to your stratagem?' Toby said.

'Some.'

'Hmm. Don't waste too much brain power on it, dear boy. I'll be deciding on your cover. All right?'

It wasn't all right at all, but he swept aside my objections.

'I said *I'll* decide, André, and that's that. It's not open for debate.'

I let him have his victory. If his scheme of things didn't suit, I could always pull out.

'You'll have to stick with my real name,' I said.

His head did a slow rotate towards me, like a traversing gun turret.

'How so?'

'I was in Gib last week and fell into conversation with a pro-independence crowd. They asked for my name, I gave it.'

His annoyance was palpable. He fingered the inside of his collar while he worked on the implications. Down the hillside a small bird gave off a cheep of alarm and was seen flirting low through the scrub.

'It doesn't really matter,' he decided. 'Your passport will be false in all but name. If there are any comebacks afterwards, or retributions, it'll be your neck.'

'You mean you're going to provide a fake passport in my real name?'

'Precisely. And that's the one you'll use for the duration of this job.'

At least that would leave my genuine passport uninfected. I shrugged.

The body heat generated by our gallop was waning. I turned up the collar of my leather windbreaker.

'Shall we go on?' I said.

'Not yet.' He was back to landscape-gazing. 'We haven't agreed on a price for your services.' His casualness didn't deceive me. The mind that framed the question was ever honed to scalpel sharpness.

'My price for destroying GIBESTÁ and saving Gibraltar from the big bad Spanish?' If he detected mockery in my words he didn't rise to it. 'It's one hell of a job. On top of that you expect me to go head-to-head against a goddam General.'

'How much, André?' His voice crackled like static.

'If I fail, my expenses and nothing more. If I succeed …'

'Yes … yes?' Impatiently.

'A million has the ring of a nice round sum, wouldn't you say?'

He lost interest in the Thames Valley to goggle at me.

'You're not serious. You can't really expect … a *million*!' A thought hit him. 'Do you mean dollars, or euros?'

'Pounds sterling. Don't be a cheapie. Isn't Gibraltar worth a million?'

Chapter Ten

Colin Baynes' unannounced visit was only welcome inasmuch as he was another Brit to converse with. Keeping conversations going in Spanish was still a strain.

Handshakes and platitudes done, he announced that he'd found a buyer for The Golden Palm, 'if you're interested.'

It was so unexpected I poured us both a double Scotch, a reflex action I regretted at once. Hell, he should be buying the drinks; he was the one who stood to make a commission second time around.

'I wasn't aware I'd put the place on the market, let alone hired *you* to sell it.'

'Word gets around.' He eased his backside onto a stool. It was raining out and his bald head glistened, the shoulders of his beige windbreaker pocked with spots of damp.

Thanks to the weather, the bar was bustling. My Fernando seemed to have managed well during my second absence, had even showed a modest profit.

'How much is it going to cost me?' I asked, resigned to making a loss on the deal.

'My buyer will pay what you paid, subject to due diligence. Are you interested?'

I was and I wasn't. Part of me got a kick out of my bar. On the other hand I would soon be off to Gib on indeterminate furlough and uncertain outcome.

'That's a lousy bargain and well you know it,' I stalled. 'I've spent thousands doing this place up. I want at least … oh, twenty grand on top to even consider it.'

Baynes shook his head. 'Not a chance. I might be able to get you ten.'

I puffed out air. Reflected some more. The business had served a purpose, set me on a new path away from the killing fields. Surely though, it wasn't destined to be my life's work.

'Are the books okay?' he asked.

'They're good, don't worry. Most of what comes in is recorded. Not much goes into my pocket.'

We sealed the provisional bargain in the manner of English gentlemen (which neither of us, for different reasons, could claim to be) with a handshake and another double Scotch for him, and mineral water for me. My drinking was still moderate these days.

'How long will it take to wrap it up?' I asked him.

'A month or so. That's assuming he agrees to the extra ten.'

'I have to go away to … er, Alicante for a few months, but I can easily get back for any signing formalities.' I stepped aside to make room for Gustavo to squeeze past. 'I'll leave my manager …' I nodded towards Fernando, hovering solicitously over a crowd of boisterous teenagers as if they were visiting Royalty, '… to run the place. He seems to be making a go of it.'

Baynes gave his glass a further tilt in my direction. 'I'll recommend him to the new owner then.'

And that was how I ended my short-lived tenure as a glorified bartender.

* * * * *

The metronome thud-thud of rock music came from beneath the street, like some great underground beating heart. The flashing neon script above the stairs proclaimed LA CAVERNA. I had visions of a seedy, smoky basement with rock star clones churning out amateurish imitations of current hits, and hordes of kids dancing like mindless automatons. Exactly the way I used to myself, a quarter of a century ago.

'This way,' Colin Baynes said and started down the stairs, clearly expecting me to follow. When he realised I wasn't, he stopped and twisted his upper body towards me.

'What's up?'

'Club music gives me a headache. I leave it to the younger generation.'

'You make yourself sound like an old man,' he said with a laugh. 'Anyway, where we're going isn't part of the club and there's no music worth mentioning. Come on ...' He made a motion with his head, urging me to stick with him, and again descended the stairs.

He had proposed a champagne dinner on him, to celebrate the impending sale of the bar, and this being my last night before heading south to the Rock I hadn't objected. If I got nothing else out of this shark I would at least have a free meal. The visit to LA CAVERNA was supposed to 'round off the evening'.

At the foot of the narrow stone stairs was a door, sturdily constructed, perhaps as a concession to the sordid environment. Three raps was our password. The door opened inwards with no visible assistance, and we passed through into semi-darkness. Beyond was a narrow ante-room where Baynes exchanged undertones and banknotes with a large, archetypal bouncer. The rock music had faded to a murmur.

'This is on me,' he whispered, as the bouncer laboriously counted the notes, which he then folded and stuffed in a side pocket of his jacket. This was our signal to proceed.

The hubbub and the music had died altogether. On our right, as we crossed a curtained threshold, was a small, semi-circular stage bathed in a red glow. It was empty, unlike the triple bank of seats placed in a crescent format before it, which were three-quarters occupied. The atmosphere was stifling, rank with tobacco smoke.

It was, of course, a strip club. I hadn't been in one since my teens, when London's Soho was at its zenith as the be-all and end-all in the art of genital display. I had heard the Internet had made live shows redundant. I began to snigger, like we used to do as kids over a dirty book. Baynes affected not to notice as he zeroed in on a couple of empty seats on the back row, but several of the audience glared at me in disapproval. Then the obligatory background music started and my sniggers were drowned by it.

The seats creaked under our weights. A body of young men passed by behind us, noisy, snorting with nervous embarrassment, and installed themselves at the front. As my eyes adjusted to the darkness I perceived that the clientele was not exclusively male, nor predominantly middle-aged, fat, ugly, nor yet wearing dirty raincoats.

'When Spain was, er ... liberated striptease became all the rage,' Baynes murmured in my ear. 'It's a long way past its peak now but still isn't considered non-U to be seen here. Quite the reverse among the younger set.'

'Well, it'll make a change. Next best thing to lying next to a naked woman is looking at one.'

For sure, lying next to an undressed woman had become a rare event for me since Cassandra had given our affair the last rites. Aside from having Elena flaunt herself on my terrace, I hadn't been giving women *per se* a lot of thought lately. Maybe I needed a shot of Viagra.

The stage was still devoid of performers. A Spanish catcall or two sounded on the front row.

'What should I expect,' I said to Baynes, 'apart from the usual boobs and fannies?'

'An unusual naked body. If my timing is right the Star of the Show is due on next. Get ready for something really special, shocking even.'

'I'm bracing myself.'

Some joker at the front chanted the Spanish equivalent of 'Why are we waiting?' As if in answer the music switched to a slow, sexier refrain, and the stage lights brightened, from hazy red to a harsh, fierce white. No subtle shadows for Spanish strippers to hide behind. This was going to be total exposure, crude and clinical.

Then, as if at the wave of a wand, she was there, centre stage. Only just out of reach of the front row. Dark brown hair, middling length, glossy and clean-looking; even darker eyes; her features were blurred by lashings of make-up but she was a good looker. Sensuous mobile lips that smiled widely, naturally, parting to make room for a serpentine flicking of the tongue.

'Something really special, shocking even.' Well, Baynes had forewarned me. What he hadn't prepared me for was two simultaneous shocks, of which the more immediate and mind-blowing was the girl's condition – at least five months pregnant was my estimate. But the visual shock of seeing a pregnant woman under the spotlights, wearing only a black G-string, a nominal black bra, and white stockings, less than a metre away from an amphitheatre of oglers, was surpassed by the shock of recognition. For the stripper was that wayward diplomat's daughter, Linda Pridham.

* * * * *

She knew the ropes as well as any pro. Undulating her body, unashamedly thrusting her bulging belly with its inverted navel like an extra nipple, holding it two-handedly, massaging it, using it as a stage prop. The white lights were merciless: every blemish on her pale skin was highlighted, even the greenish veins that scribbled across her gross belly, like the strands of a cobweb. The lights gave her whole body a luminescence, a transparency, somehow heightening her vulnerability. It could have been titillating. It didn't quite come off, not for me. Baynes, however, like the rest of the crowd, was loving it. Leaning forward, transfixed, no longer aware of my presence.

A rattle of applause had greeted Linda's appearance. Now the only sound was the throbbing background music. She moved into her act with seeming gusto, her bumps and grinds going well beyond the call of duty. Nor was she slow to discard her skimpy garments. As a finale she cast aside her G-string and assumed a prone position, to splay her thighs and display what we had paid to see: faithful to the current fashion she was bald down there, and the dusky pink of her vaginal lips were livid against her white skin. At that point I was suddenly embarrassed and averted my eyes towards the aisle. The movement caught Baynes' attention.

'Yeh, I know, I know,' he said, his voice hushed. 'You've seen it all before.'

That's where he was wrong. Any pregnant stripper would be bad enough but to sit there gawking at Linda Pridham, a girl I knew and had, to be truthful, been attracted towards, was too much. I jumped up, the seat springing back into place with a bang that earned me more than one annoyed glare. Without a word to Baynes I stalked out. If he called after me I missed it.

The street, for all the litter and garbage sacks awaiting collection, for all the late night traffic contributing its stink to the air, was fresh as wind-scoured moorland after the exhibition down below. A gentle rain was falling and there were few people about, just the odd drunk and a vagrant preparing to sleep rough in a shop doorway, arranging sheets of newsprint, finicky as any house-proud momma.

'André!' Baynes, tiresomely, had followed me out. As I turned he was emerging from the stairway. He trotted over to where I waited beneath the neon-lit canopy of some night-club entrance. He looked disgruntled at being dragged from the show.

'Are you ill?'

'No. I'll be off home in a minute. You get back inside, you might miss something.'

He joined me in the dry. 'Why did you do that?'

'Leave?' I hesitated. 'I … oh, shit, I bloody well *know* the girl. And her parents.'

'Oh.' Then, as it sank in, a deeper, more sober, 'Ohh.'

'You said it. Don't let it spoil your enjoyment though. She's nothing to you, just another stripper.' I gave him a light push on the shoulder. 'You get back in there.'

'No.' He gave a kind of shudder. 'No, I couldn't, not now. Somehow it doesn't seem to matter when they're complete strangers. If they don't mind flashing it, why quibble?' He thrust his hands deep in his pants pockets. 'But knowing the girl, even through someone else … it would be like … like …'

'Yeah, well, forget it.' I turned up my jacket collar. 'I'm off now. Thanks for the entertainment. I'll phone you a week from now.'

We shook hands.

'Er … good enough.'

'Just do what needs to be done about the bar, and be sure to keep me in the loop. You've got my cell number and my email address.'

I left him to return to LA CAVERNA or home, as the mood took him, and crossed the street, heading in the general direction of the Place José Antonio where I had left the car. When I was sure I was out of his sight I nipped into a dingy alley and doubled back to the street, emerging via another alleyful of prostitutes lurking in doorways. I received a dozen invitations in as many seconds.

Baynes was gone. I scouted round the block of darkened shops that sat on top of LA CAVERNA, seeking the club's back entrance. Praying

I wasn't too late, that I hadn't missed her. Then a door further along opened, a fire exit with a horizontal locking bar. The yellow glare from within lit up a heap of swollen black plastic bags, one of which had burst, spewing cabbage leaves, empty cans, and plastic water bottles across the sidewalk and into the gutter.

The figure that hurried out, slamming the door firmly to engage the locking bar, was without doubt a woman and without doubt pregnant. Long white-stockinged legs, a red mini-dress, red handbag. As she paused to open a striped umbrella I moved towards her but had barely got into my stride when she hoofed it down the street in one hell of a hurry. Late for her next engagement, I supposed. Most strippers work several clubs per night.

My shoes were rubber soled and she remained unaware I was pursuing her until a couple of loafers rounding a corner gave me a cheer of encouragement, accompanied by some raucous remarks. Linda's stride slackened and she spun to face me, discarding the umbrella. And, by God, had I intended her harm, I would have had good cause to regret it. From her handbag, fast as a gunslinger, she whipped a compact, black aerosol. I had just long enough to recognise it for what it was, and redirect my body away at right angles. My feet became entangled and I crashed onto the road. Car brakes squealed in evasive action. The nauseous chemicals from Linda Pridham's mugger deterrent hissed harmlessly into the night.

'Linda, it's me – Warner!' I yelled as I sprawled in the gutter. A car swerved past me, hooting. I stuck my middle finger up at his receding lights, hobbled back to the relative security of the sidewalk. Linda was staring at me in disbelief, her aerosol-wielding arm still extended in the aim and fire position.

'André Warner,' I said, rubbing my bruised hip. 'You remember me?'

She was flustered. 'Yes … yes, sure I do.'

I eased the black cylinder from her small white hand. 'You won't need this.' I smiled at her. 'Promise.'

Her hand covered her mouth. 'Holy … excuse me, Mr Warner. I didn't recognise you with the beard and all.'

'No harm done, apart from a bruise or two.' I examined the aerosol label in the glare of the nearest street lamp. ' "Defensa",' I read out loud.

She shook her head as if to collect her wits. 'Spanish equivalent of Mace. Makes your eyes run, so you can't see.'

I'd been threatened with worse.

'Look,' she said, back in control of herself. 'I'm late for an appointment. I gotta move it.'

'I know,' I said. 'Another CAVERNA?'

It was cruel but I aimed to stop her, shock her into compliance. Her mouth parted in surprise – it was a nice mouth. With a lot less lipstick it would be even nicer.

Surprise was quickly overtaken by discomfiture.

'You … were there? You *saw*?'

I nodded. 'It's no place for a pregnant girl.'

'It's none of your business, you creep,' she retorted, with some heat. She had too much strength of character to be bothered by the knowledge that I had seen all of her there was to see.

The rain was dissolving her make-up. A globule of mascara made an uncertain descent of her cheek, drawing a line to mark its passage. I retrieved her upended umbrella, held it over her.

'It's none of your business,' she repeated with less heat.

I took out my wallet. Inside was over five hundred euros in 50-notes. I extracted all but a couple, stuffed them in her still open handbag, followed by the deterrent. Snapped the bag shut.

'What are you doing?' she demanded, affront reinstating her natural spirit. 'Just who the fuck …?'

'Call it compensation for loss of earnings.' She stared, her eyes dark hollows, unfathomable. 'Now, if you'll let me, I'll escort you to your home.'

* * * * *

Home turned out to be a studio, four floors up, off the boulevard Paseo del Parque. Not a bad district to live in. Linda had probably chosen small and beautiful in favour of big and ugly. The rent would be high, even for these thirty square metres of living space.

Neither of us had spoken during the walk to where the Aston was parked. I had simply taken her arm, and she hadn't resisted.

'You must be nuts leaving a heap like this here,' she remarked, as I operated the remote door lock. 'You deserve to have it swiped.'

On the short drive to her pad she lapsed into broody reticence until, as we drew into the curb, she said curtly, 'Come up for coffee.' Not the warmest of invitations. But, chiefly out of curiosity and only secondarily out of attraction to the girl, I went up for coffee.

While she made it in the curtained off kitchenette I did a tour of the room, which took less than a minute. No pictures, very few ornaments. Two Puma tennis racquets were acquiring a film of dust in a corner, kept company by a battered pair of Nike tennis shoes. A few magazines, mostly about boats from what I could see, a 2016 Michelin Guide to Spain & Portugal; otherwise no books. The two armchairs were draped with cast-off clothing. Conclusion? Linda Pridham was an outdoor, sports-minded girl, no art lover, and tidiness was low on her list of priorities. So was cleanliness: every corner had its festoon of cobwebs. In one, the creator was in residence.

'Don't you mind the spiders?' I said as she came thrusting through the gap in the curtains, a hand massaging her flank the way pregnant women do.

She didn't bother to follow my glance but went to draw the curtains. 'Why should I? They're company. And they catch flies.'

There was something sad about considering spiders as company, even jokingly. Clearly the days of being the companion of a rich and powerful man were no more than a memory.

'Want to talk about it?' I said.

'Stripping for a living, you mean?'

'No, that's not what I meant. Though I guess it's part of the package.'

She screwed up her face. 'Package?'

From behind the curtains a kettle began to shrill.

'How do you like your coffee, Warner?'

'As it comes.'

'I only got Instant,' she said, in a tone of take-it-or-leave-it, making for the kitchen.

By the time she came back I had transferred the strewn garments to the veneered buffet and cleared space on the coffee table.

We sat at right angles to each other and drank insipid, unsweetened black coffee. Whatever traumas she had suffered and was still suffering hadn't done her looks any harm. She had scrubbed much of her professional make-up off in the car and was now in more or less her natural state. Her hair had grown some since our last meeting. If, as I once read someplace, it was a mirror of the state of her health, she had no worries on that score and the rather pallid complexion I remembered from our meeting had gained some colour. Perhaps carrying a baby did that. Weren't pregnant women supposed to bloom?

'He dropped me when he found out,' she announced suddenly, the cup against her lips. She was trembling slightly. I half-reached towards her, drew back before contact was made. This was an independent girl. She didn't need any consoling from me.

'Irazola? Is it his?'

Her glare said: you may think I'm a slut, mister, but I'm a faithful one.

'Didn't he give you … er … provide for you?'

'Pay me off, you mean, a handsome settlement for placing my snatch and tits at his beck and call, twenty-four hours a day, for nearly two years, that kind of thing?' Her hand shook and coffee slopped from the cup. 'No, sirree. I got diddly squat.'

Privately I hadn't too much sympathy. While it lasted, her liaison had been fruitful. Flash car, expensive clothes, expensive apartment no doubt. Protection from predators. Some would say she should be grateful to have had that much for as long as she did.

'What makes it worse is that I really loved the sonofabitch.' She swirled her coffee about. 'Still do, come to that. Bastard!'

'So he didn't give you any money, not even to see you through the pregnancy.'

'Not only did he give me no fucking money, pal,' she said grimly, 'but he took back his fucking apartment and his fucking car. What do you think of that?'

'I think you're fucking right to be pissed.'

She grinned weakly.

'Anyway,' I said, 'from what I've heard, strippers make a decent living. And you appeared to be enjoying yourself.'

Her cup had been midway between saucer and mouth. Now she

crashed it down with a force that transferred most of the contents onto the table.

'Enjoying it!' she choked. 'Are you screwball or what?'

Oh-oh. Seemed I had touched an exposed nerve.

'For your information,' she snarled, 'there's a greasy little slob called Hernandez who sits in the audience all night and every night whose sole purpose is to make sure us girls hold nothing back. Show the tiniest inhibition, let your smile slip a millimetre, and you're out with a capital O.' She sniffed, drew the back of her hand under her nose.

I passed her a crumpled handkerchief. 'It's clean. I only use it to polish my rose-tinted glasses.'

She blew her nose and laughed at the same time.

Floorboards creaked outside the door. I raised enquiring eyebrows at Linda.

'It's only Enrico. He's got the apartment next to mine, it's much bigger, a proper bedroom. He's queer as a three-legged dodo.' She put her coffee cup on the floor beside the chair. 'Look, Warner, I promise you I'm not one of those kinks who gets a charge out of rolling about under a spotlight while guys jerk off inside their coats ...' She paused, her expression darkening. 'And not always inside ...'

'Lay off the technicoloured description. And to answer you, no, I didn't imagine you did it for kicks. But why not go home? Your parents will take care of you.'

'Oh, sure, like I should expect them to. For Christ's sake, I'm twenty-nine. If I mess up my life I can't expect the folks back home to unmess it for me.'

Pride, that deadly sin. She'd slide all the way to the bottom before she'd accept a leg up.

'So where do we go from here, mister nice guy?'

'I hadn't thought about it. Do we go anywhere?'

'Put it this way – you just paid me the equivalent of a week's wages. I'm grateful and I owe you. So ... how'd you like to pass the night in little Lindy's ...' She broke off to chuckle, '... in *big* Lindy's bed. Or two nights, if you like.' She cocked her head sideways to consider me. 'Maybe you don't like. Is that it?'

I couldn't make up my mind.

'Never screwed a knocked-up woman before?' she said with a manufactured come-hither smile.

Now that she mentioned it, I hadn't. Not so in-your-face knocked-up, anyhow.

'Brother, you don't know what you've been missing,' she went on. She lifted her backside to free the hem of the red mini-dress, pulled the garment over her head. She wore no bra, just a black silk half-slip.

In spite of myself, in spite of her bloated belly, I suddenly wanted her. More badly than I had wanted any woman in many a month. The price of too much abstinence maybe.

'No need to prostitute yourself …' I began. Not that she would be my first.

'Don't be such an asshole. You've been living so long among Brits you've developed stiff lower lip syndrome. Stop behaving like a gentleman, for Pete's sake.'

'That wouldn't be hard. And it's upper lip, not lower.'

'Upper, lower, They're both lips aren't they? Which reminds me …'

She kissed the way she talked, forceful, no-nonsense, direct.

And a little later I discovered what it was that I'd been missing.

Chapter Eleven

When I awoke the sun was already above the surrounding tenements, bleeding the colour from the yellow curtains, driving a silver sliver through a gap at the top. Linda was up, out of sight, humming some tune.

'What'll it be, Warner? Corn Flakes or toast? Can't manage anything cooked, unless you'd like warmed-up spaghetti Bolognese.'

I shuddered. Knuckled the sleep from my eyes.

'Well?' Peremptorily now.

'Er...toast will be fine.'

'Coming right up.' I heard the clunk of the toaster. The kitchenette curtains bulged then parted to admit Linda, bearing a tray. She was naked, bloated belly and all, and completely unself-conscious about it.

'Do you always walk about like that?' I said, rising from the much dishevelled single bed.

She turned. 'Look who's talking.'

My undershorts were nowhere in evidence, so I reached for my undershorts, which were, and sat on the edge of the bed to pull them on. She watched me. She had tied her hair back with a red ribbon and was without make-up. She was a whole lot prettier without cosmetic embellishment, I decided. The pride, the independent streak, the devilment were all written there.

Later, after breakfast, she asked me if I wanted to stay on a while. No diffidence, no hesitation, just a straight invitation to play house. She'd gotten dressed to eat, a loose, smock-dress over faded designer jeans with rips in both knees.

'Do you offer bed space to all your friends?'

She didn't much care for the implication. 'I don't have any friends. Not since Julio. You're the first.' She regarded me suspiciously. 'If you *are* a friend. By the way, how old are you, Warner?'

'Over forty. Let's leave it at that.'

'You're wearing well, unless you've had work done.' She grinned to show she wasn't serious. 'Did I tell you I'm twenty-nine?'

On the young side, but did I care? About the same as any man in his forties with his sexual impulses still functioning cared about making out with a woman in her twenties.

'You're a nice looking girl, Linda,' I said. 'And it doesn't bother me that you're carrying another guy's child. But I can't stay.'

Her face closed up.

'Who's asking you?'

'It's not like that,' I said, and reached for her hand. But she wasn't having any of that. She stood up, brushed crumbs from her smock. I stood with her.

'Don't take it personal,' I said. 'I have to go to Gibraltar. It's business and I can't get out of it. Before I go, though, there's something I want to do.'

Still suspicious, unwilling after that imagined rejection even to meet me halfway, she folded her arms.

'You want to give me money?' The tone was jeering.

'No. I want Irazola to give you money.'

She arched an eyebrow, her deep-set eyes derisive. 'You got a screw loose?'

'Maybe. But I intend to go calling on him on the way to Gib and get him to do the right thing by you.'

Her laugh came from gut-level. 'When are you going to come down and join the rest of us here on Planet Earth? This isn't some story out of a romantic novel book, kiddo. There's no King Arthur, no Round Table, and you sure aren't Sir Galahad.' She hooted raucously.

'I'm serious,' I said, pasting on a serious expression.

She saw that I was.

'Hey, I'm sorry, Warner.' She started towards me, then stopped in some confusion. 'Look, I know you're only trying to help. But no way is Julio going to entertain a touch from you on my behalf. Last time I saw him he was, like, don't ever try and contact me.'

'He'll see *me*,' I demurred. 'if I just show up at his front door.

Anyhow, you've nothing to lose. Even if I fail, you won't be any worse off.'

'Chances are he'll be away on duty.' She said it as if she hoped he would.

'I'd phone to find out but that would just give him an opportunity to put me off. Best to risk it. If I draw a blank, so what? I'll have wasted a couple of hours and be out of pocket the price of a gallon or two of gas. You still won't be any worse off.'

'No,' she said in a growly voice, 'but that shit Julio will think I asked you to go round there with the begging bowl.'

That pride again.

'I'll tell him you know nothing about it.'

'Oh no, you won't. I'm coming with you. You don't think I'm going to hide behind a man's pants, do you?' Her face softened. She came to me and my arms opened of their own accord to receive her. 'Even a man as good and kind as you.'

Good and kind? This girl was great for my ego. Even if she was confusing me with somebody else.

* * * * *

Extracting money from General Irazola on Linda's behalf was not the altruistic gesture Linda assumed it to be. Uppermost of my motives was Toby's injunction to cultivate Irazola.

Keep an eye on him and report back, the sooner the better.

The issue of financial support for Linda gave me the excuse I needed to update my acquaintanceship with the General, and see where it led. If I could earn a few credits from Linda into the bargain, I wouldn't turn down the opportunity.

Long before we reached the perimeter of Irazola territory our presence on the lonely dirt road through the foothills must have been reported. Once, a helicopter came flipping by, so low I could see the pilot's mouth moving as he spoke into his radio mouthpiece. Yet we got as far as the guard house unmolested. And the two soldiers who came from behind the lowered barrier, one to each side of the car, their pistols holstered, were smiling, amiable.

'Señor Warner?' The taller of the two had sergeant's stripes. He bent to my level, looking not at me but at Linda. 'Señorita Pridham.' Pronouncing it Preed-ham. This instant recognition of Linda surprised me, until I remembered she and the general had been in harness for two years and this wouldn't be her first visit.

'You sound as if you were expecting us,' I said in my best Spanish.

'*Tu, si, por supuesto.* Your car was reported.' He stroked the edge of the roof like a used car dealer assessing its value. 'We do not see many Aston Martins here.'

'Is the general home?'

'You are fortunate. He returned from Madrid only yesterday and he leaves again tomorrow. He has instructed me to allow you to proceed. However …' A slightly embarrassed cough, '… this was before we knew the *señorita* was accompanying you. I am not sure …'

'It'll be fine,' I said as if my assurance would save him from the general's wrath.

Against my expectations he didn't pursue it. 'Very well. You may go through. I will telephone to let him know you are not alone.' He stepped away from the window. 'Arias – *levantas la barrera*!'

Arias duly went into the guard post and operated the motor that raised the barrier. We purred through onto the paved road.

'You may not be welcome,' I warned Linda.

'Well, what do you know?' Sarcasm and bitterness combined. If, as she claimed, she still loved the guy, rejection would be hard to take.

It was mid-afternoon and I was due to meet Toby in Gibraltar that evening. Whatever happened from here on, I was going to be late for that date. In the first place we were late setting off from Malaga, and then I had had to call in at the apartment in Fuengirola to collect my luggage. It was already close to mid-day before we hit the open road. Linda had sunk into melancholia and spent the journey smoking, chewing gum, and not speaking. I didn't have a lot to say myself as I tried to figure out how I might gather some useful intelligence for Toby. Yet I also genuinely meant to lean on Irazola to do right by Linda too. Maybe I was Sir Galahad after all, if only the poor man's version.

We finally rolled up before the massive front door, where we were given a wary welcome by the youthful Comandante Navarro. He showed us into a ground floor sitting room whose windows framed a vista of mountainside, the peaks tipped white. Heavy, indestructible furniture of some reddish wood, was complemented by acres of brocade, tapestries and wall-hung carpets. The bare wooden floor creaked a protest as I paced. Linda sat in a straight chair ('When you're this shape it's more comfortable sitting upright') and watched me back and forth. She was nervous, chewing gum.

'Relax,' I said, I who was drawn tight as a violin string.

Then in strutted the general. Hands clasped behind his back, the door opening before him and closing behind him, courtesy of some unseen aide.

'Mr Warner,' he said, and a formal smile tempered the stern, regular features. 'I am very happy to see you again.'

'It's mutual, General.' While still shaking his hand I inclined my head towards Linda. 'You know Miss Pridham, of course.'

The smile faded. Irazola bowed stiffly from the waist. 'Linda. They informed me you were accompanying Mr Warner.'

That formality over, he switched his focus back to me. 'Will you take some refreshment? Coffee, something to eat perhaps ...?'

'Later, thank you.'

'I'll have some coffee,' Linda said tartly. 'If I'm included in the offer.'

Irazola managed to stay on the right side of gentlemanly, but it wasn't easy for him. He picked up a telephone from the nearest coffee table, gave an order in an unrecognisable tongue.

'Let us sit down.'

I chose a very low armchair, so low in fact that you sat with most of your body horizontal and your legs extended straight out in front. If I wasn't careful I would fall asleep. After all, it had been an energetic night.

Irazola sank gracefully into an identical chair, rested his elbows on the padded arms, clasped his left fist inside his cupped right hand.

'So, my friend,' he said agreeably enough, 'we meet again. You are welcome here, as I told you when last you visited us.'

'Visited' was coming a bit strong, I thought. But I bared my teeth politely.

'Miss Pridham, however,' he went on, 'should have known better, even if you do not, than to come uninvited, with or without you as her escort.' A frown here, to register his displeasure. 'Am I to assume you are here on her behalf?'

'You assume right, General.'

He frowned more profoundly, at this confirmation.

'Look, Warner,' Linda cut in, 'no use pussyfooting around with this guy – give it to him with both barrels, if you must give it to him at all. Otherwise let's blow.'

Irazola and I both regarded her with a certain amount of shared exasperation. A proud, donnish man, he must have found her uppity attitude hard to live with. It was a miracle the affair had run for as long as it did.

'Still the same girl, eh, Linda?' he said, with a shake of his noble head.

'Don't patronise me, you bastard,' she snapped back at him. 'I'm not one of your uniformed ass-lickers.'

'Anybody ever tell you, you have a lovely way with words?' I said.

'And fuck you too, Warner,' was the predictable retort. She moved to rise. 'I'm going. I should never have come.'

'Sit down and shut up. I'm trying to negotiate for you and all you can do is explete.' She remained standing, glaring at me. I turned from her. 'General, I'm here to ask you to consider making some kind of ... allowance to Linda, as a charitable gesture –'

Linda let rip an exclamation. 'Charitable gesture – Jesus!'

I ignored the interruption. 'As a charitable gesture to enable her to live in reasonable comfort until the baby's born and perhaps for a few months afterwards. Were you aware she's been earning a living as a stripper in Malaga?'

'Yes, I was aware.'

He was cool, controlled. I had expected shock, hoped for some display of remorse.

'You don't mind? You don't care?'

'Linda can do as she wishes. She is not my responsibility.'

'That's baloney!' Now my composure was beginning to fail me. 'She's trying to make ends meet, General. To earn some fast money to see her through the last few weeks before the baby arrives, when she won't be able to work at all. And to take care of the kid when it arrives – *your* kid.'

'Who is to say it is mine? There has been no DNA test.'

'You motherfucking son-of-a-bitch!' Linda yelled, starting towards him, bent on inflicting injury.

I leapt out of the chair as best I could from my near-prone position, and intercepted her. Irazola had not budged by so much as a fluttered eyelid. He sat looking stonily up at Linda, letting me do all the restraining.

Then somebody tapped on the door. Irazola called to enter and this seemed to calm Linda, even to the extent of resuming her seat.

Coffee was delivered and served by a maid wearing severe black with a frilly white apron. A nice traditional touch. They had similarly dressed staff at Waverley House.

Irazola was smacking his fist into his palm again, slowly, his expression far away. Somehow I didn't think he was reflecting on the good times he had had with Linda.

'A gentleman would give a lady the benefit of the doubt,' I said mildly.

Linda said nothing, just breathed fire and brimstone through her nostrils.

'A gentleman would also not wish to see a former … companion in distress,' I suggested.

A well-constructed turn of phrase, I thought.

'Who's this gentleman you keep talking about?' Linda snarled.

Anger flickered briefly in Irazola's eyes, like a strobe light. He wasn't made of granite rock after all. He had emotions, like the rest of us. You just had to dig deeper than usual, break through the atavistic crust.

'Mr Warner,' he said, still socking fist into palm, but faster now, as if he were building up a crescendo. 'I resent this attempt to extort money from me. I understand your motives, you are simply trying to help.' He smiled grimly. 'Like the Good Samaritan, is it not? But you are mis … misguided. This girl is nothing to me. The past is the past and I do not care for it. She lived well for two years at my cost. I made no promises. Now it is finished and I do not intend to be blackmailed into –'

'Blackmailed!' Linda was on her feet again. This time I was ready for her.

'Leave it, Linda,' I soothed, imprisoning her windmilling arms.

'Don't put yourself in the wrong. I haven't finished with him yet.'

I had come to plead. I was equally prepared to do battle. Dismissing, in my desire to get results, the perils of fighting behind enemy lines.

Irazola was also standing now. 'You may not have finished with me, Mr Warner, but I have most definitely finished with you.'

'No, you haven't.' I hesitated. The knightly stuff had fallen flat. It was time to move on to providing feedback for Toby.

If coming here at all had been a misjudgement, I was about to compound it big time.

I opened my mouth and the following words flowed forth. 'You wouldn't like it to get out about your plans for Gibraltar, you and your buddy Ricardo.'

It was the wildest of shots, based on an overheard telephone conversation five months ago and Toby's vague hypotheses about what Irazola was plotting. Wild, but, in the event, on target. Irazola went rigid. The man was too poised, too self-disciplined to give himself away entirely. Nonetheless, whether he realised it or not, it was there, in the dilation of the nostrils and the narrowing of the eyes.

From here on in the battle was likely to be bloody. Irazola had once before demonstrated his preparedness to use violent methods to achieve his ends. Whether or not Linda and I were allowed to walk out of here would depend on my powers of negotiation. Too late, I saw that I had extended my neck too far.

'Would you care to explain that remark?' Irazola said, not conceding a millimetre, tactically speaking. His was a perfectly natural response to an inference such as I had just made.

Linda had stopped fighting me so I released her and said to Irazola, 'Do I need to?'

He moved away from me, to the coffee table. Took a boat-shaped cigar from a carved wooden box, lit up with a table lighter. Smoke obscured his face.

'In any case what you imply is nonsense. I have nothing to do with Gibraltar, and I know of no one called Ricardo.'

That, at any rate, was a definite lie. I had him on the defensive.

'It doesn't matter whether you deny it or not. I have enough proof to cause you and your Government plenty of grief. If I were to release the recordings I have of your telephone conversations, you and Spain could kiss your ambitions goodbye.'

The faintest shadow of alarm crossed his features. He must have longed to ask how I had come by my alleged recordings, but dared not without admitting culpability.

'This is all nonsense,' he said, but conviction was lacking. This buttoned-down man was as close to bluster as he would ever get.

'See here, General, your secret doings are not my concern, although I have connections with people who would be concerned.' I let that sink in, then added, 'If they knew.'

He cottoned on quick that a deal was in the offing. He was still too much of an old pro to admit anything.

A sigh, then, 'Tell me what you want.'

'I already told you – money for Linda. How about a hundred thousand euros? Enough to ensure that neither she nor the baby lack for anything for a year at least. In return …'

'Ah,' Irazola said softly, nodding. 'In return you will guarantee to keep silent about my private conversations.'

'That's about the size of it.'

He sucked hard on his cigar, stroked his jaw with forefinger and thumb. 'One hundred thousand, you say.' He seemed to come to a decision. 'Wait here.'

He strode towards the door, head erect, outwardly unruffled by the threat to his plans and schemes. He left the door open; his footfall receded.

'What now?' Linda whispered.

'Hopefully he's gone to fetch his cheque book.'

'You are deluding yourself, Mr Warner,' said a voice that was a higher- octave version of Irazola's.

A slim figure stepped through the doorway.

'Luis!' I said.

Irazola's son closed the door firmly behind him.

'I know why you are here,' he said urgently. Turning to Linda: 'We know all about you, my sister and I, though he does not think we do. Also, I was listening at the door.'

'I hope you like what you heard,' Linda flared.

'I like nothing about my father.' He came up to me and clutched at my arm. 'Believe it or not, Mr Warner, I am your ally. He will not pay you, he is going to have you both thrown into prison.' An exclamation from Linda. 'Do you understand?' Luis shook my arm, as if I were rejecting his warning. 'Sooner or later he will kill you. You must believe me, you must go – now!'

Momentarily I wavered. It wasn't that I didn't believe the general to be capable of killing, more that it was disproportionate. To kill two people to avoid paying out a hundred thousand euros, sure to be a derisory sum to a man of Irazola's financial standing, made no sense. Then it came to me. Linda was no longer even a part of the equation. This was now between Irazola and me. If the Spanish Government was mixed up in something really big connected with Gib – bigger even than Toby's rumours – he wouldn't take a chance on trusting me to honour our bargain.

'Señor Warner!' Luis pleaded, his good-looking, girlish features contorted with anxiety. No reason for him to lie, every reason for him to leave us to his father's mercies.

Linda was looking at me owlishly, awaiting my decision. Her normal self-sufficiency was of no value here.

I took her arm. 'Let's go.'

'If you say so.'

Luis was already heading for the door. Seconds later he pronounced the all clear and the three of us made a commotionless exit from the sitting room. Guarding the main door, and apparently a party to the conspiracy, was Elena, dressed in a white miniskirt and a tight black sweater that was designer-made for a figure like hers. Studiously disregarding Linda she rushed to me, clasped my hands in hers, making a statement that had no basis in reality.

'André, you are in great danger. My father –'

'Yes, yes, Luis told me.' I stifled the impulse to prise her fingers free. 'We're leaving.'

'Yes, you must leave. Immediately.' Yet she still clung to me. Maybe she hoped I'd take her instead of Linda.

Linda, tossing me a knowing sidelong grin in passing, was already following Luis through the door. Elena, scorning decorum, pushed her thigh into my groin; her lips fastened crushingly on mine.

'This isn't the time, you over-sexed bitch,' I said roughly. 'Any minute now your father will be back.'

'Yes ... you are right.' She pulled back and dragged me towards the open door. 'You must forgive me.'

A very un-Spanish drizzle was falling as we crossed the threshold. The Aston was only a few paces away, at the foot of the curved steps.

'Warner!' The summons came from behind.

Elena released me as if I had suddenly given her an electric shock. I swung round. General Irazola had just entered the foyer at the head of a gaggle of lesser ranks.

'Do not move!' he bawled. He was not armed but his aides were and, even as I watched, hands reached for holsters. With Elena back to clinging to my arm I was safe enough from flying bullets for now, and we stumbled in harness down the steps to the car. I had left it unlocked, and Linda was already in the passenger seat. Luis slammed her door shut then came rushing around the front of the car, still in a state of frantic anxiety. I didn't envy him. The wrath of Irazola senior would be his to contend with afterwards.

'Quick, *Señor*!' he yelped. Wasted words on his part. Quicker I could not go.

'Good luck!' Elena clutched in desperation at my arm as if even then she would delay my departure a few seconds longer. I flapped a vague goodbye, spared a breathless 'Thanks' for Luis as I dived into the Aston's driving seat.

II

HEAVY METAL

Chapter Twelve

The engine rumbled awake, responding instantly to throttle and I set about challenging the manufacturer's acceleration figures. The car leapt forward, Linda frantically buckling her seatbelt. In the rear-view mirror, I glimpsed uniforms surging through the doorway, Elena's white face, Luis's arm raised in defiant valediction. No shots were fired. Then we entered the curve of the driveway and their images were wiped away. Ahead, the approach road tapered to nothing in the rain and the mist. I held the car manually in second gear, winding the rev counter around the dial. More uniforms detached themselves from an outbuilding to our left, charged across the grass in a vain attempt to intercept us. Some were toting sidearms but we were already out of range.

The mist absorbed the buildings and the pursuit. Ahead lay the open road, as straight as Route 66 and nothing to bar our passage; at least, until we got to the guard house with its barrier. The barrier didn't worry me. The armed guards did.

'He must have flipped,' Linda said, her voice small with fright. 'You really got to him, didn't you, with all that crud about Gibraltar and recordings?'

'My mistake. The material was good, the tactics faulty. If I was going to threaten him I should have done it on neutral territory, not in his own back yard.'

'Too late now to change your mind.'

I felt her watching me but I kept my eyes on the road, as I belatedly locked my seat belt. Fortunately the road was straight but visibility was bad and worsening, the rain driving hard across the mountainside and lashing the side of the car as from a hosepipe.

'What are you, Warner? Not some kinda …' She sniggered self-consciously. 'You know, like a … like a spy, or something.'

Good guess, Linda.

'I'm doing a job for the UK Government,' I said tersely.

'Really? Cool. How did you get to hear about Julio plotting against Gibraltar?'

I switched the wipers onto fast-speed and left her question unanswered. A square of yellow opened up in the greyness ahead: light from the window of the guard house. My foot eased by instinct off the pedal. Vague forms took shape into uniformed guards.

'You aren't gonna stop?' Linda said sharply, drawing the wrong conclusion from our slowing down.

'Not a chance!' I rammed the pedal down. The four hundred horses under the hood responded with alacrity, and the white pole of the barrier leapt at us. When we hit we must have been doing over eighty. The pole was flimsy. It shattered in several places, one whirling section glancing off the nearside windshield pillar, fortunately missing the glass. The two guards scattered in panic to the left and right, without firing a shot.

Linda squealed, excitement not fear. 'Attaboy, Warner!'

I wasn't kidding myself we were done with Irazola yet. If my reading of him was even half-right we wouldn't just be allowed to head home as if we'd been on a picnic in the boonies.

We were now on the dirt road, the poor surface testing the Aston's ride, the occasional rut making itself felt through the suspension. I slowed to a relatively sedate eighty kph. The rain was easing, the sky paler, but there was more muck in wait ahead, rolling down the side the mountain, obscuring the summit.

In the midst of this unwelcome weather window they caught up with us. In a helicopter.

It reared up in the offside door mirror, an ugly buzzing bug, and closed in fast, skimming the ground at a dangerously low level. The pilot was either brilliant or nerveless. It flipped away in a vertical climb and I lost it.

'Was that a helicopter?' Linda demanded, peering around me.

'None other.'

'Jeepers! They sure mean business.'

A draught of damp air brushed my cheek as she lowered her window a little. The stammer of the chopper became all-pervasive, battering the eardrums. A moment later she whooped, 'They're right above us! If they come any lower they'll be sitting on our roof!'

A couple more minutes and we would be back in the murk. In front of us a great parapet extended across the skyline, and there lay invisibility. No helicopter could operate in that.

'Señor Warner!' The ululation boomed in the sky, distracting me so that I strayed off the road on to the raised shoulder.

'Oh!' Linda, even secured by her seat belt, was tossed sideways, her shoulder jarring against mine.

'You all right?' I was too busy wrestling the wheel to see to her.

'Sure.' Her voice was shaky. 'You keep your eyes on the road, and don't worry about me.'

She had guts all right. She was going to need them.

'Señor Warner!' The amplified summons momentarily drowned the noise of the chopper's engine. 'If you do not stop at once we are ordered to shoot.'

The ultimatum didn't shock me. I had been more than half-prepared for it. I had grasped the nature of the beast I was up against even before I stuck my head between his jaws. Only now it wasn't just my head but Linda's too.

I fed fuel to the vee-eight cylinders. The car bounded forward like a pouncing cat. At the very same instant a cracking-whip sound reached my ears, indistinct but unmistakable.

'Hey, they really mean it!' Linda, worldly in many ways, naive in others, was more incredulous than alarmed. 'That was a *shot*!'

I did the best I could within the limitations of resource and circumstance. The road surface was poor, made worse by the rain, and the Aston wasn't cut out for cross country work. I began to weave from side to side, varying the frequency and angle of deviation, also alternating between acceleration and deceleration. More than once I came close to running off the road. The man behind the gun, if he had any skill at all as a marksman, would soon adapt to my dodging tactics.

The note of the helicopter's engine suddenly surged and it dropped from the sky to fly alongside, on a parallel track just a few metres away. It was painted charcoal grey, relieved by the red-yellow-red military insignia at the rear of the fuselage.

'This is your final warning, Warner,' the megaphone blared. Linda reached past me and raised a defiant vertical finger at our pursuers. That would scare them off all right.

The bank of rain was rolling down on us. In less than a minute by my reckoning we would be in amongst it. A minute can be a long time when you're under fire.

The helicopter was pacing us, like an obedient dog trotting to heel. I contrived greater variations of speed, but the pilot wouldn't play. His priority now would be to maintain a steady gun platform for the marksman, easy to do in a chopper. Even as the thought struck me, a firefly of orange sparkled from the cabin and simultaneously the glass of my side window burst into fragments, spraying my head and shoulders with a thousand glass baubles. Linda yelled – she wasn't the screaming type – as the bullet exploded her window too, but outwards, away from her.

Wind and rain tore at us from both sides through the partially glassless windows, creating turmoil inside the car, and making Linda's hair do a crazy dance around her head. The helicopter had backed off a little. If that had been a warning, maybe it was the final one.

The choice was between surrendering or hitting back. I reached across Linda into the glove compartment. I operated the lever that lowered the built-in flap that wasn't put there by Aston Martin. The SIG automatic dropped into the palm of my hand.

'That's a gun!' Linda squeaked.

'Your powers of observation do you credit, honey.'

Releasing the wheel just long enough to rack the slide, I shoved the gun between my thighs, where it would readily come to hand.

'What are you doing with a gun?' Linda said, tugging at my sleeve.

'What I'm going to be doing, is giving that chopper a taste of its own medicine.'

'What! You can't do that!'

'Why not? You'd prefer they shot you, would you? Lower your seat as far as it goes and lie back. I want you out of my line of fire.'

She caught on fast. Found the seat recline switch and operated it so that she was almost horizontal. Not a second too soon. The helicopter was closing in again. I gave the pedal a blip, felt the rear wheels drift on the wet, muddy surface. Battled with steering that seemed no longer to be connected to the wheels. The helicopter swelled in size until it filled then overlapped the whole of the side window.

I yelled at Linda to cover her ears; mine would have to live with the noise. I lifted the SIG and pointed it at the chopper over the mound of her belly. The range was so short and the target so large it would have been harder to miss it than to hit it. Without taking my eyes off the road, I squeezed off a half dozen unaimed rounds from the fourteen-round magazine, fast as I could. The crash of the gun in the car's small interior, was eardrum busting. It wasn't possible to watch my shots strike home while keeping the car from running off the road. The chopper suddenly sheered away, so I guessed I had made them think twice if nothing else.

We pounded on, swerving and sliding on the wet surface, my ears not just ringing but clanging. Then the rain came down like a shutter and blotted out the world and our pursuers with it.

* * * * *

Toby, being conditioned to nothing less than the best, was lodged at The Rock, Gib's lushest and plushest hotel while I, preferring to keep a little distance between us, had taken a room at the Caleta, where I had spent a comfortable two nights during my earlier snoop around.

'Four stars are enough for me,' I had assured him. 'Think of how the Chancellor will approve of keeping my expenses down. Better for security too, that we aren't seen to be in cahoots'

Better still if he had stayed away from Gib altogether, though I didn't say so. I suspected Toby had strict instructions about monitoring my activities. So no surprise when I rolled up at the Caleta around nine to find him at the front desk, haranguing a pretty girl receptionist.

The porter dumped my bags by the desk. Toby's attention was caught by the act and relief lit up the lantern-jawed face for long enough to take in Linda's proximity to me and her state of impending motherhood. Naturally, he would draw the wrong conclusion.

'You were due here hours ago,' was his first shot across my bow, followed by: 'And who the devil is this?'

'Linda Pridham,' I said, very quickly to forestall a rude retort from the girl herself. 'A friend. Linda, meet Toby Wyatt. You're not seeing him at his well-bred best right now. But when he calms down – which he will when he's heard what I've got to tell him – you'll find he's quite civil really.'

'That's why I'm a civil servant,' Toby said unsmiling, not even acknowledging Linda. 'I'll be in the main bar. Join me in fifteen minutes. Now if you'll excuse me.' Remembering his manners, he tipped his head at Linda, made some brief comment to the front desk clerk, and went off to slake his ire.

'He seems a bit peeved,' Linda observed.

I snorted. 'He's just jealous.'

* * * * *

Alcohol, as expected, ironed the wrinkles out of Toby's displeasure. Diplomatically cajoling Linda to stay in our room, I tracked him down at the bar, where he was gossiping with an elderly British couple. Through the long window the sea was like black silk, shimmering under the light of an unseen moon, the setting overlaid by the orange-hued reflected interior of the bar.

'Brandy,' I told the barman, who was coffee-skinned, moustachioed, and probably Moroccan, like most of the hotel and restaurant workers in Gib.

'Brandy, yessir.' It came up fast and golden, and instantly soothing. I shoved my index finger in my right ear and wiggled it around. The clanging had diminished, was now a continuous hiss, like steam escaping.

'Well?' Toby demanded, as we settled in a corner seat under concealed orange lighting that made him look anaemic. 'Explain yourself.'

'I'm overdue and I'm sorry. Fact is, I had a spot of bother with our General Irazola. I nearly didn't get here at all.'

As expected and intended the mention of Irazola calmed his spleen.

'Tell all,' he commanded and gulped most of his brandy to fortify him against the worst. He always, he had once confided, feared the worst when professionals like him had to work with amateurs like me.

This was among the rare occasions when I settled for the straight truth. Toby, avidly attentive, didn't interrupt once. He even forgot to finish his brandy.

'Even when the weather closed in and they lost us I expected them to pick us up later, once it cleared. But it didn't abate until after we reached the highway, so they were screwed.'

'No difficulty at the frontier?' Toby asked, swigging the last dregs from his balloon glass. 'I would have expected them to alert the border police. Gib is a natural bolt-hole.'

'None at all. Say, now that you mention it, it was kind of lax of Irazola not to instruct the police to hold us.'

The only trouble I encountered during our return to Gib was a harangue from Linda, about having a gun secreted in the car.

'You expecting to kill someone?' she had said, and I wondered if she had somehow learned of my past profession.

'Ask no questions,' I hedged, avoiding her accusing gaze. 'Just stick it back in that compartment.'

'Why don't you just chuck it away?'

'You never know when we might meet up with your friendly neighbourhood general again.'

She saw the funny side of that and subsided into semi-manic laughter. When, finally, she calmed down, she extracted the SIG from between my thighs, adding a caress or two in the process, and shoved it back in its home. The subject was dropped. Perhaps, on reflection, she realised it might have been the gun that saved us.

'Weren't the border police even curious as to how your windows got broken?' Toby enquired.

'I anticipated that. I knocked out all the residual glass so it appeared as if they were lowered, that's all. The glass of one of the headlights was cracked from hitting the barrier, but the light was still functional and neither side even remarked on it.'

Our empty glasses were collected, another round requested. A pair of twittering old dears came and occupied the other half of my piece of couch.

'Now tell me, André, what's the idea of bringing a female companion?'

'Are there rules against it?' Before he could answer, I went on, 'If it weren't for her you wouldn't have a useful piece of intelligence on Irazola.'

'Is it so useful? It's just speculative hearsay. There isn't a deal I can do with it.'

I released a theatrical sigh, the kind that implies extreme denseness on the part of your audience.

'You don't consider his reaction extreme? You don't believe the Spanish could be cooking something up for Gib?'

'You've no solid evidence of that. I can hardly report the man's over-reaction to your vague threat as a hard fact. Dash it, André, it's barely even supposition.'

'Charge it to Room 414,' I said to the waiter as he delivered our brandies.

'Civil of you,' Toby murmured.

'It's all coming from the Treasury,' I said, grinning, as I signed the tab and tipped the waiter a 5-euro note.

Toby humphed. 'I'd quite forgotten you're on the books now. Be sure to keep all the receipts, and don't include your friend's shopping expeditions in yours.' He reached inside his blazer, drew out a well-worn but exquisitely-tooled leather cigar case. 'Care for one?'

'This is a no smoking zone,' I said, indicating a discreet sign on the wall behind him.

He turned his head and glowered at the offending notice. The cigar case returned to its place of repose.

'I still forget at times. It's gone too far, this no smoking nonsense. What next – a licence to breathe air?'

'So you're not going to take any action on my report,' I said, steering him back to business.

His shrug was elegant, as were most of his mannerisms.

'Oh, I'll put in a report of my own, all right. We never, as you well know, discount intelligence from whatever source and however questionable. Someone, somewhere, will set the dogs on General Irazola and find out what he's up to.'

'From our previous talk on the same subject I had the impression the dogs were already on him.'

'You should know better than to draw conclusions. Now – to come to the nitty gritty of your, er … mission: I'm going to bring you and Michael Vella together.'

'No, you're not. I'll do my own arranging. I told you – I've already met him.'

'Time's too short,' he said curtly. 'You have five weeks. We can't afford any leisurely preparations.'

'You don't say. So how and when and where is this arranged meeting to take place?'

'At a reception being held at my hotel tomorrow night on behalf of some fund-raising crowd. The Governor will be there and Peter Caruana, who was Chief Minister, and some people of influence in Gib society, including Vella.'

I digested this slowly.

'I would have thought the Governor and Vella would be anathema to each other.'

'Correct. But the Governor has to be seen there as representative of the UK government.'

'And Vella?'

Toby gestured airily. 'Outside of his politics and his involvement with this GIBESTÁ rabble he has many personal friends here. Furthermore, who's to say he won't succeed in his aims? Not even your machinations can guarantee his downfall. And if he does succeed everyone will want to be his friend. It's called –'

'Playing both ends against the middle, yeah,' I concluded for him. 'To be seen at the same bash as the Governor is to be pro-establishment. To chat up Vella is to secretly side with him.'

A woman's neigh of laughter behind us usurped Toby's riposte. He frowned his displeasure in the general direction of the disturbance, then said, 'You'll understand now why I wanted to be here for the kick-off.'

'Will I? You've been very close-mouthed all along, Toby. Are you finally going to tell me what I'm supposed to be?'

'Yes.' His voice sank to a whisper and he bent his head to mine. The two old biddies at the other end of the seat ceased their chatter and their upper halves swayed towards us. 'Vella has been told about you and that you're here to offer your services as an explosives expert.'

I blinked at him. 'A *bomber*? Little old me? So *that's* why my knowledge of explosives was such a necessary qualification. Don't forget that knowledge is pretty goddam rusty and I was never involved in the production side.'

His eyebrows squirmed furiously.

'We'll update you, never fear. A three-day elementary crash course has already been booked with an ex-bomb disposal officer in the Gibraltar Regiment.'

'Can I learn how to make bombs in three days?'

'The IRA trained their bombers in less.' Toby gave his glass a swirl, imbibed generously from it. 'Not to mention Isis.'

'Ah, yes, but Isis bombers don't mind getting blown up with their bombs.' I tapped my chest. '*I* do.'

* * * * *

It was well into the new day, and Linda was asleep fully-dressed on top of the bedclothes when I stole into our room on the fourth floor. Though she didn't know it, this was to be her last as well as her first night at the Caleta Hotel. Toby had been adamant on this point.

'I can't stop you womanising, André,' he had grumbled primly, 'but I'm damned if I'll stand for her sharing your room or even your hotel. It's too much of a risk. There'll be telephone calls, messages at the desk … you might even talk in your sleep.'

'You're stressing over nothing, Toby.'

But he was right. Security *über alles*. So, much as I resented being dictated to, I transferred Linda to the Rock Hotel that very morning. Her protest was perfunctory.

'You sure have funny ideas about how to treat a mistress, Mister.'

'You're not my mistress.'

Her deep blue eyes sparkled. 'You reckon?'

Chapter Thirteen

Linda was expecting to be my arm candy at the charity reception but I had to veto that idea. A bomber would hardly be likely to bring his pregnant partner with him. As a sop, I financed a clothes shopping spree, something of a necessity since all she had to wear was what she had on. As additional penance I spent the whole day with her, trailing from boutique to boutique. In the process I discovered that pregnant women are not well catered for where high fashion is concerned. Sometime during the expedition I rented a tux and accessories.

In the late afternoon we drove back to her hotel, the Aston's trunk stuffed with colourful carry bags, an excess of early spring air entering where the windows used to be. This reminded me that I needed to order replacements. Unlikely any garage in Gib would have them in stock, which meant airfreighting them from the UK at prodigious cost. I could always try adding it to my expense account.

In the single bed in Linda's room on the top floor we made love with a quiet but satisfying passion. I was still working several months of monastic regime out of my system and the visible evidence of Linda's pregnancy didn't interfere with my enjoyment. For her part, Linda showed no inhibitions at all.

Returning to the Caleta around six in the evening, I took a few minutes out to study my false UK passport, handed over by Toby the previous evening. My first and last names were the same but without the accent over the "e" and no middle name. I was now two years and a few months younger than the real me. The passport number was different. Physically I was as described in the original apart from losing two cms in height; the colour photo had not been tampered with but had been taken before I moved to Spain and I was therefore beardless. No matter, Toby opined, it added realism: people grew beards, people shaved them off. He cautioned me to carry only the fake from now on, as if I, who had owned more passports than the entire populations of some small countries, needed to be told.

For background, Toby had given me a Vancouver birthplace to account for my Transatlantic accent, and a successful businessman father but an Irish mother, which would justify a degree of hostility towards the English. I had also purportedly done a stint with the Provos, leaving when the Emerald Isle became too hot. Several actual Belfast bombings were 'loosely' attributed to me. As if I didn't have enough real wrongdoing on my conscience.

The invitation card specified 7.30pm. for cocktails, dinner at 8.15. My taxi actually deposited me at the front door of the Holiday Inn at eight o'clock on the hour. The Cameo Room on the second floor was the cocktails venue. Toby and I were to pose as only the most casual of acquaintances. The seating arrangements had been manipulated to place Michael Vella beside me.

The uninspiring Cameo Room was packed. A hundred or more, skimmed from the cream of Gibraltar society: politicians, high-ranking army officers, bankers, possibly a senior police officer or two, though these were plain clothed. And women galore, a-gleam and a-glitter, and bursting with eminence or reflected eminence. Had Cassandra been my companion, it would have been I who basked in the glow of her status, like an orbiting satellite, unable to break free from her gravity pull.

Toby wasn't hard to find. True to form he had gone straight to the top. In this instance Sir Gilbert Dover, Governor of Gibraltar, was the receptacle for his discourse. Very recently installed as Her Majesty's representative and military supremo on the Rock, he would be keen to make an impression. Not to mention anxious for the latest intelligence from inside Whitehall. None was better placed than Toby to supply it.

I ambled by, catching Toby's eye. The better to blend-in I snatched a glass from a passing tray. It turned out to have a cherry on a cocktail stick, something I can't abide. I popped it in the near-empty glass at the end of a long bare female arm that was blocking my way. The arm's owner, breathlessly recounting how 'that frightful Pearson woman' was forever dropping in on this or that pretext, and how she was quite positive she had designs on Edward ...

My meandering brought me to the far end of the Cameo Room without sight of Michael Vella. I picked up a blatant-come hither signal from one matriarch who ought to have renounced such behaviour a generation ago and, my drink still unsipped, I turned to retrace my route and all but collided with the very man.

'I saw you come in,' he said, straight off. His voice was as I remembered it, a hint of harshness yet mellow, benevolent. A minuscule Latin accent indefinably hinted at non-English genealogy. 'It is you, isn't it?'

He had taken hold of my arm; there was strength in his fingers.

'It is me,' I agreed.

'No.' He waggled his handsome silver head. 'I mean … it was you, you helped Andrea, my daughter when she …'

The memory revived my emotions of the moment. The girl's youth and the manner of her death still haunted me on occasion.

'I tried,' I corrected. I stuck out a hand. 'Warner.'

'Warner? André Warner?'

'Call me André. You're expecting me, I believe.'

'You know who I am?' Then, before I could answer: 'Yes … yes, of course you do.' He did a quick scan of guests within earshot. 'We have to talk. You may be able to help us. Time is very short.'

'The Madrid Conference, you mean?'

'Yes. Whatever agreement they come to will weaken our campaign, possibly destroy GIBESTÁ altogether. We –'

I motioned him to silence. 'Not here. The place is full of unfriendly ears.'

'You're right. I'm sorry, I'm not used to being a conspirator.'

I edged off centre stage, nearer the wall. 'We're booked to sit together. Did you know?'

Strata of amusement fanned out from the corners of his eyes.

'I should, since I arranged it. But, as you say, we won't be able to talk freely anywhere here. When can we meet?'

We agreed on ten o'clock tomorrow evening, at his apartment. He produced a wallet, fumbled a card from it while I studied him anew. He was a good bit taller than me, spare of frame yet broad. The thin grey moustache was slightly asymmetrical, trimmed short at one end by a wart or carbuncle the size of map pin head. There was an air of the swashbuckler about him. You could visualise him with a cutlass between his teeth and a bandanna tied to his head, leading a boarding party.

A bald man, his pink dome framed by bushy wings of black hair, eyes made small by rimless glasses, was watching us from the other side of an exclusively male circle. His face, though unremarkable, triggered a memory cell.

'Is that Peter Caruana?'

Vella tracked the line of my gaze. The bespectacled man suddenly became engrossed in the causerie taking place within his group.

'That's right,' Vella confirmed. 'Our past Chief Minister never misses an opportunity to lend his support to a worthy cause. Especially if there's a free night out attached. The man on his left –' grey-haired, more rimless glasses, sober blue suit, '– that's Keith Azopardi, GSD Party Chairman. Who knows, may be our next Chief Minister. They'll be curious about you.' He fingered the lapel of his midnight blue dinner jacket.

'Mmm.' It had already occurred to me that the Whitehall mandarins might not have taken Gibraltar's leadership into their confidence. If Fabian Picardo and Co. were unaware of my true rôle they could inadvertently foul up the works. I lodged a mental note to mention my fears to Toby.

Around us, a general drift towards the open doors was taking place. Caruana's group had split up, though one of their number, tall, lean, with Slavic features, had lingered to drain his glass and was observing me over the rim. When I stared back at him he gave a secretive smile before turning to follow Caruana and the others.

'Come on,' I said to Michael Vella. 'We don't want to attract attention by being the only ones left standing.'

I deposited my untasted drink on a side table and we joined the traffic flow to the dining room next door.

We had been allocated seats midway along a table with our backs to the wall. Vella was on my left, nearer the VIP table, which was at right angles to the rest. Toby, seated opposite, was between a woman who might have been attractive had she got rid of her Dame Edna spectacles and done something about her teeth, and a sallow-skinned, shifty-looking Latin, with the persona of a slave trader. More likely he was the most respectable man there. The immediate circle was completed by an elderly spinster type, who was silent until we began eating and then spoke non-stop with her mouth full, keeping up a constant spray of food particles.

The courses, which were numerous, ebbed and flowed and conversation with it. Vella drank steadily, mixed his wines indiscriminately, and became progressively withdrawn. Understandable. With his daughter so recently laid to rest he could be excused a certain bitterness. It said a lot for his grit that had not been deflected from his cause.

The evening would clearly have wound down to an uneventful close but for the speeches. Peter Caruana, as former and much-respected Chief Minister was due on first. We were all sitting back, some with loosened ties, to relish our brandies and liqueurs when a table-top mike was set up before Caruana, and he duly rose to a mixture of mechanical applause and a few good-natured groans.

He was not, he assured the room, second chin quivering, about to make a party political broadcast, nor did he intend to drone on for hours. No, it was merely to cast a few pearls of praise over the orphaned children's charity in whose aid this gathering had been organised. He was confident that our donations would be put to effective use.

He prattled for about fifteen minutes. By now, Sir Gilbert was shooting furtive glances at his watch so I guessed Caruana was past his allotted time. Somebody must have sent him a coded signal, because he brought his monologue to a conclusion in a couple of terse sentences and resumed his seat to lukewarm applause.

It was now the turn of Sir Gilbert Dover. His role was non-political so he was not expected to talk along controversial lines.

Just shows how wrong you can be.

It all started harmlessly enough, with reference to the honour of being appointed to represent Her Majesty in this important strategic outpost, blah-blah-blah. I was almost dozing off when the diminutive Governor inserted into his peroration a swipe at GIBESTÁ which had all the subtlety of a punch in the nose, and had me snapping out of my snooze as if an alarm clock had gone off beside my ear.

'Before closing,' this masterpiece of provocation ran, 'I wish to speak briefly about the recent violence that has been visited upon this peace-loving country. I am confident that I speak for ninety-nine per cent of the population of Gibraltar, in condemning it and, equally, the source from which it springs.' A low growl came from the back of Vella's throat. His hand twitched, accidentally upsetting his liqueur glass; a yellow stain fanned out over the white tablecloth. I seemed to be the only one who noticed. All eyes were turned towards the top table. Caruana, seated on the Governor's left flank, was frowning down at his plate.

'Over the past few weeks the Government of Gibraltar has been subjected to a great deal of loud invective. We have been told that … independence –' The way he enunciated the word you might have thought he was talking about child molestation, '– is the only course that will bring security and prosperity. Yet those who mouth this propaganda know full well that without the deterrent of British military support the Spanish would simply stroll across the border and put an end to all notions of independence. Nor would our neighbours be content with a mere *Anschluss*, leaving us to get on with the business of living. Make no mistake, ladies and gentlemen, citizens of Gibraltar, your country would be occupied by the Spanish army and likely to remain that way!' He cleared his throat, running spread fingers through his receding pepper-and-salt hair. 'As for prosperity, under Britain you already have the security and prosperity that the pro-independence factions trumpet about. It is uncertainty and poverty they would visit on you.'

Vella had heard his fill. Sir Gilbert had paused in his speechmaking to give his rimless glasses a vigorous polish when the hurled salt cellar smacked fair and square into his midriff. The glasses shot from his hands. He blinked short-sightedly out across the room.

'Lackey!' Vella, the launcher of the missile, was up on his feet, swaying ever so slightly but otherwise in full command of his faculties. 'You bootlicking jackal!' Gasps all around. All faces were turned towards Vella now. I tugged at his cuff but he yanked his arm free so savagely a button tore away in my fingers. 'All you want is to keep us under your thumb. Bloody colonials, that's all we are to Britain!' His voice was a bellow, needing no artificial amplification.

The Governor's glasses were back on his nose. They somehow increased his gravitas if not his height.

'You may posture all you like, Mr Vella,' he retorted, his voice reverberating through the speakers, causing feedback. 'The people of this country don't want and certainly don't need your blustering rhetoric –'

'How do you know what they need!' Vella raged back. 'Don't pretend you aren't going to sell us down the river in Madrid five weeks from now!'

This accusation was heresy of the highest order, and was greeted by indrawn breaths. Toby was lounging back in his seat, appraising Vella, a vague smile playing across his lips. He would be enjoying the show, enjoy being in the wings. The reactions of those with more at stake were less phlegmatic: Caruana was signalling frantically to some aide, while Sir Gilbert's wife seemed to be pleading with her husband. An unidentifiable VIP a few places along from Caruana, was also now standing, shaking a fist at Vella. Camera flashes were going off all round. Two uniformed police officers, one of each sex, came through the doorway in a rush. They were intercepted by a guest who pointed Vella out to them. They moved in. More cameras flashed.

Vella was still ranting but the general hubbub was blurring his oratory, robbing it of impact. The police officers were closing in. I got up and physically pushed Vella down into his seat. So complete was his surprise he didn't resist. His mouth locked open.

'The police are here!' I had to shout to make myself heard over the furore. 'You'll be out on your ass if you don't shut up.'

'I don't care.' He threw off my restraining hold, rose again, to resume his verbal onslaught on the hapless Governor. The male police officer, a flat-capped sergeant, reached Vella, seized him roughly.

'Look, sergeant …' I said, rashly intervening. 'Mr Vella's loaded, he doesn't know what he's doing.'

'Stay out of this, sir,' the sergeant said, keeping just to the right side of courtesy. A glass whizzed past my ear, caught Vella on the cheekbone, shattering and drawing blood. He flung the sergeant aside, sending him spinning into me. The woman police officer grabbed at me, I thrust her away, instinctive self-defence.

'André ... stay out of it!' came the wail from Toby across the table. He might as well have been on the other side of the world for all the use he was to me. A full-scale brawl was now in the making. Vella and me against the rest.

Down I went, like a thrown caber. I remember getting in one good kick that raised a satisfying howl. Payment for that minor triumph was in kind and in multiples. Then the lights went dim and finally out altogether. On me, that is.

Chapter Fourteen

'Feels good to be a free man again,' I said to Toby, as he met me in front of the Irish Town police headquarters. It was morning and I hadn't slept at all in my cosy little cell.

'You've only yourself to blame,' he chided. A car was waiting at the curb, rear door open ready to receive us. It was a nondescript conveyance, a military green Vauxhall with a dent in the offside wing and a driver in army uniform with corporal's stripes. 'A breach of the peace charge is not going to look good back in London.'

'Stuff London,' I retorted, across the car's roof. 'It wasn't my bloody fault.'

'Not your fault it started, but did you have to get stuck in? How's your head, by the way?'

I explored the swelling on my forehead that was the outcome of its meeting with the floor of the Cameo Room.

'Pulsating gently.'

The Vauxhall pulled away and rounded the corner into John Mac Square, where Michael Vella's daughter had met her end. It was sunny, if on the breezy side. It lifted my spirits to be a free man again.

'Did they let Vella out too?' I asked.

'Yes. The authorities wanted the police to hang on to him but they couldn't justify it on a drunk and disorderly charge. He'll appear in court in the fullness of time and be duly fined.'

'What about charging him for assault? That salt pot he chucked at Caruana. It would solve a lot of problems if they found an excuse to jail him until the talks are over.'

'More likely it would mean martyrdom,' Toby said moodily. He leaned forward. 'Corporal – take us out to the Point, will you?'

'Right, sir.'

'The Point?' I queried. 'What is it and why are we going there?'

'A place where no eavesdroppers lurk, dear boy. For your final briefing.'

So we went to 'the Point,' or to accord it its full title, Europa Point, the European mainland equivalent to England's Land's End.

'Your lady love phoned me just before I came to collect you,' Toby said as we settled on a bench with an outlook across the Strait of Gibraltar.

'Linda? Why was that?'

'Heard about you on local radio. She was quite worried. Panicky almost.' He nipped his nostrils thoughtfully. 'Seems ... fond of you. Doesn't say much for her taste.'

I crossed my legs, contemplated the rumpled pants of my rented monkey suit. My night in a police cell had been hard on them.

'Linda Pridham is the most independent-minded representative of her sex I've ever come across. If she's fond of me it's because I'm her meal ticket at the moment. As soon as she's brought Irazola's brat into the world she'll latch onto a new sugar daddy. A billionaire at least.'

Tony was amused. 'How cynical you've become of late.'

We were alone with the lighthouse and a pair of twelve-pounder guns mutely rusting away on their circular emplacements. Across the strait was Africa, rising from the horizon on a bed of haze, brooding and mysterious, the higher peaks lost in a halo of cloud. Nearer, a white-hulled ferry was sliding across the sparkling water, heading into the Spanish port of Algeciras.

Toby, with his customary foresight, had thought to bring binoculars.

'You can see Ceuta,' he announced after sweeping the panorama.

'Ceuta? You mean that itty-bitty piece of Spain over in Morocco?'

'Spain's equivalent to Gibraltar. No sign of them ever giving *that* up.'

'You want me to go over there and see what I can do?'

He grinned without taking the glasses from his eyes. The strong breeze coming off the sea whipped his thinning locks into a frenzy and he brushed at them impatiently, tutting with annoyance.

'Coming to the point of coming to the Point,' he said, chuckling discreetly at his own whimsy and undeterred by my sigh. 'Let's work out your next step.'

'Before we do, you'll be pleased to learn that I'm meeting Vella and his cronies this evening, at his home.'

Toby lowered the binoculars. 'Good. And to further give credit, by taking Vella's side in last night's rumpus you'll have established your credentials with him. You'll see – from now on you'll be able to do no wrong.'

'Do you imagine,' I said, 'I didn't think of that?'

He gave me a slow stare before breaking into a guffaw. 'Oh, André, when will I stop underestimating you? There I was, deluding myself you're acting out of conscience or a sense of fair play, when all the time you're simply calculating the odds. You're better versed in the art of guile than I gave you credit for.'

Let him go on thinking so. It might even be true. The real truth was that I even didn't know myself half the time.

'Tell me, what did you do after leaving MI6? Before you bought the bar.'

It was a question I was often asked. My replies varied, but were never truthful.

'I was in the waste disposal business.'

'Is there money in it?'

'Sure. Millions to be made.'

'Really.' More nods, contemplative now, as if he were weighing up a career move. 'I would never have guessed it.'

Before he started digging I reminded him why we were here.

'Quite so. So you're to meet up with Vella tonight. By then I shall be gone, of course. Any questions on the reporting procedure?'

'No, all is clear. All communications through Major Ribble at the Governor's office, for his and the Governor's ears only. All reports to be verbal, unless the amount of detail necessitates an using the overnight bag, in which case coded to OM/G4 with a priority sticker. No emails. No faxes. No pigeons. Routine check-in every Wednesday night and Saturday night at 22.00 hours.

'The same Major Ribble will act as my personal quartermaster,' I continued. 'Notably for the supply of the … er … explosives. They'll come from the Base, I suppose. I report to him tomorrow morning, eight am. sharp, for my bomb-making tutorial. So far, so correct?'

'Go on.'

'In case of emergency my contact will be Chief Superintendent Mascarenhas at Irish Town Police Headquarters. In all cases my bogus passport is the recognised form of identification coupled with the codeword "Sideshow". If I have to go to ground in a hurry and can't make contact with Mascarenhas, I go to 35, Lime Kiln Terrace and ask for Tommy. Show my passport for identification, quote codeword "Sideshow blown."' I flicked a glance at the inscrutable profile beside me. 'Have I left anything out?'

'You have not,' he said, without looking at me. 'I don't suppose you're willing to give me a preview of the method.'

'You suppose correctly, Toby, old pal.'

Fact was, I hadn't firmed up any ideas yet, though a germ of one was already scurrying around inside my head, like a hamster on a treadmill.

'Toby … about my masquerade as a bomber. You and the bigwigs back home do realise that I may actually have to plant a bomb or two in the course of duty. Have you thought about that?

'Then plant with discretion, dear boy.'

'My God,' I said, drawing the words out. 'You lot really don't care a bent cent, do you?'

'Do *you*?'

Oddly, I did a bit, though I would never be able to convince him of it.

The ferry slipped from sight behind the curve of the headland, leaving the sea empty, molten silver where the sun struck it. A man and a woman, casually dressed in bulky sweaters and jeans were wandering past us down the slope towards the cliff edge. Something about the man's loping gait and angular frame was familiar. He was on the thin side for his height, with near-white hair, whereas the woman was small and plump with a bottom that wobbled. In physique they were exact opposites.

'Someone you know?' Toby didn't miss much.

'That man …' I shook my head. 'Have a feeling I've seen him before.'

Toby studied the descending couple. They had their backs to us. 'Here in Gib, you mean?'

'I think so. It doesn't matter anyway.'

But it nagged at me. All the way to the airport, on the other side of the peninsula, where I saw Toby onto his flight. All the way to The Rock Hotel, to lay Linda's worries to rest. All the way through lunch and afternoon, until, in the aftermath of lovemaking, with the pink sunlight of early evening crawling over our naked bodies, I remembered. Remembered the man with the Slavic looks, who had been so interested in me at the charity ball.

That he should be out at Europa Point with his girlfriend the same time as Toby and me brought out the suspicious side of my nature. Gib wasn't so vast that coming across the same people more than once wasn't a believable coincidence. Yet …

Linda, snuggling into my armpit, her skin lightly chilled as the temperature fell, sensed my preoccupation.

'You're not being your usual attentive self, Warner,' she complained, stroking my chest. 'Things on your mind?'

'No. Nothing at all. Except … this.'

'Oh!' And a few moments later: 'Mmm, ye-e-es, I like that.' Her loins squirmed against mine. As always she sat astride me.

'More comfortable for a gal my size,' she explained unnecessarily.

'Fine for you. But the two of you are a lot to support.'

'Weakling,' she said, laughing. Often when she laughed she tossed her head and her soft, peat-brown hair rippled sinuously. She bounced more energetically still.

Later, in the darkness and afterglow of contentment, I asked, 'Do you feel okay?'

'Sure,' came the drowsy reply. Then, coming alert: 'What do you mean – okay?'

'The baby. Have you seen a doctor at all?'

Silence.

'You should. Go tomorrow.'

'Sucks to you, Warner. Don't go giving me orders.'

'Suit yourself.' I rolled onto my side, away from her.

For a while the only sound in the room was of our breathing. Now and again a car buzzed past on Engineer Road, its headlights briefly chasing a white square across the wall.

A hand slithered over my shoulder, squeezed lightly.

'I'll go tomorrow. Promise.'

I turned and hugged her. She sighed, her cheek nuzzling my neck, like a puppy seeking attention. She wasn't as tough as she would have people think.

'Got to go home soon,' I reminded her.

'Louse. I was hoping you'd forgotten. Will you come back here afterwards?'

I found the tip of her nose with my lips. 'Better not. I'll be round first thing in the morning though. We'll have breakfast together. Go for a swim in the pool.'

'No, we won't. It's empty.'

* * * * *

Single detached dwellings standing on individual lots are scarce in Gibraltar. Despite a certain amount of land reclamation, space is at a premium, much of what there is being in the hands of the military and therefore unavailable for development. Consequently, like most of his fellow Rock dwellers, Vella had to make do with an apartment.

My iPad's Google map pinpointed it on the lower side of the Alameda Gardens and almost directly opposite an open-air theatre. Comfortable walking distance from the Rock Hotel. All the better. Walking is the least obtrusive form of motion and hardest to tail.

The apartment block was three-floors high, manifestly upper echelon, and Apartment 6 was at the top. No security precautions, no electronically bolted gates or outer doors. I had heard tell Gibraltar's crime levels are classed as very low, albeit on the rise like everywhere else.

Vella opened the door within seconds of my thumbing the buzzer. 'Come in, Warner,' he said, warmly. 'I mean André. It is André, isn't it?'

'Most people call me that when they're being polite.'

We crossed a plush-carpeted entrance hall, so ill-lit that the design of the sombre wallpaper was indistinguishable, to a door standing ajar at the far end. A vast living-cum-sitting room lay on the other side: low slung armchairs, mahogany table, buffet, geometric bookshelves. A shelving unit, also of mahogany, laden with more books, TV, music centre, etc. Pottery ornaments throughout. Michael Vella had conventional bourgeois tastes.

The table was spread with papers. Around it were four men.

'We meet again,' the man furthest from me said, with a small chuckle. He was in shadow so I moved forward, to see him better: it was the old man from Catalan Bay Village.

'You remember me?' he said. He was better dressed tonight in a finely checked suit, knitted silver-grey tie. A different person.

'Sure do. El Jefe, right?'

'And me?' The voice belonged to a younger man, more casually dressed.

'Peter, isn't it? Good to see you again.'

Easy to tell he was pleased I had remembered.

'How are you?' he said, 'I am glad we are to work together.'

'That hasn't been decided yet,' Vella said sharply, a reprimand.

Peter looked resentful but held his tongue.

I was introduced to the two other members of what I gathered was the GIBESTÁ Inner Council: Benjamin and Maurice. No last names were given, would have been superfluous anyway – all the movement's leading lights were on record, down to the maiden names of their mothers, in the intelligence report distributed at the committee meeting in London. Benjamin Levy – "Ben" – was somewhere in his thirties, eyes small and darting behind pebble-lensed glasses, bony features. Maurice Pilcher was older, of Vella's generation, with a spare tyre that was putting pressure on his shirt buttons, and wild blond hair.

'Drink, André?' Vella asked, as I took my place at the table. Bottled Carlsberg lager was the only beer going, so I conformed.

'Here's to an independent Gibraltar,' I proposed, sloshing lager into a chunky half-pint tankard.

They loved that.

'To business then,' Vella said decisively from the head of the table. Just below his left eye was a neat Band-Aid patch, legacy of a thrown glass at the charity gathering. His first scar of war.

'For your information, André, we five constitute the decision-making body within GIBESTÁ; we're the executive, you might say. There is a lower council, with voting rights, but for all practical purposes what we say goes.' He smiled, a friendly, manly smile that relieved the severe jawline. 'Whatever we agree here tonight will be official party policy within twenty-four hours.'

'I believe you, believe me.'

'You have been recommended by a … let us call him a Whitehall ally. Some of us are impatient for results, we feel we must force the hand of the British Government. Our first objective therefore is to have the Madrid Conference called off. Our second objective is greater autonomy, on a par say with Scotland. Our third and ultimate objective, complete independence. Also like Scotland would like to be.'

He squared the thin sheaf of papers before him.

'All clear?'

'Optimistic,' I remarked, and five sets of eyes fixed on me, quizzing.

'André …' Vella hesitated. 'I don't wish to be discourteous but you are not here to comment on our strategies or offer advice. We don't seek to recruit you to our cause, merely – possibly – to employ you. It is a mercenary we need, not a disciple.'

'Good enough. I apologise. Tell me what you want from me.'

Vella drew his chair closer to the table, swallowed several times. 'What we … what some of us want, is a campaign of violence against the authorities. In black and white terms, a series of bombings, directed against government and police property, spread over the next four to five weeks. For that we need outside expertise. Not only on the grounds of technical knowledge but because I …. *I* …' He tapped his chest, glared a challenge around the table, 'have decreed that no member of our movement shall have a direct hand in any violence.'

It was a form of self-delusion, even of hypocrisy, but having had my wrist smacked once for expressing an opinion I just bobbed my head in understanding.

'GIBESTÁ must remain pure,' Peter (surname Vitale) said sneeringly. 'Pah! His daughter is killed in the streets and still he says we must not soil our hands.'

'That's enough!'

'We should have the courage …'

El Jefe (full name Eduardo Goncalves) rapped his knuckles on the table top. Peter immediately fell quiet.

'Mr Warner is not concerned with our internal squabbles. For him this is a simple question of yes or no, do we wish to use him. If it is no, then he can leave with our apologies for wasting his time.'

Vella was nodding gently like a treetop in a gust of wind. Even he yielded to El Jefe's authority.

'Well, gentlemen?' My gazed passed around the table. 'Do you want to use me, yes or no?'

To do what I had been signed up to do, I badly needed a 'yes'. Yet to try and persuade would be out of character for the mercenary I was supposed to be. Toby had led me to believe it was a foregone conclusion.

'We vote,' El Jefe declared, and Vella signalled his reluctant accord.

'All in favour of the bombing campaign, as proposed by Peter,' he said in a husky voice, 'raise their hands.'

Peter's shot up, as if he couldn't wait. Ben and Maurice were only a beat behind. Vella and El Jefe sat motionless, eyeing each other from their opposite ends of the table. Then, with a kind of shudder, El Jefe lifted the lower part of his arm, his fingers spread and trembling slightly.

'I vote to bomb,' he said.

Vella's face was expressionless.

'All those against the bombing campaign,' he intoned, like a speaking computer, and with an air of weary surrender put up his hand. 'The motion is carried by four votes to one. We bomb.'

'Should we now vote on hiring André?' Ben's enquiry was of nobody in particular.

'Let's take it as understood, shall we?' Vella said dully. 'We don't have a flood of applicants, and the more people we interview the greater the risk of a security breach.'

A grandmother clock on the wall behind Vella ding-donged the hour as he spoke. I kept my face bland, my relief damped down.

'Good.' Peter was animated, already thrilled at the prospect of demolishing City Hall and the Central Police Station. I suppose every successful political pressure group needs its hard-line fanatic but the breed frankly scares me. They'd blow up the world to further their cause.

'Are you going to take me on trust?' I asked, amazed that credentials had not been demanded at the outset.

'We have to,' Vella answered simply. 'If you're an impostor you'll have proof and to spare that you are who you claim to be. If you're genuine, you have no need of it.'

Such faith offended my sense of professionalism.

'Now that we are all agreed, let us make a start.' Peter was on the edge of his chair, flushed and twitchy with excitement. He shuffled through his papers. 'I have a list somewhere –'

'Not so fast,' I said, an edge to my voice. 'Before you raze the town we have to settle my terms. It takes two sides to make a bargain. How do you know you can afford me?'

Doubt replaced elation.

'What will it cost us?' Peter said with a show of pugnacity. He had taken my acceptance for granted, he hadn't even considered the price tag.

'Yes,' Michael Vella said, perhaps entertaining a private hope that my rates of hire would be unaffordable. 'What is your fee?'

Pitch it too high and they would go elsewhere; too low, and suspicions might be aroused. I had already given the subject careful thought.

'Twenty thousand euros per job all in, materials included.'

Maurice looked shocked. His flabby cheeks wobbled as he gave a violent shake of the head.

'At that rate twelve bombs will empty the coffers.' Which placed Maurice in charge of the Treasury.

'Twelve bombs will be enough,' Vella interposed, adding, in the ensuing hiatus: 'Perhaps more than enough.'

'I haven't finished,' I said. 'Ordinarily I would expect a bonus on completion – say fifty thousand.'

'What!' The exclamation came from several quarters at once. Only Peter showed unconcern. He gulped his lager, leaving a moustache of froth which he licked away slowly, like a cat after a satisfying lunch of mouse.

'However …' I said, with pause for effect, 'I am prepared to make the bonus conditional on your achieving independence, if that will help. Once you're in power you'll have all the resources of government to call on.'

Vella left his chair and, hands thrust in the pockets of his immaculate navy-blue pants, walked half the length of the room and back. His silver hair sparkled as the multi-branched ceiling light played over it. On the floor below, a dog, perhaps roused by his footfall, started barking.

'Suppose we say two hundred and fifty thousand total, for six weeks work.'

'Open-ended, you mean?' I made a face. 'I couldn't agree to that, especially as I'll be supplying the materials – explosives don't come cheap. There has to be a limit to the number of incidents.'

'All right then.' This from Peter, embarrassingly anxious to seal the contract. 'Twenty bombings, absolute tops.' He glanced worriedly at Vella, as if fearing he had overstepped the mark. 'All right, Michael?'

Vella shrugged in resignation.

'All right with you, André?' Peter demanded.

'It'll have to be,' I grunted, 'if that's the best you can come up with.'

Still manifestly unhappy at the prospect of violence and the likelihood of collateral fatalities, Vella went and stood before El Jefe in a final appeal.

'Jefe … ever since I was capable of thinking for myself I have been against violence. I have observed the Irish Republican Army, the Basques, the Corsicans, Baader-Meinhof, Isis, and all those other Muslim terrorist groups. In no case … *no* case … could I bring myself to even condone it, let alone sympathise or approve. In fact, I have always despised them and their indiscriminate bombings. Now you ask me to commit our political movement to as many as twenty bombings of our own. To destroy what we wish to build up and nurture. Even to kill. Because there will be deaths, there are always deaths … innocent people. I have led you this far without recourse to such methods –'

'And see where it's got us,' Peter snorted.

'Now you ask me,' Vella went on, addressing only El Jefe, 'to lead us along a path of planned, premeditated destruction with no certainty of success. How can you expect it of me?'

El Jefe ruminated at some length. 'My friend,' he said finally, 'this matter is not about people or buildings. Our aim is independence, the chosen vehicle is GIBESTÁ. People are incidental. Even you, son of my closest friend, are incidental. You are liked, respected, admired. No one is better qualified than you to lead us through what will be difficult times. No one is more likely to keep the respect and admiration of our people when all around is violence and death. But you are not indispensable. We have voted, you have lost. You must either accept the voting of the Inner Council or you must go.'

Vella's head bowed.

'You are right,' he said with a tremor in his voice. 'I must shut my eyes and my ears and steer a straight course towards our goal.'

'It is the only way,' El Jefe agreed.

Spoken like true fanatics.

There they sat, the battle-scarred sage and the peace-loving idealist. The one having long lived by the creed that mountains are moved only by deeds and moved fastest of all by deeds of violence; the other, his conscience giving him hell, yet, being human, attracted by the power that would accompany success. I pitied him. Win or lose, let there be a single innocent victim and he was doomed to lifelong torment.

'This is all very moving,' I said, with a fabricated yawn, 'but we've yet to settle the method of payment. I don't give credit. I want ten per cent up front and instalments of ten more after every two bombings. Agreed?'

Peter took it upon himself to agree and Vella, by his reticence, underwrote the commitment.

'Good,' Peter said, smacking his palms together ostentatiously. 'Let us now proceed with the practical arrangements.' He had a handwritten list before him. 'These buildings are all soft targets …'

Chapter Fifteen

It was after two in the morning, the streets lifeless, glossed with rain, clean-smelling. Down in the dockyard the glare of floodlights. Beyond, across the blackness of the bay, the lights of Algeciras twinkled. My footsteps were unnaturally loud, drowning all other sounds. So much so that I slowed every fifty paces or so to listen.

I was rounding the corner into Europa Road, just a few hundred metres short of The Rock Hotel, when I spotted him. Or them. A shadow, flitting across a patch of light under a streetlamp. Muggers? I kept going.

'Muggings don't happen here,' Mike Manders, front desk manager at The Rock had assured me smugly.

If I accepted that and accepted too that I wasn't about to become a blemish on that admirable statistic, I had to conclude that I was under professional surveillance. Possibly friendly. I suspected Toby wasn't above keeping tabs on me.

Crossing the road, hand in pocket nonchalantly jingling a few coins, I psyched myself up to deal with enemy action. I was weaponless though the Aston was close enough to rectify that omission if I made a run for it. Above The Rock Hotel's long flat roof the real Rock towered, black against the indigo of the night sky. Around the summit clouds clustered, made luminous by the moonlight.

The hotel was served by an uphill ramp. There I came to an abrupt halt, pivoting on my heel. A tall figure didn't react quite fast enough, ducking behind a low wall.

No use keeping up the pretence of unawareness now. I went up the slope to the hotel parking lot at a fast lick, unlocking the car from twenty paces. I started up, over-revved in my urgency, reversed fast out of the line of cars to swoop back down the road to where the snooper had gone to ground.

There was some loose gravel on this section and I made a lot of commotion by braking harshly. I sat there with the doors locked, the engine chugging and my foot hovering over the accelerator pedal while I scanned the area where I had last seen the mystery man. A couple of wheeled garbage bins stood behind the low wall. I waited, I watched.

Either my Mr X was still there, crouching behind the bins, or he had cut and run. If he was still there, he might be armed, he might be prepared to use it. Confrontation meant commotion; maybe some public-spirited soul would summon the police. If by then I had a corpse on my hands, my cover here in Gib would be just as dead.

I opted for discretion, much as running away went counter to my instincts. I gunned the Aston back up the ramp and parked back in my slot. Out of the car, I listened, heard nothing, looked around and saw nothing, and went inside.

It was a warning to be heeded. Interested parties were sniffing around. Be they British, Gibraltarian, or Spanish. The rules of the game had been rewritten. To stay in business I would have to adapt to them.

The snag was, I didn't yet know what the rules were.

* * * * *

The evening after my recruitment as official bomber to GIBESTÁ the organisation put on its biggest most impressive demonstration yet: over three thousand people were estimated to have flocked to Convent Place to hear an inflammatory speech by Vella. I watched, from the semi-darkness of an upstairs room of the Governor's residence, in the company of Lennox Ribble, Signals Corps major, who was also my link-man. Vella's pulpit eloquence flowed through the open window, into the room and around us, and it was potent stuff. Advance notification, if you could read between the lines, of hard-line tactics to come.

'If circumstances require we should take a violent road we will not shrink from it!' This was received by a gale of cheering and hooting. The guy was a gifted orator, all right.

Ribble, a pale, ginger-haired man, short of stature, with a calm efficiency that impressed me, clicked his tongue.

'Listen to them. Put a rabble rouser with a cause in front of any crowd in the world and they'll howl for war.'

'Until they get it, then they'll start howling for peace. Why don't the police break them up? Causing an obstruction or something.'

A wan smile formed on his pale face.

'You should know better than most. Vella's to be left alone. In any case you don't stop a man like that by gagging him.'

Vella spoke for nearly an hour. When the speech and the succeeding near-hysterical ovation were over, the crowd, instead of dispersing went on what appeared to be an impromptu march, off down Main Street, towards the shopping mall. Only Vella, with a few adherents, one of whom I recognised as Maurice, remained in the square, holding an outdoor conference. A solitary helmeted policeman circled them, the rest of the law's representatives having left with the mob. Two men in overalls were loading Vella's mike and a collection of amplifiers into a station wagon, and two others were dismantling the platform from where he had delivered his speech.

'It's going to get worse,' Ribble observed, 'before it gets better.' He cocked his head towards the window. 'You hear that?'

Mingled with shouts and cheering was the smash of glass breaking, not once in isolation but a succession of shatterings and with each of them the cheering swelled in volume.

Ribble drew the plain green drapes and switched on the ceiling lights.

'You're not going to make matters any better, are you?' he said morosely. 'It's all right for you – you can scuttle off back to wherever you came from when you've settled with Vella. The ones who are left behind will have to pick up the pieces and stick them back together again.'

'Yours and mine not to reason why, Major. You've got three days to make a fully paid-up bomber of me, starting tomorrow.' I sketched a farewell. 'Now I must wish you *buenas noches*. Do I leave the same way as I entered, or do you have a choice of secret exits?'

'If I was to tell you that they wouldn't be secret any more,' Ribble countered, which was as near as he had come to humour all evening.

* * * * *

The damage was superficial but extensive. I walked Linda down a sun-warmed Main Street and glass crunched underfoot. Teams of labourers were sweeping it into heaps in the gutter. Police were everywhere, mostly prodding around in looted shop windows. A shop selling radios, cameras, and suchlike had been gutted, the stock reduced to lumps of congealed plastic. Passers-by ogled the scene in a kind of stupefied disbelief.

'You said Gibraltar wasn't at all like England,' a well-dressed elderly woman was heard to complain. 'No football hooligans you said, no vandalism, no teddy boys …' Her voice, petulant, accusatory, dwindled away in the distance, and was superseded by static from a patrolling constable's short-wave radio.

'Roger,' the policeman acknowledged into the mouthpiece. 'I'll proceed up City Wall Lane and report back in five minutes. Over and out.'

'It sure is a shame,' Linda said, clinging tightly to me for fear of slipping on the glass. 'It's a pretty little town. People are shits, aren't they, when it comes down to it?'

'Some have more failings than others,' I conceded. 'Some are easily led.'

'Yeah.' She seemed genuinely distressed. A social conscience was a side of her I hadn't come across. I hadn't really given much thought to her deeper emotions, to what made her tick. Even pregnant, she was nice to look at, nice to make love to, and I felt an obligation to see her through a difficult period. Deeper motives, if any, hadn't yet surfaced.

She glanced up and caught me looking at her as we walked. She grimaced. 'Look like hell, do I?'

'Shucks, no,' I said, which made her laugh. 'You look … swell.'

She patted her bulge. 'Well, I'm swelling for sure.'

She was wearing a knee-length patterned shift, that smoothed out the bulge without eliminating her other curves. Modestly heeled shoes with ankle straps flattered her legs and at the other extremity, her hair, now of a length to sweep her shoulders, was tied back with a broad red band. No beautifying aids. She could do without.

Her real pleasure at the compliment was there in the wide white smile and the glow that came to her cheeks. Yet to her it was natural to hide it behind some throwaway remark.

'What are you after, Warner?'

'Stop playacting, Linda,' I said. 'There's no need for it with me, not anymore. I've got you sussed, so you can let the real you out of the bottle.'

The eyes that were the blue of the ocean deep widened. For once she was caught with her guard down. She stopped, her arm pulling free of mine.

'Who is the real me, Warner?' she said, her tone vicious. 'The dupe who screws around until some jerk puts one up the spout? The easy lay? The stripper? Are all of those the real me?'

Some youths sitting on a bench goggled at her. I piloted her past them. She was stiff as a waxwork and inclined to dig her heels in.

'How do you get off coming the caveman?'

'Shut up,' I growled 'and don't be so fucking sensitive.'

Her resistance vanished. She squeezed my arm.

'You told me off once for bad language. So I stopped.' She had too. Why hadn't I noticed? 'Now *you're* doing it.'

'I apologise. Come on, let's have a coffee – if we can find a bar that hasn't been looted.'

We found one at the bottom of Main Street, near the market. Outburst forgotten, Linda took it upon herself to quiz me over what I was doing here on the Rock. Her tone was bantering, yet she couldn't entirely hide her real curiosity.

'Where do you keep taking off to? Is that Toby creep your boss? You didn't talk to him as though he was.' She tapped her coffee spoon against her teeth while keeping me under scrutiny. 'Is it to do with all this independence baloney I keep hearing about?'

'Mind your own business,' I said easily, and took her hand in mind. 'Don't ask, and don't want to know. Stay clear, stay clean.'

'Clean!' Her voice was a derisive hoot. 'You're about fifteen years too late, fella. I got derailed while I was still in eighth grade and I've never looked back since.'

'I'm not talking about morals, dummy, I'm talking about politics, about governments. About craze for power, and manipulation and exploitation.'

'Big woyds for a gal from Noo Joysey.'

'Is that where you come from?' Glad of the change of subject.

'Where I was born. Most of my life we jetted between California and Washington DC.'

Her hand squeezed mine. She was smiling, relaxed, could have passed for any conventionally happy mother-to-be. Her flare-ups burned out fast.

'You know something, Warner … I kind of like you.'

It was my first glimpse of the inner Linda. Of the kernel inside the shell she had built up around herself. She had more to say, I sensed it, so I stayed quiet, encouraged her with my eyes and my touch.

'Yeah, I guess I owe you one hell of a lot. You're a nice guy under the tough cookie shell. Shame about the beard.' She gave my chin growth a mild tug. 'In fact …'

'More coffee, sir?' the waiter's timing was right on the nail. It saved Linda from getting in deeper than either of us was ready for. By the time our cups had been replenished the mood had flown and she was back behind her armour plate, back to the scathing witticisms.

'No pow-wows to attend today?'

I shot a glance at my watch. I was due to meet Ribble at one, to begin re-learning about how to blow things up.

'I'll be tied up after lunch until about six, then I'm yours to command until the same time tomorrow.'

A briefing with Vella and the others had been set for Monday next. The bombing itself was provisionally booked for the following Friday. Plenty of opportunity in between times to work out my plot within a plot, the downfall of GIBESTÁ.

We left at a quarter to twelve for Linda's appointment with a Doctor McGrail, whose surgery was down near the Queensway Quay Marina. As we strolled along the sunny dockside, bustling with boat owners and early season tourists, Linda said, with casual and disarming innocence: 'Any chance we're being stalked?'

My instinctive reaction was to look over my shoulder. I suppressed it.

'That's a strange question,' I stalled. 'One of your secret admirers?'

She sniggered. 'I can always hope. I don't seem to rate much of *your* time.' She twisted her head round to look behind. 'There was a tall fair-haired guy with a short fat woman. Ha-ha-ha! It just occurred to me they'd make a dandy stage act. They went by the coffee bar a couple of times. You were sitting with your back to the street, you remember.'

Lax of me. It was basic teaching for all undercover operatives: keep your back to the wall and your front to the wide open spaces. It used to come natural to me to watch my back, but since I moved into the hospitality business the discipline had atrophied.

'Are they tailing us then?' I said.

'They were. They've gone now. Funny looking pair. We used to meet quite a few East European diplomats when Dad was working in Washington. They all seemed to look alike: fair or light brown hair, blue eyes, badly dressed. One of them took a special liking to me.' She shuddered. 'He tried to entice me into an empty office – I was eight at the time. I don't actually remember it, thank God.' She pulled me to her, laughing gaily in her innocence of the schemings of governments. 'Anyway it's ridiculous. Why would a comedy act be interested in us?'

* * * * *

With Toby off my back I restored Linda to the Caleta Hotel. To keep some kind of faith with his no-cohabitation ruling, I booked her in a separate room, just a few doors down from mine.

'You and your goddam security,' she groused, when I gave that as an explanation for our apartheid. 'It's like starring in a spy movie. We aren't, are we? In a movie, I mean.'

'If that'll make you happy – yes, we are making a movie.'

Wrong note – too patronising.

'Don't talk to me as if I was some snot-nosed kid!' she blazed, dropping the dress she was hanging to slam me against the balcony doors.

'Then don't keep asking!' I shouted back. 'What you don't know you can't tell!'

She calmed instantly. 'Is it that serious then?'

'If it wasn't, do you think I'd pay for two rooms when one would do?'

That tickled her sense of humour.

'You sure do have a point there, Bonzo.'

* * * * *

I had mulled over sending a query to London about possible Russian interest in me and my mission but decided that to do so on such flimsy evidence (a Slavic-looking guy may be tailing me) would only invite some scathing riposte. Best leave it lie for now. Await developments.

Between moving Linda back into the Caleta and my rendezvous with the GIBESTÁ executive, I did little to justify my fee beyond learning anew how to construct a bomb, courtesy of Ribble. In my free time I toyed with ideas for rendering the movement defunct. I didn't progress far, not with Linda in near-constant attendance, insistent on exploring the Rock. We did the things most tourists do: visited the ruined Moorish castle with its life-size models of who-was-who in ancient Gibraltar; rode the cable car to the Top of the Rock restaurant to see the city spread out below, clear and precise as in a street plan, the great hook of the bay, dotted with boats, the blue-grey mountains above Algeciras. Descending via steps, we fed the famous Rock apes with apples which they discarded after a couple of bites, and nuts which they spurned altogether. We walked the casemates – the battlements that were originally built along the along the sea's edge but now stand hundreds of metres inland, thanks to ambitious and ongoing reclamation projects. We lunched on grilled swordfish at Le Trattoria del Pescatore and dined on king-sized T-bone steaks at Biancas. Most of all during these two days we explored each other, inside and out, cementing the growing bond between us.

So close had we become that when Monday evening came and I dressed – leather windbreaker, denim jeans, roll-neck sweater all in obligatory black – Linda tried to dissuade me from going, even to abandon 'whatever the hell you're mixed up in'.

I didn't take her entreaties seriously. As a result, our goodbyes were frigid and I drove around to the other side of the island in poor humour, inwardly berating the female of the species. Resolving to untangle the entanglement before the bud became a flower and ending it became impossible.

'You're late,' Peter, who answered the door at Vella's apartment, accused.

'Yeah, all of five minutes,' I snapped back.

'Never mix women with business,' El Jefe chuckled as I took my place at the table. They were five as before, seated as before.

'What are you talking about?' I said belligerently.

He laid a thick, knobbled finger along the side of his nose, winked.

Was that a subtle admission that the comedy duo was in the pay of GIBESTÁ? If so, it was irritating but not beyond reasonable.

'Take no notice of Eduardo,' Michael Vella said. He looked tired this evening. The lines around his mouth were deeper and his skin looked grey, like old parchment. 'He is only envious.'

'I do not deny it,' the old man said. 'I am surprised, however, that our friend here should encumber himself, considering what he has come here to do.'

'It was accidental,' I said, thinking that El Jefe was a sight too perceptive for his and my good, and that some explanation would allay any latent worries. 'It started out as a favour for a friend. It ended up as a bloody great commitment that I'm stuck with for now. Don't worry, she knows nothing at all. And she doesn't go wherever I go.'

'Gibraltar is a small place,' Peter pointed out. He directed a hard stare at El Jefe. 'Too many ears flapping, too many old women gossiping.'

'Eduardo is right to be concerned about security,' Vella intervened. 'Now, gentlemen, shall we get down to business?'

No drinks were proposed. This was not a drinking matter. Peter spread a blueprint across the table.

'This is our first target – the Post Office in Main Street,' he announced. 'In my opinion the bomb should be sited about here.' With a pencil he indicated some spot inside the main chamber.

I leaned over the plan, studied the various entrances and exits.

'Technically I don't see why not. Subject to my checking out the real thing, you understand.'

'Of course,' Vella said. 'We presumed you would need to inspect it. This is why we chose the main chamber rather than, for instance, the sorting room. No need to break in to look it over, or take any risks.'

'Thoughtful of you. Do you want the bomb to go off in daytime or night-time? And at what hour?'

They all looked blankly at me.

'What I'm trying to establish is – do you want casualties? If so, how many? Two or three? Twenty or thirty?'

'No!' The word exploded from Vella like a bursting bag. He came up off his chair so fast it toppled backwards with a crash. The dog in the apartment below set up a yapping. 'I want no casualties! None!' His eyes swept the table like twin searchlights. Only Eduardo didn't shrink from him. This was Vella at his most intimidating. The very strength of his opposition to violence set him apart from its advocates. Half of me wished he could convert them, even though this would make my services redundant. He deserved better than bombs.

With an effort that made his whole frame tremble he brought his emotions under control.

'I am a realist,' he said then, in a subdued tone. 'If we use bombs, sooner or later people will get hurt, even … even killed. This I understand and, though I personally opposed the bombing campaign, accept. What I will not tolerate is any act of violence that deliberately targets any human being, be they friend or foe. Is that understood?'

This question, a challenge almost, was for the Council as a whole but it was especially directed at Peter – Peter the hawk, the hard-liner. Every movement has at least one. So long as they're restrained they serve as a useful makeweight to the doves. It's when the pacific policies fail and the lone hard-liner gains converts to his cause, and the clamour grows for more action less words, that the bombs and the bullets take over, and the spilling of blood begins.

I had seen it happen more than once as an officer of the SIS, and could see it happening here if I didn't succeed in my mission to subvert it, whatever the outcome of the Madrid Conference.

'You've answered my question,' I said to Vella, hoping to remove some of the friction from the proceedings. 'The bomb must go off when the Post Office is closed and the risk of any passers-by getting caught in the blast is minimal.' Vella dragged his stare from Peter and brought it to rest on me. 'Between three and five in the morning then,' I concluded.

'If that is your advice,' Vella said, a shade huskily, as if his invective had strained his vocal chords.

'Which means we can't plant it inside the building?'

Vella's silver eyebrows made interrogation marks.

'Why not?' Peter, less equivocal, demanded.

Maurice got in ahead of me: 'We'd have to break in if it's to be done at night.'

Peter's shrug was eloquent. 'So? Is breaking in so difficult?'

'Post Offices,' I explained without condescension, 'are built along similar lines to banks. It would be goddamn near impossible to gain entry quietly. At that time in the morning any significant noise will carry all the way to Algeciras.'

'Meaning?'

'The bomb must either be left inside the building during the day, set to go off at the required time, or we must place it outside.'

'Not inside,' Vella said promptly and firmly. 'If it malfunctioned, went off early …'

'Also it might be discovered,' El Jefe said, more focused on success than risk to life.

'Okay,' Peter conceded. His sole concern was that no obstacles should prevent the bombing from going ahead.

'Outside the building then.' Vella was making sure there would be no misunderstanding.

'What will you use?' El Jefe asked me. 'For explosive.'

This interest in the mechanics of the task enhanced my suspicions that the old man had once seen active service in some form. At the time of the Spanish Civil War even his parents would have been infants, therefore it would have been in the sixties or seventies, perhaps as a mercenary in the Congo or Yemen.

'Gelignite,' I said, then, anticipating his request for specifics, elaborated: 'A plastic water gel.'

'How much?'

'Say five kilos? Ought to make a big enough bang without spreading the damage over too wide an area.'

He didn't disagree. Asked next about the detonators.

'Tetryl. Electrically primed. I'll use a delayed action, naturally – a timer.'

'Naturally,' El Jefe echoed with a chuckle that told of experience. 'Where will you obtain your materials?'

My look alone was enough. He hadn't seriously expected me to say.

'You will need help,' he suggested.

'Yes,' I said flatly. 'You volunteering?'

'I will help' Peter's offer was instantaneous.

'You know explosives?'

That was too much to hope for.

'You can teach me,' he said with that fanatical eagerness of his. I agreed I could teach him. Might as well let the blind lead the blind.

'Very well,' Vella said, though no one had sought his assent. 'Will you need anyone else, André?'

'Look-outs. Front and back of the building, working to prearranged signals. Can do?'

Vella gave a slow nod. 'I will come myself. Ben – what about you?'

Ben didn't look wild about the prospect but nodded firmly enough.

'Shall we proceed to the next stage then, gentlemen – the operation itself?' There was a general murmur and shuffling of bottoms. 'In which case I pass the Chair to André.'

I stood up and began to speak, wishing I had faith in what I was doing, a belief in the cause I was pretending to serve. In the recent past my world had been black and white. Contract offered, contract accepted, contract executed. One less transgressor in the world. Now I was in the thick of politics and governments, in amongst grey writhing mists of lies and trickery and betrayal. I served no one, no cause, beyond self-interest. Like an actor, I was working to a script, reading lines, following directions.

The covenant I had made was beyond recall. It was no longer a matter of money, it was about keeping faith and damage limitation. I would do what I had been told to do and groomed to do, and hope to come through with my integrity intact, maybe not quite smelling of roses but at least avoiding the stink of infamy.

Chapter Sixteen

It was a fine night for a bombing: a clear sky, thick with stars like fluorescent smoke, the faintest nip in the air, leftover from a winter that in these southerly latitudes was never more than notional. Three o'clock on a Friday morning and Gibraltar was dead. Somewhere in the warren of streets the mewling of a baby's cry. Down towards the docks there was activity, the desultory clank of machinery, the whirr of a crane's motor, a pneumatic drill at work on some task that couldn't wait until daylight.

'The dockyards work around the clock,' Peter remarked, voice hoarse with tension, as we huddled side by side in a recess in Bell Lane, a narrow passage connecting Main Street with the upper town. Though I was personally immune from arrest for the crime I was about to commit, my nerves were tauter than a tripwire. Failure tonight might mean failure of my mission. If my efforts were ever to bear fruit, the bombing was obligatory.

Nearby, in the general direction of Irish Town and the Central Police Station, a footfall. I held my breath. Doing it 'under the noses' of the police appealed to the hothead in Peter. I didn't share his enthusiasm.

The footfall ceased. Someone coughed – a subdued, forced cough – once, twice, three times. All was clear along Irish Town. Almost immediately a nose was blown, so close I felt Peter twitch beside me. This was the Main Street signal, Vella's watch, and the more dangerous of the two lookout positions. All clear there too.

'Let's go,' I said, nudging Peter.

The five kilos of plastic explosive were contained in a New Balance-branded carryall, slung crosswise over my shoulder. I slipped around the corner into Main Street, hugging the shadow of the building. Peter, in charge of the detonators, the timer and such tools as were necessary, stuck close to me; so close my heel connected with his shin and prompted a snort of pain. His own fault, so I didn't apologise.

His function as my "assistant" would amount to little more than handing me the right materials in the correct sequence, quickly and noiselessly. I had spent hours schooling him, ultimately with his eyes shut, forcing him to identify items by touch. To avoid detection we would have to work at high speed, to locate and prime the device in a matter of seconds rather than minutes. To linger would be fatal. I had timed us at sixty-five seconds dead in an artificial situation, both of us working blind. Under pressure we might well balls it up, nervousness might turn fingers into thumbs. Consequently, I was allowing a minute-and-a-half and keeping my fingers metaphorically crossed.

We scuttled into the doorway, crouched behind the joined pillars of the post boxes with their EIIR Royal Mail logos. Peter's bag made a metallic clink as he set it down incautiously on the sidewalk.

'Sorry,' he breathed. I let it go. What else could I expect from an amateur?

The street was empty. A white plastic bag tumbled by, propelled by a flutter of wind that died as fast as it was born. In a Main Street jeweller's doorway, about thirty metres from the Post Office, Vella was watching. We were totally reliant on his warning us of an interloper.

My bag joined Peter's. It was pre-unzipped, because zippers make noise. I slid my fingertips under the block of jelly in its plastic container, lifted it clear. Respectful but firm was the technique, as explained by Ribble. Show it who's boss, don't be afraid of it. On its own it was inert.

The container was semi-transparent, the kind used to keep food fresh. Plastic in plastic, I mused irreverently. I prised off the lid. It came free noiselessly.

Peter was crouching beside me, almost imprisoning me against the double glass doors of the Philatelic Shop that shared the outside foyer. My finger tapped his knee and instantly there was cold metal in my palm: an all-aluminum tube, about ten centimetres long – a detonator. I would use two, the second as insurance, though Ribble assured me that British Army-issue detonators are not prone to failure. Oh, yeah? My MI6 experience disagreed.

Both detonators were already wired up. With the plastic box positioned at the base of the double doors, where they met, I pressed them into the gelignite, which consisted of fifty 100-gram slabs packed tight to form a single block. Plastic explosive has the consistency of putty and I had already excavated two holes to receive the detonators. It was therefore only a matter of thumbing them down into the plastic until they were flush with the top, leaving the wires protruding. The wires, or more accurately the integrity of their connection to the terminals, were the weakest links in the chain between trigger and explosion. I had made the connections personally, tested them to not-quite destruction.

Peter was holding the timer. His hands were trembling a little. Not fear, I was sure of that, more likely exhilaration. His first bombing. Wow! Now he was a true revolutionary, a partisan, a guerrilla even. I don't believe he had ever stopped to weigh the consequences of what we were doing. He was carried along by the certainty of right-ness. The cause was just, the means therefore were justified. Amen.

I found myself wondering if Linda was lying awake, wondering in her turn about me. I had left at nine: 'I'll be late – don't wait up.' Her farewell kiss had been lingering, designed to delay, dissuade even. On the outside she was all bravado as usual; within, I sensed a fearfulness. She was less secure than she pretended.

'Don't forget where's home,' she joked, yet her eyes held uncertainty not humour.

Most of the ninety seconds I had allowed had been used up. The timer was pre-set for ten minutes. Little enough time to get clear of the area, yet more than ample for the bomb to be discovered and the leads ripped from the timer. I offered the timer box to Peter. Let his be the symbolic hand to start it off. He divined the thought behind the gesture, his teeth flashing white.

This was the point of no return. No hesitating, no misgivings, he rammed the button down as if it were the plunger of a detonator box. We were committed. In just ten minutes we would make history and the front page of world's press.

Then Vella showed, stepping out of his assigned doorway and setting off towards us. Just a man in a hurry to get home.

Also a warning. Someone was coming!

Peter and I gathered up our bits and pieces, slid along the wall past a shop with a boarded up window, a casualty of the recent demonstrations. It had a shallow doorway, the scantiest of refuges. Nevertheless, we had to chance it. Whoever was coming might well spot the bomb. Worse, might be within injury range when it went off.

Peter had been peeping around the edge of the boarded-up window for a sight of our night-time stroller. Now he let out an exclamation. 'It's a bobby!'

'Easy now,' I hissed sharply, dragging him back into the recess. I carried no lethal weaponry. Our self-defence system consisted of a sock and a few pounds of sand. Marry the two and you have a highly efficient blackjack, a trick among many taught by MI6.

The policeman was not suspicious. He was ambling, now and again testing some shop door. He was also on the opposite side of the street. So far, so good, but that white plastic box stood out all too starkly, only partially screened by the post boxes. A slip-up on my part, not to have used a darker container.

I checked my watch: only six minutes left. Our safety margin was eroding to nothing. The policeman still ambled. He was in no hurry, he had the whole night to fritter away. If I didn't take the initiative all three of us would go up with the bomb.

'Stay here,' I ordered Peter. I didn't doubt his fortitude or his willingness to help, but he was still an amateur and a volatile one at that. I moved out into the open, crossing the street at a tangent, on a convergence course with the policeman. My sudden materialisation startled him, his saunter faltering.

'*Buenos dias*,' I hailed, forcing a casual tone.

'*Señor*,' he returned neutrally.

'I have just arrived here,' I said in Spanish, by way of explanation. I stopped an arm's length short of him. 'Is there a hotel …?' That was when I hit him. Bringing the sandbag out from behind my back in a sweeping curve, connecting with the side of his skull, just below the rim of his helmet, which promptly flew off.

In real life people do not go down without a murmur when sandbagged on the skull with a solid object. Not unless you can place the blow in an especially vulnerable spot. The policeman didn't even fall, merely staggered against the wall, gasping, arms stiffly outstretched, like a high wire walker. I hit his now unprotected head again and he crumpled untidily, still conscious but all co-ordination gone. A third tap, to the temple, and finally he was out. He looked peaceful lying there on the sidewalk. He might have been taking a nap.

Less than a minute left.

I signalled to Peter, huddled in the doorway.

'Let's go.'

He came at a run, lugging the two bags. The sign on the side street read Tuckey's Lane. We had just rounded the corner into it, stumbling in our haste, when two loud bangs ripped the night apart.

Peter let go a hushed whoop. 'We did it, we did it!'

'And we'll be done for it if we hang around here,' I cautioned him. A light came on in the second floor of an apartment building up ahead, then another, higher and to our left. Dogs started barking here and there.

But for the incident with the policeman, our ten minutes' grace would have been ample for us to reach the battered but roadworthy van that was our getaway vehicle, parked a short sprint from the Post Office. Peter would have driven me to my hotel and gone on alone to his home in Catalan Bay Village. No sound plan is without a contingency clause and this was where Peter came into his own. He led us at a trot down a dank alley between darkened buildings. It terminated a street's width from a flight of stone steps that wound upwards between the blank walls of two tenements – there are many such steps in the town, short cuts to its upper levels. We bounded up them, as perfectly co-ordinated as partners in a three-legged race, tool bags clinking. Haste would make us conspicuous, but had to be risked. The priority was to get clear of the immediate scene, before the police mobilised and began rounding up all stray persons as a matter of routine.

Out of breath, we arrived at the top of yet another flight of steps. Paradise Ramp announced the sign. A haunt for courting couples maybe.

'Over there.' Peter said, snorting with exhaustion. He indicated more steps, narrow, curving up into a dense pack of buildings. Sirens were hee-hawing down below in the city centre.

We were crossing the road, the bulwark of the Rock black against the starry night, when a voice hailed us. I had the sandbag out even as I turned to meet this new threat.

Peter, reacting fast, restrained me. 'It's all right, André. He's one of us.'

A fair-haired man in a donkey jacket loped towards us, grinning.

'That wasn't much of a bang,' he said, and there was only relief in his voice. 'Hello … Mr Warner. Nice to meet you again.'

It was the guy called John, last met on a bar terrace in Catalan Bay Village, during my exploratory visit.

'Let's get under cover,' Peter urged, sounding nervous for the first time since the explosion.

John grunted agreement. 'Follow me,' and he took off up the steps.

We had covered perhaps two-thirds of the distance to the top when he veered off to the right where a door stood open, the room beyond dimly lit by a table lamp. In the doorway was a woman wearing a dressing gown. She retreated inside to admit us.

Peter, last to enter, closed the door, locked and bolted it.

'My wife,' John said, as I took in the details of the small but neatly-kept room. The woman was petite with black braided hair and in an advanced state of pregnancy. She greeted us with a tentative 'Hello.'

'We stay here tonight,' Peter said, stripping off his jacket, making himself instantly at home.

This was part of the back-up plan. Like it or not, I was temporarily dependant on Peter and the goodwill of GIBESTÁ to stay clear of the law.

'Would you like coffee?' the woman asked, in uncertain English. John gave her an approving look.

'Coffee would be great,' I said, smiling at her to put her at ease. She smiled back and went off through the only other door, in the rolling gait that seems to come with late-stage pregnancy.

'Tomorrow morning we will take you to your hotel,' Peter said to me, fishing a packet of cigarettes from his discarded jacket. He and John lit up.

'Did it go smoothly?' John enquired.

'Exactly as planned,' Peter boasted, drawing hard on his cigarette, the tip glowing like a firebrand. He didn't mention the policeman.

'Now they will take notice of us.' John's grin split his face. 'We have shown our claws. They will not dismiss us so lightly.' He looked at me. 'We must have more bombs, and soon. We will force independence down their throats.'

'Bravo,' I said. 'Spoken like a true fanatic.'

Puzzlement altered his features. These were not the sentiments of an ally.

Peter said, 'You sound as if you do not approve. Yet it was you who placed the bomb.'

'Don't get confused about the difference in our motives. As Michael pointed out to you the other night, a mercenary isn't obliged to commit to the cause, or even sympathise with it. Bombing is only a means to achieve your objective. It can happen that the end and the means sometimes become blurred, so you can't tell one from the other.' We were all sitting now, three points of a triangle. 'You understand what I am saying?'

Peter scratched the point of his chin, fingernails abrading stubble. 'Not exactly.'

'Just don't get so fond of bombs that you forget why you're using them.'

At that point I left off moralising. The coffee came and I drank it. It held tiredness at bay for a while longer but I eventually dozed off in the chair and there spent what remained of the night.

* * * * *

The morning papers had been typeset before the bombing took place, and written reporting was confined to a Stop Press section at the foot of the front page of the *Gibraltar Chronicle*, a few strictly factual, unemotional lines. They reported the discovery of an unexploded bomb at the Post Office. It mentioned the detonators that went off but failed to set off the explosive device. The policeman I had pretended to sandbag got a mention as the hero of the day for having disarmed the bomb. That same policeman, who was really a bomb disposal expert, had disconnected the detonators from the plastic the instant Peter and I left the scene. The two bangs we had heard were the detonators going off.

In terms of outrage, the failed attempt was as effective as a successful bombing would have been. People in the street interviewed by Rock Radio, the local station, expressed shock but not all of them condemned it. A sizeable minority were in favour of any action that would promote independence and keep the Spanish out. The radio station stated that they had earlier received an anonymous call, allegedly from a GIBESTÁ spokesman. Whilst no responsibility was admitted for the bombing, the spokesman had spelled out GIBESTÁ's singular requirement: an immediate commitment by Britain to negotiate independence.

As arranged the "policeman" was also given airtime. He told of how he was knocked down but not out, and managed to stagger over to where the bomb had been placed and extract the detonators.

The reporter, noticeably awed, asked how he knew how to disarm the bomb.

'I used to be with a bomb disposal unit in the army.'

That took care of any questions that Vella and co. might have been inclined to fire at me over my failure to blow up the Post Office.

Later I tuned the TV in to Gibraltar News and watched Vella being intercepted by a reporter as he left the Central Police Station after 'helping with enquiries'.

'Was GIBESTÁ responsible for that bombing attempt?' the reporter fired at him, no attempt at subtlety.

'We do not approve of violence,' Vella had replied stonily. Which was as good a non-answer as I had heard in many an interview, and in his individual case was not a lie. He would make a brilliant politician.

'But was the bomb yours?' the reported persisted.

'GIBESTÁ has no bombs.'

'I'll rephrase the question – if the Government don't agree to negotiate with you, will there be more bombs?'

'I am not in a position to say,' Vella stonewalled flawlessly.

Other questions were fended off with equal skill. Vella was urbane, co-operative, and in no hurry to slip away. It was the press who tired of the verbal duelling and in the end let him pass through their ranks.

Later on they seized other GIBESTÁ interrogees, including Peter. They mostly lacked Vella's finesse at deflection but the crumbs they cast at the pack were no fatter. In turn they made their non-committal statements and nobody hearing them would be in any doubt about where the blame lay.

* * * * *

The call from Vella himself was not unexpected. I had just returned to the Caleta from my restless night in an armchair, and was about to step into an elevator when my cell did its warbly thing. Before answering, I tucked myself into a discreet corner, out of earshot of the front desk.

'What happened, André?'

'You heard the news report. A policeman got brave.'

It was fortunate for the veracity of the report that Vella had been present when the policeman had interrupted our bomb planting. No need to invent an explanation.

'So it would seem. As it happens, for propaganda purposes, the attempt to bomb has been almost as effective as if we'd done the job. And speaking personally, I'm happy that we got away without any damage to property.'

He was happy, the Government was happy, and no doubt the insurers were ecstatic not to be facing damage claims. Most importantly, my credibility as a bomber was intact.

* * * * *

'You could have buzzed me,' Linda said, pouting, as we strolled along the Catalan Bay beach, barefoot, carrying our shoes.

I apologised.

'I was worried,' she grumbled on.

I apologised more abjectly. We diverted past a ruined sandcastle. Linda kicked at it, sand puffing from her foot. She had painted her toe nails blue, I noticed.

It was afternoon, and my lesson periods with Ribble were over and done. Now I could devote all my attention to Linda, which after all was no hardship. We had the beach much to ourselves. A lone windsurfer was trying to work up speed from a catspaw of wind. Blue skies, blue seas. The stuff dreams are made of on a foggy winter's day back in Britain.

'Were you mixed up in that bombing business?'

'No.' The lie came smoothly from much practice. 'I wasn't mixed up in that "bahming" business.' The exaggerated imitation of her accent brought her out in a fit of giggles.

'So if you weren't trying to blow up the Post Office what were you doing, out all night?'

'Never you mind. What I wasn't doing was cheating on you.'

The hackles, predictably, shot up.

'Who the hell cares if you were?'

'You do.'

She was so taken aback that her usual responses let her down for once. I put an arm about her waist, what was left of it.

'And I'm glad you do,' I went on.

We stopped in perfect concert. Shoes hit the beach. She entered my embrace quite naturally. Her thighs pressed mine and suddenly I wanted her.

'Oh,' she said. 'You're growing.'

I kissed her hard on the mouth. She strained against me.

'Don't pretend you're surprised,' I said as I came up for air.

'But here? It's such a waste!'

The hotel was a literal stone's throw away. Linda demonstrated that being pregnant didn't necessarily slow you down if the motivation was strong enough

Chapter Seventeen

Breakfast is my favourite meal. The day lies ahead, virgin, unsullied, ready to be used or squandered according to inclination, the mind and body bursting with stored energy.

Linda had gone up to her room for the performance of ablutions, I had lingered in the restaurant for a second *espresso*. Now, emerging from the breakfast bar, I drifted across the lobby to browse through the picture postcards. Debated whether to shoot one off to Cassandra. What should I say? Wish you were here? Get better soon?

'Mr Warner … André?'

I turned to confront the speaker and received a jolt like an electric shock.

'*Luis …*?'

General Irazola's son grinned and nodded. 'You did not expect to see me again.'

'Well, no, not here, at any rate. What brings you to Gibraltar?'

'You.' The reply was female. Elena Irazola side-stepped into view from the other side of the postcard rack. Her eyes sparkled mischievously. She was the practical joker of the two, the sort to get a kick out of playing a trick.

'Elena. Fancy seeing you here.' Although my mind was playing football with the possible motives for the arrival of the Irazola twins, I kept my expression bland.

Which became difficult when Elena delivered a smacking kiss to my lips.

'Where is your girlfriend?' she asked, eyebrows hoisted in wide-eyed innocence.

'Upstairs.'

'Can we talk?' Luis said, and added, 'In private,' nodding pointedly at a stooped old guy who had come to stand beside me and was pawing through the postcards.

'In my room,' I suggested and we took the elevator to the third floor.

'Marvellous view,' Elena commented, going straight out on the balcony. She was wearing grey designer jogging pants and sweat shirt. Luis was dressed retro-style in narrow slacks and a chocolate coloured blazer with wide lapels.

I sat on the edge of the unmade bed. 'Talk,' I said curtly.

Elena turned and leaned her bottom against the balcony wall. 'We are on your side, André, let us be clear about that.' She lit a long, tipped cigarette, dribbled smoke from her nostrils. 'We are not your enemies.'

It was true that without their help Linda and I might now be prisoners of the General. Or worse than prisoners. Still I was mistrustful. People change sides. Alternatively, their ostensible disloyalty to their father might well be part of some fiendish scheme to do with Gibraltar. Currently, I was suspicious of all and sundry. That, in part, was what I was being paid for.

'How did you know I was here in Gibraltar, at the Caleta Hotel?'

'My father,' Luis answered.

That was jolt number two. 'How is the General?' I said while assembling my thoughts.

'He knows all your movements,' Elena said, watching me closely as if monitoring my reactions.

'How? And why?' Though perhaps the why was unnecessary. In his mind I posed a threat. He wasn't to know I had already relayed all I knew to Toby, and that I wasn't being taken seriously.

'The how is by means of informants stationed here in Gibraltar.'

'Are you saying Gib is infested with Spanish spies?'

They both shrugged. Luis sat down, interlocked his fingers, fixed his gaze on the carpet.

'Our father does not tell us everything. All we know is that he claims to have connections in Gibraltar and that these connections notified him of your presence. They also report that you are associating with leading members of the GIBESTÁ movement.'

Connections. It might mean anything from the Spanish Secret Service to a casual paid informer. It might mean a tall Slavic guy with a dumpy female companion. My confusion was growing.

'As to the why –'

Luis broke off as there came a brusque tap at the door. Linda walked in in her usual breezy fashion.

'Oh! Hey, excuse the interruption.' She was about to back out when recognition set in. She stared in disbelief.

'My God, it's the Irazola kids!'

'Come in, Linda,' I said resignedly. 'No reason you shouldn't be in on this.'

She backed up against the door to close it and advanced into the room, joining me on the bed. The gesture statement was not lost on Elena. Her mouth twisted. She turned her back on us, flipping her half-smoked cigarette over the balcony.

Luis, effecting not to notice, said, 'My father thinks you know something of our Government's plans, something to do with Gibraltar, the Madrid Conference …' He frowned. 'I am not sure myself what is going on or what it is you know that is of such importance. However, we offered to come and see you and find out.'

'You don't say. You've got a nerve telling me you've come to interrogate me on behalf of your old man. You figure I would obligingly reveal all my secrets, just like that?'

'Kind of optimistic,' Linda inserted.

'I am not such an *inocente* as that,' Luis said with some affront. 'That was a ploy to win his approval. We are not here to in search of information, we are here to supply it.'

There are moments when my intellect is slow to get into gear. This was such a moment.

Luis, noting my confusion, didn't try to hide his amusement. 'For … private reasons, we are prepared to … to give you information which has to do with our country and Gibraltar.'

I was catching up fast now, the agent-provocateur side of me stimulated by this unasked-for gift.

'Do you speak for both of you?' I glanced meaningly at Elena, whose back was still stiffly presented, arms folded.

'He does,' she said grudgingly, without looking round.

With the morning sun gathering strength and beaming directly into the room it was becoming uncomfortably warm. I removed my jacket while pondering furiously and getting nowhere.

'But you're Spanish,' I said finally, more mistrustful than ever, unable to conceive of any motive that could justify such double perfidy, betrayal of both parent and country.

'No!' Elena's cry was as someone in physical pain. She stormed in from the balcony, planted her curvaceous frame before us, long legs forming an A, arms akimbo. 'No –' more moderately now '– not Spanish.'

I still couldn't figure what other nationality would bear ill-will towards Spain.

'So what are you – Portuguese?'

Her face tightened, her lips drew back off her teeth giving her an unholy, savage look. I sensed Linda draw back.

'*Euskara*!' she spat the word, but with more pride than I had ever heard anyone speak of their race. 'We are Basque!'

* * * * *

Beyond that revelation about the Irazola family tree I learned little of what was prompting the twins' treachery. Maybe being Basque was enough on its own. Of all the enemies of Spain, past and present, the Basques were arguably the most relentless, the most implacable. They conceded no allegiance to the Spanish Government and its Head of State, the monarch. They conceded no commonality with Spain, not historical, social, dynastic, nor linguistic. The Basques are truly a people unto themselves.

When digging for explanations proved fruitless I gave up and let the Irazola twins get on with the purpose of their visit. Elena was reluctant to speak in front of Linda, but Luis saw no harm in it. Which led Elena to fling up her hands, as if to wash them of the consequences, and withdraw once more to the balcony, there to smoke and brood away her disapproval and present her shapely bottom to admirers.

The gist of the information they were willing, no, eager, to supply was that the corps that went to make up the South Regional Operational

Command of the Spanish Army were on “special manoeuvres” out at some unpronounceable lake twelve kilometres north of Algeciras. The corps, of which Irazola was *generalissimo*, comprised two divisions: one infantry and one armoured. Plus a unit of Anti-Insurgency Helicopters.

‘Expecting a revolution, is he?’ Linda had asked, sarcastically.

‘Maybe starting one,’ Luis replied, without drama.

Linda sobered at once.

‘Are you serious?’ I said, not yet convinced this wasn’t just some mischief-making escapade, or, much more likely, a baited trap.

He was serious, he assured me, and from then on, curiously, I didn’t question his sincerity, not even privately. Something about him carried conviction. He was too intense to be other than straight.

‘You mean a Russian-style revolution?’ Linda said, pop-eyed.

‘No, not a revolution against Spain. But the outcome will mean war, as surely as I sit here before you.’

The manoeuvres, if Luis’ interpretation was correct, were a screen for an invasion of Gibraltar. When he said it, flatly, in exactly that many words, I was astonished at how readily I absorbed and accepted the feasibility of such an act.

‘Will it take place before or after the Conference?’

Luis shook his sleek, handsome head. ‘My father tells us little. Most of what we learn comes from spying on him.’ A glimmer of shame here. ‘Listening at the door, listening to his telephone conversations, things like that.’

‘What made you start spying on him in the first place? Surely not because of this difference between you over allegiance to the Basques.’

On the balcony Elena stirred. I thought for a moment she was going to speak.

‘There is more to it than that, of course.’ Luis spoke with a quiet dignity. ‘But it is a personal matter, a family matter. I can say no more than that.’

‘All right,’ I said. It troubled me slightly but pushing too hard might stop the flow altogether. ‘All right, Luis. Tell me more about this supposed invasion.’

He puffed out his cheeks. ‘What more is there to tell? It has not been possible to obtain details. Our father is very discreet, very secretive.’

I asked whom the general took his orders from.

'De Cadalso seems to be the main contact. He has twice been to the house and Papa has spoken often to him on the telephone.'

I tried shock-treatment.

'Where do the Russians fit in?'

'The *Russians*?' If Luis was acting it was of Academy Award standard.

'Somebody called Lavov or Lavrov and somebody called Vladimir.' It was my only lead, garnered from that overheard telephone call at Irazola's house.

'Yes, I *have* heard these names. You think the Spanish Government is working with the Russians?' He sounded incredulous.

'Far-fetched, I know,' I agreed with a wry grin. 'But I have reason to believe your father has met up with this Lavov in St Petersburg.'

'He went to Russia?' Luis exclaimed, still sceptical.

Elena came stalking back inside, still smoking, still magnificently moody.

'Now I remember you asking me about de Cadalso, the day I came to your house …' Her voice tailed off as she glanced at Linda, perhaps recalling that she too had come to my house that day. 'I wondered about it afterwards. I wondered if you were some kind of agent perhaps.'

'I wasn't. Then.'

'And now?'

Linda's head also turned towards me. My answer concerned her at least as much.

I hesitated. They wouldn't accept outright denial and I would lose much goodwill by it. I settled for a limited truth.

'I am doing a job here in Gibraltar. It has nothing to do with Spain and not at all with the Basques.'

Nor was I sure I wanted to plunge into whatever cauldrons were bubbling across the frontier. The Irazola twins had made me a gift of an opportunity that, had military intelligence still been my line of business, I would have seized two-handed. But even if their reasoning was infallible and Spain was indeed about to mount an invasion of the Rock, it was outside my jurisdiction. My terms of reference did not extend to private adventures. Yet to keep that knowledge to myself and blithely go on with my GIBESTÁ assignment was to reduce my function to that of a mindless machine.

Then too, I remembered Toby's secondary brief – keep tabs on Irazola.

'Presumably you're giving me this information so that I can somehow prevent the invasion from taking place.'

'We have no wish to see Spain grab Gibraltar,' Elena explained. 'As Basques we can empathise with the people here. They must not suffer what our people have suffered.'

'Noble sentiments.' I wasn't being sarcastic either.

'How do we know you're not just making this up?' Linda said crisply. 'About these army manoeuvres, I mean.' She touched my hand. 'It could just be a load of hogwash, Warner.'

Elena glared at Linda, but held her tongue.

Luis, with controlled asperity, said, 'To what purpose, Miss Pridham?'

'Maybe you're bored out of your minds – how the hell do I know? It just sounds fantastic to me.'

I sensed she was appealing to me to stay out of it. I stood square on to Luis, trying to see beyond the good-looking veneer. His eyes held mine, no wavering, no weakness.

'Okay, Luis, I'm nearly convinced. But I want to see this invasion army for myself. My people don't give credence to second-hand intelligence. They have to have it handmade, gift-wrapped, in wide screen technicolour before they'll even open the package.'

'I understand,' Luis said. 'We will take you. We will show you.'

'Okay. When?'

'Now. It is an hour's drive, maybe a little more.'

'I'll need my camera to film with.'

Elena shook her head. 'A cell phone is good enough.'

'My camera's telephoto lens will be a lot better. It'll give us higher definition, and longer running time.'

'As you wish,' Luis said, as I went to fetch my camera bag from the closet.

Luis was beginning to bother me. Not because I doubted his word. It was his motives that caused my misgivings. He was too wound up, too feverish. As if he was expecting trouble.

My suspicious side was privately seeking a reason to delay, to ask advice, to make proper preparations. For a start, re-entering Spain might not be good for my health now that Irazola knew my whereabouts. He could have primed the border police to look out for me.

The headstrong side of me dismissed these qualms and my petty niggles about Luis, and said, 'Okay, let's go.'

Linda jumped up off the bed as if it had bitten her. 'I'm coming with you.'

'In your condition? Forget it.'

'We will have to go some distance on foot if we are to make our approach unobserved,' Luis warned her. 'It would not be possible for you.'

'Then I'll stay with the car,' Linda snapped. She flounced around the bed and snatched my car keys off the night table. 'There. Now you won't be able to stop me. If you go you'll have to use their car and I'll be right behind you from A to Zee.'

* * * * *

We went in the twins' car anyway – a silver Audi 4WD station wagon with Spanish plates, it was less conspicuous than my Aston – and Linda came with us, she and I sharing the back seat. Elena drove. We were held up for ten minutes on the road out of Gibraltar; an RAF maritime patrol aircraft was taking off from the airport. Since the runway intersects the only exit from the Rock all road traffic comes to a standstill for the duration. We were further delayed for over an hour at the frontier while the Spanish guards played their usual games and checked every car minutely. No special interest was shown in me when I presented my bogus passport, bearing my almost-real name.

We enjoyed a fast run past La Línea and around the top of Algeciras Bay, swinging right towards the mountains onto the A381 *autovia.* Linda's hand rested high up on my thigh, fondling occasionally, trying not to smirk at my reactions. My anger over her trick with the keys had only partially abated, coming as it did from plain, honest worry that she would come to harm through her lack of mobility. All I could do was wring from her a promise to vamoose back to Gib in the car, if our escapade went belly-up. This wasn't some kid's goof-off and I wasn't in it for kicks. Irazola had already shown his fangs. If he ever got his hands on me again, the weather couldn't be relied on to save me. And what I was about to commit was, in any country's book, a hostile act.

In some respects, I was a fool. But I felt it was my duty. Not just to my employers, but to Gibraltar and its innocent citizens, who had no idea what was being cooked up for them.

Okay, an honourable fool then, which was marginally better.

As the road climbed clouds were beginning to form in big bunches, like cauliflowers, each with its own smear of rain trailing beneath. I checked that the Sony digital camera with its various accessories was snug inside the shoulder bag, ditto the binoculars in theirs. A well-kitted out spy was I.

'Sunny Spain,' Linda muttered as the first drops spattered us.

The village of Los Barrios, a mixture of old Andalucian and tacky tourist villas, fell away into the valley behind. Below and to our right the river, like a discarded length of rope, muddy and swollen with rain, descending in a serious of rapids. This was wild country. It didn't seem possible that the busy coastal highway lay a mere five minutes' drive to the rear.

Beyond Los Barrios we exchanged the highway for a narrow country road, complete with potholes. We met no other vehicles and made fast progress in a continuous shallow climb, Elena holding the car in third, negotiating the bends on lightly squealing tyres.

We crossed a bridge, the river wider and more turbulent here, and pulled over onto a meagre shoulder. Elena switched off the engine.

'From here we must walk,' she announced.

'Fine,' I said, 'but leave the keys with the car.'

'You can be the driver in case we have to leave quickly,' Luis said to Linda. 'Like the getaway car in a bank robbery.'

Linda's smile was forced. 'Count on me. I'll keep the motor warm and my powder dry.'

He looked bemused but didn't ask for a translation. We all got out. The rain had eased to a fine mist. Visibility was poor for photography, zoom lens or not.

As if reading my mind, Elena said, 'This will pass – look.' She pointed towards a long bare ridge. Above it a swathe of blue was squeezing out the grey. 'That is where we are going. The lake is to the right of that ridge. You cannot see it from here because it is on higher ground. The main camp is beside the lake.'

'I would have expected more military traffic.' I said. Right on cue a helicopter, a gnat on the strip of blue, rose up from the vicinity of the ridge and stayed there, hovering. It bought home the nakedness of the terrain. From above we would stand out like boils on a bare backside.

Linda, too, was alive to the dangers. 'This is crazy, Warner. You won't get ten yards before those guys up there spot you.'

Elena made an airy motion of the hand and said, 'You cannot see it from here but there is a ravine running up the side of that ridge. That is the way we will go. We will be invisible from above, I promise you.'

'I've got to go, love,' I said to Linda and tried to exude confidence. 'You can see that, can't you?'

'Yeah,' she said, resigned. 'I can see that, you goddam dupe. It doesn't mean I got to like it.'

'Make sure your cell phone is switched on.'

She patted the only pocket of the artist-style smock she had taken to wearing, her only sartorial concession to her condition.

'Switched on and fully charged.'

'A bit like its owner.'

'Is that a compliment?' She touched her lips fleetingly to mine.

'Don't leave the car,' I said. 'If anything goes wrong …' Alarm flared in her face. 'I mean … it won't, but if it does, scoot.'

'Is there nobody I can go to for help?'

Was there? It was a gold brick to a dud cheque that Toby's crowd would disown me after this. Government bodies always disassociate themselves from failure. Break the rules at your peril – that was the first and most inviolate commandment.

'Try Michael Vella. Everybody knows him in Gib.'

And then we were off, moving at a trot. The chopper had flapped away northwards and we made it to Elena's ravine just ahead of that big band of blue that was so welcome yet so dangerous to us. Sunlight raced down the ridge to meet us. Elena, who was leading, made a brief halt to put on sunglasses. I did likewise. I flicked her a sidelong grin but she ignored me.

To the crest of the ridge was maybe five hundred feet. The going was rough, the bottom of the ravine consisting of small boulders and fragments of stone. I stubbed toes frequently and ricked an ankle more than once. Then the sides of the gully began to taper inwards, eventually down a hair crack, obliging us to abandon it for the bleak hillside. The sense of exposure was unnerving: it was like wearing no clothes in a blizzard.

We came to the highest point, a flat mesa of rock topped by a pyramid of boulders that had not been visible from the road.

'You see.' Elena drew these to my attention in triumph. 'Under there we will not be seen.'

'Under where?'

She was about to explain when the flip-flop of another or the same chopper wafted over us. The machine itself was not yet in sight but definitely coming closer.

Elena was the quickest thinker among us.

'Come quick!' she yelled and was up and running for the boulders.

It was a near thing. As we drew close to the boulders I saw that the underside of the two largest formed a shallow arch, just about high and wide enough to accommodate a prone body or two. Beneath the arch was a depression, in which rainwater had collected. This did not deter Elena who bellyflopped into it without ceremony. Luis went next, me last, loaded as I was with camera and binoculars. Then the air above us was shredded with noise as the helicopter crossed the ridge, directly overhead. In a line, in our cosy little puddle under the two great slabs of rock, we lay still, panting.

'That was lucky,' Luis said, snorting with relief, as the clatter died away.

It struck me we were leaning pretty damn heavily on luck. Too late now to start applying scientific precautions.

The rock surfaces around us were slick from the recent rainfall, and steaming in the sun's heat. I wiped my palms on the sleeves of my windbreaker and again wondered at my sanity in being here. To the north, where a higher, more rugged ridge joined two moderate peaks, a second helicopter was circling lazily. There was no vegetation hereabouts to speak of. Just the blue mirror of the lake and the river that fed it, a scrawl in a beige landscape.

Oh, yes, and the biggest concentration of military hardware I had ever seen.

Chapter Eighteen

'See!' Elena pointed downwards into the basin of the valley. 'Now do you believe us?'

The binoculars' 10X magnification reduced two kilometres to two hundred metres. I panned across rank upon rank of tents, a row of Portakabin-style buildings, parked vehicles galore: jeeps, trucks, personnel carriers, AFVs, towed guns, two fuel bowsers; plenty of heavy metal too in the shape of about thirty tanks, two distinct types. Their grey-green paintwork gave off a dull sheen. Helicopters stood around, the rotors of two of them were revolving slowly, warming up. Their fuselages all bore the legend FAMET, in square white letters.

'That's the Army Aviation division,' Luis explained when I asked about it. 'Nothing to do with the Air Force.'

The whole encampment measured perhaps a kilometre by a half, and I could readily believe it contained thirty thousand troops, or three divisions. About what you'd expect for a full general in peace time.

'What did you say this unit is called?'

'Papa is *generalissimo* of the Southern Regional Command,' Elena replied. 'Although the Spanish Army has only one regular soldier to two conscripts, the ratio here is nearer fifty-fifty. Papa has some influence with the General Staff of the Army, also with the Defence Minister, as we have told you.'

'What do you think, hey?' Luis' eyes on me glowed like live coals.

I set the binoculars aside, extracted the camera, careful to keep it clear of the puddle.

'Impressive. It doesn't prove they're about to invade Gibraltar though. Maybe they're on manoeuvres.'

Elena expelled a 'Pah!' of disgust. Luis, more tolerant, no chips on his shoulder, checked off the points on his fingers.

'There is what we already know, the three of us between us, about my father's secret negotiations. Secondly – army manoeuvres have never been held here before, they have always been in the Campo, far to the north. This is private land, not Government-owned. Thirdly – never so many men, never more than two brigades.'

So far I wasn't all that impressed with the reasoning. It was too circumstantial. I extended the zoom lens, took a squint through the viewfinder. With the sun out the definition was excellent. The unit numbers on the vehicles showed up distinctly.

'Fourthly,' Luis chanted, 'there is *matériel* down there that does not belong to Papa's command.'

'So what?'

'Normally he would have one armoured brigade and one infantry. Down there is the equivalent of two of each.'

Still so what? was my internal reaction.

'Go on,' I said.

'Go on? What's to go on?' Luis was growing excitable, the Latin in him bubbling up. 'Papa's command has been increased by two brigades, only they are not new brigades, but a doubling in size of the two he has already. They carry the same numbers. This has never happened, except perhaps in time of war.'

'Maybe I'm not as bright as I thought I was, but what are you implying?'

'That somebody wanted to strengthen his force *secretly*. They wouldn't dare simply transfer two brigades from another regional command, it would be noticed by the High Command. Instead, they have reinforced existing units, probably from several different regions, so that on paper the number of brigades here is the same as always. This way they build the strength they need to invade yet contain the knowledge. Now do you see?'

'Yes.' And I was finally beginning to 'see'.

Elena loosed off an ironic cheer.

'You can't expect him to understand the workings of the Spanish Army,' Luis said in my defence.

'I don't suppose there could be some other explanation?' I said.

Luis blew out his cheeks in exasperation. 'Why look for other explanations? You already have the correct one.'

With the lens set at maximum zoom I sighted the camera and panned slowly left to right across the valley. Then re-setting normal vision I did a reverse sweep, from right to left.

'Do you think you have all you need?' Elena had borrowed the binoculars and was tracking a helicopter across the far ridge.

'Unless you think we should count heads,' I cracked, but she didn't respond, intent on the helicopter.

Luis was already backing out, slithering on his stomach.

'All clear this side,' he announced, seconds later. I wriggled out after him; Elena brought up the rear, the glasses dangling from her neck in the water. We were all soaked down our fronts. I stowed the camera and at a crouch we headed for the ravine. It opened up before us, the cover it provided like a welcome home. As we scrambled over the lip, I lost my footing and came down hard on sharp chunk of rubble. My 'Ouch!' made Elena titter, the heartless bitch.

In single file we jogged down the hillside. Below and to our left the Audi came into sight. Linda was perched on the hood. I thought I saw her wave. Unease fluttered in the pit of my stomach as I saw how close we had parked to the encampment. The chopper patrolling this area must have spotted the car, must have questioned its presence in this remote spot.

'Wait,' Luis, last in line, called. He had halted and was staring down into the valley that ran from the tip of the lake down to the road. 'Look – a jeep.'

No need for the binoculars: it was a jeep, sure enough, with four occupants. Fairly rocketing along the dirt track that served the encampment. It had, I judged, about a couple of kilometres to travel before it reached Linda and the Audi. It would be hidden from her until it was clear of the end of the ridge, and by then it would be too late for her to react.

Resuming jogging, I yanked my cell phone free of my jeans pocket. Pressed the button for Linda's number. It buzzed as the call went through, but only feebly.

'It's no good here,' Elena said, coming up alongside me. 'Reception is very poor.'

She was right. My cell's screen displayed only a single bar on the reception grid, and even that was flicking on and off. I listened in, but heard only static.

I could see Linda. She was looking up the hillside, shading her eyes. I signalled manically. Wasted energy. Even if she could see my gesticulations they wouldn't mean anything to her.

'Come on!' I put on a spurt, leaping from boulder to boulder like a baboon.

'No!' This from Luis; he and Elena had dropped back. 'Come back, Mr Warner! You will be caught.'

He was probably right but I wasn't about to run out on Linda. The camera case thudded against my chest as I went blundering down the ravine. It would have to be junked before I ran into the soldiers.

'Come back!' Luis, fainter now, a despairing note.

No chance of my reaching or even coming within hearing range of Linda before that jeep got to her. I worked this out in my head as I continued my reckless descent. A red herring was needed and I was the only one available. Without slowing, I swerved towards the side of the ravine, scrambled up it, sliding in the loose scree, and out onto the hillside where they couldn't miss seeing me. Still running and in full view, I took a beeline for the Audi.

I had temporarily lost sight of the jeep; now it emerged from an outcrop of rocks, and the soldiers spotted me at once. The engine note altered, revs dropping then, decision made, it swung decisively from the track and came at me, bouncing on the rugged terrain. Out of the corner of my eye, I saw Linda start forward, hesitate, then back-pedal towards the car. I had bought her an escape route – I hoped she had the sense to use it.

The jeep well and truly lured in my direction, I turned from it and retraced my steps at speed towards the ravine. The Irazola twins were nowhere in view. The jeep's engine, straining in low gear, rose in volume behind me. My only hope of avoiding capture lay in the ravine, as crossing it in a wheeled vehicle would be an impossibility. It wouldn't be necessary either if the soldiers had orders to shoot. With that disturbing thought I started zigzagging.

The jeep's engine was howling, the front bumper almost within bumping distance of my backside, when I tumbled into the ravine. My fall was softened by something human, with soft curves – Elena, curled up below the overhang. She gave out a sequence of yelps as we rolled down into the bed of the gully in a tangle of limbs, finishing up with her chest in my face. In other circumstances a possibly erotic posture.

We groaned in chorus. She called me something in Spanish. It didn't sound complimentary.

Luis was there too, a little higher up the gully, pressed against the side. He didn't look at me. Paralysed with fright, I supposed. I supposed wrong, as it turned out.

The jeep had gone quiet. Voices filtered down into the ravine. I was upright, unhurt, and brushing damp dirt from my pants when four soldiers arrived on foot at the lip of the ravine. Their leader wore sergeant's stripes and a pistol at his belt. He was thick gutted, moustachioed, cocky. He grinned at me from above, grinned even more widely at Elena, who was still on her bottom, her T-shirt the worse for wear, exposing flesh and a white bra strap. The three troopers, sub-machine guns slung from their shoulders, whistled appreciation. One of them worked the zipper of his fly, blatantly suggestive.

'*Ustedes vienen conmigo*,' the sergeant said, his Spanish patois not easy to decipher. I interpreted it to myself as 'You come with me.' He hadn't yet spotted Luis, still crouched under the projecting lip of the ravine.

Elena told the sergeant what he could do with his order. He didn't take amiss, merely motioned to his underlings.

'Bring them out. Maybe we'll have some fun with this spitfire, heh?' He whistled appreciation. 'Look at those tits.'

'Tell them who you are, Elena,' I urged her. They wouldn't dare fool with the daughter of their commander-in-chief. If she heard me, she didn't react.

'*Esta* Señorita Irazola,' I said, adding that she was the daughter of '*su general*'.

They roared with laughter. Either they didn't believe it, or they weren't impressed. The trooper with the agitated zipper lowered himself gingerly over the edge of the ravine, the other two queuing up to follow.

That was when Luis, still tucked away beneath the lip, made his move.

He sprang away from the side of the ravine, agile as a cat, and screamed something short, sharp, that might have been '*frezas de putas*!' approximately translatable as whores' shit. The troopers didn't take offence. Maybe the fat automatic Luis had lined up on them accounted for this. He held it as if he was born to it, two-fisted, straight-armed. Not a muscle trembled.

To a man the troopers looked towards the sergeant. He had paled but some of the discipline held fast. He clapped a hand to his holster and that was his last act on earth.

You could see from the chubby grip of Luis' automatic that it held a sufficiency of rounds. He used three on the sergeant – more than adequate: the heavy slugs picked the man up and tossed him away down the hillside. His men made vain efforts to unsling their sub-machine guns but they were a maladroit lot; the zipper operator dropped his and his screech of grief singled him out as Luis' next victim.

I didn't count the gunshots but fifteen was about right. Luis fired them all. He fired until the slide locked open and his gun was empty. By then he didn't need it any more. Quiet was restored but for the echoes of the gunshots racketing along the ravine.

Throughout the brief slaughter I didn't move. I was at forty-five-plus degrees to Luis' line of fire and therefore safe from all but the most errant of shots. And none of Luis' shots had been errant. As far as I could tell every single round struck flesh. The three troopers lay in the bed of the ravine, motionless, a dishevelled heap of uniforms. Death had seemed to shrink them. Luis, dispassionate, expressionless, was wreathed in gunsmoke. It clung to him in tendrils, though the whiff of cordite, initially strong, soon dispersed.

'Well,' I said, to break the thrall that bound us. 'That was a pretty thorough job you did there, Luis.'

He let out a breathless giggle. His eyes were sparkling, bright as agate chips. He didn't speak, just worked the action of the automatic to return the slide.

Elena, also outwardly unmoved by the slaughter, said, 'We must get away from here. They will have heard those shots.'

'I don't think so,' I said, surprised at my own calmness, the ability to think rationally still intact. Maybe I was too inured to violent death, most of it at my own hands. 'The ridge is between us and the camp, and there's the noise from the choppers.'

But reinforcements had been summoned before the shootings. As we clambered from the ravine a second jeep with a truckful of troopers in tow was bouncing along the dirt road, following the same route as the first.

'Come on, quick!' I rapped, and scrambled out of the ravine and into the jeep, whose engine was obligingly ticking over, all ready to roll. I spared a glance for the road and the Audi: it was still there. It wasn't enough to have saved Linda once, I was going to have to do it all over again.

Elena swung in beside me while Luis piled in the back. I heard the unmistakable clunk of a magazine rammed home. The vicious little hoodlum had come prepared for a major campaign. And to think I had crossed the frontier in the same car as that armoury! The moral impact of the multiple murder hadn't hit me yet. I was still just relieved to have been spared a repeat interview with Julio Irazola.

'Down the hill to the road,' Elena commanded. In any case we had no alternative. Twice I crunched the unfamiliar gearbox, then we took off. In the mirror I saw our pursuers alter course and come lurching after us.

The hillside was not built for motor vehicles and jeeps sure don't go in for soft springing. Every rock, every irregularity in the terrain came up through the chassis to the top of your skull. My backside spent more time in the air than on the unpadded seat. At least I had the steering wheel to cling to. Elena gripped the top of the windshield with both hands but was nevertheless thrown about plenty. Luis in the back had the worst of it, the expletives coming in an endless stream.

At intervals during this blundering descent I darted a sideways glance towards the Audi. It hadn't moved. For God's sake, Linda, get out of there! Leave the heroics to me. I resolved to head deeper inland as soon as we hit the road, in the hope of drawing the pursuit away from her. But Elena saw it differently.

'The other way!' she bawled in my ear as we smacked onto the tarmac, wheels skittering on the still wet surface.

'Stuff you!' I roared back, and crushed the accelerator to the floor.

The shadow of a mountain on our left closed over us. Elena, accepting the inevitable, sank back in her seat.

Luis' head bobbed up in the mirror.

'It's okay, Mr Warner,' he said, slapping my shoulder. 'I agree we must think of Miss Pridham.'

'You're a stand-up guy, Luis,' I said and meant it. The little punk might be gun happy, he might even be plumb crazy, but his heart was in the right place.

The road took us first west, then north, away from the valley and through a narrow defile. Our pursuers, less reckless perhaps, fell back and lost visual contact. The helicopters worried me though. It could only be a matter of minutes before they came to hunt us down, like hounds after a coursing hare. Sure enough, after we had covered perhaps ten kilometres, Luis let out a warning cry.

'Here they come.'

Two of them, in echelon. They were weaving over the open countryside, one on each side of the road, while we were still under the shelter of the mountains and would be hard to spot in our grey-green livery.

'There!' Elena indicated a track, no more than parallel ruts veering off to the left, passing a coppice of trees, just big and thick enough to hide us. I wrenched at the wheel and in less than a minute we were ploughing into the coppice.

'Do you think they can see us?' Elena wondered, as we sat under the trees' canopy while the slender machines buzzed low overhead without break in their flight path.

'No,' I said, 'but if they've any savvy at all they'll realise these trees are the only hiding place within miles.'

Luis shook his head. 'Not so, my friend. There are some olive plantations across the valley. Plenty of places to hide there.'

'I hope you're right,' I said, to the dying stammer of the two choppers. 'Because if you're not, they'll be back.'

It was reasonable to assume the jeep and truck would be waiting for feedback from the choppers. When none came, hopefully they'd give up and go home.

We stayed under the trees for some hours. The choppers came back after an hour or so but passed a safe distance from our refuge. I made attempts to call Linda on all our cell phones but reception was still too weak.

With the onset of evening the rain resumed, bringing an early nightfall. Now we were safe until daylight. We erected the jeep's canvas top and, Elena driving, quit the trees and carried on up the valley. Where we were going wasn't even discussed, and I for one didn't care. Simply keeping out of the clutches of the Spanish Army was ambition enough for now. So I just sat there, clinging on to the windshield, thinking about Linda, hoping she wasn't passing the night in the vengeful custody of her former lover.

Chapter Nineteen

Aesthetically the house was a wreck: extensions sprouted from every angle and the whole dump was coated in several different shades of *crepi*. A wistful palm tree flanked the front door, no doubt wishing it was somewhere more congenial. From a sagging clothes line hung a pair of singlets and a towel.

It was also a lonely spot. A good five kilometres from the nearest village, no neighbours, no view of the sea, awful roads. It was perfect.

'Foreigners,' Luis observed, reflecting aloud my own thoughts. 'Only foreigners would have a home in such a place. The price must have been very low.'

'A house is a house,' Elena said, ever the practical twin. 'And it has a garage. We must get under cover. They will still be looking for us.'

The sun was still down behind the hills to the east but already its rays were bathing the sky. We had not travelled far under the protection of darkness. A blow-out, a flat spare and no means to inflate it had spoiled our plan for a dash east and then south to Algeciras before dawn, there to lose the jeep and ourselves in the vortex of a big city.

'It's occupied.' I pointed out. A decrepit Citroën 2CV was drawn up alongside the garage.

Luis did that breathless giggle thing and patted the gun at his belt. 'It does not matter. They will do as we say.'

I had forgotten about the gun. Yesterday was remote, it had happened to somebody else. Even today was surreal. This was some other guy, tired and mud-plastered, crouching in a roadside ditch, accessory to four murders, now contemplating forcibly entering someone's home.

I was hungry though, and the house represented shelter and food. If nothing else, we could eat. And we did need to get under cover. The four bodies would have been discovered. The hunt would be on in earnest.

Being a fugitive was not a new experience. I had been a fugitive before. What got to me was the irony of it. All the years of killing and getting away with it, to end up on the run for someone else's killings.

In the event our unlawful entry was painless. We walked in on the owners of the house while they were still abed. We allowed them to get dressed under nominal supervision, sat them down at the kitchen table. They were in their sixties and they were scared, but not scared witless. We didn't terrorise them. Luis let them see the gun, then stowed it away, making no threats. No need.

They were Dutch and retired, seekers of an inexpensive place in the sun. Name of Sloothaak. Anneloes and Maurits. They spoke little Spanish, rough and ready English, so we conversed in that language. How long would we stay, please? Not long, I assured them, a day, maybe two.

The interior of the house was spick and span but poorly furnished, with Ikea well-represented. Two bedrooms, living room, kitchen, bathroom. The shower worked fine and we used it in turn, consigning our muddy garments to the washing machine. Borrowed dressing gowns served to keep Elena and me decent; Luis wrapped a bath towel round his waist.

A phone was my next urgent need. The house had a land line but it was disconnected or out of service. Sloothaak confessed to have been unable to pay his Telefonica account for three months. Cell phone reception was no better here, and in any case the battery in mine had died along the route.

'Why don't we take their car and leave now?' Elena suggested as we breakfasted on slightly stale bread rolls and an assortment of jams. The Sloothaaks had been banished to the living room, leaving the door open. 'They'll be looking for a jeep.'

'Ever heard of road blocks?' I returned. 'They've probably called the police. You can't kill four soldiers in peacetime and expect them to be written off as battle casualties.'

Later that morning a chopper came over, circled the house at scarcely more than roof height. The palm tree fluttered like a ragged flag and the whole building vibrated, rattling the knives on our plates. A tortoiseshell cat came in through a cat-flap in the kitchen door as if a firework were tied to its tail and streaked across the room, presumably en route for its favourite bolthole.

The chopper zoomed away abruptly, maybe satisfied, maybe not. Luis laid the automatic on the table. It was as I had thought, a Heckler & Koch, the USP model, a pattern designed for military use. I toyed with the idea of disarming him but let it go. Making an enemy of him wouldn't get us out of this mess.

'You will not stay long please,' Mrs Slothaak said worriedly, as she cleared away the dishes. Less philosophical than her husband, she was red-eyed from weeping.

'Not long,' I assured her for the umpteenth time.

In the event we stayed for seven days. After twenty-four hours a routine was established. We took it in turns to keep the Slothaaks company. Contact with the outside world meant a ten minute drive. No visitors came that first day. The Slothaaks had no television either, and no computer, only an ancient transistor radio and a CD player. We tuned in to national and local stations for the news. No mention of any multiple killings. A security clampdown? Always possible. The Spanish authorities wouldn't be keen to advertise any incidents that might alert the British to the presence of a large military force next door to Gibraltar. The obvious explanation didn't hit me until much later.

The sleeping arrangements were easily sorted. Elena slept in the second bedroom while Luis and I shared the living room. Luis, being slightly smaller, took the two-seater couch. I wallowed in the luxury of a wobbly Z- bed the Slothaaks exhumed from sundry junk in the garage.

The second morning, late, we had a postal delivery. We watched from behind the thin net curtains as the postman shoved a solitary envelope in the box on the gate post, and roared off in his little yellow van as if he couldn't wait to get away from the place.

Otherwise our isolation was undisturbed. The radio stations remained mute on the subject of the killings.

The weather was settling into its spring regimen. The sun shone uninterruptedly during our second day at the house. After a sleepless, uneasy second night I rose early ahead of it. Went out to sit on the log pile in the garden. Still wondering and worrying about Linda and whether she had made it back to the safety of Gib.

'You couldn't sleep either?' Elena emerged from the kitchen door, tartan patterned dressing gown a size and a few too large, bare ankles protruding below. She lit a cigarette, eyed me coolly.

'Luis thinks we should leave,'

'I know. I disagree.'

'There were no helicopters yesterday,' she said, meandering about the lawn. The grass stubble was damp with dew, making her feet glisten.

'It's too soon.'

'You are too cautious.'

For a while she said no more. The sun appeared over the mountains, splitting the sky. Elena, standing back to it, became a featureless cut-out. I shaded my eyes.

'Why don't you sleep with me?' she said, with her usual lack of subtlety.

My commitment to Linda was the reason. So as not to hurt Elena's feelings I came up with a different one.

'Luis might not like it.'

'Luis? Hah!' Her tone was scathing but, tellingly, she didn't dispute the point, so maybe I was on the mark.

'How old are you, Elena?'

'Twenty-four. Why?'

'You know how old I am?'

She made a show of studying me, head cocked, eyes appraising.

'Thirty-five?'

My laugh was hollow.

'Not since quite a few years.'

'Age is unimportant. I prefer mature men to boys like Luis.'

Signals of a familiar kind were flashing again. I steered the conversation away from them.

'Aren't you afraid?' I asked,

She flipped her cigarette into a bare laurel bush. It continued to smoke, a lazy spiral in the windless air.

'Of?'

'Being caught. Imprisoned.' I paused to let it penetrate. 'For life maybe.'

'There are worse things than prison. Dying, for instance. And loving. Loving is a form of dying too.'

That was too esoteric for me. Another change of topic seemed due.

'Why did you get involved in this invasion business? You didn't make it up, did you?'

'Maybe. Who knows? Luis believes it, but then Luis is a hothead.' Her laugh was uncertain. 'As you have seen for yourself.'

She left me then. Proud, head erect, the daughter of a general, rising above the ill-fitting, shabby dressing gown.

A sparrow fluttered down to perch on the top strut of the Sloothaak's rustic fence. Chattered at me friendly-like.

I went inside.

* * * * *

'We must buy some food,' Luis said, throwing open cupboard doors, one after another. 'We cannot live on sugar and butter and herbs.'

'Every week we shopping go.' Sloothaak spoke timidly, as if fearful of retribution.

'Ja, every week we go,' his wife concurred, nodding.

So shopping we went. Sloothaak and I, in the Citroën, to the little market town of Casas Viejas. We bought fresh fruit and vegetables, fish, bread, milk, bottled water, and a welter of canned and dried food for the longer term.

Sloothaak became increasingly agitated as the pile in the supermarket cart grew.

'Why you buy all this? You say you going away soon.'

'Just in case.' My disarming smile didn't work. His worried frown stayed in place. 'We'll leave whatever we don't eat. Just think how much you'll save. There's enough here for two people for a month.'

'Please?' I had spoken too quickly for him.

'Don't worry,' I said. But he did worry. He spent the whole thirty-minute ride back gnawing at his knuckles. I concentrated on my driving.

A helicopter had been prowling over the house in my absence, three passes and a close scrutiny. The cat hadn't stopped shaking since.

'See what I mean,' Elena said to Luis. 'It is too soon. They are still searching for us.'

That was Day Three. No more helicopters came after that and by the seventh day I was ready to concede we could up sticks, provided we moved by night.

'We'll have to borrow your car, I'm afraid,' I told the Sloothaaks. Hands were wrung.

'But what shall we do without our car?'

It was a moot point. The jeep had been left in a wood, some distance from here, so was no use to them. I gave Sloothaak a few hundred euros from my shrinking store of cash. Luis made some vague promise about paying someone to bring it back.

Elena snorted. 'And tell the world we were here?'

'They'll tell the world anyway,' Luis said. 'The postman at least.'

'Let's take them with us,' I proposed.

'And afterwards?'

Luis settled our dilemma that very evening, and his solution was pure in its simplicity.

It happened at dusk. It was a peculiarly still evening, the landscape reddening in the sunset, an atmosphere of expectancy cloaking the shabby little house and its square of garden. The slightest sound carried across the valley and beyond. It was a desolate spot all right. At a certain level the Sloothaaks were to be admired.

Traffic was scant on the track that served the house so any hint of it put us on immediate alert. Apart from the postman we had seen only a couple of motor vehicles during our stay. Once, a tinker in a flat cap had shambled past, leading a very old mule laden with assorted ironmongery. We didn't answer his knock on the door. On another occasion a boy of twelve or thereabouts had cycled by, a fishing rod strapped to the crossbar, to return just ahead of nightfall.

'From the plantation,' Mrs Sloothaak told us dolefully. According to them the orange plantation was the nearest habitation, three kilometres away on the road to Casas Viejas.

Luis and I were outside, debating the fate of the Sloothaaks, when the burr of an engine broke the stillness. We listened to it, half expecting it to fade. But, no, it came on, not even slowing for the bends, of which there were many.

'Inside,' I said with quiet urgency to Luis. He nodded, pulling the automatic from his belt as we hurried indoors. More killing wasn't on my agenda. Once again I considered relieving him of it, and once again I let it go.

Elena met us at the door. 'There's a car coming …' Then she noticed Luis' gun, and saved her breath. 'What shall we do with the Sloothaaks?'

I thought fast. 'It may not be coming here. Put the old woman in the bathroom and stay with her, hold a knife at her throat or something. Mr Sloothaak can answer the door. Luis can be a guest of the family, I'll stay out of sight.' I grabbed the fearful Sloothaak. 'You may have a visitor. Act naturally and you'll come to no harm. We're leaving tonight, remember. Just act naturally,' I emphasised, 'and we'll be gone for good in a few hours.'

I wasn't sure he understood. I could only hope.

Through a crack between door and jamb in the Sloothaak's bedroom, I could observe the hallway and the front door. Sloothaak's co-operation was the key factor. The gun at his back and the knife at his wife's throat ought to keep him cooperative. But under stress people are unpredictable creatures. All too often they don't play the parts you cast them in.

Through the bedroom window I saw the car drive up. My heart lurched. It was the Guardia Civil, the country police. Not so quaint in appearance as they used to be since they abandoned their tricorn hats in favour of French-style *kepis*, they were unquestionably the law in these parts. To back up their authority, they carried guns.

The engine cut out. Doors slammed. Footsteps, voices, then the rap of knuckles on wood. Sloothaak shuffled past; Luis would be covering him from the living room, the door ajar like mine. Please, God, let both of them keep their heads.

The hinges creaked as Sloothaak opened the front door.

'*Buenos tardes, señor.*' The greeting reached me quite distinctly. '*Siento hablar molesto. Ha visto …*'

Sloothaak couldn't go through with it. His terror must have communicated itself to the policeman. I saw him stiffen and reach for Sloothaak.

'*Señor*! *Qué pasa*?'

The second policeman swore – '*Mierda*!' His hand flashed to the gun at his waist.

From behind and to my right Luis fired. Sloothaak caught the first bullet. The centre of his back grew a red-bordered hole and he crumpled, dead before he touched the floor. The policeman who had spoken first took a bullet in the chest. It mashed him into his colleague who got off a single shot that thumped into the wall outside. Luis came out, running, still firing at the fallen policemen.

'Luis!' I blundered into the hall, catching a handful of his jacket. 'No more …'

He tore free of me. For a fleeting, gut-emptying moment I though he was going to shoot me too. He pointed the gun at me, his hand shaking, his features contorted, unrecognisable. I backed off. He uttered a few jumbled words that made no sense to me, and ploughed on to where the policemen lay, one motionless, the other alternately groaning and coughing blood. Luis put a stop to all that. At point blank range he put a bullet in the brain of each man. Economic, you could say.

The killings themselves were no shock to my system. I was even beyond grieving for lives unnecessarily ended. It was Luis' eagerness to kill that was so sickening. Compared with him, Peter Vitale, self-styled Action Man and proponent of violence, was an innocent babe. Luis was deadly in a way Peter, for all his fanaticism, could never be. Luis was a true psycho.

Nor was it over yet. He strode back towards the living room, no sign on his face of pity or remorse. I watched him dully. Woke up too late to his intent. Woke up to a woman's terrified screech and the now familiar crash of the automatic – once, twice, rattling windows in their frames.

'Christ, *no*!' A surge of dread propelled me through the living room with its tacky laminated furniture, to the bathroom.

Elena was splayed against the wall as if she had been hurled there. She looked dazed, but was apparently unhurt. Luis was standing legs apart, gun held stiffly, still smoking, the stink of cordite sharp in the confined space.

As for Mrs Sloothaak – poor, terrified Mrs Sloothaak – her husk was sprawled messily at the feet of her slayer. Her heart must have stopped instantly for there was only a small seepage of blood from the hole in her scrawny chest.

The top half of Luis' slim body was rotating towards me when I hit him. My punch landed on his cheek bone, tearing the skin. He reeled the length of the bathroom, cannoning into the wash basin and bouncing off. He tripped over his victim, cracked his skull on the rim of the bath and subsided to the floor. Out cold. The gun came to rest under the wash basin; Elena only had to stoop to retrieve it.

But she wasn't interested. Her stare was blank.

'I t-tried … to stop him,' she croaked.

I massaged my hand. It was my first experience of tackling a killer dog with bare knuckles.

'I'm leaving,' I said flatly, coldly. 'Coming?'

Her dazed look faded, her eyes acquiring focus.

'I … can't. What about Luis …?'

'Suit yourself.' The bond between twins is often said to be almost supernaturally strong. I didn't stick around to put it to the test.

Apart from a few toilet items I had bought in Casa Viejas the house contained nothing of mine. I collected my windbreaker, and with it the keys to the Citroën, from the coat rack in the hall, stepped over a fresh corpse or two, and got clear of that place just as fast as deux-chevaux could transport me.

Chapter Twenty

The Cessna's undercarriage skipped lightly on the tarmac, the impact barely felt. Then we were freewheeling along the runway, the pilot letting the speed fall off without braking.

'Thanks for a smooth flight,' I said as we parted company at the cabin door. I was his only passenger.

'Pleasure, Mr Warner,' he said. He spoke with an Afrikaner accent.

I stepped onto the apron of Gibraltar airport into the unwelcoming arms of Major Ribble.

'A fine mess,' he said. 'A fine mess.'

No hello, no enquiry after my health.

'Good of you to come, Major,' I returned. Civility costs nothing.

I was excused the usual immigration formalities. Ribble drove me to the Caleta Hotel in a Navy Land Rover. As we travelled east on Devil's Tower Road, passing the Holiday Inn on our left, the Rock on the right casting its shade over us, he demanded an explanation for my absence.

'What the fuck were you doing in Spain? Do you realise what it cost to smuggle you out? False documentation can't be provided at a moment's notice, you know. And pilots who make a living out of illegal transportation don't grow on trees.'

'Then why didn't you leave me to rot?'

He honked through his nose. 'My orders were to place myself and all facilities at your disposal. I took that to mean I was to rescue you if you needed rescuing.'

'I needed rescuing,' I admitted with feeling.

The speed at which the machinery for my removal from Spain had been activated, once I had telephoned my plight to Ribble from a payphone, was heart-warming. A follow-up call to Linda's cell phone was less productive. I was asked to leave a message, and that's what I did.

With my cell phone's battery dead she wouldn't have been able to call back.

Ditching the Citroën in a supermarket parking lot in the town of El Puerto de Santa Maria to confuse any pursuit, I took a bus to Jerez and found a greasy hotel whose proprietor was induced with most of my remaining euros to overlook the usual reporting procedures and let me hang on to my passport. Next morning, shortly after sunrise, I was met by a Man with No Name outside the Cathedral, who exchanged my current phoney passport for a new phoney passport in the name of Eric Donaldson, a wad of money for emergencies, and verbal instructions to be at the airport at five o' clock that afternoon. My old passport, still needed in Gib, would be returned via the diplomatic bag.

Easy when you know who.

I had blown some of the money on new clothes. Afterwards I took in a movie – Brad Pitt and Leo di Caprio in 1960s LA, speaking fluent Spanish without moving their lips – and was at the airport at a quarter to the hour. The rest was anti-climactic.

As Ribble filtered us into the Caleta parking lot behind a minibus I kept a lookout for the twins' Audi. It was there all right, next to the Aston. Linda had done good. I was looking forward to our reunion more than I cared to admit, even to myself.

'What's next?' Ribble enquired jeeringly as I dismounted. 'A trip to the Canaries perhaps?'

'You're forgetting your place, Major,' I said.

He bristled.

'I'll be in touch.' I added a farewell nod.

He drove off in a surfeit of revs and resentment.

Message at the desk. Would I contact a Mr Wyatt in London. No surprise there. Same old Toby, fretting at the lack of contact, anxious for feedback. The message was three days old.

'Is Miss Pridham in?' I asked Harry at the front desk.

His gaze roved over the keys. '313? No, not in her room at any rate.'

'Yes, funny that.' This was from an over-made up blonde woman, one of the reception team. Past forty and dressed twenty.

'What's funny?' Harry and I said together.

'Miss Pridham didn't spend last night in her room. In fact …' she sucked at a pencil while she thought, '… I don't believe I've seen her since breakfast yesterday morning.'

Harry crooked an eyebrow my way.

'I can't understand that,' I said. 'Her car's outside, the Audi. Well, it's not her car exactly, it belongs to some friends, but she's using it.'

'Oh, she walks quite a lot,' Blondie said brightly. 'She said exercise was good for pregnancy.'

My next line of enquiry was a trip upstairs to check her room for a clue to her whereabouts or a message. The keys to the twins' Audi were on her night table. Her purse was absent. Next I searched my own room, not expecting much and finding even less. I descended to the ground floor and used the keys to search the interior of the Audi. Another blank. Back in my room I plugged my cell into the charger and called hers again, with the same non-result.

From the hotel I transferred to the adjacent village and the beach hoping to spot her. Worry piling up like thunder clouds. One crisis over, another begins. And over the horizon more thunder clouds in the shape of Toby and his masters. Impatient for news, anxious for progress. I had news for them all right, of an impending invasion of the piece of real estate they were determined to hang on to. But it wasn't what I had been recruited for.

Night fell and still no Linda, and her cell remained switched off. I dined alone at the hotel. Worry killed my appetite and the waiter raised eyebrows over the amount of picked-over food I sent back to the kitchens. Usually I cleared my plate.

Afterwards I found a niche in the main bar, cuddled a glass of Scotch and wished I were cuddling Linda instead. Hard drink and introspection go well together, I find. So I drank and introspected about eight deaths that, in part at least, could be laid at my door. Dwelling on them made me feel hollow, so I drank faster to take away the feeling. I introspected too about an invasion that might or might not be going to happen, and about my duty to contact Toby and alert him anyway; about how I was neglecting my mission here in Gibraltar. But these were peripheral fleabites compared with my introspection about Linda.

The telephone call came virtually on the stroke of midnight, as if it had been timed. They paged me. I took it on an extension in the bar.

Expecting Toby and a right royal roasting.

Instead I got a man whose English was too punctiliously modulated to be his mother tongue.

'It is good that you have returned. The young lady will be relieved.' He mispronounced his diphthongs: relee-eved.

'Who is this?' I demanded, words slurring. Drink had made me dull.

'This is someone who is taking care of your lady friend.'

The dullness suddenly morphed into brightness. I didn't ask him to repeat it.

'Say what you've got to say,' I snarled into the receiver. The barman, wiping out a beer glass, gave me a startled look. I swivelled away to present my back to him.

'You will come here,' my caller instructed, 'alone, unarmed, and tell no one where you are going. Is that understood?'

'Get on with it, you piece of shit,' I said through my teeth.

A tinkle of laughter, like tiny bells.

'Piece of shit.' He chortled. 'You Americans are so amusing.' Then, the tone reverting to businesslike, 'You will leave immediately. Here is the address …'

* * * * *

Exactly as ordered, I left immediately and drove hard and fast, taking the tunnel road out towards Europa Point. Wind Mill Flats, was my destination, and the barman had directed me with the aid of a foldup tourist map, which he then donated to me. Inside the car I opened the hidden compartment at the bottom of the glove compartment, and hooked out the SIG by its trigger guard. The P365 is what's known as a carrygun, by virtue of its compact dimensions. It was still grown-up enough to hold ten rounds in the magazine plus one in breech. I rammed it down my pants waistband, in the small of my back. Uncomfortable when driving, but comfort wasn't a priority right now.

On the other side of the tunnel were some buildings tucked into a notch in the hillside – military married quarters was my guess. I passed them by. It was a clear moonlit night, the sea tranquil. Further on, more married quarters, climbing the hillside. Squares of light from their windows made holes in the darkness. Here, according to my directions, I had to perform a complicated manoeuvre, sharp left, down a hill, left again and yet again. I missed the initial turn, realised my error when the headlights panned across a hospital sign. I reversed in the hospital driveway and doubled back.

No more mistakes. I passed under a bridge. A tunnel loomed, a black toothless scream in the night. As I entered it the Aston's exhaust throbbed back at me. A bat flipped across the windshield, was tossed aside like a scrap of cloth. Just beyond the tunnel exit, on the left, was a parking lot, and beyond it a beach lit up by two feeble streetlamps. I turned off the road, parked the Aston carelessly and slid out.

'Good evening, Mr Warner.'

The voice was that of my recent caller. He was standing in a patch of shadow under a tree. His clothes were drab, merging with the background, only his disembodied face revealed. His hair was fair, his height well above average. I knew him then – the guy with the Slavic features and the roly-poly girlfriend. Not a total surprise then. The gun he was pointing at my gut wasn't a surprise either.

He gestured at me to raise my arms. His frisking technique was thorough. It told me I was up against a pro, and needed to respect that fact. Naturally, he found the SIG. He hefted it in his hand, but didn't comment.

'Come with me, please.'

It was too early for gung-ho moves that might increase the risk to Linda. Wait and watch and eventually would come an opening.

He had a penlight and flashed this on and off as we climbed up the rockface with me in the lead, to the promontory that abutted onto the beach. No words passed between us. The climb was easy, via a narrow path to the top. Once there he kept the penlight off, letting the moonlight guide us. The edge of the married quarters estate was quite near. I could actually hear music and laughter. A party was in progress. I wished I was there.

We went across the top of the tunnel, made a U-turn and came to some steps, cut into solid rock and leading down. The penlight flashed, illuminating a door, steel like that inside the tunnel but without padlocks. I realised then that I had been given false directions, most likely as a precaution against my passing them on.

The door opened more easily than its condition would have suggested. Within was light, weak and diffused, and more steps. My captor remained mute. I assumed we were entering one of the old galleries with which the Rock is honeycombed. Not quite. It transpired to be a natural cavern, with only the enlarged entrance bearing marks of man's hand. Such places were often used as munitions stores during the last war.

With each step the shimmer of light became stronger. The steps unwound gradually, as if we were descending inside a round tower. At the bottom we made a right-angled turn. From somewhere came a continuous hiss.

We had landed in a long, high-ceilinged vault of a cave, lit by several butane gas lamps, which explained the hissing. Crates were piled in a far corner; closer at hand, some beams, thick as railway sleepers but much longer, were loosely stacked. Black with filth, they looked as if they had been here since the cave was discovered. It was dank and chilly, how I imagined the inside of a tomb would be. Underfoot, no flooring, just compacted dirt.

In the cave were two women. I recognised the guy's plump partner, now dressed in workmanlike one-piece coveralls, too tight all over to be flattering. Her straight black hair was done up in an untidy knot, secured by black ribbon.

The second woman was Linda.

Linda naked, her back to me, the dimples in her bare buttocks emphasising her helplessness and the indignity.

Linda, head drooping, dangling from a rusty chain bolt, fixed to a beam across the ceiling, her feet at waist level.

Linda, suspended by her thumbs.

The gun was still covering me. Oblivious of it, I started forward, driven by a blind intent to help Linda, to release her.

'Stay where you are!' the guy commanded. The woman moved to block my path. She produced an automatic, toylike but sure to be loaded with real bullets.

I may have faltered but I was still going forward when the woman re-directed her pistol downwards.

'Come further and I will shoot you in the foot,' she said in impeccable English, and her tone was calm and measured. It was a douche of cold water on the heat of my madness. It was effective in stopping me.

'Tell me what you want,' I said hoarsely, 'and let her down.'

'That is precisely it,' the man said. I was still facing Linda. Behind me came the snap of a cigarette lighter. 'You have grasped the point very quickly, Mr Warner. You tell me what I want, and we will let her down.'

'Linda,' I called out. 'Linda – speak to me.'

No reply, only the hiss of the gas lamps. Then ever so slightly her head lifted once, twice. She was alive, however tenuous the thread.

'How long has she been up there, fuck-face?' I demanded of the guy.

'Please do not insult me,' he said, so cheerfully that again came the urge to rush at him and wrap my fingers about his thin neck and squeeze until my ears popped from the pressure … 'My name is Petrov.'

'How long … fuck-face?' I said. Considering that he was armed, and had Linda at his mercy, it might have been smarter not to taunt him. Rage was making me incautious.

'How long?' Lips were pursed, as if in genuine contemplation. 'An hour or two. Or maybe three. Not long by our standards.'

'State your terms, for Christ's sake.'

He was in no hurry though. Making me sweat was part of the thrill. The longer he dragged it out the readier I would be to do his bidding.

His teeth glinted. 'You may take your time.'

'Take your time,' the plump woman echoed.

She had acquired a broom handle and was rubbing it up and down between Linda's thighs. Linda didn't respond. She hung there, slack and unmoving, like a carcass on a hook. Her skin was pale with a pearl-like translucent sheen; an even paler bikini pants-shaped band linked hip to hip.

I turned to face Petrov, forcing detachment into my voice as I said, 'You won't make me more cooperative by prolonging it. Tell me what you're after and let's be done with it.'

Behind me came a gasp, more of surprise than pain. I spun round. The woman had the broom handle hard up into Linda's crotch, impaling her. As I watched she moved it up and down inside her. A slanted smile on her face to go with her warped mind. Her free hand still held the gun.

Blood was pounding inside my head. I was about to go for Petrov, gun and all, when he rapped out a single word of command to the woman. Looking sulky, her fun spoiled, she lowered the pole.

'Stop right now,' I grated, 'or you're a dead man. '

'Ho, ho, brave talk,' he said, cigarette between lips. 'It is I who hold the gun, my friend, not you. I could kill you now and it would disturb me no more than if I had trodden on a slug. I would be happy to kill you. I would sing with joy –'

'Okay, okay,' I grunted. 'You've made your point.

'If you will permit me to finish. I was about to say that I have no orders to kill you other than in self-defence. How I interpret self-defence is, however, my decision alone. In any case, there are some injuries that can be inflicted to which death would be preferable. In my country, we are experts in death by excruciating, unimaginable pain.'

'In Russia you mean?'

'It is of no consequence to you which country I represent. You do not, as you British spies say, need to know.'

In the subfusc light his features were gaunt, almost skeletal. He looked the part of the degenerate creep he was.

Petrov's female satellite had retreated to some dingy recess. Now she returned, carrying a tubular steel chair that she set down before me, a metre or so from where Linda dangled.

'Sit,' the woman ordered. Petrov ratified the order with a twitch of gun barrel.

A roll of duct tape was produced. This was my last chance of fighting back before they immobilised me. But these were old pros. Petrov stood well out of reach, toting both his and the woman's weapons.

'Resist and your woman will suffer,' he warned,

Dead or disabled, I would be no use to Linda. In some trepidation I sat in the steel chair. While the man kept me covered the woman taped my wrists to the chair arms and my ankles and calves to the front legs, and my torso to the chair back. She was thorough; she got through the entire roll. When she had finished I could just about move from the neck upwards but that was my limit.

'So, then, Mr Warner, we come to the moment of truth … of *your* truth.' He was leaning against the wall now, the little automatic lined up with my belly button. He tossed the other gun back to the woman. 'You will explain what you are doing here in Gibraltar. I want your brief, the identity of your controller in London, your contacts here, your contacts with GIBESTÁ. I want to know about the bombing and the source of your materials. I want to know where you have been since 21st April. I want to know the nature of your relationship with the Irazola son and daughter.'

'That all?' I said sourly.

'To begin with. And the faster you tell, the sooner Miss Pridham's … er … discomfort will be relieved.' He wagged the automatic. 'Let me warn you in case you attempt to deceive me, I already have much information about you and your network. If you tell one single lie which I know is a lie, I shall have to assume all that you say is lies … are lies.' His stumble over the syntax gave me a childish spurt of pleasure. It didn't last. 'In this case, Miss Pridham will be punished on your behalf.'

I took his threats seriously. Pros seldom bluff, except at poker.

So I gave him information. I interwove truth with lies, half-lies, and inventions. I took a chance that his knowledge would not conflict with my fabrications.

He listened with seeming absorption, nodding at intervals. When I finally ran dry I had spun a convoluted web of political machination and deceit that was by no means all fantasy but was just misleading enough to confuse him.

'So … let us go through it again.' He started to walk in small circles. While he walked, he talked. He re-capped my fiction near word for word, displaying an enviable faculty for recall.

'Is that correct?' he queried at the end of his recitation, coming to stand in front of me, screening Linda's lower limbs. 'Have I understood the situation correctly?'

I assured him he had.

He smiled then. It was a threatening smile, devoid of humour.

'Liar.' He slapped me lightly, left cheek, right cheek. It wasn't meant to be painful, just mocking. 'Think again, my friend. For a start, you are not a civil servant but a private citizen, employed by the British

Government in an undercover capacity. Your controller is a man called Tobias Wyatt, an English spymaster, not Richard Kirkland, who is your Prime Minister's personal aide. We also know that you carry a Canadian passport. There are other discrepancies in your story but those will do for a start. Ana!' This to the woman, who, with unabashed glee, began to do things with the broom handle. Petrov stayed between me and Linda, blocking my view. This time Linda's gasp was of real pain, and the gasp became a short, sharp cry. Her body writhed, dragging at the chains.

'Stop!' I shouted, sweat springing to my face as if it were I, not Linda, who was suffering. I wrenched ineffectually at the tapes around my wrists. The chair slid backwards but I remained firmly attached to it. 'If you know so much, why this farce? What do you expect to gain by hurting her, you fucking pervert?'

Petrov tut-tutted me. 'So much foul language. You Anglo-Saxons are so limited in your forms of expression' He signalled to the woman. Linda's squeals tapered off in an undulating moan.

'Regrettably there are gaps in our knowledge,' Petrov said, 'and neither of you will leave here until you have joined them up. And whether you leave at all will depend upon how co-operative you have been.'

'I've told you all that matters,' I said, desperate to save Linda from further agonies, yet manacled to the "rules of the game" as surely as I was taped to this chair. 'All right, so I changed a name or two. I've told you the truth about my brief, about GIBESTÁ.'

The lamps hissed on. Linda whimpered. After so long suspended it was incredible that she remained conscious. The strain on her thumbs and her arms, what with the added weight of her unborn child, must have been unbearable. Petrov considered me, the thin smile still pulling his mouth out of shape. He had put the gun away and was trimming his fingernails with a pocket clipper.

'I would like so much to believe you, my friend. Really, I would. But if I report back what you have told me and it is shown to be false in so much as a single comma, I will be discredited. My masters, like computers, are not forgiving of errors. Now, come along, Warner – one more little effort, just for Miss Pridham. You don't want to see her hurt, do you? Badly hurt, I mean.'

Linda's head lifted fractionally. 'Warner …' Whether she meant to plead or hurl defiant expletives I never learned, for she slumped once more, beyond even speech. It spurred me to flex my arms, in an eye-popping attempt to snap the tapes. There wasn't a millimetre of slack.

'Linda,' I said, speaking round Petrov. 'I've given them all I have. There's nothing else, I swear …'

I swear. The lie left a foul taste. I couldn't live with it. So I fed Petrov more semi-factual pap. Now he had almost the whole box of tricks. All I held back was the true intentions of the British government, and my true profession. Like before, he let it permeate.

'Look …' I scoured my memory for harmless data that would sound more valuable than it was. 'I'm not a professional. I'm an investor. It's years since I worked in a regular job.'

'We know all about you, and your Spanish bar, and your cover.'

His nod to the woman, Ana, was the signal she was waiting for. She went to work with a will, loving her job. Linda squirmed suddenly and violently, lifting her knees to waist height.

'No!' Her voice was high and thin. 'My baby …'

'Well, Warner?' Petrov was smiling. The click of the nail clipper was louder than ever. Sweat coursed down my temples and down the back of my neck.

'There's nothing else, I promise you …'

I swear, I promise. What a regular, stand-up hero I was.

Petrov stepped aside and I was now able to see what was happening. Linda was impaled on the broom handle, the lower part of her body swivelling in an effort to break free. But short of raising herself a good foot she and that handle were inseparable.

'Don't do it, Petrov,' I pleaded. 'She's pregnant. You'll harm the baby.'

He was impassive, his eyes shrouded. 'I will count to five, Warner. One …'

Click-click went the clipper.

'Two …'

The Ana cow was actually wetting her lips, anticipating the thrill to come.

'Three …'

'You bastard!' I yelled. 'I've told it all, for fuck's sake!'

Linda gave a little cry, like a hurt child. 'André … don't let them … Oh God!… No!…'

It flashed inconsequentially across my mind that she had never called me André before. I hopped my chair forward, as if to get closer to her was to somehow lessen her suffering.

'Four.'

I hurled myself, chair and all, towards Petrov. A hopeless, fruitless last throw. The chair overbalanced. I hit the ground, the worst of the impact softened by the thick layer of dirt, but winding me just the same.

'Five!' He pronounced it with relish. I twisted my head to look at him from down in the dirt. His gaze shifted from me to a point beyond Linda. His nod was so slight I might have imagined it.

The shriek that followed hit the ceiling, travelled lengthways and sideways and when it could travel no further it resounded back towards the centre, in waves. When it abruptly ceased it left behind a vacuum in which all that could be heard was the resonance in my ears.

'Ah, you scum,' I groaned. 'You stinking pigs.'

Yet they stank no worse than me. For their masters they raped my girl with a broom handle. For Queen and Country I let them.

I didn't see or hear them leave. I simply sensed, after a while, that I was alone – alone with Linda, that is, be she dead or dying. Movement wasn't possible in any direction. So I lay there, breathing dust and listening to a distant dripping tap. That and the hiss of the lamps were all I had to listen to.

It sank in, infinitely slowly, that it wasn't a dripping tap I could hear, nor was it distant. It was close, a regular tick … tick … tick. Investigation was impossible but I could slither round, through a full three hundred and sixty degrees if necessary, by using the foot that was in contact with the ground like a paddle. It took a while and in the process removed most of the skin from my ankle bone.

The blank far wall entered my vista. Closer at hand were a pair of bare feet, toes turned in, somehow childlike. I watched the bright red dewdrop form and detach from the instep to splash into a spreading patch that glistened in the light of the gas lamps. My eyes traced it back to its source, via a red tendril to the top of her inner thigh, where the flow was stronger, thicker, branching out in places into tiny tributaries that wandered among the fine down on her legs.

The discarded broom handle, red-smeared from the tip for a good quarter of its length, lay in the dirt. I felt physically sick. My stomach churned and gorge hit the roof of my mouth.

'Linda?' My voice was a squeak a mouse would have disowned. I dragged up phlegm to clear my vocal chords. 'Linda … speak to me, for God's sake, speak to me!'

No response. Unconscious, maybe worse. I was in no position to help her. Duct tape is impossible to tear or stretch. My limbs were numb, even my body felt detached. Only the brain still functioned. And the voice.

So shout, you fool. *Shout.*

I shouted. I bawled at the top of my voice. The drip of Linda's life blood slackened and dried up. Which might be good news or bad, no way of telling. The lamps thankfully continued to provide light.

I shouted until my throat was raw and my lungs ached and a thirst such as I had never known came over me. I also, perversely, pissed myself.

But eventually somebody did come.

Chapter Twenty-One

Hospitals are not my favourite places to hang around. Whether it's the smell, or the association with disease and pain, or simply all that white paint, I've never analysed. But once inside, even as a healthy visitor, I can't wait to escape.

The Naval Hospital in Gib was no different from its civilian counterparts except that the majority of its nursing staff was male. The surgeon was a few years my senior, slight of build, his naval rank concealed beneath a white topcoat which he wore unbuttoned. We discussed Linda in the cream-walled corridor by the reception desk with its hulking orderly.

'She'll live,' the surgeon assured me. 'Couldn't save the baby though, I'm afraid.' He treated me to a practised look of sympathy. For simplicity's sake I had posed as the father. 'It was a boy. The womb was ruptured, there was a loss of fluid, you see. In any case the foetus was only twenty-six weeks –'

'Skip it,' I said, more brusquely than was warranted. 'How serious are her injuries?'

He hesitated.

'Come on, doc, give it to me straight.'

'Well, she'll get over them all right, and probably quite quickly. The external damage is mostly confined to her thumbs … the ligaments have been quite badly deformed but they'll heal in time. The facial bruising …' (Linda had been beaten, though not too brutally) '…is just skin lesions, no permanent scarring.'

'And the internal damage?'

He folded his arms, studied his shiny toecaps. I noticed a bloodspot on the sleeve of his white topcoat. It made me think of Linda, of her blood spotting the dirt …

'As I said, rupture of the womb ... it's unlikely she'll be able to bear children.' An expletive exploded through my teeth and he laid a consoling hand on me. 'I'm really sorry. We've done all we can to repair the damage. She's young, healthy, she'll recover fast. A week, ten days at the most. She lost a lot of blood, but we've replaced that, of course.'

'That's fine, fine.' My attention was elsewhere, wondering how precious to a woman was the ability to bear children. Very, I suspected. Yet another ruined life to be laid at my door.

'You haven't yet explained how she came by her injuries,' he said, looking stern.

'I'm not going to,' I retorted.

Nettled, he said, 'The police will have to be notified anyway. Clearly some kind of assault took place.'

'Superintendent Mascarenhas.' The name provided by Toby. 'Call him. He'll vouch for me.'

The doctor drew himself up and managed to add an inch to his modest stature. 'That will be my decision, not yours. This is a military establishment, may I remind you. She should really have gone to St Bernard's. If it hadn't been an emergency, we would have had to turn her away.'

'This has to do with national security,' I said irritably, his officiousness beginning to rile me.

Fortunately he took me at face value. He narrowed his eyes at me, and said, 'Very well then. I'll see what I can do.'

I caught his sleeve as he made to depart. 'While I'm here, may I see her?'

Five minutes was all they allowed me, and no talking. Not that she was capable of holding a conversation: heavily sedated, not yet emerged from the anaesthetic. A saline drip was suspended by the bed, delving into her arm. Her face, always pale at best, was as white as the crisp night-gown they had dressed her in, relieved only by dark smudges under her closed eyes and the purple flare of her bruises. So deathly was her pallor that I half-doubted the evidence of the heartbeat monitor, despite the bleeps that came from it at one-second intervals, and felt constrained to check her pulse. It was there all right, pitter-patter, feeble but regular. I stooped to kiss her, a tenuous meeting of lips. Hers moved, formed the faintest of smiles.

'Warner …?' Her eyes stayed shut. 'That you?'

'Who else are you on kissing terms with?' I said.

* * * * *

Major Ribble was waiting for me in the reception area in the company of a portly, rosy-cheeked man with coal black hair, who looked as if he had been sleeping in his clothes. Ribble introduced him as Superintendent Mascarenhas.

'You move fast, Superintendent,' I said as we performed the usual rituals.

'London seems to regard you as a VIP,' was his terse comeback, in accented English. 'I was told to jump if you said jump.'

'You look done in, Warner,' Ribble commented without sympathy.

I was also matted with grime from many hours spent on the cavern floor, not to mention ravenously hungry, having partaken of nothing more substantial than machine-dispensed tea and a machine-dispensed packet of tasteless biscuits, since the ambulance deposited me at the hospital around dawn.

Ribble, Mascarenhas and I had been allocated a minuscule windowless office, fitted out with utilitarian steel furniture in warship grey.

'Are you going to tell us about it?' Mascarenhas asked, lowering his bulk onto a tubular chair not dissimilar from the one to which I had been taped for half the night.

'Why not?'

I told them all that had happened since my return from Spain, without mentioning the reasons for my absence over the border. When I began to describe what Petrov and his sadistic sidekick had done to Linda, Ribble blanched under his tan.

'Is she all right?'

'Not good, but she'll pull through. Looks like she can forget about being a mother though, of this or any other kid.'

'Christ, that's tragic.'

Mascarenhas was more conditioned to brutality.

'We shall need to interview the young lady,' he said, jotting in a small black notebook.

'No, you don't,' I said firmly. 'She stays out of this. Anything you want to know, you ask me.'

He made no attempt to contest the point, coming as it did from a VIP.

'How did you escape?' Ribble said.

'I shouted for help.'

He gaped. Mascarenhas looked up from his notebook, disbelieving.

'Are you serious?'

'Sure I am. Luckily for us there was a guy, a hobo, crashed down for the night in another cave linked to ours. He freed me and helped me release Linda – the chain was hooked up to the ring bolt with a spring clip. He also helped me carry Linda to my car. I gave him some money, about fifty euros.'

'Do you think he was an immigrant?' Other of Mascarenhas' instincts had been aroused. Now he would want to conduct two investigations simultaneously.

'Later, Superintendent,' Ribble said, sighing. 'Let's not get side-tracked. I'd like this Petrov character and his girlfriend picked up.' He fixed me with a reproachful gaze. 'I'm rather surprised you didn't report this sooner, Warner. They've probably slipped across the border by now.'

He was probably right. I was too whacked to care.

'If you have all you need from me I'd like to go back to the hotel and get steam cleaned.'

'This Petrov character …' Mascarenhas' police pencil was poised as if in anticipation. 'Will you describe him, please? The woman also.'

I obliged, down to the mole I had noticed on Petrov's neck.

'Somebody must know him,' I added. 'He was at the charity dinner at the Holiday Inn a couple of weeks ago. He would have needed a formal invitation to get in.'

Mascarenhas jotted anew.

My duty to the authorities done, I made good my exit. Ribble caught up with me in the parking lot.

'You'd better have this,' he said as I unlocked the car. He slipped me my fake Andre Warner passport without the accent over the "e". 'Be sure to return the Donaldson one. It's needed elsewhere.'

'Roger. If GIBESTÁ haven't got cold feet about bombing their way to power I'll be in the market for more plastic within the next day or so.'

'Yours to command,' he returned with a grin and waved me away.

But I was not destined to luxuriate in a steaming bath yet awhile. As I pushed through the swing doors of the Caleta Hotel I bumped into Michael Vella.

'André!' His hand folded around mine, strong and firm and sincere. 'What happened to you? Where have you been this past week?' He took in my grubby demeanour, raised an inquisitorial eyebrow. 'You look as if you've been in the wars.'

'My apologies, Michael. I had to go and see an old friend in need. I only expected to be gone a couple of days, otherwise I'd have notified you.'

'We must talk.' He guided me through the reception lobby, into a corner of the Catalan Lounge Bar. 'My colleagues want to step up the bombing. They have voted to place a bomb every other day from now on.' He massaged the back of his neck. He looked as if he had passed a sleepless night or two. 'I'm still against it at a moral level, yet … we must do something. Time is so short. Our followers are demanding action.' His shoulders drooped. 'I'm afraid if we don't make a breakthrough very soon there will be real violence, possibly killing in the streets.'

'You'll end up under martial law.'

'Quite.' Glumly. 'The last thing we want is curfews, bans on meetings in public places. Martial law would finish us.'

We agreed to meet that evening at his apartment.

Finally making it to my room, I decided on a bath instead of shower. Cossetted by the hot water, I fell asleep only to wake to the shrill of the telephone. I wrapped a towelling robe around my hot wet body and got to the phone before it gave up. Predictably, it was Toby. I should have let it ring.

'I'm here in Gib,' he announced, sounding short of breath as if he'd run all the way. 'Flew in this morning. Richard Kirkland is with me.'

'How cosy for you.' I was still drowsy, the knell of doom too distant to detect.

'Put your humour in cold storage,' Toby said with gravel in his voice.

'You're to get over here immediately.'

'Where's here?'

'The Convent.'

The Governor's HQ. I was going up in the world.

'Don't feel like it. I've had a hard night.'

'You'll be collected – two pm prompt.'

The line went dead.

Rebellion stirred within me like the rumbling of a dormant volcano. Stirred but didn't erupt. When all was said and done, Toby and those above him were paying my wages and therefore entitled to order me about.

So I confined my defiance to my garb: sneakers, jeans, and an open-neck checked shirt, crumpled from too many days in a suitcase. Rounded off the ensemble with my black leather biker's jacket, always good for thumbing your nose at the establishment. Finally I removed the chip from my camera and zipped it away in my breast pocket. If nothing else I would be able to barter forgiveness with it.

My escort consisted of two hefty redcaps. They treated me more like a miscreant than the VIP Mascarenhas said I was, delivering me to the very door of the Governor's office. Inside, the three of them lined up against me: Toby, my calm-water friend; Richard Kirkland, the Prime Minister's private aide and hatchet-wielder. His own skin was all that would concern him. And, most exalted of all, there was the shiny new Governor: Sir Gilbert Dover, doll-like, politico-military, a career hybrid.

I had never been inside the Governor's sanctum before. It was tastefully done out in a mixture of English and Spanish, a lot of white woodwork on the walls. A blue and brown carpet, probably of Moroccan origin, well-worn so that the pattern had lost all definition. The floor was of wooden squares, laid diagonally, alternating light and dark in tone, and polished to military brilliance. Through the windows were treetops, the roof of the opposite wing of the building, and a piece of the Rock's tablecloth cloud. It was warm and the window was open, letting in the rumble of traffic and a variety of birds in full chirp.

When we were all seated around the egg-shaped conference table, including me, the inquest began. Kirkland fired the ranging shot.

'Explain,' he said, immaculate in pinstripes, every fine blond hair in place, 'your protracted absence, your lack of progress, and your relationship with the son and daughter of General Irazola. In that order.'

Toby was staring, you could say glaring, at me. No support to be expected from him.

'Well?' Kirkland rapped. 'What are you waiting for? A sign from above?'

'Balls to you, Kirkland. I was just trying to decide whether I should walk out and leave you all to catch the shit when it hits the fan.'

Toby shifted in his seat. His complexion was bilious.

'I suggest you confine your remarks to what's relevant, Warner,' Sir Gilbert said mildly.

'Then keep this creep off my back.'

Kirkland glared. Toby unbent enough to allow himself a flicker of a smile.

'All-righty,' I said, 'keeping it in chronological order, let's begin with my absence. Acting on my own initiative, I went to investigate a report of an unusual build-up of Spanish forces near the frontier.'

I stuck to the military statistics and left out any theorising. Let the "experts" do the figuring. I also omitted the sundry killings to which I was technically an accessory. It would all come out in the end, this dirtiest of dirty washing, but for now I wanted to concentrate their minds on the tanks and the guns and what they meant for Gibraltar.

Of the three of them only Sir Gilbert seemed at all troubled by my narrative.

'The reinforced armoured divisions and preponderance of helicopter gunships does indeed suggest something … er … abnormal is going on.'

Kirkland was mute, tapping steepled fingers against his chin. Toby murmured agreement, blew his nose into a handkerchief with the family crest woven into the corner.

'You all seem very calm about it,' I said, slightly uptight. I had run a substantial personal risk in following up the twins' tip-off. From the reaction of these three I might as well have stayed home.

'Spreading alarm with apocryphal stories might be just a blind to divert us from your failings in other areas,' Kirkland ventured with more than a hint of accusation. 'Are you sure you're not exaggerating the numbers?'

'Or mistaken.' Toby, more charitable.

I unzipped my pocket and flicked the chip across the table. Kirkland snatched it up.

'What's this?'

'Proof.'

The trenches of worry on Sir Gilbert' s brow deepened.

'You took pictures?'

'Video. How else to convince you I'm not "exaggerating."'

Kirkland's thin red lips formed an arc of dislike.

'Even if it bears out your assessment of the strength of the forces it doesn't prove Irazola's the C-in-C, or that it's anything more sinister than an exercise.'

'Irazola's C-in-C of the Southern Regional Command. If you have particulars of the regimental units it comprises you can check them against the numbers on the vehicles. Some of the shots are close-ups. In addition to which …' I let my gaze traverse the three of them.

'Yes?' Kirkland said irritably.

'You mentioned the Irazola twins. It was thanks to them I was tipped off about this. The only reason they knew about it because their father is commanding the force.'

Kirkland and Toby glanced at each other; Sir Gilbert merely looked enquiring.

'The *Irazola* children told you about these manoeuvres?' Kirkland spoke stiltedly, as if he found the words difficult to pronounce.

'Hard to credit, I guess, but true nevertheless.'

Kirkland exploded. 'Hard to credit! My God, Warner, if you aren't the fucking limit! Are you so gullible, man? Do you really think General Irazola's own children would rat on him, not to mention betraying their own country? You must be retarded.'

This wasn't quite running along the lines predicted.

'They explained that –' I began, only to have Kirkland chop me off with a hand slapped palm down on the table. Sir Gilbert winced at the mistreatment of Crown furniture.

'Explained it!' Kirkland laughed. 'I'll bet they did.'

'They're Basques, you see …'

'I don't care if they're Buddhists, you raving half-wit!'

If Toby hadn't stepped in then I might well have punched Kirkland, Prime Minister's crony or not.

'Hold on there, Kirkland,' he said in that steady calming manner of his. 'I don't think André has the full picture.'

'Nor have I, for that matter,' Sir Gilbert asserted with some feeling.

Kirkland made a gesture that implied disassociation. Abandoning his seat, he walked over to the window and planted himself there, back to the meeting, stiff with silent outrage.

'The Irazola twins are a pair of mischief makers,' Toby told me. 'The boy is a notorious adventurer who's already been in trouble with the police: suspicion of running drugs from Morocco, suspicion of implication in that frightful cinema bombing in Madrid last year and others since, suspicion of helping supply guns to various terrorist factions, and more. If it weren't for his father's position and influence he would have been serving a life sentence several times over by now.'

I could have added multiple murder to that list. Didn't dare.

'As for his sister, she's not much cleaner.' Toby shook his head; a lock of hair parted from the main mass and drooped over his forehead. 'Numerous affairs, a terminated pregnancy, rabid left winger, arrested several times for assault during demonstrations.'

'You seem to know a lot about them. Sounds more like scandal mag gossip than hard fact.'

This earned me a reprimand from Toby. 'Gossip forms part of the dossier of every subversive. Surely you were with the Secret Service long enough to have learned that much.'

'Why is the government so interested in a couple of delinquents?'

'Because Spain is a member of NATO. Officers of general rank of all member countries are screened periodically. That means their families too.' He spaced out the words as if he were addressing a child.

'Don't say it as though I should have known. Before this I was purely your sister's boyfriend. Your sleazy little world is foreign to me.'

Toby's face twisted in a sardonic smirk.

'Things haven't changed that much since you were part of our sleazy little world.'

My experiences in Finland on behalf of MI6 should have warned me of that.

'Got that straight now?' From Kirkland, without changing his stance.

'Some things I have to know. I'm doing a job for you in Gibraltar?'

'That's debatable.'

I shut up. I was fed up of being talked down to, made to feel like a small boy caught raiding the larder.

Sir Gilbert, who gave the impression of being as ill-informed as me, took up the cudgel.

'I'm not quite so ready to dismiss Warner's report as you two gentlemen seem to be. I'm responsible for the security of Gibraltar. Any potential threat should be investigated.'

'Waste of resources,' was Kirkland's terse dismissal, while Toby murmured concurrence.

'Better to waste a few resources now than wait until we face a full-scale conflict,' Sir Gilbert countered, to my silent cheers.

Kirkland returned to the table, incredulity radiating from him. Sir Gilbert regarded him gravely while tapping his fingers gently on the table surface, his gaze steady. Lilliputian he may have been, cowed he was not.

'Do you mean to tell me,' Kirkland said, 'that you attach credence to this invasion business?'

'Not necessarily. But nor do I believe in discounting unlikely possibilities.'

'Now look here, Sir Gilbert, we don't want you mounting commando raids into Spain when we're about to start talking to the buggers about Gibraltar. Right, Toby?'

'Spot on. Can't be done, Sir Gilbert.'

'I rather fancy I'm the best judge of that.'

Kirkland gripped the back of his chair, his knuckles white against the skin; I noticed the backs of his hands were quite hairless.

'Now listen to me, Sir Gilbert. You are not to make any forays into Spain whatsoever and for whatever purpose.' His index finger jabbed. 'That's an order and within an hour I'll have it made official.'

The fires of battle blazed in Sir Gilbert's piggy eyes. While he and Kirkland slugged it out I kept myself amused studying the assorted artwork spaced around the walls – portraits of monarchs past and present, studies in oils of the Rock from all conceivable points of the compass, and of course an election-year portrait of Mother Theresa, parrot-beak nose prominent. Otherwise forever to be known as Madam Brexit.

All of it a cosmos away from my old uncomplicated world of drug barons, mob rule, and vendettas. I was almost nostalgic for it.

Sir Gilbert lost the contest. He was too remote from the seat of power, and Kirkland and Toby too close to it.

The Great Spanish Invasion of Gibraltar having thus been publicly denounced as mischief-making on the part of the Irazola kids in cahoots with gullible Warner swallowing it as the genuine article, next on the agenda would be the stalled GIBESTÁ project, Operation Sideshow. Censure would be the least I could expect, now that I had nothing of value to show for my week's R & R in Spain.

Unless friend Petrov was a card of some value.

'How do you explain the presence of Russian agents here in Gib?' I said, making it a throwaway remark.

Sir Gilbert gave a kind of twitch. 'Russian agents? *Here*?'

'You mean this Petrov character?' Toby showed no special concern. 'We've read the police report on the abduction of your … er … friend. A nasty business.'

'Have they been picked up, him and his floozie?'

'Slipped across the border in the small hours. They were on Czech passports, posing as tourists. No reason to detain them at the time. You didn't see the police until much later, as I understand it. '

'I was pretty tied up,' I said, acknowledging my delay in alerting the police.

From a personal angle, it was an even greater pity that Petrov had made it into Spain. Thirty minutes alone with the Russian, with him bound to a chair instead of me, would have given me a lot of satisfaction. Inability to conceive would have been the least of his injuries.

'Nobody told me there were Russian agents here,' Sir Gilbert complained.

'We didn't know ourselves until an hour ago.' Toby said, in a consolatory tone.

'You didn't answer my question,' I pointed out to him.

'Why the alleged Russian presence, you mean?'

'We don't know the answer,' Kirkland cut in. 'It'll be investigated.'

The rays of the evening sun suddenly surged into the room, laying an oblique swath of light. Sir Gilbert's head was outlined against it, strips of pale pink scalp highlighted under the meticulous comb-over.

'Which brings us to the topic for today, André,' Toby said, with a modicum of glee, as if relishing the dressing down he was honour bound to deliver. 'Your progress report on GIBESTÁ.'

'I've been away,' I protested.

'Now you're back. We know what you've achieved so far.'

'Now we want to know what you're *going* to achieve.' From Kirkland. He couldn't resist stamping his authority all over me.

'What about a drink first?' I said in my best ingratiating voice. 'Gin and lemon, if you have it.'

If I was going to be hammered – which I surely was – I might as well cushion the blows with some Government booze.

Chapter Twenty-Two

Bomb number two was to be bigger and louder. It was to be placed so as to demolish part of the Supreme Court, just down the road from the Governor's residence. It was meant to be a nose thumb at Sir Gilbert who, thanks to a warning from me, would be nowhere in the vicinity when the ten kilograms of HE went boom.

The afternoon of the day before the planned bombing I paid my ritual call on Linda, now in her third day of convalescence. Her recovery had been faster even than the consultant's best hopes.

'They build 'em tough in NJ,' she grinned, when I commented on her vitality.

On my previous visits our dialogue had been limited, the pain-killing drugs dulling her intellect. Today she was altogether more vibrant. She made no reference to the events that had brought her here, nor to the loss of her child, if that loss had penetrated through the sedatives they were still pumping into her. She was as yet still ignorant of the permanent damage. That unpleasant duty was mine alone. Part of the hair shirt I had to wear for having failed first to protect her and then to save her when – possibly, though not certainly – it had been within my power.

All this said, I felt I owed her an explanation about my mission, an end to the secrecy. She was now, albeit unwillingly, a part of it. So, without pausing to soul search, I told her as much as I dared. It was a major breach of the Official Secrets Act that, if it got out, would earn me a long spell behind bars.

Her eyes grew enormous as I unveiled the scenario. Few people can credit the dirty tricks that democratically-elected governments get up to, though Watergate should have dispelled all illusions.

A hushed 'Yikes!' was her gut response to it all. Then a short period of reflection. 'You mean you've been cosying up to this GIBESTÁ lot just to bring them down?'

Not contempt, just awe.

'Look, honey, this is new territory for me. When I was in the Secret Service I worked overseas, keeping an eye on the Russians, the Chinese, and the Middle East.'

'All right, James Bond, I'm impressed. But why should your lot imagine that this independence movement will weaken their position at these talks you mentioned? Independence wouldn't mean Gibraltar was pro-Spanish, just neutral. Governments are so bloody neurotic and self-centred. It's unbelievable.'

'It's a weakening of the pro-Brit stance Gib has been so famous for, that's all. The Spanish will count it a factor in their favour and they'll exploit it, be less inclined to settle for a few cosmetic concessions – which is all our side is prepared to offer.'

Linda reached for a bottle of Lucozade at the side of the bed, became snarled up in the drip hose. I disengaged her, took over the job of pouring.

'Want some?' she asked, between gulps.

'Only if you've got some gin to lace it with.'

'Warner …' When the tumbler was empty. 'When that bomb was planted, the one that didn't go off, you were, like, it's nothing to do with me.' She tugged nervously at the high neck of her unbecoming night-dress. 'It *was* something to do with you, wasn't it?'

Today was coming-clean day. 'It was me, period. I'm sorry I had to lie when you asked before.'

'But where's the sense in it? Are bombs supposed to make people want independence?'

'It's more complex than that.' To elaborate would be to invite the bawling out I had so far escaped. 'Let's just say there won't be any more.'

'Hey, on the level? You mean you're gonna quit?'

Her incredulity was not misplaced.

'I wish. But this job's not for quitting, honey.' I left the bed to stretch my legs. The window was full of the grey upsweep of the Rock, as yet untouched by the morning sun. 'But I'm done with bombs. I'm going to bring it all to a conclusion some other way. And don't ask how. There are still limits to what I can tell you.'

Or want to tell you. I was ashamed of what I was about to do. Shame alone wouldn't deflect me though. That would take an Act of either God or Government.

'While you were away I met your Michael Vella,' she said. 'He came to the hotel looking for you.'

I remembered Vella complaining about Linda's reticence.

'There were two of them,' she added. 'I forget the other guy's name. Behaves like a volcano about to go off.'

'Peter Vitali. He represents the hawk faction of GIBESTÁ.'

'Ah. Vella, I imagine, is the chief dove.'

I wondered what Vella had said to lead her to that snap assessment.

'I liked him a lot,' she went on. 'This place could do a lot worse, I reckon. He's got to be a better deal than your Brits and those pathetic creeps who run the show now.'

I aimed a pretend sock at her jaw. 'Marxist.'

'Woman beater.'

To steer the talk away from the subject of GIBESTÁ I went on to relate how I had failed to convince my principals that an invasion was looming and how they had converted me into believing I was the victim of a hoax.

'No way was that a hoax!' Linda said, with a vehement headshake. 'Listen, I may not go a bundle on Julio's kids, especially Elena, but I'd stake my reputation they weren't just goofing off. What happened that day, after you conned those guys in the jeep to chase you?' She gnawed at her lower lip. 'I heard shooting before you took off. Did anybody get hurt?'

I returned to the bed. Springs creaked when I sat. It was a very old iron bed, old enough possibly to have seen service during the great siege of 1727.

'Not on our side. And it wasn't my doing.'

'You didn't need to tell me. You're no killer.' She leaned forward to land a smacking kiss on the tip of my nose. 'Lady killer, maybe. Ow!' She sank back fast into her pillow rubbing her stomach tenderly. '*Ooh*, that hurt.'

'Shall I call the nurse?'

'No panic. Just a twinge. They warned me to stay still.' She grinned roguishly. 'Never could get the hang of it though. What happened to the Irazola kids anyway?'

'We split up.' It came out too fast to be natural and earned me a probing appraisal. She was shrewd enough not to pursue it.

'So don't tell me. Tell me something else though, Warner …' Head tilted, eyes bright and quizzical. 'What's in this screw-up for you?'

'It's a job and I'm being paid,' I said. 'If I'm going to be hundred percent honest with you, I was also in the market for some action. I was running a bar, and it wasn't really my thing.'

'A bar? You're right, it doesn't sound like you.' She chewed on that for a few beats. 'Did you do anything between quitting the spy game and running the bar?'

What had she said? *You're no killer.* Goes to show you're no judge of character either, Linda.

'I got religion.'

She spluttered with mirth and was still gurgling when a nurse backed in toting a trayload of lunch and ordered me off the premises.

* * * * *

For all its stout aspect the door of Michael Vella's apartment was no challenge to a housebreaker: an ordinary Yale-type cylinder lock vulnerable to a strip of plastic carved out of a bottle of wash-up liquid. A light downward pressure along the curved edge of the catch whilst nudging the door panel with my knee and I was inside. A breeze. It still brought me out in a sweat.

The apartment was unoccupied. I had watched Vella leave ten minutes earlier, driving off towards the town centre in his Mercedes wagon. After he turned the corner I made no move for five minutes in case he'd forgotten something. It took five more to gain entry to the apartment block and stage my break-in. I had allocated a further twenty in which to secrete away the parcel.

Guided by the slender beam of my penlight I crept through into the living room. The freezer was my objective. As was to be expected it was in the kitchen, in a corner. The upright kind with wire frame trays, which didn't suit my purpose as well as a horizontal model would have done. No matter. Penlight between my teeth, I dragged out the lowest drawer, removed packets of frozen this and that, mostly vegetables. He was partial to asparagus if the profusion of packets was any guide. Powdered ice sprayed across the tiled floor. Couldn't be helped, I was bound to make a mess no matter how careful I was, so no sense in going slowly.

The tray emptied, I unslung the bag from my shoulder. Ten kilos made a sizeable parcel – too sizeable, I discovered. Fortunately it had been split into five 2kg packages. I rammed three into the back of the empty drawer, loaded the frozen food packs back in until I ran out of space. It was a shoe-horn fit and the drawer protested as I pushed it shut, showering more ice granules over my hands and the floor. The two residual packages I returned to my bag.

I checked the time. Ten, eleven minutes had gone of my allocated twenty. Now, a dust pan and brush and a cloth, and I would be gone, leaving no mementoes of my passing. Warner the phantom burglar.

Vella's kitchen was a modern fitted job and the broom cupboard was easy to spot – the only full-height door in the line of cupboards. It did not, however, contain a dust pan. Four minutes to go. Improvise, improvise, In the course of seeking a makeshift dustpan I came across the real McCoy, under the sink, complete with clipped-on brush.

A set of headlights from a turning car lit up the wall with its pinewood slats and the low-slung ceiling light over the table, then all was dark again. By now my jaw was aching from biting on the penlight. The ice crystals had travelled far and wide. I swept them into the dustpan and mopped the floor dry with a couple of segments of paper towel torn off a roll by the sink. The ice and the sodden towels went in a swing-top bin. My last act was to return the utensils to their cupboard.

I was heading for the door when the unmistakeable sound of a key sliding into the lock cylinder rooted me to the spot. I snapped off the penlight and, before disorientation set in in the ensuing blackout, nipped around the freezer and flattened against the side of it. Bloody thin cover. Let him take but a few paces into the kitchen and I would be discovered.

'Take a seat,' Michael Vella said to persons unseen. 'I'll just slip into something more comfortable then I'll join you.'

'Take your time.' The voice was Ben's. 'We're early anyway. Is Warner coming?'

'Not tonight.' Vella's reply was indistinct. 'Nor Peter, nor Eduardo. Tonight's meeting is off the record. Just between the three of us.'

'Now I'm intrigued.'

Me too.

Glasses clinked somewhere. I only hoped they wouldn't come looking for frozen carrots.

'You want some of this, Maurice?' Ben, doing the drinks.

'Go on then. Just enough to settle the butterflies, huh? No more'

I crept out from behind the freezer cabinet. I placed Ben and Maurice in the living room, Vella in his bedroom. The entrance hall and front door were in full view of both rooms. Safer then to delay making a break until they were all closeted together, preferably behind a closed door, even though sticking around heightened the prospect of discovery.

A smacking together of hands and Michael Vella's booming voice: 'I see you've made yourselves at home. Let's get straight down to business then.'

'Hear, hear.' This was Maurice. 'I am in trouble from my wife; we have guests coming tonight. What is so urgent that it could not wait until the weekend?'

'Just this, Maurice. I want to cancel tomorrow's bombing, and stop the campaign altogether. Either you agree or I will resign.'

What was this? A schism in the making? My hands mentally rubbed together. It could only be a nail in the coffin of the movement.

Ben was the first to react. 'You're bluffing.'

'Call my bluff and you'll see.'

'Why isn't El Jefe here? Have you told him?'

'I don't need Eduardo. All I need is you two to vote with me and the bombing stops.'

'To hell with you.' Ben, angry. 'Do you think you are indispensable?'

'Not quite. But if I was to step down now, GIBESTÁ would never recover, certainly not before the Madrid talks.'

The freezer motor burped into action right by my ear and I only shot a foot into the air.

'Why now, Michael?' Ben had gone from a snarl to a whine. 'Just when we are beginning to win.'

'Win?' Vella's voice was a lash. 'Nobody wins when you use such methods, can't you get that into your heads? What is left to win if you have to smash and destroy on the way. All we shall inherit is rubble and a people to whom violence will have become acceptable as a means to an end. Listen, both of you: when our political rivals seek to remove us, as they will surely do one day, will they not feel justified in using the same techniques? In time our country will be as synonymous with perpetual violence as Northern Ireland was, or Syria is.' A thumped fist. 'I will have no part of it!'

While my brain was assimilating this development the kitchen light came on, dazzling me and paralysing me in one. Footsteps, coming closer, then the easily recognisable opening of the door of the fridge, which stood next to the freezer. Now I had good reason to be grateful that Vella had chosen an upright model.

I held my breath while Vella – it was sure to be him – rummaged in the fridge. He was whistling softly through his teeth, no tune. A tearing of polythene, the fridge sighed shut. Now, surely, he must come past me to the sink and it would be all up with me, cover and plot both blown.

But he didn't come to the sink. When the kitchen light snapped off I slid to the floor, weak with relief. The talk in the living room was now muffled, the words indistinct. Vella, bless him, had closed the door. Regret at being shut out of the evolving drama took second place to the need to put distance between me and Vella's freezer.

Lights were on in the hall, which eased my exit. I slipped out, retaining the door catch with my little strip of plastic to prevent it from snapping back. A fast descent, three stairs at a leap, to the ground floor. In the street, I set a brisk pace towards the town centre, past the cable car station, to pass under the ramparts at Southport Gates. A clock chimed ten. The evening was still young, if only I had someone to enjoy it with. Officially though, I wasn't even here. I was an unperson.

The Three Owls bar in Irish Town was bustling and noisy. Noise is great cover for private phone calls. I tapped out a number on my cell phone. A single bleep and the receiver was lifted.

'Mascarenhas.'

'Sideshow. Go ahead.'

End of conversation.

* * * * *

Vella was arrested later that night for possession of explosives with intent to cause injury to person and property. For good measure Ben and Maurice, who were still with Vella when the police swooped, were also taken into custody.

'What a coup!' Toby, phoning from London, crowed. 'Masterful. You've excelled yourself, André .'

'Yeah, thanks.' I felt flat. Dirty, too. 'He was planning to call off the bombings.'

'Who – Vella? Irrelevant, dear boy, irrelevant. It's debatable whether they did his cause more harm than good anyway.'

I skipped my morning visit to Linda. She would wonder why, but I wasn't up to the inevitable inquisition. She had a knack of making me look inside myself and not like what I saw. Same as Maura used to. Not that I required any external assistance right now.

While I was sipping an aperitif in the hotel's Arcadia Bar I was paged to come to the front desk. It was Peter. White faced, lower lip protruding aggressively. More volcanic than ever.

'How did that stuff get into Michael's flat?' he hissed within earshot of a lobby-full of staff and guests.

'Are you trying to get me arrested?' I snapped back, fuming at his lack of discretion. I hauled him away from the desk. The hall porter stood back in alarm as we crashed through the swing door and into the parking lot.

'Don't say anything,' I warned him.

The rough handling seemed to sober him. He shook free of my grip and we strode stiffly along the road, the Great Dune on our right, soaring up to the crest of the Rock.

'Now,' I said, as we cleared the hotel precinct, 'what are you trying to tell me?'

Peter's lip curled. 'You mean you had nothing to do with planting explosives in Michael's freezer?'

Long practice in living a life of double identities had made me adept at manufacturing outrage. 'Why do you assume that? Shit, man, we're on the same side.'

'You're on nobody's side. I realise that, even if Michael doesn't. And obviously it was you. Who else has access to explosives?'

My derisive laugh was also manufactured.

'Any number of your enemies, including the Government.'

That quietened him for a moment. He laid a hand on my arm, forced me to a standstill.

'Do you deny it then? It wasn't you?'

'Is it likely, schmuck? I mean, you haven't even paid me for that last bomb yet. Would I be so dumb as to bite the hand that feeds me?'

'You might. If ours *is* the hand that feeds you.'

He left me before I could drum up a riposte, to stalk back towards the hotel. I let him go. His suspicion was unsurprising, his shrewd insight goddam disturbing.

I stepped over the low wall at the roadside, located a suitable rock for perching on. The sea, sunlit, winked at me. An old man was fishing from an overhanging crag, making frequent casts, reeling in fast, obviously using a spinning lure. The ozone smell was clean and pure, and made my private world all the grubbier by comparison. What sickening irony that Vella alone of the GIBESTÁ hierarchy had opposed the bombing campaign and, ultimately, had been prepared to stand on his principles, and yet it was he, not Peter, not Eduardo, who now languished in the can and stood branded as a terrorist of the worst kind.

Well done, Warner. As neat a frame-up as anyone could wish for. Pat yourself on the back, celebrate a little; better still, celebrate a lot. The Government treasure chest is at your disposal.

It almost made my old profession as an assassin seem honourable.

The fisherman had made a catch: a strip of silver was threshing at the end of the line, dodging his clutching hand. At length he got a grip on it, discarding the rod to free the hook from the gasping mouth. He cackled wheezily in his triumph.

My next move was not so clear cut. It didn't necessarily follow that the incrimination of Michael Vella would lead to the demise of GIBESTÁ. Assuredly it would weaken it, cause some loss of momentum that, with the talks now looming, could prove fatal to its cause. For the present though, all I could do was sit on my butt and let developments develop, so to speak.

Depressed, I retraced my route to the hotel. As I entered the parking lot a multi-coloured cab pulled up at the hotel entrance. A girl dressed in leggings and a short jacket got out. She stared at me, a slow smile creasing her face.

'Hello, André,' Elena Irazola said. 'I've come to collect the car.'

Chapter Twenty-Three

The Irazola twins had barely entered my thoughts since I parted company with them. I had wiped them from my memory, as one does a particularly unpleasant nightmare. The impact of the murders committed by Luis had faded to a distant ache.

'How's Luis?' I said.

Her expression clouded.

'He is well. He is at home.'

'Got away with murder, did he?' I said harshly. 'Daddy must carry a lot of influence.'

The taxi drew away and she came closer. My olfactory senses were titillated by her perfume. The rest of me wasn't. The prospect of a romp with Elena no longer appealed.

'It is nothing to do with Papa. No one knows Luis did what he did. Nobody saw us clearly enough to identify us except those four soldiers.'

'No, that's right. And they're all dead.'

'Can we talk? Without anger, I mean.'

That made me cool down fast. Elena wasn't responsible for her brother's misdeeds and I had no cause to suppose she condoned them. Hadn't she even tried to prevent him from killing the Sloothaak woman?

So I apologised. We took tea on the terrace, overlooking Catalan Bay, all very civilised. She had come, I discovered, not only to pick up her car but to deliver a message.

'Who from?'

'It is in writing.' She dug in her shoulder bag. 'From my father,' she said as she placed the white envelope on the table before me.

I was tempted to let it lie but my curiosity was too strong. Inside was a card, printed in fancy italics with the general's full name and, below it, an address I didn't recognise.

It read, in a precise hand that was of nearly the same standard as the printing:

Mr Warner

May we meet? Elena will say when and where. I owe you an explanation.

Your servant.

And a signature that bore no resemblance at all to the rest of the handwriting. The 'servant' bit was pure irony.

'Meet for what?' I asked Elena, my mind racing with the implications and whatever else minds race with when confronted by an unexpected situation.

Her eyes over the cup were solemn.

'He didn't say.'

Another attempt to muzzle me, perhaps for good? Not that he would know it, but he had no cause to nibble his nails over me. I had revealed all there was to reveal about him and his schemes, and the lack of interest from high quarters had been resounding.

'He doesn't say where.'

'Anywhere but here. In La Línea if you like.'

'Not a chance. He's not getting me back into Spain.'

'But he cannot come here. He dare not. Someone would recognise him. How would a Spanish general explain a visit to Gibraltar?'

'Inspecting the fifth column?'

A small line of irritation formed at the bridge of her nose.

'Be serious, André.'

Two small blonde girls rushed out onto the terrace squealing, one in the pursuit of the other.

'It's mine – give it back!'

'Shan't, it's mine!'

Once around our table then off back into the coffee bar. The squeals faded.

'Kids,' I said, in that indulgent tone the kid-less use on such occasions.

'What reply shall I give Papa?'

I thought about it. Was there any point? It wasn't the risk that bothered me. Not much, anyway. But risks should only be run for a purpose. Whatever Irazola wanted, it wasn't to make me a gift of his invasion plans.

Then that old professional curiosity came peeking through, like a shaft of sunlight following a downpour.

'All right. Tell him I'll see him in La Línea. We'll meet on the beach tomorrow, next to the border fence.'

'André …' Her voice was strained. It didn't sound like her at all.

'Are you all right?'

'I didn't want to see you. I wanted to collect the car, leave the note at the desk, then call you later for your reply. That's how it was supposed to happen.'

'But you have seen me. What's the difference?'

Her face crumpled, losing some of its loveliness.

'That *is* the difference, *mi cariño*.'

* * * * *

The La Línea beach at six in the morning was sparsely populated. A pair of joggers at the sea's edge preceded by a Lassie-type collie, were the only life forms in sight to ease my solitude. They trotted up to the wire fence that marks the start of the neutral zone between the two frontiers, coming round in a wide circle, their rhythm unbroken. A glance for me, squatting on a rock, as they padded by in perfect harmony, their dancing shadows misshapen in the rising sun.

It wasn't a very clean beach. It smelled of dead seaweed and faintly of sewage from the processing plant on the Gibraltar side. Litter density was about average for Spain and included an overturned supermarket cart with its castors missing.

The collie bounded over to investigate me. A sniff at each of my feet in turn before chasing after the joggers with a 'wait-for-me' bark.

The sun unstuck from the horizon. The sea was calm, slapping idly at the shore. To my right the Rock rose sheer, even the taller buildings at its base puny and frivolous by comparison. The gun emplacements high up were like empty eyes, watchful, yet with nothing to watch. The days of battle were long past. Even the solitary sentry patrolling the frontier had been dispensed with. Only the customs post and a few strands of wire stood between Spain and reconquest of the Rock. In short, it was vulnerable.

I rested on an elbow and imagined the sequence of events if Irazola was bent on marching in: seizure or destruction of the airport would be the key to a successful invasion. Control of the airport would make external reinforcement of the Royal Gibraltar Regiment, the Rock's only military unit, impossible. To bring troops in by sea would take too long; it would be all over before they embarked. Mobilisation alone would require a minimum of one week.

The more I examined the situation the more certain I became that Gib could only be defended if it made preparations. If the defences were strengthened and more men and especially more materiel were shipped in before hostilities opened.

But these were ridiculous suppositions! Spain wasn't going to invade Gibraltar. It was unthinkable, on a par with the Irish Republic invading Ulster. Spain and Britain were allies and joint members of NATO. They hadn't been at war since … since … the Peninsular War? Or was that Napoleon? European history was a shaky subject for me. Anyway, not for centuries. Okay, so Gibraltar was a running sore, it still wasn't worth a Falklands-style adventure.

'*Buenos dias, Señor* Warner.'

He had approached with such stealth I had been unaware of his presence. Had he been so minded, he could have killed me and I would have died by an unknown hand. A chilling thought.

'Good morning, General.' I stood up, brushing sand from the seat of my pants. We shook hands, warily, as if we each of us were handling a container of nitro.

'Thank you for coming,' he said in his flawless English.

He was not in uniform but in riding breeches and a grey corduroy blouson that was loose enough to conceal a gun. He looked alert and very fit. He had a lot going for him, whatever his ambitions. It was a shame that we were adversaries instead of allies.

Beyond him, where the sand became scrubby grass bordering the beach road, was a figure, perched on the hood of an olive green sedan. Indistinguishable but clearly more than mere bystander.

'Yours?' I said to Irazola, indicating the figure.

He didn't follow my look, simply nodded.

'Say your piece,' I growled.

He dipped inside the blouson. Defensive instincts instantly aroused, I stiffened, backed away, creating space to manoeuvre. But the hand emerged holding nothing more deadly than the well-remembered leather cigar case.

His chuckle was soft, but not reassuring.

'Did you imagine I would shoot you, here in full view of the town?' He swept an arm towards the concrete carbuncle of La Línea.

'No sane person would,' I conceded, 'but then you might be a madman.'

He took that in good part. 'I might,' he said, as I declined a cigar from the proffered case, 'but the possibility doesn't trouble me. I feel perfectly sane, That's all that matters to me and my men.'

He lit his cigar; he left the band in place, as always.

'We are civilised men, are we not, Mr Warner?'

'*You* may be, General.'

My answer took him slightly aback. Some of the self-confident ooze left him. When he spoke again the timbre of his voice was less cocksure, a trace more respectful.

'We know the reason for your presence in Gibraltar.'

'Is that a fact?' A little boat was putting out to sea on the Gibraltar side of the neutral zone. Over there, maybe a hundred metres away, was safety. Right then I envied the man in his little boat.

'To establish my bona fides,' he continued, 'I will tell you that I know you are here to break the GIBESTÁ movement. I will also tell you that I approve. Speaking personally and off the record, that is.'

That was unexpected.

'You surprise me. A trend towards independence is reckoned to be helpful to Spain's cause.' I was giving away no secrets. The Spanish Government would have figured that out for themselves.

'That is the conventional view.' He inspected the glowing tip of his cigar with a nonchalance that didn't convince me for a second. 'I don't suppose, by any chance, you were mixed up in the deaths of four of my men about two weeks ago, up in the hills behind Algeciras.'

'That's a funny question. I'm a civil servant, sort of. I don't go around killing soldiers.'

'Civil servant? Hmm, I wonder if that's what you really are.' He walked a short distance away from me, his riding boots crunching in the sand. He had small feet for a man, I noticed. He rotated slowly, cigar gripped between his immaculate teeth, profile on to me. It was a clean, classic profile, the nose straight and just the right length, the jaw assertive with no loose flesh beneath.

'So you were not there, spying for your Government, when my men were murdered?' A hint of anger in his voice now, well-contained.

'Spying on what?' The creation of distance between us was not accidental, only meant to appear so. Even more so than me, he was wise to all the tricks. We were both old dogs, only he was older and therefore more cunning.

His line of questioning so far was ambivalent. Was he investigating the deaths of four soldiers or plumbing the extent of my knowledge? If his forces really had been assembled for an invasion he had to know if the secret was out. If I thought he would accept it, I might have told him that the powers-that-be knew all, and didn't rate his chances of success.

'The day you brought Linda to my house,' he said, in an apparent switch of subject, 'you made some wild accusations. You realise it was all nonsense.'

'All of it?'

'Most of it. You took a few bare facts and mixed them with a great deal of hypothesis. Jumping to conclusions can be dangerous.'

'As you demonstrated.' The sand was so soft my feet were slowly subsiding into it. I shifted position. He watched me warily.

'General Irazola,' I went on, getting exasperated by the fencing, 'you asked me to meet you and here I am. So far all we've done is exchange chit-chat. Either you tell me what you really want from me or I leave right now.'

The blood rushed to his face. He glanced towards his unidentified companion. The latter seemed to tense as if in expectation. Waiting for a signal perhaps.

'I want to know,' Irazola said, 'how much you have learned and whom you have told.'

A last appreciative pull on his cigar before he flicked it away, three-parts unsmoked.

'We're wasting each other's time,' I said coldly and set off for the road. Irazola himself didn't budge but his companion stepped out smartly to intercept me. As we drew closer I observed that he was tall and very slim and most of all very familiar.

Petrov.

The VP-70 hammerless automatic Ribble had supplied as a precaution was not merely to make me feel better. Petrov was also armed, and only a fraction behind me on the draw. I was close enough to make out the fat silencer that almost doubled the length of his automatic. Silencers are less effective than propaganda would have us believe, but out in the open like this it would do an adequate job of finishing me off, without disturbing the peace.

We both stopped. It was a classic standoff situation. A man was cycling along the road that led to the beach but even as I watched he turned into a side street between two apartment blocks. The rest of the town was not yet up and about.

'Do nothing impulsive, my friend.' Irazola had moved up behind me and spoke into my left ear. 'My gun is also silent.'

'But mine isn't,' I reminded him. 'And when I start using it everybody will know what's going on here, including my people.' I aimed a nod at the Rock as if to imply we were under observation.

A low chuckle.

'You are right. I am only bluffing.'

'I'm not. I haven't killed anyone for a year at least.' To Petrov, now within conversing range, I said, 'Hello, fuck-face.'

'Be careful what you say, Englishman.'

'Tortured any more pregnant women lately?' I said breezily.

His sallow features remained as impassive as a carving.

Irazola frowned. 'Torture? You talk in puzzles.'

'Riddles, actually,' I said. 'Your friend Petrov is a throwback to your famous Inquisition. He could teach you Spanish a thing or two, couldn't you, Petrov?' As I spoke I rammed my automatic into the man's mouth, barrel foremost. It pulped his lips, carried on through his front incisors, and pushed them down his throat. He screamed and gagged at the same time, which can't be easy to do, and let go the nasty big pistol – I caught it before it hit the sand.

Retching and gurgling blood, Petrov sank to his knees. Irazola stepped forward to his aid, then had a change of heart when I jabbed him in the solar plexus with the silenced snout of Petrov's gun. Most men would have doubled up. Irazola wasn't most men though. A whoof of pain and an involuntary backward skip were the only effects.

Petrov was still choking on ingested molars and blood. His mouth was a scarlet pit and he was clawing at it with red-tipped fingers.

'Does it hurt, Petrov? Consider yourself lucky. If this wasn't such a public place it would be your balls down your throat, not your teeth.' So saying, I kicked the kneeling, swaying form in the fork as hard as I ever kicked a football. He didn't even scream. Just folded up, instant and total blackout. Too bad. I'd have liked to see him suffer some more, the way Linda had.

'Now you'll have to find yourself another inquisitor, General.'

Irazola lowered his gun. Arguably he could have shot me when I kicked Petrov. His failure to react told me he wasn't as confident of his immunity as he pretended.

'That much was true anyway,' I said. 'You are working with the Russians.'

He snorted. 'You're jumping to conclusions.'

'You would say that, wouldn't you?'

A car engine whirred behind the nearest apartment block but failed to fire. An empty bus rumbled around a corner, diesel engine clanking. La Línea was coming awake. Irazola holstered his gun hurriedly, more proof that even a Spanish General wasn't above the law. I stooped and used Petrov's pants leg to wipe the gore from the muzzle of the VP-70 before following Irazola's example.

'I could have you arrested for carrying that,' Irazola said.

'Go ahead. And explain him.' I stirred the comatose Petrov with my toe. 'And how both of you happen to be carrying silenced pistols.'

He squared his shoulders. 'We will meet again,' he said, with conviction, as if it were pre-ordained.

'Count on it.'

'I must remember not to underestimate you next time.'

In the rosy glow of that accolade I watched them go, Irazola supporting Petrov. They made for the olive green sedan. Irazola even flipped me a salute as he drove off. I hung around until the car turned off the road and its engine noise faded into oblivion.

A grey cloud had settled over the Rock, motionless as if tethered there. I walked to the sea's edge. No spectators. No one to see me lob first Petrov's pistol then the VP-70 over the wire to land in the sand on the Gibraltar side. The reverse of the method I had used before crossing into Spain a short while ago. At 5.30am. no one had been around to witness the deed. Now it was after seven, and joggers and strollers were about. But if someone found the two guns, at least they would be our finders, not theirs.

On the Spanish side of the frontier post Elena was waiting for me.

'You're up early,' I said in greeting.

'I came with Papa. Is everything all right between you and him?'

'We haven't kissed and made up, if that's what you're asking. He wants to know how much I know.'

'About the invasion?'

'Presumably. If there is to be an invasion.'

'You still question it?'

'Yes,' I said bluntly, aware that a border policeman was taking an increasing interest in us. 'Some of my associates suspect you may be pulling our legs.' We were speaking Spanish and I used the expression '*tomar el pelo*.'

Her disbelief refuted it.

'Why should I do that?'

'*Por gusto vivo*?' For kicks.

'Pah!' She threw her hands up. 'You do not deserve to be helped.'

'You're probably right.' I made as if to go on.

'Wait,' she said. 'Let me give you my telephone number. When you finally become convinced that Luis and I have told the truth you may need us again.'

The prospect of needing the murderous Luis was scary. But I took the card from her, consigned it to my wallet.

She angled forward to kiss my cheek. 'Take care, André. However this turns out.'

'You too. If ever your father finds out what you're doing you may discover that blood isn't always thicker than water.'

I crossed the border on foot, waved through by a yawning border police officer, and walked down to the Gibraltar side of the beach to recover the two automatics.

* * * * *

It was a simple enough equation.

Irazola, a Spanish general, and Petrov, a Russian agent of some sort, maybe now on sick leave.

Irazola plus Petrov equals Spain plus Russia.

The equation couldn't be that simple. Spain, at its most left wing, was a Social Democracy, albeit of post-war vintage. Spain would not climb into bed with Russia and Vladimir Putin.

Longer, deeper deliberation. My conclusion was that not even the prize of Gibraltar would induce Spain to alienate herself from her military and trading partners in the Western World. The price was too high.

So approach it from a new angle, dummy: why employ a Russian agent to do your spying and torturing when you have a whole Army Corps of trained Spanish muscle men at your beck and call? Why buy allegiance, when you already have it for free?

Possible answer: because a deal had been cut and Petrov was there to represent his country and make sure it was honoured.

Speculation, speculation, speculation. It led to the conclusion that Spain and Russia were in cahoots, a hypothesis that didn't add up. When I got up from the breakfast table to pay a call on Linda I was still no further forward in my theorising. Still no nearer truth and reality. All that could be said with certainty was that under the ever more scummy surface of the stagnant pond that was Gibraltar, something was seething. The rattle of sabres was in the air, and the spit and crackle of musketry, and it was daily growing louder. If I wasn't careful I was going to get caught in the crossfire.

* * * * *

On my previous visit to the hospital I had brought Linda's iPad and she was toying with it when I popped my head around the door. Her smile was less brilliant than usual, not much more than a reflex.

'Oh, it's you,' she said, and offered only her cheek for me to buss. 'I've been watching that demonstration outside the Governor's house on Sky news.'

The demonstration she referred to had been organised by GIBESTÁ the previous evening as a protest against the arrest of their leader. Some scuffles had taken place and here and there a window had been smashed. In most respects though it had been an orderly affair. According to which estimate you believed, as many as seven thousand Gibraltarians had participated, over twenty percent of the indigenous population.

'What's up?' I asked as I pulled up a chair.

'If I ask a you a direct question will you give me a direct – and truthful – answer for a change?'

My mind engaged gear, trying to predict what was coming.

'If it doesn't put me in breach of contract. I've already been a heap less discreet with you than I should have been. Don't make me betray secrets, honey.'

'Secret or not I've got to ask: were you responsible for what's happened to Michael Vella?'

I took refuge behind a veneer of surprise. 'What makes you think I might be?'

'Something you said the other day. You talked about bringing your job here to a conclusion. You were kinda shy about saying how.'

I remembered. I studied her, She was paler than usual, her eyes pink around the edges and slightly bloodshot.

'Have you been crying?'

She sat upright with a jolt, bringing her face up close enough to mine to rub noses. 'Don't give me any bum steer, Warner. Just level with me – was it you? You're the bomber, you've got access to explosives. If figures that you must have planted them on him!'

'Leave it, Linda. I told you – I can't talk about it.'

She twisted away from me. A handkerchief appeared from under the sheets and she blew her nose into it.

'It sucks,' she said, two words only, but steeped in recrimination. 'I don't care what your motives are, it's a lousy, lousy deal you gave that poor sucker. How can you live with yourself?'

'The world's a dirty place.'

'Sure it is, it's a stinking sewer. But that doesn't mean you got to go swim in it. You don't need to do this, Warner.' It was a plea straight from her heart. The caring Linda, making a rare showing.

'Don't delude yourself. Vella will stay behind bars until the authorities decide he can be set free. It's out of my hands.' I reached for her, but she shrank away. 'Surely you can see that.'

'Is it out of your hands?' Her look was withering. 'Couldn't you publicly confess? They wouldn't dare arrest you, after all you're one of ... one of *them*. They might kick you out of the ... what do you call it ... Civil Service. But so what? I tell you this, buster, I'd sooner make a living flashing my snatch at a roomful of jerkoffs than doing a tenth of what you do.'

Stung, I retorted, 'And you'd still be doing it if it wasn't for me. And who are you concerned about anyway – me or Vella?'

That flustered her. She made some uncoordinated movements with her hands, finally said, 'You ... both of you. Vella I hardly know, but he strikes me as a good man ... sincere ... you remember that word? But it's you I worry about. You're too good for this cruddy business.'

'Linda ...' This time she didn't shrink away but let me take her hand, let it lie limply in mine like a dead fish. 'It's a job of work I'm doing, like any other. It's in the interests of the people of Gibraltar.' Did I really swallow that? 'It's in the interests of world peace and security.' More baloney. And if *I* wasn't convinced how could I hope to convert her. I shifted tack. 'Look, maybe this isn't the right time to say this but I thought maybe ... you and I could –'

'Don't say it, Warner!' she flared. 'You're goddam right – this isn't the time. I need to think, sort things out in my head.' The appeal in her eyes touched me. 'So do you. My God, so do you.'

* * * * *

I took the Aston at a faster lick than was safe up narrow, climbing Queens Road, the sprawling city below opening up as I left the Rock Hotel and the Casino in my wake. The tip of the runway poked into sight below, thrusting out into the blue bay. A battered van coming towards me slowed and cowered into a recess in the road to let me past; the Aston needed a lot of space and I wasn't in a forgiving mood after Linda's harangue.

At the barrier, I handed over a £20 note to gain access to the Upper Rock. From there I travelled by obligatory taxi to the Upper Galleries, part of the thirty miles of tunnel bored and blasted through the Rock by the British army.

Peter had phoned while I was brushing my teeth. He urgently needed to meet me and it was peremptory summons, not a request.ne

'Where?' I said. 'Better be discreet.'

'St George's Hall.'

'Is that in the town?' I asked, still unfamiliar with much of the geography.

He laughed coldly. 'It's not a building. It's part of the Upper Galleries, the tunnel system. Anyone will tell you how to get there. When you enter the tunnel just keep to the main thoroughfare, you can't miss it.'

When I pressed him to say what it was about, he clammed up.

'Two o'clock, right?'

It had begun to rain when the taxi dropped me at the observation platform by the entrance to the Upper Galleries. I wandered to the edge of the platform, to look out over the low wall, out past the airstrip and the frontier, to La Línea and beyond, the Costa del Sol lost in the mist and rain. The strip of beach where I had met Irazola was monochrome, and it was hard to tell where the beach ended and the sea began.

A taxi crested the slope behind me, engine labouring in too high a gear. As I moved away from the wall it turned into one of the parking spaces, an old Peugeot with faded paintwork and a digit missing from its licence plate. No other cars; it was not a day for sightseeing.

Inside the galleries it was well-lit, and I was greeted by a life-size model in a glass cage of a "World War 2 tunneller", a member of the Royal Engineers whose skills had excavated most of the tunnels. Opposite, a blue plaque proclaimed this to be the Windsor Gallery, the work of a Sergeant Major Ince of the Military Artificers. It had been completed in 1783. Gibraltar was packed with history, inside and outside the Rock.

The floor was uneven and sloped downwards. I passed several more effigies of garrison troops and engineers. It was cold and my breath steamed the air but by setting a brisk pace I managed to stay warm. At intervals I came across gun embrasures, in which huge naval cannon were installed. Plaques were also a regular feature. One self-congratulatory testimonial read:

"*When the great siege ended in February 1783 this gallery was 370 feet long with guns mounted in six embrasures. The Duc de Grillon, who had commanded the enemy forces, when shown the gallery later, said 'These works are worthy of the Romans'.*"

Behind me I could hear other visitors, their voices carrying down the tunnel in whispers. The sound effects were akin to the interior of a cathedral. I buttoned up my jacket, shivering a little, and plodded on, still descending.

A vast chamber opened up on my left, having six … no seven gun ports. St George's Hall. Another plaque commemorated the holding here of a dinner in honour of the visiting US General Grant in 1878. 'Big deal,' I could just hear Linda sneering.

No Peter in evidence. That was okay, I was ten minutes early. I stepped over the rope barrier and did a quick scout of the chamber, working clockwise around the gun ports. The drop outside was sheer and the outlook stupendous – or would have been on a clear day. A dumpy jet airliner was lumbering along the runway to line up for take-off.

The seventh and last gun port was narrower than the rest and overlooked the road to Catalan Bay Village and the Caleta Hotel. The precipice immediately below the embrasure shelved away from the opening at an angle of perhaps seventy-five degrees, forming a shallow V in which some small plants and tufts of wiry grass clung in defiance of all normal pre-requisites for growth.

Behind me, in the chamber, a rush of feet. I turned away from the gun port, more in curiosity than alarm. I found myself in the midst of a group of figures. Before I could react my ankles were grasped and I was thrust upwards, backwards, and outwards through that hole in the mountainside, and into space.

Chapter Twenty-Four

I experienced a single blinding burst of terror as my head and flailing arms emerged into the damp air, my upper body gyrating in flight. The sky swung in an arc, the Rock's summit appearing momentarily to be capsized, the sea now overhead like a solid expanse of cloud.

An involuntary yell escaped me. Hard unforgiving limestone thudded into the base of my spine, expelling another, louder yell, of real pain. The sky ceased to tilt and my upended world of grey cloud and grey sea, flecked with white spume, stabilised. An upside-down ship was at anchor at the extreme limit of my vision, phantasmal in the drizzle. I was disorientated, no longer sure which was up and which was down. I felt dizzy then sick. My fingers scrabbled for purchase but found precious little in the slick black rock face.

I became slowly aware that I owed my present precarious security to the same grasps on my ankles that had launched me out through the embrasure. I peered up between my legs. A pair of hands was wrapped around each of my ankles, their owners' faces not on view. My pants bottoms had slid to my knees exposing my lower legs; my skin in that area was very white. Now I felt faintly ridiculous as well as afraid, a sign I was recovering from the initial shock. A face filled the space between my shoes, foreshortened by my angle of vision, but still familiar.

'Hello, Warner. How do you like it down there?'

Stay calm, don't get panicky.

'Hello, Peter.' Being head over heels made it difficult to speak naturally. 'Be a pal and pull me in, will you? I'm getting wet.'

An unsympathetic snigger from Peter.

'He says he's getting wet,' he relayed to unseen third parties, prompting a ripple of laughter.

The clouds beyond the summit were in jumbled motion, an optical illusion perhaps, since it was a windless day. Nausea bubbled up (or was it down) again, and was harder to quell. It was as if I were standing on nothing, walking on air, defying gravity. If I tilted my head backwards I would be able to see the road far below. I tried it and was immediately hit by vertigo. I gulped air. Tried to compose myself, to still my fluttering guts.

'What do you want from me?' I yelled. Nobody was listening. Peter had withdrawn his head, and only the two pairs of hands remained, all that separated me from death by falling from a high place.

To my relief, Peter's face again appeared in the embrasure. 'A confession will do.'

'What confession?' My searching fingers brushed against a tuft of grass clinging to a crack in the rock. I tugged it and astonishingly it held. It wasn't much, the roots would be near the surface and it would never bear my weight. But it was better than thin air.

'It's game over, Warner. You planted those explosives in Michael's flat, didn't you? Admit it and we'll bring you back inside.'

At that moment I would have admitted to child murder if it would have satisfied him.

'All right, all right,' I croaked. 'I admit it. Now for Christ's sake pull me in.'

The laugh was mocking now. 'And have you deny it the minute you're safe? We're not simpletons, you bastard. You've given us what we wanted. Now you're expendable.'

One ankle was released, leaving me suspended from a single pair of hands.

'No, wait!' It was as near a scream as I had ever managed.

'Goodbye, Warner.'

The remaining hands released me and I began my slide: my feet slewed sideways, the corrugations in the rock face chafing the exposed calves of my legs, my body pivoting on the tuft of grass that was my only lifeline. By some miracle the tuft didn't immediately tear loose. My lower half slithered further until I was near-horizontal. My arm holding the grass tuft was now at full stretch and the plant was bearing the greater part of my full weight. I sensed rather than felt it loosen fractionally. I grubbed frenziedly with my free hand for a hold: a crack, a nodule of rock, anything.

'André!'

My first inclination was to turn my head to the source of the call. But I was now so precariously balanced, with one foot caught on a slender ledge, that I was afraid to make the smallest movement.

'André – it's Michael!'

I groaned. Had he come to gloat over my demise?

'André, I'm going to tie my belt and my tie together and make a line. If you raise your other hand you'll just about be able to reach it.'

I was too shit scared to speak even as hope flickered within. Then the tuft that was taking my weight began perceptibly to shift. Hurry, Michael! From my new horizontal position I could look straight down the side of the Rock. A miniaturised red car was travelling along the shore road leaving faint tracks on the wet surface. Rain sprinkled my face as the drizzle intensified. It served to emphasise the dryness of my lips, the constriction of my throat brought on by extreme fear. The roots of the tuft were tearing away, I could feel them snapping one by one, breaking free of the tiny patch of earth that sustained them …

'Here – catch!' Something flicked my cheek. 'Get a grip on it – quick! That clump of grass is coming loose.'

Didn't I know it.

Now, like it or not, I had to move. Gingerly I brought up my free hand to seize the trailing end of what turned out to be his tie, winding it around until all the slack was taken up. The tuft tore loose the very instant I put weight on my new lifeline, and to make matters worse the general disturbance dislodged my foot from the narrow ledge.

'Christ!' It seemed as if the whole mountainside was on the slide. Clods of earth and a cascade of small stones hit me in the face. Like a pendulum I swung free, held by nothing more substantial than Vella's tie and the strength of his arms. Dangling, helpless, wholly reliant on a man I had tried to destroy. For poetic justice it took some beating.

'Try and find a foothold!' Vella's voice was ragged. He was taking my full weight. 'Hurry!'

His urging was superfluous. My toes were already foraging for purchase.

'There, to your left and above. There's a small ledge of some sort.'

My foot groped diagonally upwards and there it was, literally a toehold. But by laying my foot lengthways along it and pushing upwards I made a useful amount of vertical progress and took some of the strain off my saviour. Now I was able to look into Vella's eyes; his handsome concerned visage was puce from the strain of bearing my weight. I pulled in more slack. What was the breaking strain of a tie, I wondered.

Unaided I located a projection of rock at knee level. It wasn't much but it sufficed to lever me to within arm's length of the gun port.

'If you pull … same time … I push,' I wheezed, 'I can … reach the port.'

'Right … right.' His wheeze outdid mine. 'Together then – now!'

In conjunction we push-pulled. I went up like a launched missile, so fast that my forehead butted his chin and sent him sprawling backwards into the chamber.

'Sorry,' I said, grinning fatuously and delightedly, the lip of the embrasure tucked securely under my armpits, my head and shoulders inside the chamber.

'I've a good mind to let you stay there,' he said ruefully, testing his jaw with cautious fingertips.

From there on, exhausted though I was, I could have managed alone but I didn't spurn his final helping hand. I fell into the chamber, cracking both knees on the floor and hardly feeling it. Vella collapsed, completely done in, his breath sawing, his chest going like a mechanical bellows.

'Thanks,' I said, the word seeming drowned by the wild thud of my heart. It also seemed inadequate.

He gave a shake of his head, sucked in a great lungful of air, then said: 'Keep your thanks. It's explanations I'm interested in.'

* * * * *

We cabbed back to the parking lot by the barrier and sat in the Aston, the drizzle making runnels on the windshield, nothing ahead but grey soggy space. The mountains of Spain across the bay were invisible.

'I ran into Peter and the others leaving the gallery,' Vella told me. 'He claimed you admitted planting the explosives at my apartment. Is that true?'

Now mostly recovered from the trauma I was again thinking like a devious, scheming Government stooge.

'It's true I admitted it, not true that I did it.'

Bewilderment built up while he digested this.

'You mean you admitted to something you didn't do?'

'Wouldn't you in the same circumstances? Goddammit, I thought I was buying my life.'

He thought about that for a good minute then a smile broke lazily through. 'Perhaps I might have done the same,' he agreed, 'in the same circumstances.'

'Thank God you came along when you did.' I mopped ineffectually at my sodden hair with a Kleenex. 'How did you come to be there anyway? I heard you were a guest of Her Majesty.'

'I was released this morning. The police accepted that the explosives were planted in my apartment.'

Poker-faced, holding back my dismay, I said, 'Just like that? You mean the police think I did it too?'

'No, you're in the clear.' A sad expression stole over his face. 'Maurice confessed.'

That rocked me. 'Maurice! Surely he … but no, that doesn't make sense. If he really was responsible Peter would have had no reason for doing what he did to me.'

'Precisely.'

Rain drummed on the roof, a sudden intensifying. The cloud base had now descended so low we were sitting in it. The windows began to film over with condensation. I started the engine and the windshield defogger.

Vella gave himself a sort of shake. 'Maurice confessed purely and simply for the sake of GIBESTÁ. Because – and I speak in all humility – a change of leader now would be the end of us. He was prepared to go to prison so that I could continue leading the party.'

To hell with Maurice for a self-sacrificing busybody, was my private professional reaction. Thanks to him my scheme was now blown. Vella, wrongly-accused, would stand higher than ever in the esteem of the people of Gibraltar.

Then, through the frustrated rage, a reluctant respect for Vella began to penetrate. That a man could command such devotion that his followers were willing to offer themselves up as sacrifices. It humbled me. It also demeaned me and made me shabby. The bile of self-disdain rose in my mouth.

'How did you come to be there, in the gallery, when they chucked me out? Not that I'm complaining, just wondering.'

'Peter met me when I was released, said he was convinced you were the guilty party and that he was going to, er … make you talk, was the way he put it.'

'You can't fault his methods,' I grunted.

'I tried to stop him, but, well, Peter is an impetuous person. He dropped me at my place and went off in a great hurry. I was worried. I thought I should warn you. You weren't at the hotel so I went to see Linda. She said you had left about an hour before, said something about going up to the Galleries.'

To think I had so nearly lied to her about the venue.

'Your persistence saved my life. So again … thank you.'

'Even if it was you who planted those explosives, I couldn't have let them kill you.'

'Well, it wasn't me.' The lie, overlaid with the right degree of hurt and earnestness, wasn't quite effortless. I despised myself anew. This game of deceit and counter-deceit had never been one that I enjoyed playing, even when it was part of my profession. At least killing was clean and straightforward and didn't involve betrayal of people I liked and respected. 'Believe me, Michael. All right, so I blow things up for money, so I'm short on moral scruples, but even people like me have codes of honour. We don't cross our employers.'

His cell phone trilled. He clucked, extracted it from its belt holster and frowned at the screen.

'The bloody *Chronicle* again,' he muttered. 'Let them wait.' He disposed of the cell and his eyes swivelled back to me. 'It occurred to me … to us … that you may have other employers.' He cleared his throat self-consciously. 'Other employers, that is, with a prior call on your services.'

'Peter made the same accusation.' For a short while the only sound in the car was the whirr of the defogger fan, drowning the engine's purr. The car throbbed faintly, the powerful engine chafing to be away. Like me. Away from Gibraltar, away from the mire of politics and plotting. 'I think I can prove whose side I'm on, if you'll let me.'

'It's not necessary. I'm willing to accept your word.'

'No, I want to. But I need for you to meet someone … a Spanish girl and her brother.'

'You want me to go into Spain?' he said dubiously, as if fearing a trap.

'No, I'll get them to come here.'

'All right, André. If you think it will do some good.' He checked his watch. 'I really must go now; there is much to do.'

'Will you still need my services?'

I hoped he would say no. I couldn't see how going on posing as a bomber would help me succeed in my task. I had shot my bolt. The Warner cupboard of ingenuity was bare.

'We'll talk about it tomorrow.'

We arranged to meet. He got out and walked slowly to his car, parked askew across two spaces. And as he walked, a proud, statesmanlike figure, his silver hair glinting with moisture, it sank in how great was the debt I owed this man. The man whom I had betrayed, who had saved my life.

Slower to penetrate came the uncertainty, tentative at first then ever more insistent, about my mission and my loyalties. Suddenly, I was no longer sure whose side I was really on.

III

A ROCK TOO FAR

Chapter Twenty-Five

Toby called from London where, unlike Gibraltar, they were enjoying a heatwave.

'Another foul-up, André?' It was not a reproof. His voice, even from a thousand kilometres away, was tired, dispirited.

'If the police here weren't so quick at accepting false testimony Vella would still be safely in the slammer.'

And I would be dead.

'If-if-if. I've heard it all before. That man … what's his name?'

'Maurice Pilcher.'

'Yes. I gather he had already made his so-called confession public before seeing the police. They could hardly hush it up after that, could they?'

A suitable answer escaped me.

'Now that Plan A's failed, is there a Plan B?' Toby went on. 'Are you going to deliver at all?'

'I'm working on it.'

'Work fast. Five days from now the British delegation arrives in Madrid; ten days from now the Conference begins. You're on a short fuse. And so am I. And so's the PM.'

'Leave it with me.'

Unusually, he took it no further. Resigned, perhaps, to failure.

'One other thing, Toby,' I said, breaking into his goodbye. 'Did you look at the chip I gave you?'

'Chip? Ah, yes, the *fameuse* record of the Spanish Army preparing to wage war on us.'

'Well?' I said, when he didn't elaborate.

'Our experts agree they're genuine …'

'You don't say. Charitable of them.'

'...but that they don't prove where, or more pertinently, why. Added to which, we've warned you about the Irazola progeny. They're a malicious pair, not to be trusted.'

'Message received, Toby. No sense in depleting the Treasury further with pointless telephone conversations. Give Sam a goodnight kiss from me.'

I was mad, but not that mad. Still sitting on a fence of my own, between belief in an invasion and the urge to dismiss it as fantasy. Why I should bother in the face of such establishmental apathy beat me. I suppose deep down, however much I might decry it, I was a man of integrity. It was inborn or inbred, I don't know which, and I was presumably stuck with it.

I dressed soberly in my charcoal grey suit, settled a dark blue handkerchief in the breast pocket, and went to dine alone. Alone by design for once. I had much to mull over. Including the unprecedented rift that had been driven through my loyalties.

* * * * *

The venue for my meeting with Vella was the GIBESTÁ headquarters, an office in a disused bonded warehouse on a rundown wharf behind the Royal Gibraltar Yacht Club. It was not a spacious office and the seven of us made a tight fit.

We sat at a small laminated-top table that was overdue for retirement – the members of the GIBESTÁ hierarchy minus Maurice, ranged against Elena, Luis, and me. Luis had a large band-aid on his left cheek, where I had socked him. The sun had returned, but little of it percolated here. The only light was a bare LED bulb, too bright to look at.

Elena and Luis had willingly agreed to attend for the purpose of verifying what I was about to reveal to the GIBESTÁ council. Their vendetta, or whatever it was against their father, burned as fiercely as ever, it seemed. I had insisted on checking Luis for weapons but he was clean. Maybe he didn't want to push his luck by transporting a gun across the frontier a second time. With or without, he still made me jittery.

The meeting opened, not with an introduction by Vella, but to

Peter's blurted 'To make it clear where I stand, I –' He tapped his chest forcefully like a woodpecker going at a tree, 'have not changed my mind about you, Warner. I only regret that Michael took it upon himself to save your life!'

'Shut your mouth,' I said, with equal asperity. 'Ask yourself would I be here if I were the Judas you say I am?'

'You admitted it! Anything else is of no importance. Can't you see that?' he appealed to his fellow council members.

'Enough!' Vella imposed his authority on the gathering with that single word. 'These people …' He indicated the Irazola twins whose expressions reflected their bemusement, '… have not agreed to meet us to listen to your hysterical spluttering.'

'No, indeed.' From El Jefe. 'For my part, I am … what is the right word? … eager to hear why they have come. How do we know they are not spies? The Spanish Government would pay well for inside information on GIBESTÁ.' He smiled, rare for him, exhibiting an array of worn molars.

'My brother and I are Basques,' Elena announced, with the same blazing pride I remembered. 'The Spanish are our enemies. We are prepared to help you because we do not support their policy towards Gibraltar.' Chin up, every shapely centimetre the rabid revolutionary, she surveyed the four GIBESTÁ leaders and there was something scathing, even contemptuous about her regard. 'And because … of a personal matter.'

'May we be told what it is?' El Jefe said. 'This personal matter.'

'No.' Elena said shortly. I warmed anew to her. In spirit she and Linda were much alike: gutsy, hot-blooded, inveterate rebels.

'Let's get on with it,' Peter grumbled, 'farce though it is. What marvels is the famous Mister Warner going to reveal to us?'

'Just this, Peter – Spain is planning to invade Gibraltar.'

If stunned silence was the reaction I had wished for I should have been well content. Even unflappable Eduardo had no slick comeback to offer.

Four pairs of eyes swivelled from me to Elena and Luis.

'It is true,' Luis confirmed. 'An invasion force has been assembled twenty kilometres from your frontier. It consists of thirty thousand men and a considerable amount of armour.'

I felt sorry for Michael Vella. Here was this honourable, peace-loving man, being told that his plans for an independent Gibraltar were about to be consumed in the flames of battle, his precious GIBESTÁ and with it his whole *raison d'être* made impotent and irrelevant. His features caved in. He seemed to shrink in stature.

'How did you come by this … story?' Though inside he must have already accepted the truth of it, he couldn't bring himself to do so publicly.

Luis answered. 'The *Generalissimo* of this force is our father, General Julio Irazola.'

Collective shock rippled through the committee. No one spoke for several seconds. At length Vella roused himself sufficiently to say to me, 'Can you vouch for this?'

I nodded. 'All of it. I've met General Irazola, I've known Elena and Luis six months, and I've seen the invasion army with my own eyes. Not only that but I've passed the word along.'

'To whom?'

'Someone with influence at Westminster.' At this Vella perked up. I fashioned an apology with my hands. 'Before you pat me on the back, Westminster was not impressed by all accounts. Dismissed it as fantastic.'

It still rankled, that dismissal. Notwithstanding the infamous reputation of the Irazola twins, any hint, however vague, of another Falklands in the making ought to have merited further enquiries.

'Do you mean,' Peter said, his tone incredulous, 'that the British Government is aware of this invasion plan and don't intend to do anything about it?'

'Not quite that. They simply don't believe in it.' I didn't say why. Slighting the Irazola twins would only weaken their credibility.

'Do *you* believe in it?' Vella asked.

The question was inevitable. Much as I would have preferred to duck it, I also wanted to tell him the truth. He deserved at least that much. If only I was sure what the truth was. Mentally I ran through the supporting evidence: the Irazola twins' own conviction, be it real or pretended; the presence of such a large force with its unheard of preponderance in armour – if Luis was to be believed; General Irazola's apparent courtship of Russia; his attempts to silence me, to dig out of me how much I had uncovered of his scheming.

Everyone was watching me. As if my belief was the lynchpin on which the next move turned. If so, it was a large responsibility. All manner of wheels might be set in motion if I backed the twins.

'Yes, I believe in it,' I said at last, in a voice that sounded unlike my own. 'I think they're going to invade Gibraltar.'

Peter opened his mouth as if to refute it, then changed his mind and instead rose and moved across to where a wall map of southern Spain hung.

'Where exactly is this army?'

'A little to the west of north of Algeciras,' Luis answered. 'Find the town of Los Barrios, there is a lake to the north west.'

Peter traced a route on the map with his forefinger. 'I have it.'

'They are camped by the lake.'

Peter's breath whistled through his teeth. 'They could be here in a matter of hours,'

Vella joined him and together they bent forward to quiz the map.

'Even sooner than that,' Elena said. 'They have helicopters – many helicopters.'

'Not troop carriers,' I countered. 'Or not big ones, at any rate. The most they could transport at a single uplift would be, oh, five or six hundred men.'

'Not enough,' Peter conceded. 'They would need to outnumber the garrison here by two-to-one to be certain of victory.'

'The garrison has no tanks, no artillery to speak of,' El Jefe reminded him. 'No fighter aircraft.'

'We're bloody defenceless,' Ben growled, fishing out a packet of cigarettes. He handed them round; only Luis took one.

'That's what it amounts to,' El Jefe said.

I said, 'If they landed only five hundred men at the Top of the Rock restaurant, you would never shift them without air support.'

Vella came away from the map, brow puckered in thought. 'Their main force would come in via the isthmus. Which means we would have only two or at the most three hours warning.'

'And only then if you have Irazola's camp under surveillance by someone equipped with short-wave radio or a cell phone,' I said. 'Otherwise, how will you know when they're coming? If we could find out their timetable that would be better.'

'Either way, we're finished,' Vella said gloomily. 'How can we stop or even delay that many men with tanks.'

'By proving to the British that the invasion is a fact.' El Jefe put his deft finger on the only effective solution. 'We cannot defend ourselves.'

'Nevertheless, we must try,' Peter declared. 'We must make preparations in case all else fails. We must form a militia.'

Vella looked dubious, fingering the carbuncle that disfigured his upper lip.

'You won't stop an army corps with shotguns and air pistols,' I said. 'All that will happen is that people will die.'

'Needlessly,' Elena pitched in. 'My father will win, no matter what you do. Even if you arm every man, woman, and child in Gibraltar.'

This aroused Vella's pacific instincts.

'There are not guns enough here to arm a hundredth of the civilian population. Resistance would be pointless.'

'Have you no pride?' Peter almost shouted. 'I for one, won't surrender without a fight!'

'Nor I,' Ben said.

'Nor I.' El Jefe's impassive gaze passed over us all. 'Better dead than enslaved.'

'You exaggerate,' Vella rumbled, 'but I agree we must not meekly accept the inevitability of invasion. We need the British. As you said yourself, Eduardo, we must somehow make them take notice.'

'Meanwhile, I do not intend to sit around to wait for the tanks to roll down Main Street,' Peter fumed.

Returning to his seat at the table, Vella gave the twins a direct look.

'Will you help us? Will you be our spies and secure the necessary proof – proof that will convince the British and make them act?'

'We can try,' Elena said unhesitatingly, and Luis nodded assent. 'But we cannot guarantee to succeed.'

'About the invasion date,' I said, waving air space in Ben's cigarette smoke. 'Logically the general's zero hour must be linked to the

Conference, which is due to start on 8th May. Now, which would make the most sense politically and militarily – for the Spanish Government: to launch their invasion before, during, or after the Conference?'

There was silence while six intellects sifted through the options. A ship tooted in the harbour. Some small creature scampered overhead. My own stance was already thought out but I wanted to hear others' before I aired it.

'Not before.' Luis was first to contribute. 'They would be branded as out-and-out aggressors, like the Japanese at Pearl Harbour. The talks have to be held and must fail. Only then will they have justification for using force.'

'I agree,' Peter said. 'The diplomatic avenues must always be explored before resorting to arms. Even Hitler made a pretence at settling his differences with Poland before he attacked. In any case, the King would never allow it.'

El Jefe startled us all by thumping his balled fist on the table.

'You fools!' he hissed. 'All that you say of the King and Government of Spain is true. But what makes you think they will have any say in it when the day dawns, hey?'

'What do you mean, Jefe?' Vella said, a frown creasing his brow.

'Are you not familiar with the history of Spain? How did Francisco Franco come to power? You think there are no more Francos left in Spain? Hah! It is not so many years since that crazy Tejero tried to reinstate a dictatorship. There are many who disapprove the monarchy's liberal attitudes and those of Sanchez and his socialists even more so. Suppose the King and the Government will have no say in it. Suppose the military do it first and tell them afterwards.' Eduardo's tiny twinkling eyes roamed around the table, came finally to rest on me. 'Or suppose they just get rid of them all.'

* * * * *

The following three days were notable only for my enforced inactivity and their culmination in Linda's discharge from hospital at her own behest. Thinner, paler, shaky on her legs. The hospital authorities declined all responsibility.

'Make sure she stays off her feet as much as possible,' the surgeon said in an aside to me.

Though an agreeable enough habitat, the Caleta Hotel was hardly suited to convalescence. Nevertheless, Linda's room was made as comfortable as possible and I negotiated terms for a member of the staff to be placed effectively at her beck and call.

Sex was banned of course for several weeks, which meant no homecoming romp between the sheets. Aside from which something had gone missing from our relationship. The former natural camaraderie was forced, stilted. It was as if we were actors on a stage, playing second-rate, cardboard parts, speaking lines learned by rote. I didn't air my disquiet. Hoped it would pass, whatever it was.

After that first uncomfortable day I spent more of my time out, leaving Linda to recuperate in solitary. She didn't protest.

The fourth day after her return, as I was squeezing the Aston into too small a space outside the hotel, I spotted her coming up the road from the direction of the village. Leaving the car, I went to meet her. She was wearing a summery dress of some burnt orange colour decorated with brown whorls that was new to me, and her steps were cautious. Slim once more, as she was they day I chased her on the highway those months ago. Her colour was unusually high. She looked preoccupied but happy.

'Hello there,' I said, and she started, jolted out of her reverie. But her smile was ready, almost the old Linda.

'Hi. Lovely day.'

'So are you. Lovely like the day.'

Her arm slipped through mine.

'I went down to the beach. It's my first time out of the pen, you know that? I wanted to surprise you.'

'It worked. Now you can return to your cell like a good little inmate. Do you want me to carry you?'

'Like a bride over the threshold?' Snigger. 'So long as we go slow and easy I can manage.'

It was going to be all right between us after all. Some psychological scarring from her injuries was to be expected. The surgeon had prepared me for it, impressed on me the need for tolerance and compassion. I was to make no demands on her for some while. Certainly the matter of her infertility was not to be mentioned without prior medical advice.

'Tonight we'll dine in the restaurant,' I proposed. 'If you feel up to it, that is.'

'Sure.' Her acceptance was mechanical, short on enthusiasm. 'It's a date.'

Be patient, I reminded myself.

* * * * *

Vella came round that same evening, seeking news. I had finished dressing for dinner and joined him in the Arcadia Bar for aperitifs. I hadn't heard from Elena and Luis so was unable to throw him any crumbs.

'Peter is forming a militia,' he said darkly. 'He doesn't believe your friends will obtain the proof we need or that even if they do the British Government will act on it.'

Secretly I half-subscribed to Peter's view. I brooded for a moment, sipping my gin and lemon.

'Give them two more days. If we haven't heard by then I'll … I'll …' What would I do? What *could* I do?

Vella's smile was grim. 'That's what I was afraid you would say.'

'I'll talk to my London contact again.'

'Excellent idea,' Vella snorted and poured three fingers of Scotch down his throat in a single draught.

* * * * *

London was ahead of me. I was recalled to the Foreign Office that very same evening, the message coming not directly but via the Governor's residence in the form of a fax message in an envelope delivered by a military policeman. Harry brought him into the bar.

'I was told to wait for a reply, sir,' the redcap said, stiffly to attention, brass buttons winking, webbing stiff with blanco, not a crease out of line.

'At ease, corporal,' I said. 'This is civilian territory.'

Significantly the message was from Kirkland. Had Toby washed his hands of me?

Filching a sheet of hotel notepaper, I scrawled a reply: *Coming first available flight,* and signed off 'W'.

I broke the news to Linda, sitting across the table and looking luscious.

'I'd better let Vella know,' I mused aloud, forking an endive.

Later, munching my way through a chateaubriand steak in brandy sauce, I mentioned that Elena or Luis might call the hotel.

'Can't you give them your cell number?'

'I don't know theirs, so no. If they do call, and you speak to them, tell them I'll be in touch as soon as I come back.'

'When will that be?'

'Christ knows. They might even arrest me for treason or abusing my expense account or something.'

She tittered. I wasn't so sure it was a tittering matter. Kirkland was reputed to be a vengeful bastard.

Later still, over a cairn of chocolate mousse, she said without preamble, 'It was a boy, you know.'

'What was?' Then it clicked before she could answer. 'Oh.'

The medic at the military hospital had already wised me up to the sex of the unborn child but I didn't let on to Linda. At a loss to find the right words of solace, if there were any right words, I covered her hand with mine. She managed a flickering smile, but her eyes told a different story.

A boy. Not an it, a him. Now it seemed more like murder than miscarriage.

Chapter Twenty-Six

It was 1st May. Seven days to go before the Madrid Conference. From tomorrow the British delegation would be installed in the Spanish capital for the customary "acclimatisation" period. Was it to be farce or tragedy – or a tragic farce?

A new all-electric Nissan Leaf whisked me from a grey, humid Heathrow by some circuitous but uncluttered route, in total silence. Spooky. My driver was thin and taciturn, and dialogue between us was scant. I had trimmed my beard close to the skin, put on the most City-fied suit at my disposal – the charcoal grey three-piece – and was as well equipped to deal with the likes of Master Richard Kirkland as any failed undercover agent could be. As we drove past St Paul's, the greyness was beginning to disperse but it wasn't until we turned into Whitehall that the sun finally parted the murk and made its bow.

The Foreign and Commonwealth Office in Downing Street was virgin territory for me. The exterior is no more grandiose than the PM's residence next door but one; inside it's another story. Here the aura of Empire still prevails. Here is the pinnacle of the mountain of wealth that Britain's colonies had spewed forth in their heyday. Here reposes power, though much reduced nowadays. The colonies are mostly gone and the wealth has evaporated like the morning dew in midsummer. But within the solid stone walls of the Foreign Office it was as if London, like Greenwich Mean Time, was still the hub on which the world turned and that, no matter what changes were wrought elsewhere, here was forever.

Portraits of monarchs, militarists, and ministers glowered down at me as I mounted the wide staircase with its rich red carpet, a step behind the black-suited usher. I was shown into an ante-room on the second floor, the window taken up with St James' Park. The park was peopled with all the usual walks of life: mothers and nannies with baby carriages, joggers, early season tourists, hand-in-hand couples, the inevitable down and outs, all contributing their own shade of colour.

The door opened behind me. I pivoted on my heel leisurely.

'Come in, Warner,' Kirkland said, impeccably groomed as ever, a double-breasted dove grey suit with generous lapels and a regimental tie.

I brushed past him into the office of the Foreign Secretary. It was furnished as befit the status of its occupant: red leather chairs, walls panelled from ceiling to floor, a vast oblong desk with a red leather top. Table lamps with fancy earthenware bases were dotted here and there, all of them lit despite the stream of sunlight.

'Good afternoon, Mr Warner.' The Foreign Secretary stood up, tugging at his jacket, as if he, not I, were the underling.

His handshake was middling firm. None of Kirkland's unconcealed dislike in it.

'We haven't met, have we?' he said as we all sat, Kirkland taking up position on my right flank and crossing his elegant legs.

'I haven't had the pleasure, Minister.'

The rather watery eyes regarded me gravely, a sort of sizing-up. At close quarters the mouth was slightly weak, in contrast to the aggressive jawline. His dark hair was faultlessly groomed. He was reputed to work out in the gym three times a week, and certainly he was slim and fit-looking

Kirkland picked up a grey folder, finger-thick, from the edge of the Foreign Secretary's desk. It was a folder I was familiar with – my personal dossier, blemishes and all.

'Would you like a resumé, Minister?' Kirkland said, at once pompous and ingratiating.

'Not at all. I'm perfectly happy to take Mr Warner at face value.'

'Indeed his track record to date shows him to be resourceful, imaginative, and ruthless.' I could hardly believe this was Kirkland describing me. 'Against this, he tends to lack thoroughness and is considered by his operator to be insufficiently security-conscious.'

Before I could protest, the Foreign Secretary said in a purring voice, 'His attributes clearly far outnumber his failings. I am always suspicious of people without failings.'

'To err is human,' Kirkland concurred.

This was marvellous. I had expected vilification and I was getting pats on the back. I slid a little lower in my soft, all-embracing leather armchair. All it would take to round off my contentment was a glass of cognac and a few dancing girls, non-PC though that would be.

'So, Mr Warner,' the Foreign Secretary said, smoothing his hair, an unnecessary and slightly effeminate gesture. 'You come highly recommended. Toby doesn't dish out bouquets freely.'

I levered my body forward from the depths of the armchair. 'Recommended for what? Or don't I need to know?'

'Of course you need to know. Provided you remember that this conversation and all that follows are governed by the Official Secrets Act.'

'I already signed it.'

'Good – you remembered,' Kirkland said, the nearest he was likely to get to whimsy.

'You're to go to Madrid,' the Foreign Secretary said. 'With Kirkland.'

'Am I?' My well-being tottered slightly. Was this some kind of punishment? 'What about Sideshow.'

'Sideshow is being sidelined,' Kirkland informed me in another stab at whimsy. 'A change of policy towards Gibraltar.'

'What change?'

'We're going to offer the Spanish sovereignty.'

'What!' I sat up fast. 'You mean you're selling out?'

'No!' The Foreign Secretary's affability dropped from him like a shed skin. 'Realpolitik, Warner, realpolitik. Sovereignty with a ninety-nine years leaseback to the United Kingdom. Long enough to guarantee all living Gibraltarians and all but a small minority of their children a lifetime of continued British rule.'

'They'll never agree,' I said, too numb to think coherently. 'GIBESTÁ … You'll have a Civil War on your hands.'

Kirkland gestured dismissively with my file. 'Don't be so alarmist. The Gibraltarians will be – how shall I put it? – sold the idea.'

He was talking with all the lofty assurance of the ignorant. What did he know of the resolve of such as Michael Vella and the hot-blooded nihilism of Peter Vitale? A betrayal of this magnitude could only strengthen the independence movement, the entire populace of the

Rock would swing its weight behind GIBESTÁ. Thirty thousand people makes for a lot of resistance.

'Leaving aside for now the probable backlash,' I said, 'why the change of heart?'

'Politics moves in ways too mysterious for you to understand,' Kirkland sneered. His hitherto concealed esteem for me didn't extend to trusting me with secret material.

The Foreign Secretary differed. 'I think you're wrong there, Kirkland. Let's kill two birds with one stone and have our friends join us, shall we?' He flipped a switch on his intercom and asked for 'our visitors' to be shown in.

These proved to be a tallish, middle-aged man with a droopy grey moustache, and a smaller, younger, and obviously junior compatriot. Both American.

'General Arnold Krefting and Mr Willard Branklin.' The Foreign Secretary announced. 'Gentlemen, may I introduce André Warner. At the present time Our Man in Gibraltar.' The touch of humour was wasted on the Americans but drew an unctuous smile from Kirkland.

'Glad to know yuh, Warner,' the general's accent was mid-Western, unrefined by his exalted rank. Willard Branklin had the clipped intonation of a Columbia-educated man, less drawling, closer ethnically to my Canadian English. He had the apologetic manner of a small-town lawyer.

When we were all seated once more the Foreign Secretary went on to explain to me, 'General Krefting is here incognito as Special Envoy on behalf of our friends across the Atlantic who, naturally, are concerned about the issues at stake regarding the Rock.'

'The Strait of Gibraltar is vital to the whole Western Alliance,' Kirkland interjected, inclining his head towards me.

'I'm not a schoolkid,' I said, mildly irritated. 'There's no need to give me a lesson in military strategy.'

The Foreign Secretary said, 'It's necessary you appreciate that security considerations for the West as a whole override all other considerations, including the right of Gibraltar's inhabitants to self-determination.'

'Not many years ago Margaret Thatcher launched a war over another piece of rock and the right of its inhabitants to self-determination.'

'Forget the Falklands. The priorities were different.'

'That's a fact – they were political, not military. Avoiding loss of face, it's called, I believe, not to mention being evicted from government at the next election.'

General Krefting moved restlessly. 'Say, gennelmen, this sure is fascinating but my time's kind of short. Let's get the show on the road, huh?'

The Foreign Secretary relinquished the floor with good grace and the General, thanking him ultra-politely, said to me, 'An unofficial approach was made to us by the Spanish Ambassador in Washington last week, warning that unless the Conference between you guys produces what they call an acceptable result, they're gonna break off diplomatic relations with Britain and review their policy towards NATO.'

'They're playing poker,' I said, addressing the Foreign Secretary.

He shrugged.

'Poker or not,' Krefting said, his voice grating, 'we can't afford to call their bluff. Spain is still officially classified a Grade 3 Democracy, which means it's considered potentially unstable, what with the unrest in Catalonia, and the Basque truce likely to collapse anytime soon. To put that in perspective, Greece, Poland, and Croatia for instance are likewise Grade 3, Portugal is Grade 2, while other western European states are Grade 1.'

'And Britain?'

My levity earned me four baleful stares.

'It's in all our interests to avert any crisis in Europe, unconstitutional or otherwise,' Krefting resumed, 'and especially any weakening of the Alliance. Are you with me?'

A nod was sufficient.

He continued, 'We've asked your government to make a major concession on sovereignty. We would have preferred a condom.'

'Condominium,' Branklin corrected.

'Yeah, thanks, Will. Never quite got the hang of that word. Sounds like Latin for a rubber.' Laughter broke out in the room. 'Anyway, your boss here says no go, so it's to be a transfer of sovereignty with leaseback.'

He didn't fool me with his disarming country boy act. It often suited

American diplomats, I had found, to let their British counterparts think of them as straw-munching yokels.

'A condominium may sound more attractive and less of a concession,' the Foreign Secretary elaborated for my benefit. He left his desk and went to stand before the nearest window, parting the net curtains like some nosy old crone checking on the neighbours. 'But joint rule is riven with practical difficulties. Inevitably it leads to dispute and the two parties are quite likely to end up where they started, at daggers drawn.'

'Where does the US stand in this?' I asked Krefting. 'Whose side are you on, or is it the usual "even-handed" diplomacy?'

He guffawed. 'There speaks the voice of cynicism.' He leaned forward in his chair, aimed a long finger at me. 'Now, listen to me – like it or not, my country provides the overall umbrella of security for the free world and that means, rightly, we got the biggest shout. Biggest clout, biggest shout, right, Will?'

Branklin murmured an affirmative.

'Consequently …' the finger was going like a hammer-drill, 'if little guys like Britain and Spain can't get their act together, Uncle Donald has to make decisions for you in the interests of the Alliance as a whole. It's like being the head of a family – we gotta keep the kids from squabblin'.'

The Foreign Secretary cleared his throat, visibly piqued to hear Britain's status so depicted. But it was essentially the truth. In the arena of foreign affairs, Britain and most other west European states were little more than American satellites.

'Having said that, we sure would like it a whole lot better if Gibraltar stayed under British military control. The solution we've gone for will give everybody a bit of what they want: NATO avoids a crisis of confidence, Spain gets a deferred sovereignty, Britain retains her presence, and the people of Gibraltar go on for the next ninety-nine years as if nothing had happened.' His tone implied 'after that, who cares?'

'Let's face it,' the Foreign Secretary said, 'sovereignty with leaseback isn't much of a sacrifice. None of us here will see the sun rise on a Spanish Rock.'

As if that were all that really mattered.

'It's a neat little package all right,' I conceded. 'I only hope the

Gibraltarians will see it your way.'

Michael Vella wouldn't, of that I was sure. Peter would go ballistic.

The Foreign Secretary wrinkled his prominent brow. 'There's no reason to suppose they won't, is there?"

'Especially,' Kirkland said, 'if it's presented as a *fait accompli.*' He would say that, the smug bastard. 'It worked with Hong Kong, on a much larger scale, even though the occupying power is a dictatorship, whereas Spain is a democracy.'

'Has Spain been told what's going to be offered?' I asked.

'Not yet.' From Branklin. 'It'll be negotiated during the talks.'

'Made to look as if we're giving the earth, the moon and the stars, I suppose.'

Krefting clapped his hands together in delight. 'You got it, fella. Here – have a cigar.'

They were Macaduno Portofinos, seven inches of the finest Havana leaf, in a tube of the finest aluminum. I declined with thanks. He lit up, and nobody drew his attention to the THANK YOU FOR NOT SMOKING notice on the Foreign Secretary's desk.

For a few moments all was quiet in the panelled office but for the sucking noises from Krefting as he drew on his cigar. The efficiency of the soundproofing reduced the world outside to a whisper.

Then I reactivated the debate by saying, 'I still maintain Spain's bluffing. They had a referendum on NATO in the eighties. The Government would fall if they tried to renege on it.'

'It's a gamble we're not prepared to take,' Krefting said, spilling ash down his tie. 'Besides, there's more to it than just this threat to withdraw from NATO. In fact it's the main reason you've been brought in on this.'

'Should I be flattered?'

'You most surely should. As I understand it you're employed in a private capacity. It couldn't happen in the States, no way would an outsider be allowed in on something this sensitive, even a former operative. But it seems like you're the principal source of the information, so ...' He made circles in the air with the cigar, renouncing the consequences and depositing more on his tie.

'What information?'

Krefting's surprised look was directed at the Foreign Secretary.

'It's all right, General,' he soothed. 'Warner had good reason to suppose we'd rejected his reports on the subject.' Taking slow measured steps he returned to the centre of the room, propped his behind on the edge of the desk from where he could command the stage. 'We think you're right after all,' he said to me. 'We think they're going to invade.'

* * * * *

The American delegation was long gone, evening was on us, the sun now sunk behind Buckingham Palace. The Foreign Secretary's leather-topped desk was overrun with empty coffee cups and plates. Elsewhere were maps of Spain and Europe, open laptops, and a copy of the latest NATO Military Compendium. Jane's Fighting Vehicles and other military reference works had spilled over onto the floor. Kirkland's laptop screen was full of secret data about the military status of Spain and the availability of UK armed forces.

After the Americans, others, including the Minister of Defence, had come and gone: mostly military strategists. They had produced blown-up stills of my amateur movie and grilled me on this helicopter and that armoured car until I was in a daze and could no longer associate the hardware in the photographs with what I had retained in my memory. When at last they left me in peace, with only the Foreign Secretary, the Defence Minister – female and blonde with a built-in sardonic smile – and Kirkland to contend with, I felt brainwashed.

'You should have expected to be thoroughly debriefed,' Kirkland remarked unsympathetically, pouring coffee for the four of us.

'In case you've forgotten, you dismissed my report out of hand. Implied the Irazola kids were playing a joke on me.'

'Don't be deluded,' the Defence Minister said. 'I'm still not entirely sold on it.'

I sipped coffee. It tasted like top-quality dishwater.

'You aren't? Then why all this high-powered stuff with the Americans and half the brass in the British Army?'

'We're being prepared, like good little boy scouts,' Kirkland said.

'Or girl scouts,' This from the Defence Secretary, standing up for her sex.

'Quite,' Kirkland acknowledged. 'As of now we rate the chances of an invasion at sixty-forty against, and even then only if we prove intransigent at the Conference. But these odds are high enough to warrant taking certain precautionary steps.'

The Foreign Secretary, tie loosened, said, 'And since we aren't going to be intransigent, there will be no need to invade.'

The reasoning was solid. I couldn't argue with it. Others, not in this room or even in this country, might.

'I suppose,' I said, still assembling my thoughts as I spoke, 'that the offer of sovereignty plus leaseback will be enough to satisfy the Spanish.'

They seemed startled at the possibility that it might not.

'They can hardly expect more,' the Defence Minister demurred, winding a tendril of blonde hair around her index finger. 'If we concede sovereignty their *casus belli* is nullified.'

'Are we scared of fighting them?'

His discomfiture was considerable. 'Not scared militarily, no.'

'Politically then.'

'Why should we be?' A typical politician's answer.

'It's a cliché, I know, but I never thought I'd live to see the day when Britain would back down from a scrap with Spain. Whatever happened to the Armada spirit?'

The Defence Minister just grimaced.

'Realities of the age,' Kirkland said coolly. Strangely, he appeared not to share the Foreign Secretary's dismay at the prospect of surrendering the Rock.

'Why does all of this require me to go to Madrid?'

'You'll be going with Kirkland as special adviser on Gibraltar,' the Foreign Secretary answered behind steepled fingers. 'Much as it may go against the grain, GIBESTÁ is a factor which will have to be taken into account during the negotiations and your first-hand knowledge of the movement and its leading lights will be invaluable. Additionally, thanks to your extended stay on the Rock, you must have some idea of the mood of the Gibraltarians. The Spanish will be impressed, which is what we want them to be. Your relative fluency in their language will be an added bonus. As you are aware, Kirkland also speaks Spanish like a native, on account, I imagine, of his wife – his very lovely wife.'

Kirkland made a show of unbecoming modesty. 'Thank you for the dual compliments. I accept the one about my wife, at any rate.'

I drained my cup. 'Terms still the same as Sideshow?'

The Foreign Secretary blinked. 'What terms would those be?'

'Yes,' Kirkland cut in with a warning contraction of his pale eyebrows. To the Foreign Secretary he said unctuously 'I'll fill you in later, Minister.'

Meaning that my fee had short-circuited the ministerial approval process.

'Are you going to brief me now?' I said, diplomatically changing the subject.

'Outside of this office, if you don't mind, Kirkland,' the Foreign Secretary said, almost apologetically. Standing up abruptly, he stuck out his slender hand. 'Thanks for all you've done … attempted to do, Warner. It wasn't your fault it came unstuck and you more than made up for any failure in that direction with your intelligence on the Spanish invasion plan.'

'No black marks?' As if I cared.

'Not even a grey one as far as I'm concerned.'

Promotion prospects still good then.

Chapter Twenty-Seven

Madrid was hot and seemed hotter still in contrast to the cool of an English spring. Unlike Kirkland and me, the city's inhabitants were dressed for it, their light loose clothes contrasting with our wool suits. The heat bothered Kirkland and when we stepped out of the taxi before the modern and sumptuous Princesa Plaza Hotel, he was pink of hue and perspiring.

After a beer and a freshen-up I took a stroll down the long boulevard that ran past the front door of the Palacio Real – the Royal Palace. It was early evening, the first inkling of the drop in temperature that nightfall and eight hundred metres of altitude would bring chilling my bare arms. The streets were noisy but cleaner than those of London, and signs of neglect or dilapidation were absent. On the contrary, the majority of the populace had a distinctly prosperous look.

I walked as far as the Palace, a stone building of three storeys with square colonnades built into the walls. Architecturally-speaking, not dissimilar from Buckingham Palace, except that a busy thoroughfare passed within a few metres of the front door. The lower windows were pink with the glow of sunset, making them appear to be lit up inside. No members of the Royal Family waved to me from behind them.

Opposite the Palace I turned left into a plaza of lawns and flowers and shrubs and a monument of an armour-clad rider on horseback. I mounted the ring of steps at its base and read on the plinth that the rider represented was in fact a woman and a queen to boot – the Renanda Isabella Segunda de Bourbon no less. Spain's Boadicea? Behind me a tourist snapped off several pictures in quick succession, his garishly-dressed wife posing at the base of the plinth.

'Move a little to the left, dear... no, my left not yours ...'

'How the hell am I supposed to know, you moron ...!'

Marital bliss at its finest. I passed on to a bench beyond the statue, where I sat and watched the world go by for a few minutes. As the sky grew darker the nip in the air on the Iberian plateau grew in proportion. Most other promenaders were better prepared, with windbreakers and sweaters. None of them was within hearing range so I extracted my cell phone from my hip pocket and selected a number from the contacts list.

Michael Vella might have been waiting for my call: the receiver was lifted even as the ringing began.

'Warner,' I said without preamble. 'Any news from the Irazola kids?'

'Nothing. Are you still in England?'

'Madrid.'

A gasp. 'How … what …?'

I overrode his expostulations.

'Just listen, Michael, I'm trying to help you.' I checked again for potential eavesdroppers, was reassured. 'A friend in high places let something slip over dinner. I fed him enough alcohol to loosen his tongue further and I can tell you that the British Government now definitely does accept that an invasion might be in the offing.' It was a feeble tale but in his anxiety I hoped he wouldn't notice. Now for the crunch – to tell or not to tell that Gibraltar was going to be dumped, albeit on a leaseback basis. I had spent the previous night mostly engaged in an internal tug-of-war between my natural liking and respect for Vella, not to mention the personal debt, and my professional obligations. In tipping him off I might even be guilty of treason.

'André, are you still there?'

'Yeah.' I came to a decision and hoped it was the right one. 'Michael … listen carefully. The Spanish are going to be offered sovereignty –' His anguished 'No!' reverberated against my ear drum. I silenced him brutally. 'You can wring your hands later. It'll be subject to leaseback, ninety-nine years is the favourite, which means it won't happen in the lifetime of any living Gibraltarian, nor in the lifetimes of most of their children.'

He swore obscenely, a rarity for him, serving to underline the strength of his antipathy.

'It will mean an insurrection,' he said, his voice bitter. 'You'll see.'

'Talking like that won't help. It's up to you to make sure it's accepted.

You're the only one who can convince your people it's the best of all possible options. Or perhaps you'd prefer an invasion.' My tone was harsh, with an undertone of irony.

'Yes, I would.' The blunt statement shocked me momentarily. 'Then the British would be obliged to defend us.'

It was a twisted kind of reasoning that advocated independence yet *in extremis* called upon the protective umbrella of the imperial power whose sovereignty was so hateful. I said this much to him.

'I have to be pragmatic. Under British rule, GIBESTÁ has a chance of achieving some form of autonomy, under Spain we have none. After having finally regained control over us, do you imagine they would be prepared to even recognise the existence of an independence movement?'

He was right, of course.

A squat elderly man in braces and beret came shuffling over and plonked down at the other end of the bench. An unlikely snooper, but why risk it?

'I've got to go. I'll keep you posted.'

'Where can I reach you? What are you doing there, in Madrid, anyway?'

'Business.' Let him draw his own conclusions. 'I'll try and find out more. My friend's a member of the British negotiating team, staying at the same hotel. Don't try to contact me.'

He didn't speak for a long moment, then, 'André …'

'Yes?'

'I'm grateful for what you're doing for us.'

Damn right he should be.

'Think nothing of it. I'm repaying a debt.'

'What debt?' To him there was no debt. That was the kind of man he was.

'Goodbye, Michael.'

Back at the hotel I called the Caleta and asked for Linda. She was out, I was informed. Out where, I wondered, worry nibbling at me even as I hung up. She had no business being out, still wasn't recovered from her injuries.

Thanks to Linda I had been able to some extent to banish Maura from my daily flashbacks. Now I was haunted anew by the possibility that I had only exchanged one unrequited receptacle for another.

* * * * *

'The Conference opens the day after tomorrow,' Kirkland reminded me unnecessarily as we breakfasted matily together. 'So I propose we meet our team today. Get it over with. It's bound to be a bore.'

So maybe he and I had more in common than I had figured.

Our chauffeured Mercedes limousine, long as a bus, swept us through the city with unconcern for intersections and other obstacles, to the Cuidad Universitaria – University City – in the northern suburbs. Here was a city within a city, modern tower blocks rising from landscaped gardens, the youthfulness of the trees evidencing its newness. We left the broad *avenida*, doubled back on ourselves and passed back underneath it. A few complicated turns later we careered into a parking lot, overshadowed by a squat oblong of a building bearing no identification whatsoever.

'This doesn't look like a university,' I remarked, as we abandoned the limousine.

'It isn't. It only pretends to be.' Kirkland didn't elaborate. 'It was chosen for the talks in preference to some more prestigious venue in the city centre because it's easier to protect.'

'Who needs protection – us?'

'Gibraltar is an emotive issue. Fanatics are likely to emerge from the carpet fluff. Especially if the talks look like failing.'

'But they won't fail. Not on our account.'

'The Spanish don't know that yet. We aren't about to shoot off every arrow in our quiver before we even sit down at the conference table. They have to be seen to fight for their sovereignty and we to squirm giving it to them. Get the picture?'

Devious was too mild a term for what was afoot.

A semi-circle of stone steps led up to multiple doors through which people were constantly passing, many of them in police or military uniform. Two soldiers with shoulder-slung machine pistols prowled the terrace. They scrutinised us, but made no effort to apprehend us.

Inside was different. In a plasticky emporium we were directed to a desk, searched rather perfunctorily, checked against a list, approved, and handed cards with clips that bore our photographs, names, and status: I was a "Foreign Office Executor", which I guessed was a mis-spelling of "executive".

'They seem organised enough,' I said, as we followed a gun-toting soldier to an elevator, where three or four other civilians waited.

'Yes, to give credit where it's due, the Spanish are taking it very seriously indeed. They can't afford to risk any bad publicity. Any violence against the British delegates might harden Britain's attitude and lose Spain world support and sympathy.'

Up we went, bodyguard and all, to the second floor and a long room with many windows that faced towards the centre of the city: the two hundred and fifty metres tall Cuatro Torres in the business area were outlined sharply in the crisp morning air. The UK delegation, six strong, were already in debate, established in a tight group around a corner of the hollow-square table. Although they had been notified of the secondment of two "advisors" to their team, the leader, Malcolm Crabbe, MP, Foreign Office Minister and late Chairman of the Operation Sideshow committee, was not welcoming.

'Who needs you?' he groused as we offered breezy 'Good mornings', and sorted out seating.

'Perhaps the Foreign Office is afraid we'll be outnumbered,' some team member suggested. Other, less polite suggestions came in its wake.

'We take no part in the actual talks unless you call on us,' Kirkland said, spoken like a true diplomat. 'We're here to advise on technical aspects.'

Crabbe sniffed. 'Such as?'

'And to observe,' Kirkland dodged, slippery-smooth, 'and report back.'

'You hear that, chaps? We've got a Fifth Column amongst us.'

The 'chaps' evinced a suitable level of affront and clattered coffee cups.

'Milk or cream, Denis?'

'Pass the pot, will you, there's a good fellow.'

They couldn't have cared less. This was just another junket, a few weeks high living in Madrid: plush hotel, NQA expense accounts, plenty of leisure time.

I was too preoccupied to pay much attention to the round of introductions: despite my injunction not to contact me, Vella had called my cell phone, very late the previous night. The Irazola twins had turned up soon after our conversation with some new and supposedly sensational material that they would not divulge until they had discussed it with me. They were driving to Madrid today for that very purpose. Naturally, I speculated for hours on what it might be, and slept little as a result. In fact I was having a run of bad nights. There was too much conflict inside my head. Linda, Vella, Irazola, GIBESTÁ, treason, uprising, war … all of it spinning round like a great turbine, ever faster, too fast to control.

The negotiating team talked around us for the next half hour, Kirkland occasionally slipping in some germane comment that was promptly discarded. My own contribution was zero.

'Excuse me,' I said at some stage in the dreary repartee, in sudden need of solitude. Nobody acknowledged. I slipped out into the corridor. Our escort was still there, picking his nose. He jerked sloppily to attention.

'I'm going outside,' I informed him. '*Voy fuero. Vale*?'

He insisted on riding back down to the ground floor with me and seeing me out of the building. I walked through the surrounding gardens, hoping to clear my mind of clutter, returning at length to the front of the building and a wooden bench.

Cars and taxis came and departed, and people detoured around me, intent on their own affairs. Alone, free of distractions, I began to put my thoughts in order, in particular about whose side I was really on and whom I was fighting for. In truth, that was what was really at the root of my dolour. I had made mistakes, some big, some small, but to pass state secrets on to an outsider such as those I had passed to Vella was to put my conscience through hell. And Vella, by all recognised definitions, was an enemy of the state. He who is not with me is against me. Justify it, Warner, I said to myself, square it with your professed virtue if you can.

I couldn't.

So I continued to be plagued by guilt. Continued, that is, until two arms came from behind and wrapped around me. Female arms.

'Day dreaming, André?'

'*Elena*?' I freed myself and stood up.

'I've missed you.' Her kiss was uninhibited, like most of her behaviour. Her declared fondness for me was flattering considering the age discrepancy, so I kissed back with a suitable amount of ardour. She looked ravishing with her hair caught back in blue ribbon and just enough make-up. Under an open corduroy blouson she wore a white ribbed sweater that stuck to every undulation of her torso, and skinny jeans that made her appear taller than she was.

Luis was with her but remained discreetly at a distance. Now, with the intimate phase over, he came up, swaggering a little as was his style. We exchanged greetings.

'Hello, André. I am happy to see you again.'

I gave him a wary nod as I shook his hand. He was less immaculately turned out than usual, his chin shaded with stubble, his white shirt overdue for laundering. It was hard to credit that this was the same honcho who had gunned down eight people with such sickening glee. The flesh-pressing gave me the same feeling you might get from grabbing a 20,000 volt cable. Instinctively my eyes wandered over the lightweight sports jacket in search of bumps that might mean a weapon. No obvious protrusions but that didn't put me at ease: the jacket was open and hanging loose on his slender frame, and a pistol worn in the small of the back is all but undetectable.

I said, 'Vella told me to expect you, but how did you find me here? It can't be a coincidence, surely.'

'The hotel told us.' Her eyes went from me to the building. 'I know this place well. My father comes here sometimes for meetings.'

'Speaking of your father, have you seen him lately?'

'Not since we found out what is really happening,' Luis replied ahead of Elena. 'We have much to tell you.'

'So I gather. Do you want to talk here and now?'

But Luis was no longer paying attention. He was staring down the path to the parking lot, towards an approaching group of mostly uniformed men. A cluster of camera-toting newsmen paced them, filming as they went. Two civilians were cutting across a lawned area on a converging course; one of them called a greeting.

'*Hola*, General! You are late, but I forgive you!'

'You are wise to do so, my friend. I have brought a division of tanks as my personal bodyguard!'

The voice, jovial, affable, was familiar. I looked harder at the uniformed group.

'It's *Papa*!' Luis whispered, pointing like a retriever. 'He is here!'

The group broke up as it met the two civilians, revealing at its core General Irazola, magnificent in dress uniform, a broad white smile cleaving his tanned face.

'Did you know he was going to be here?' I asked Elena.

'We knew he was coming to Madrid, that was all.'

The group, now some dozen strong, plus the scurrying cameramen, was heading for the entrance where the two sentries were already ramrod-backed. In the midst of the uniforms I recognised another adversary – Petrov. Puffy of mouth and sickly of pallor. Good! The group moved on and Petrov passed within touching range of me, heedless of my presence.

Then Luis was pushing past me, eyes fixed on his father; eyes that were blind, burning with a terrible intensity.

'Now I will expose him for what he is!'

'Luis!' Elena caught his sleeve. 'Luis, no! This is not the time.'

He didn't even check in his advance. 'Irazola!' he shouted, as if to a stranger rather than his procreator. Irazola was still moving forward at the head of his party, head bobbing as he talked to a fellow officer. Others were turning, as yet only curious, towards the source of the cry.

'Irazola ... *traidor*!' Luis' voice rose to a howl that instantly stilled all conversation. He quickened his step, his finger pointing accusingly at his father.

'Luis!' Irazola, startled but unafraid. 'What are you doing here?'

A young officer flanking Irazola detached from the group and ripped open the flap of his holster, his other hand raised in a warding-off motion. His gun glinted as he pulled it free. Luis was not for intimidating. It could have been an action replay of the incident on the hillside overlooking Irazola's military encampment. From somewhere inside his clothing, like a magician plucking a rabbit from a hat, Luis produced an automatic of the same pattern that had served him so well before. Behind me a woman screamed. I started towards Luis, not sure what I hoped to achieve, only conscious of a desire to prevent another massacre.

The officer's gun was levelled. Irazola saw it at last.

'Wait!' he roared and the officer hesitated, fatally as it turned out. Luis fired, a rapid spewing of bullets, cutting the officer down and others behind him. Panic broke out. Most of the group threw themselves flat. People elsewhere on the plaza were running, everywhere and anywhere. I saw Irazola go down, then I was down too, bowled over by someone in full flight. Shoes trampled on me, including a stiletto heel that crunched agonisingly into the base of my spine. More shots rang, the flat thud of Luis' heavy automatic alternating with the crack of a lighter cartridge. Blood splattered on my pants leg, hot even through the cloth. Automatic fire now took over from single shots, probably the two sentries. It was like being in the middle of a battlefield.

The gunfire ceased, not a gradual petering out but an abrupt termination. The hush that came after was filled with moans and weak cries for help: '*Socorro*! *Socorro*!' More distinctly, someone called: '*Un medico – rapido*!'

I lifted myself cautiously off my belly, cast around for Elena. She was on her knees behind me, her expression stunned.

'Are you hit?' I got up and went to her, helped her to her feet. She leaned weakly against me.

'I am all right. Where is Luis?'

Luis was on his back, the automatic detached from his open hand. He was looking into the sun – looking without seeing. For Luis there would be no more sun. The line of red holes evenly spaced across the front of his white shirt looked like the buttons of a clown's costume. Too many holes for him to have survived. Elena let out a sobbing gulp and fell across him, calling his name, shaking him. I didn't try to restrain her.

The carnage was extensive. Blood splattered the paving stones on the pathway and there were dark patches on the grass. At least half-a-dozen forms lay still. Irazola was not one of them, sitting up, nursing a bloodied arm, tended by a crouching uniformed aide. The two sentries stood slightly apart from the fallen group, guns held out as if they expected the dead to rise up and attack them. I couldn't see Petrov. Hopefully Luis had disposed of that piece of filth.

Then Irazola, staggering upright, caught sight of me. His face was pale under the tan, the sleeve of his tunic saturated with blood. He shook off the concerned ministrations of his aide to stumble over fallen bodies towards me.

'So.' Just the one word. It spoke volumes. He glanced down at Elena, sprawled across her brother's corpse, sobbing. No emotion afflicted the severe, manly features, neither pity nor remorse.

'He was a fool,' he said, half to himself. 'A fool and a dreamer.'

He could have added psycho to the descriptive.

Elena lifted her head. To my surprise there were no tears, only an emptiness that slowly transformed to hate as she and her father locked stares the way duelling stags lock antlers.

'You did this,' she accused, her voice thick with desolation.

'He did it to himself,' Irazola replied, not without justification. 'These are his just desserts.'

'How can you say this? He is your *son*!'

'Not by blood, as well you know. In any case, by this act he lost the right to be considered as my son.' He swung on his heel and with his good hand beckoned the aide and the two sentries. They came at a lope, eager to please.

'Escort my daughter and this … gentleman to a safe place,' he ordered.

That his concern with our well-being was purely euphemistic became apparent when the sentries covered us with their sub-machine guns.

Elena put up a scrap but was easily overpowered by the aide and one of the sentries. I, seeing no point in resistance, went quietly, hustled through the gathering crowd of gawkers who, taking us for the instigators of the slaughter, spat and catcalled and jostled us.

We were bundled into an Army Land Rover, the sentries accompanying us. Two more soldiers, newly arrived, got in the separate driving compartment and we took off fast. Elena sat slumped, a resigned expression on her face. As we pulled out of the parking lot a trio of ambulances came howling down the highway exit ramp, lights flashing dementedly.

'I'm sorry, Elena, about Luis,' I said, speaking English in the expectation that our guards would have limited command of the language.

'It is not your fault,' she sniffed, head bowed. 'It was his destiny.'

Destiny or not, I was the catalyst. No loss to the world at large, Luis was Elena's only family as well as her twin. They had been close, as twins are supposed to be. This realisation prompted me to hug her to me, to give such comfort as was within my power. Her body shuddered as it conformed to mine. She wept a little after that, yet soundlessly, and for the rest of our ride the creak of the van and the occasional thump of its tyres on some rough patch of pavement were the only sounds.

Chapter Twenty-Eight

Our initial destination was an airfield, just outside Madrid, where we were locked up in separate cells for several hours. I was fed, watered, and I assumed Elena received the same treatment. No thumbscrews. I was told nothing.

Late in the afternoon an army officer whom I recognised as the General's adjutant, my old acquaintance Comandante Navarro, came for me with a detachment of troopers.

'No questions,' he rapped when I tried to quiz him. Elena was brought out. She dredged up a weak smile for me, then we were escorted out past curious air force personnel to an executive-type turboprop aircraft with military markings. Inside the narrow fuselage we were kept apart.

We flew in a southerly direction as far as I could judge, for there was no sun, merely a lighter patch of sky over the horizon to our right. The flight lasted less than an hour and as we began our descent I glimpsed the sea through the windows on the opposite side of the cabin. It was late afternoon and runway landing lights had already been switched on below. The FASTEN SEAT BELTS sign blinked and in a matter of minutes we were touching down.

Another Land Rover, the long-wheelbase model. Elena and I sat facing each other from the bench seats, guards on either side. It was too dark now to distinguish any feature of the surrounding countryside. Presently I gave up the attempt and catnapped instead. The road surface was poor, occasionally atrocious, but I must have dozed because the next thing I remembered was my shoulder being shaken. We were there, wherever there was.

I climbed down from the Land Rover and nearly laughed out loud. We had been brought to the General's headquarters-cum-residence. I had come full circle. They even took me down to the same cell. Elena was hauled away in another direction. So far, she was getting the same treatment as me, Irazola's daughter or no, though I couldn't believe we would share the same fate.

It was no warmer in my little cell than it had been when last I occupied it. On this occasion though I was dressed to cope with it. Lacking other diversions, I nodded off.

They didn't come for me until the small hours. Two soldiers plus the sadly still-alive Petrov.

Plus Richard Kirkland.

* * * * *

The interrogation room had been decorated since my previous visit, probably to hide bloodstains. It smelled of paint and the flaking patch by the light rose was no more.

'How does it feel now?' Petrov sneered from behind a screen of foul-smelling cigarette smoke. I was back in the interrogee's chair, he leaning against the wall. The two soldiers were behind me.

'Looking at you,' I said with a bravado I didn't feel, 'I feel slightly sick.'

'Soon you will feel sicker.' His lips were swollen, I noticed. They would help hide the new gap in his teeth. His reshaped mouth had given him a lisp.

'Something happen to your mouth?' I said, idiotically goading him. His face contorted. He stepped forward but Kirkland, a passive audience until now, restrained him.

'Later, Petrov,' he said. 'If you must.'

'Are you going to tell me more?' I said to him. 'Or shall I guess?'

Kirkland jangled coins in his pocket. 'Guess.'

'All right. I don't like you all that much, Kirkland, but I'll give you the benefit of the doubt: Petrov is really one of us and General Irazola is in secret collusion with the British Government, and we're really all good guys, working together to bring about a peaceful solution to the Gibraltar problem. How am I doing?'

'If you like it, you stick to it.'

Kirkland was grinning. Petrov, too, though his was more wolfish, more anticipatory. Petrov had special plans for me.

'On the other hand,' I said, 'maybe the only good guy is me and the rest of you are up to your hairlines in this invasion. Though quite why you would need to invade when sovereignty is going to be ceded to Spain anyway, is beyond me.'

'Ah,' Kirkland said, eyes creased in amusement, 'there, as Hamlet had it, is the rub.'

'Your rub, not mine. If my second guess is anywhere near right, it makes you, Kirkland, guilty of treason.'

'Don't be so innocent, Warner. I don't work for Britain. I'm not even British, I'm South African, and my wife, it might interest you to know, is Julio Irazola's sister.'

I let the shock-horror subside before saying feebly, 'Well, aren't you the dark horse?'

'You should know all about dark horses. The rôle you've been playing these past weeks is no different from mine. We just work for different sides.'

It was fair enough comment.

'So who *are* you working for? The Spanish or the Russians?' I shot a meaningful look at Petrov.

'If I might be permitted …' The voice came from the door.

'Hello, General,' I said, turning to face him. 'I'm flattered. I didn't expect a personal visit, what with you mobilising for an invasion and all.'

'I can always make time for my friends.'

'Yeah, you already said. We should have been on the same side.'

'And I was serious.' He dismissed the two guards and came before me, right arm in a snow white sling, not otherwise the worse for yesterday's bloodbath. He was in full combat kit, complete with boots and holstered pistol at his waist.

'Strange, don't you think,' he said to me, 'that our relationship should begin and end in the same room?'

'Significant, not strange.'

'Have you told him?' he asked Kirkland. The latter shook his head.

'I thought you would like that privilege, General, since you expressed a wish to see him before you leave.'

Irazola smiled approval and said to me, 'It is a mark of my respect for your talents and resource that I have come to enlighten you in person. But as a prelude to my explanation I should tell you that the Madrid talks have been cancelled by the British. The excuse they give is security issues, after my stepson went berserk at the University. Happily, the cancellation has no impact on my plans. Cancelling is almost as satisfactory as failing to reach agreement. It is enough to justify our act.' He smoothed his hair down with his free hand. 'You have suspected for some time, have you not, Warner, that we are going to invade Gibraltar? Ever since you were informed of it by my late unlamented stepson and ungrateful daughter – whose punishment incidentally I have not yet decided on.'

'You realise the risk you will run if you go ahead with this farce. You'll end up at war with Britain.'

'You are forgetting something. Thanks to my brother-in-law, Ricardo – the man you know as Richard Kirkland – we can launch our attack on Gibraltar with impunity. No military response can be expected from your Government.'

So Kirkland was the mysterious Ricardo. I treated him to a contemptuous stare. It wasn't enough to make him immediately announce that he was switching sides.

'That still doesn't explain why. If you know that much you also know you'll be given sovereignty anyway. You don't need to invade.'

Irazola clasped hands behind his back, a small frown puckering his forehead.

'If I were acting on the orders of our new Prime Minister, the good, honest, sincere Pedro Sanchez, I would agree with you. But that is not the case.'

Mystified, I said, 'Whose orders are you acting on then? Vladimir Putin's, I suppose.'

Petrov gave a little cackle. Even Kirkland, or whatever his real name was, did an exaggerated eye roll, maybe in despair at my naivety.

'For a man of your supposed intellect I am disappointed by your lack of understanding,' Irazola said. 'I am nobody's lackey, my friend. It is I who am directing the invasion. The Russians, whose interests Petrov represents, are providing financial support and such other support as will be required when I establish my government. No more than that.'

'*Your* government?' I stared stupidly at him.

His slow headshake was the kind that means 'I give up.'

The dawning came so slowly it was painful, as if hidden behind a screen of fog, thinning only gradually but the process accelerating until a sunburst of comprehension blasted through the murk and I could see clearly what I had failed to see: that Irazola was going to stage a military *coup d'état* on his own account. He was going to overthrow the Spanish Government and set himself up as the new General Franco!

And all along I – and others – had supposed that the invasion was Spanish Government-inspired, that Irazola was merely the chosen tool. As I got used to the idea, questions began to formulate in my mind. For instance, why invade Gibraltar at all? Was it to divert attention away from the real object? Or were the coup and the invasion linked?

Then I saw it. It unfolded before me in all its fiendish brilliance, like coming to the last page of a detective novel with an unintelligible plot.

Irazola glanced at Kirkland and Petrov. 'Now he has it. It is written on his face.'

'Give the Spanish people Gibraltar and you won't even need to fight for Spain,' I said. It was masterly. For an instant so fleeting it hardly registered I wished I were part of it.

'The invasion was originally scheduled for the first of June,' Irazola explained, 'by which time it was foreseen that the talks would have reached a stalemate, as they always have in the past. When I learned of your Government's new stance on sovereignty it became necessary to drastically revise the timing for the invasion. Obviously I could not afford for the sovereignty decision to be made public.'

So much for the breathing space that Vella and I had counted on.

'So when do you move?'

'In approximately …' Irazola raised his slim gold wristwatch to eye level, '… fifty-eight hours from now, that is at 0500 hours on the 10th of May.'

Not long enough for the Brits to come to the rescue even if they were so minded.

'We expect to overcome all resistance, such as there is, by noon. There is nothing you can do to stop us. Even if you picked up the telephone this very moment and called your own Prime Minister and even if he believed you and reversed his policy of non-intervention, we cannot be stopped.'

Today was 7th May and it was Thursday. My mind did the maths, fast forwarding to the 10th. Sunday. Day of rest. The day when the system of government and law and order is at low ebb. Military, police, emergency services, all at only half-strength.

'The King,' I said, a last vain appeal. 'Felipe. He'll never install you as Head of Government.'

The mirth was long and loud and unanimous. Irazola reached over the table and patted my shoulder.

'When Petrov has finished, er … amusing himself with you, he will leave for Madrid. Two days from now the King of Spain and his family will be on their way into exile under guard and the Prime Minister under arrest. By Saturday there will be no more King of Spain, there will be only me, only Generalissimo Julio Irazola, *Presidente*!'

With his clenched fist he pummelled his chest. The room seemed to shrink and he to swell in stature, adopting already the mantle of Dictator and ruler of Spain and conqueror of the British.

'You'll never pull it off,' I said, without conviction. 'You're no Franco.'

'This is true, alas. Franco was unique. But through me he will again rule over Spain.'

'*Through* you?' It sounded to me as though he was suffering from a dose of megalomania.

'Yes, my friend. Through me.' He walked to the door, swung round as he opened it. 'You see, Francisco Franco, though he never acknowledged it, was my father.'

* * * * *

My mind was so stuffed with Irazola's multiple revelations that the bleakness of my own future was briefly relegated to second place. Only when the door closed behind Irazola, and Petrov peeled his back off the wall to amble over did I start to worry about what lay in store for me.

Without any specific plan of resistance I got to my feet, clutching the chair. Petrov sniggered. Kirkland casually, as if he were taking out a cheque book, drew a slim automatic from inside his jacket. I prodded the chair legs at Petrov. He side-stepped easily, nimble as a ballet dancer.

'Put the chair down,' Kirkland said quietly, 'or I'll have to shoot you.'

I put the chair down but not submissively as Kirkland would have it; I chucked it at him legs foremost. He corkscrewed away to avoid it. Petrov came for me but made the error of reaching for his gun whilst on the move, tying up his right arm and upsetting his balance so that when I upended the flimsy table in his path he ran right into it. His mouth opened and I saw that where had once been teeth was now only space. He reeled, clutching at the overturned table and getting tangled up in it. Down he went, with the table on top of him.

The Russian being out of the running for as long as it would take to extricate himself, I closed in on Kirkland, judging him the lesser opponent in a roughhouse. Avoiding the thrown chair had brought him to his knees. He managed to get off a single wild shot that ripped through my sleeve before I kicked him in the ear and ended his participation. The door flung open. The two guards, alerted by the din, barged in, flourishing their machine pistols. For their efficacy such weapons rely on saturating the immediate vicinity with lead, controlled shots being near-impossible. Any sprayed gunfire would be as fatal for Petrov and Kirkland as for me. I only hoped these two were smart enough to appreciate it.

Their IQ ratings were never put to the test. As they stood in the doorway, crouching, uncertain how to deal with the situation, a gun cracked in the corridor beyond, several rapid shots. The soldiers crumpled, clutching their legs and howling their displeasure.

Half a face appeared tentatively around the door. Elena!

'Come, André!'

But Petrov had crawled out from under the table by now and wasn't in a forgiving mood. He took a pot-shot at Elena, but half a face makes a poor target for an unaimed pistol. Elena bobbed back out of sight as I chopped down on his arm with the hard edge of my hand. I expected it to break his grip on the gun at the very least, so it was a surprise when the hand, with the gun still attached, came winging towards my skull. Elena saved me again with a lucky shot that definitely struck flesh and blood. Petrov grunted, and reeled against me like a drunk. I thrust him away. His legs buckled and it was all over with him, maybe terminally. I hurdled the sundry fallen forms – the still and the squirming – and stumbled to the door.

'You're a bloody marvel!' I hugged Elena, and she, responding to my display of affection according to her instincts, clung to my neck and kissed me so hard I was sent staggering back into the room, with the muzzle of her gun jammed up behind my ear.

'Not now!' I squawked, before we went down with a crash over Petrov's body.

'Make love to me,' she growled, biting at my neck.

'What – on top of a corpse?' I disengaged her arms. 'You're as mad as your brother. Come on, we've got to get out. Somebody must've hear the shooting. There's a guy upstairs …'

Elena's chortle put a stop to my protests.

'He's sleeping on duty,' she said, now chewing at my ear. 'And this place is soundproof. It wouldn't do for soldiers to hear prisoners being interrogated. They sometimes scream, you see …'

But for her intervention mine might have been joining the ghosts of screamers past.

We got up and I kicked the machine pistols away, out of reach of the two groaning guards. For good measure I gave them each a firm tap on the temple with the butt of Elena's pistol. Peace descended.

'That was an efficient bit of shooting,' I said to Elena. 'It must run in the family.'

It was a thoughtless, even cruel remark. She became subdued.

'I never shot anyone before. Luis is … was my twin, but I don't share his violent streak.' Her fingers brushed a lock of hair from my forehead. 'I did it for you.'

Her admission humbled me into silence.

'Did my father come to see you?' she asked.

'Yes.'

'And he told you … everything? That the invasion is his and his alone, that he is going to kill the King, and is working with the Russians for them to supply oil and weapons after the invasion.'

'Because he expects a trade embargo against Spain?' I said.

She nodded. 'It seems so.'

'Have you known this all along?'

She stepped away from me, affronted. 'Of course not. It was only two days ago that I fixed my recording machine in the room where Papa holds his meetings. As soon as I discovered the truth I tried to contact you. This is why we came to Madrid, Luis and I, to tell you.'

'I'm sorry,' I muttered, abashed and a little ashamed, 'and I'm sorry about Luis.'

Moisture filmed her eyes.

'I am trying not to think about Luis or I shall cry and you will have to comfort me in that special way. We must be practical and plan our escape before the guards are relieved.'

'Are there any other prisoners in here?'

'Oh, yes. Perhaps ten, twelve.'

Ten was nowhere near enough for what I had in mind. But the alternatives carried an even greater risk. I checked my watch: it was after four. Dawn was only an hour away. Our chances of escape would be higher under cover of darkness.

'You have an idea?' She bit her lower lip, excited now. She was easy to excite. 'What is it, André?'

'We're going to stage a mass break-out,' I replied melodramatically.

'A *mass* break-out? With only a dozen prisoners?'

All right, so it was a lousy idea. It was the only one I had.

Chapter Twenty-Nine

The grass was damp and the air still. Above, a sky embossed with explosions of cumulus that sent shadows chasing sunlight across the swooping hills and along the valley where an insignificant little river meandered. Between the crest of the hill, where we were, and the bottom of the valley, was situated the airfield that we had happened upon by chance.

It occupied a wide shelf of land in the hillside below us. On the runway a small piston-engined aircraft; others were lined up in echelon on the apron. I counted ten sleek combat types with twin tail fins, and a trio of smaller jets with elongated cockpit canopies, two-seat trainers probably. All of them sported red fins and noses. Inside a painted landing circle on the near side of the only hangar a large grey helicopter was parked. On top of it, a figure, crouched over the rotor mast. Of the scattered buildings the obligatory hangar was the largest. Next largest was two storeys high and shaped like a shoe box, with lots of windows. Crew quarters, was my guess.

Elena and I sat side by side in the damp grass. She was smoking her last cigarette, while I assessed the chances of approaching the airfield unseen. Suddenly she emitted a rich chortle.

'Oh, André, did you ever see anything so funny as that man trying to run with his pants round his ankles?'

It was true that the incident had provided a few seconds of comic relief in what was otherwise a desperate venture. In the event our escape had not quite gone as intended. The prisoners refused to co-operate in staging a break-out, fearing the reprisals they would incur. Smart guys. So we had commandeered the guards' machine pistols and forced them out at gunpoint. A couple of bursts over their heads set a stampede in motion, and they scattered far and wide across the courtyard. We had expected the guards to give chase and sure enough they spilled out of their quarters, some of them in night attire, but instead of attempting to round up the fleeing miscreants they started picking them off. Consequently, the confusion we had banked on to cover our own escape never happened.

It wasn't until all the reluctant escapees lay still, either dead or hugging the concrete in terror, and the guards, calling to each other, were converging on the fallen, that an opportunity presented itself.

'Go!' I had yelled to Elena, and, bless her pluck, she darted off without the smallest hesitation. I went off after her, clutching the machine pistol, though there couldn't have more than a few rounds left in the magazine. Darkness was our friend. At the outset too, the prison building screened us. When we had covered a half kilometre or so we risked a halt to check our rear. No movement, no suggestion of pursuit.

'We've done it!' Elena was ecstatic.

'Getting clear is only part of it. As soon as the sun comes up we'll stand out like flies on a white ceiling, then it'll be game over.'

Luck continued to favour us though. South from the base to the perimeter fence turned out to be about three kilometres. The going was easy, just gentle slopes up and down. They did come in search of us eventually of course. The judder of a helicopter advanced and receded. We saw its searchlight traversing the countryside but they never came near enough to catch us in the beam.

Dawn came and the crimson orb of the sun rose on a bed of mauve clouds.

'We must try and get back to Gibraltar,' Elena proposed.

'No point,' I said. We were resting in a hollow, lost but content for now merely to be free. 'Your father's troops will be on the move by now and if the frontier hasn't been closed it certainly will be by the time we get there.'

'Don't call him my father,' Elena said, tugging savagely at a tuft of spiky grass between her knees.

'How do you mean?'

'He's not my father. He's my *padrastro*.'

'*Padrastro*? What's that?'

'Irazola married my mother when my real father died.'

'Ah. Step-father, we call it.'

'Now perhaps you'll understand,' she said, turning those enormous brown eyes on me; eyes that embodied sadness and grief and great beauty.

'Understand what? This hate campaign against your father, sorry, step-father? Well, no, Elena not quite. It can't be just because he isn't your real father and because he's rejected his Basque origins, if he has any. Shit, when your mother abandoned you to run off with her lover he looked after you, didn't he? You ought to be grateful –'

'You're wrong,' she interrupted, stoney-faced. 'Mama didn't abandon us.'

Then the story, too long withheld, came out in a garbled rush.

Maria-Elena Irazola had left her husband not to run away with her lover, for there was no lover, not then. She left because she could no longer tolerate her husband's cruelty, both physical and mental. Their relationship, Elena explained, was that of master and servant. Her duty by the standards of Irazola's warped values was to indulge his whims and attend his needs day-in, day-out. The sadistic belt-lashings that arose out of her failure to meet his standards as he perceived them, were frequent occurrences. Elena and Luis too had tasted the belt, not once but many times.

This had gone on until, one day, when their mother, defending Elena, had struck back by taking a heavy poker to Irazola's skull and fracturing it. Afterwards she packed bags for herself and the twins and decamped for Barcelona. Irazola did not pursue them. They spent the next three years living in semi-squalor, their mother ultimately peddling her not unattractive body to keep them from starvation. Until she picked the wrong type of customer and finished up literally in the gutter with her throat gaping open and her blood mingling with the effluent of the city.

'But why did the General take you back?'

'There was no one else. Our real father was dead. By law Julio Irazola was our next-of-kin, our legal guardian. Also, by then he had appearances to think of.'

'What appearances?'

She brushed her fringe away from her forehead. 'He was an

ambitious officer. To abandon his step-children would be a black mark against him. He wished to appear magnanimous … forgiving.'

It was a dismal tale. I remembered the brittle atmosphere on the night I had dined with the General, the strong impression that the banter was spurious, staged for my benefit.

The sweat produced by our run was beginning to cool. I shivered in my inadequate and much-abused lightweight suit.

'And is he really Franco's son?'

'Probably. His mother was a whore. He took her name. It is said that Franco paid her to keep quiet.'

I drew her to me, stroked her black hair. 'Poor Elena. You must really hate him.'

'More than I can say. More even than I love you, André. He killed my mother and now my brother. Now I have no one except you and I don't really have you, do I?'

I couldn't meet her gaze. I wanted to be kind, yet I owed her too much to prevaricate.

'You are in love with Papa's woman, aren't you? With Linda.'

'I wouldn't call it love. Sure, I'm fond of her, but it goes no further than that.' It would have been a cruelty too many to tell her that my real love was on the other side of the Atlantic. I took her chin in my hand, held her eyes with mine. 'Let's get out of this mess and then we'll see. You're a beautiful girl, and I admire and respect you. However this ends, I will always want to be your friend.'

'Hah! Say no more, André.' She got up; the seat of her jeans was dark with damp from the grass. 'You are right, we must first save ourselves. Afterwards, let us see what the fates have in store.' She turned up her collar. 'What do you wish us to do now?'

I rose, more slowly, my joints stiff. 'Get going.'

We didn't have to travel for long. Barely twenty minutes more trudging up slopes and down inclines before we crested a ridge, and there below us was the airfield, and our ticket back to the Rock.

* * * * *

The little piston-engined aircraft was zipping down the runway. It took off, climbing in a near perpendicular ascent, banking southward. The busy vibrato of its engine dwindled to nothing.

Somehow we had to make it to Gib before nightfall. To warn anyone who cared to heed us of the imminence of invasion. I voiced the thought to Elena.

'This was what I imagined you would say. It makes me love you all the more.' She came to me and laid her cheek against mine. 'You are so brave and unselfish.'

Yeah, a million pounds worth of unselfish. Just being brave was enough for me.

While I was basking in her eulogies a solution hit me.

'We'll fly there.'

'Oh, yes? Scheduled or charter?'

'I mean it. We'll steal that helicopter.'

She didn't take me seriously. 'Will we? And an obliging pilot to go with it, presumably.'

'We've got guns.' I shook her by the shoulders. 'Down there will be pilots.'

'Of course. Why not?' She did a little caper. 'You are very smart, André. Kiss me.'

Kissing her was the easy part. The hard part was to come. We were intending to hijack a military helicopter in daylight without resources and the most meagre of armouries: two nearly-empty machine pistols plus Elena's revolver which had but a single cartridge to its name.

'You realise we're not equipped for a long campaign,' I said as I swept the terrain yet again in search of cover. It was as bare as the open sea.

'Don't be defeatist. Those are air force men down there, not soldiers. You will only have to wave a gun at them and they will fly you around the world.'

The man on top of the helicopter had descended to the tarmac and appeared to be wiping his hands. If he was just a mechanic, he was probably no use to us, so we would have to go hunting for our flyboy.

I was still worrying about how to cross that patch of bare hillside without being spotted when the sun abruptly went in and the far end of the runway seemed to blur over and then to dissolve.

'Look,' Elena said excitedly. 'It's getting misty.'

On all sides the landscape was fading, losing colour as the curtain of mist rolled in and over us, stilling the chatter of birds, isolating us as effectively as if we were marooned in space. God was still batting for us, it seemed.

'We must go immediately,' Elena said, and was almost out of sight before I started after her.

'Do you think we can fly in this?' I asked her as we jogged side by side down the slope.

'Oh, yes. It's only a sea mist. It will soon clear.'

As we went lower the mist thickened and we almost ran into a fence, a man-high, heavy-duty mesh affair. I punted Elena over the top, hand cupped under her butt, then scrambled over myself, hoping it wasn't wired up to an alarm system.

Elena reassured me. 'They use guard dogs.'

'What!' I gripped the sub-machine gun and glanced to the left and right, expecting some Baskervillian hound to materialise out of the curtain of grey.

'At night only,' she added with a playful grin.

'Why are you so goddamn cool and collected?'

The question was rhetorical and without waiting for a response I carried on down, the gradient flattening out as we neared the runway apron and the mist now thickening to real fog.

A building loomed on our left. Elena tugged me away and the murk sucked it back in. Then instead of grass there was tarmac underfoot and our running feet were audible. Too audible. We stopped in perfect coordination, a few metres short of the helicopter. Voices, deceptively close or deceptively far away. Mist plays tricks on the auditory senses. I lined up the machine pistol, doubtful I would actually use it, even in self-defence. Whatever taste I had ever had for shedding blood had been sated years ago.

'Raul, *es bien*?' came a disembodied cry.

Raul shouted back that he had just about cracked the problem and threw in a grumble about it being wasted effort as nobody would fly in this muck.

We crept forward, took cover behind the chopper. A blurred silhouette in the fog morphed into the red fin of an aircraft with a fat, slab-sided fuselage. Under the nearer wing was Raul, obviously a mechanic. He was on one knee, tinkering with the starboard wheel, an open cantilever tool box to hand. His colleague was nowhere in sight, presumably hidden by the bulk of the aircraft.

'The charger unit is plugged in,' the other mechanic called.

'They won't be flying in this, I tell you,' Raul insisted, grunting as he tightened some nut with a spanner.

'It's only ground mist.'

'It's all the excuse they need to sit around in the mess playing cards.'

Away to the left was the flight control tower, lights burning at its upper windows. If anyone was to look out now, fog or no fog, we were done for.

'*Finito*,' Raul proclaimed. 'Let's go.'

The clatter of tools being dumped in the tool box. We ducked back behind the chopper in case they were going to pass our way. Footsteps, murmured conversation decreasing in volume as they made off, towards the hangar.

'You OK?' I said to Elena.

She grinned an affirmative and by unspoken command we headed for the shoe box building. A glass door on the long side facing us led into a lobby with another glass door that opened up on what I guessed was the Spanish equivalent of an officers' mess. It was occupied by a dozen or so uniformed men, whose heads turned towards us in complete synchronicity, like a well-choreographed stage act.

'Who are you?' one said; he was a bit older than the rest, with receding hair and a burgeoning paunch. Not a pilot then.

'What do you want?' another asked.

The machine pistols were down by our sides. We raised them to gut level, so they would get the message that we weren't just delivering groceries.

Elena was quick to come to the point.

'Which one of you is the helicopter pilot?' she demanded.

Nobody owned up. Elena grimaced and looked at me for guidance.

I beckoned the paunchy officer to come over. He hesitated. I wagged the gun. I daren't waste bullets on a demonstration.

He came, dragging his feet.

'I want to know who is the helicopter pilot,' I said. 'If you don't tell me in five seconds I will shoot one of your colleagues.'

He paled. I started the countdown, but got no further than two. The pilot who had spoken second, indicated a tall, lanky guy with too much hair, wearing a flier's blouson.

'It's him. No need to shoot anybody.'

Elena summoned the lanky officer over and interrogated him about flying the helicopter. His nods and monosyllabic affirmatives were good enough for me.

'He's coming with us,' I announced to the room at large. 'If anyone comes after us they'll be shot.'

'They might come after us in a fighter,' Elena warned.

Outside the fog was thinning. If conditions continued to improve, Elena was probably right. A couple of the pilots exchanged whispers. Elena silenced them with a curt command.

It was going to be tricky, the outcome uncertain. In our favour, Gib was only a few minutes flying time away. Worst case scenario we could put the chopper down anywhere reasonably level.

Elena took charge of our pilot, asked him his name.

'Teniente Torres,' he said, tone and expression surly.

'*Vale*, Torres. Outside and no funny business.'

While she shepherded Torres out of the mess, I hung around covering the remaining pilots, so as to let her get to the chopper before they could take action or phone for assistance.

I gave her a couple of minutes, then reversed out through the inner door. The pilots just stood there, watching me but making no effort to interfere. My backside bumped into the outer door. A final macho glare to terrify them into immobility, and I plunged through the doorway.

The chopper was in sight now as the mist continued to disperse. Our abductee was just going through a doorway in the side of the fuselage, with encouragement from Elena's machine pistol.

I glanced back at the mess. Several of the pilots were moving towards the door. I fired a single shot through a window. The shattering of the glass was more dramatic than the gunshot, and the pilots scattered, diving to the floor.

I started forward at a run. When I reached the chopper Elena and

Torres were already inside; he was getting settled in the left-hand captain's seat, Elena standing over him. The controls and instruments were arranged along a black oval panel in front of the seats, and in a second panel between the seats. The Perspex bubble of the nose canopy was sub-divided into a number of individual panes.

'Get on with it,' Elena snapped at Torres, making sure he could see the machine pistol.

While he got stuck in with what I assumed were the pre-flight checks, I stayed by the open door to discourage the others. I also used the lull in activities to check the state of the magazine of my gun, thumbing the rounds out into my cupped hand. The count was four plus another in the breech. Too few to waste on automatic fire.

More action inside the building, some of the braver souls now venturing outside. Two at least held pistols. I popped off an aimed shot just above their heads. Glass sprayed, and the group flung themselves flat once again.

'How much longer?" I called over my shoulder to Elena.

'Two minutes.'

I heard the pilot chanting Spanish stuff, most of which being aeronautical-ese was a mystery to me. I caught the words '*freno*', '*bateria*', and '*rotor*' but the rest was just monologue.

'*Darse prisa*!' I heard Elena yell at him. Hurry up.

A mumbled response from Torres, then more monotonal chanting.

Somebody fired at us from the mess. I heard the bullet clang against the sliding door panel, metal striking metal. I retreated from the doorway. A second shot, a second clang. If they kept it up sooner or later a bullet would find me. I crouched, to reduce the target size. I didn't want to kill anyone, but if it was them or me …

Overhead the rotor began to crank, very slowly. A rumble, was followed by a clatter as the engine fired. I decided waste half of my remaining ammunition, and peeping around the edge of the doorway, loosed off two shots, at the handful of officers who were now advancing cautiously towards the chopper. Down they went yet again, although some of them fired their handguns, mostly missing the chopper. If they were fighter pilots the Spanish Air Force needed to step up its target practice.

The rotor was going at a lick now, making the old familiar slapping sound. The floor under my feet shifted and I braced myself against a bulkhead. More bullets pattered against the fuselage. Then abruptly we left the ground, the floor vibrating, and unseen metallic stuff rattling. Hanging on to the head restraint of the left hand seat, I peered through the front canopy. The runway and green-brown areas of grass on either side were falling away. The parked fighters shrank in size as I watched, became toylike.

Torres seemed relaxed enough, his right hand gripping a short control stick and stirring it lightly; his left hand was down beside his seat, also in action. I felt the chopper respond, the floor tilting upwards towards the front as he increased the climb rate at some muttered instruction from Elena, accompanied by the jab of a gun muzzle in his neck.

She moved to the co-pilot's seat and strapped herself in while keeping Torres covered. She grinned at me; she seemed to be getting quite a kick out of our little escapade.

'Sit down and fasten the straps,' she ordered me.

Behind her seat was a passenger seat. I flopped into it, buckled the straps. We were now well above what was left of the mist, skies all around blue and free of clouds. A perfect day for vacationers. Some object struck the windshield and was flipped way leaving a mark like a dead insect. It didn't bother me. Any moment now we would be out of range, even of a rifle.

'Looks like we made it.' I said to Elena.

Her eyes sparkled.

'Isn't it fun?'

To her we were just goofing around, playing a practical joke on the Air Force. I hoped they would see the theft of a helicopter in that light.

We were accelerating forward now, the note of the engine rising and the rotor at full hammer. Somewhere in the array of dials and digital readings must have been a ground speed indicator but it wasn't evident. Digits flickered and tumbled and winked in profusion, confusing me but hopefully telling Torres all was well.

Hills and a large lake were rolling past beneath us, and beyond the lake was the sea and a town, possibly Sotogrande. To my right the Rock, less impressive from up here, was obscured by its habitual low cloud.

'Can you tell what's our altitude,' I asked Elena, shouting to make myself heard over the thunder of the engine.

She prodded Torres. '*Quantos metros de altura temenos?*'

'*Ochocientos*,' he grunted.

Eight hundred feet. If it mattered. If we were shot down at any altitude above sea level the outcome was likely to be fatal.

We hadn't seriously discussed tactics. I assumed we were going to land at Gib airport.

'Unless you'd prefer to come down in the sea,' Elena said, with a terse laugh.

'We may need clearance to land? We'd better tell Torres. Or maybe not, if your people will be listening in.'

'They'll guess anyway.'

Torres fired a question at Elena, too fast for me.

'He asked where he's to go.'

I told him to head out to sea, to mislead the Spanish radar. The summit of the Rock edged past on our right. I could see the red cabin of the cable car en route for the top. A straight dash for the airport, capitalising on our start, might have been a smarter move. I wondered how long it took to scramble a fighter. Five minutes? Three? No, that would be from a state of readiness. Those fighters I had seen were not parked for instant getaway.

I peered through the Perspex. Behind and below us Irazola's forces would be preparing to break camp. They wouldn't move until nightfall, using darkness to cloak their advance. From their encampment to the frontier was not much more than an hour, even for the heaviest armour. I visualised the tanks rumbling down through the pass on their way to the coast, steel dinosaurs in the night, tracks squeaking and squealing. I imagined the shouted orders, the cursing, the milling confusion that goes hand-in-hand with a major military exercise, the inevitable mishaps: a jeep toppling into a ditch, a tank carving the corner off a wall, one troop-carrier shunting another.

Up here in the blue though, all was calm apart from the racket from the engine. Then the radio stuttered, the staccato jabber too fast for me to translate.

'What are they saying?' I shouted at Elena.

She shushed me. More rapid fire dialogue, then she said, 'They are sending up two fighters. They have been instructed to shoot us down on sight.'

'Christ!' I wasn't even wearing a parachute. 'Is this thing armed?'

Elena relayed the question to Torres.

'*Si.* Two heavy machine guns. The fighters will be carrying air-to-air missiles however.'

The radio went quiet. I scanned the sky, swivelling my head from side to side. Notwithstanding that a visual sighting would serve no purpose, since those fighters could outpace us many times over. Likely as not a missile ploughing into the fuselage would be the only notice we would receive.

We were beyond the coast now and ahead was all water. Elena instructed Torres to descend and head back for the airport by the shortest straightest route. The priority now was to get down before we were shot down.

He nodded, glanced over at me as if for confirmation. We began to turn in a wide circle and lose altitude. Our view of the sea was replaced by a view of the Rock and the runway at its base. We were not far above the surface of the water now, flapping over a small sailing boat, a line of white faces following our progress.

Elena turned in her seat to face me. 'André …'

'What is it?'

'I love you, *mi cariño*.'

No honest reply would have been adequate, so I reached out and rested a hand on her shoulder to try and convey my feelings for her, even if they didn't quite add up to love.

Maintaining wave-skimming height, Torres was on his final run for the airport, the sun bursting into the cabin with the brightness of a phosphorous shell. The north face of the Rock was on our left, growing in magnitude with every passing second.

A patch of sea up ahead shivered as if in a spasm. Now you see it, now you don't. I stared at the spot, but it told me nothing. Then the chopper gave a shudder and there was a sound of tearing metal. I glanced over my shoulder. A jagged rent had appeared in the sliding door. So that was what 'shoot on sight' meant.

Torres shouted, 'They're shooting at us!'

Cannon fire was less deadly than a self-homing missile, which was all you could say in its favour. Or so I deluded myself until the second burst left a gaping hole a few feet behind me. The chopper rocked, swinging like a pendulum. The sea was suddenly very, very close. We flew on, shuddering and clattering, the Rock closing in on us at a frightening rate. A slender aircraft suffused the screen going from left to right, too close for safety, too fast to change course. A screeching of metal to metal followed, accompanied by a loud bang. Our aircraft quivered and the fighter went cartwheeling spectacularly across the surface of the sea, throwing up arcs of spray from its extremities, like an aquatic catherine wheel.

God knows how, but Torres kept his nerve. It felt as if our machine was shaking itself apart as we thundered over the water, the airport coming up fast. Then the second fighter appeared on our right, two o'clock high. It flicked past, going too fast to engage us. Now it was already swinging across the sky in a semi-circle, coming back for the kill.

Gibraltar airport was no more than a kilometre distant. To land we had to reduce speed, which would have made us sitting-duck targets. To stay aloft was a no more enticing prospect and would only prolong the inevitable. Our craft was in poor shape, creaking and vibrating; some of the instruments were doing a war dance and an orange square of light was flashing from the control panel. Behind my head an alarm was wailing. Torres seemed to be fighting the stick with both hands wrapped around it.

We were facing approximately west, the isthmus of land between the Rock and Spain the slenderest of threads, the runway tapering to vanishing point out in the bay. Our altitude was virtually zero, all Torres had to do was keep us aloft and fly in a straight line for less than a minute.

A feeling of helplessness came over me. We were entirely dependent on Torres and I wasn't enjoying it one bit.

'Here he comes!' Torres warned. I looked in all directions but saw nothing. A faint drumming, like distant hooves, and something exploded in my face spraying me with warm fluid. Elena cried out and we wobbled violently, the airport runway no longer in view. I called her name, struggled to get free of the harness.

'Don't … move.' Her voice was hoarse, barely audible. 'I'm … all right.'

The chopper stabilised, Torres continuing to perform miracles in keeping us aloft. Elena was motionless, kept in place by her harness. If she was hurt there wasn't a damn thing in the world I could do about it.

Cold air was funnelling up between my legs, and fluid continued to sprinkle me from some unseen source. The fighter had gone into a zoom climb after the attack. When it reappeared it was off to port, a speck that doubled then quadrupled in size, gobbling up the airspace between us at a prodigious rate. Ahead, the runway was close – so close it seemed that all we had to do was sink down onto it. Instead we shot upwards as if snatched by some giant lifting device and the fighter, moving too fast to conform, passed beneath, the patter of its cannon cutting off short. It was a brilliant piece of flying by Torres who then brought us down so fast I left my stomach behind. Under my feet something was banging about. I got the impression the fuselage was about to tear itself apart.

'Are you all right?' I asked Elena but my voice was drowned by the general din. The machine pistol slid off her lap and hit the floor with a clatter.

The runway broadened to an arrowhead shape as we homed in on it. A twin-turboprop aircraft in drab military grey was sitting on the tarmac in front of the airport buildings, its props whirling discs. Stay there just a moment or two longer, I cautioned in my mind. People were pouring from the buildings, rushing to the side of the runway to stare.

A yelp of rubber, a bounce before finally settling. We were down, fifty metres from a goggling line of spectators who came rushing over to render aid. The rotor was slowing. Torres was tilted sideways, his head resting against the Perspex, as if he had dozed off. Blood covered the right side of his head and his shoulder.

Tendrils of smoke oozed lazily from under the control panel. I had by now discovered the quick-release button of the harness and was out in a flash, clambering over the seat to get to Elena.

Her body had been hit at least twice by shrapnel. There were two distinct wounds and she had bled so much that her clothes were saturated with it; little of the original colour still showed.

Her head had flopped back, her eyes were closed, the sweeping black lashes lying like little fringes on her pale cheeks, below the big fringe. Not a mark on her pale face. At peace. And in her peace she was the most beautiful creature on earth.

'Elena,' I said, uselessly, helplessly, my voice breaking with emotion.

'Hey you – get out of there!' The shouting was accompanied by a hammering on the fuselage. 'She'll go up in a minute.'

I laid my hand along Elena's cheek. 'No, she won't,' I murmured. 'She's not going up ever again.'

Smoke belched out from under Elena's seat; smoke interspersed with tongues of flame. The heat seared my leg. I didn't feel a thing.

Afterwards they told me they had had to drag me out.

Chapter Thirty

'Mild concussion,' the doctor pronounced. 'First degree burns to upper right leg, minor bruising and lacerations. You're a lucky man by all accounts. Finish those dressings, will you, nurse?'

'Never mind that,' I said, sitting up on the bed as the nurse fussed around me. I was clad only in undershorts and socks. 'What day is it?'

'Day? Friday.'

'The 8th?'

He nodded. My watch was still on my wrist: it was ten minutes after eleven and room was sunny. Thirteen hours had gone by since we landed. We? Where was Elena?

Then it all came back to me, vivid as a nightmare. Especially the blood … Elena's blood … blood everywhere …

'I have to get out of here, see the Governor.'

'You're not going to see anyone,' the doctor said warmly. 'You need at least twenty-four hours rest for the concussion alone.'

The nurse was spraying sealant on the burned area of my leg. It was ice-cold but it did the job. She kept skimming nervous glances at me, as if she were unsure of my mental stability. I was in what appeared to be a small private ward, probably at the St Bernard's Hospital which was closer to the airport than the Naval Hospital.

'Didn't anyone tell you what happened at the airport?'

'Only that you crash landed,' the doctor said. 'Now if you'll just lie still …'

'You goddam fool!' I seethed. 'We were shot down by a Spanish fighter.'

His calm bedside manner slipped. The nurse was no longer spraying.

'I … I don't understand,' the doctor said, a crack appearing in his shell of officiousness.

'You will soon enough. Get me a car – with a driver if you think I'm not fit to be at the wheel. I have to see the Governor right away.'

I could see he was still unsure whether to humour me or send for a straitjacket. In the event he humoured me. My wounds were dressed in what was probably world-record time and the doctor himself drove me round to the Convent.

Then my problems began. The Governor was having a working lunch with the Chief Minister and on no account to be disturbed. The Sergeant of the guard refused me entry and when I brushed him aside and entered anyway I was seized by two soldiers and placed under arrest. Which did at any rate gain me admittance, if only to a small basement room furnished with a wobbly bench and a table. My fortunes took a turn for the better when, at my insistence, my old accomplice Major Ribble was sent for.

I wasted no words on greetings.

'Did you hear what happened at the airport?'

'Something about a Spanish plane shooting down a chopper.'

'Correct. I was in the one that was shot at. The pilot and a … a friend of mine, were killed.'

He tweaked his moustache anxiously. 'What's going on, Warner?'

'Explanations will have to wait. I have to see the Governor right now.'

'I don't know about that, old man.' Typical. Protocol and red tape would be the death of Gibraltar yet. 'He's closeted with the CM. Can't you tell me what it's about?'

'War, Ribble,' I said bleakly. 'War is what it's about.'

* * * * *

The Governor made no effort to suppress his displeasure. As it happened, his session with the Chief Minister was over but another appointment was waiting in the wings. Ribble was dismissed with a mild rebuke, and Sir Gilbert received me alone in his private office. It was cool and peaceful there. The threat of an invasion took on a mildly ludicrous aspect.

'I've sent for Kirkland to join us,' the Governor said as I made myself comfortable.

'It may be a long wait, Governor. When last I saw him he was lying on the floor in an interrogation room at General Irazola's HQ.'

The Governor boggled. 'You mean he's been abducted?'

'No, I mean he's defected.'

'What!'

I gave him a potted rundown on Kirkland's background and loyalties. As the extent of the Prime Ministerial aide's perfidy was unveiled the Governor's brow darkened and an expletive passed his lips.

'Is all this true?' he said, when I had run dry.

'It can't be proved, but it'll come out eventually. Meanwhile, Governor, there's a more pressing item on the political agenda.'

'Go on.'

I went on. He heard me out and no interruptions.

When I had recited my piece he said, 'We already discussed your invasion theory at some length, as I recall. Surely the concessions that are to be made – and incidentally no one in Gibraltar apart from Mr Picardo and I are privy to the details – have removed that threat.'

'That's the whole point. The invasion is part of a military takeover of Spain, it's nothing at all to do with the elected Government. Why do you think I was pursued here by two fighters and shot down?'

'A serious infringement of Gibraltar airspace,' Sir Gilbert asserted, thrusting his modest chin belligerently.

'Balls to your airspace – with respect, sir. You've got to alert the Government … both Governments, British and Spanish. King Felipe may be in danger too.' Though I was sure Petrov had been eliminated, his demise on its own wouldn't remove the threat to the King.

Sir Gilbert rested his elbows on the arms of his leather swivel chair and regarded me balefully.

'You are quite sure about all this, I hope, Warner. It's a great responsibility you're asking me to shoulder.'

'Sir Gilbert,' I replied, my patience tottering, 'it is now one-forty five pm on 8th May. On Sunday morning, approximately forty hours from now Irazola's tanks are going to roll across the frontier, across the airport runway, and down Main Street. Behind them will come a division of troops, with a couple more in reserve. Your skies will be full of helicopter gunships, and warships will mount a blockade. Do you want to be remembered as the man who handed the Rock over to Spain?' I was guessing about the blockade but it was reasonable to assume that Irazola had allies in the fleet.

'All right, Warner.' A profound sigh, as if he were humouring me. 'Point made. I'll call the Foreign Office. Then we'll see.'

I had always known he wouldn't move without authority from HQ. I sat down uninvited in one of the crescent of chairs drawn up before Sir Gilbert's desk.

His face darkened. 'I'd rather you waited outside, if you don't mind.'

He forestalled my protest by stabbing the buzzer of his intercom. Ribble came in, so promptly I suspected him of eavesdropping at the door.

'Mr Warner will wait in the ante-chamber,' Sir Gilbert said unsmilingly. 'And you are to remain with him.'

My banishment lasted through three cups of Government-brand tea. It was approaching three o'clock when Sir Gilbert came out of his office. He was paler than when I had left him.

'Well?' I fired at him.

'Come in, will you?'

Back in his office he said without prologue, 'We are to let events take their course. No precautions are to be taken and nothing done which might be construed as provocative.'

'Provocative!' I almost gagged on the word. 'You mean we let them stroll in and raise the Spanish flag over the Rock?'

'There are difficulties.' Sir Gilbert was clearly unhappy with his brief. 'The Spanish Prime Minister is away in South America, the King cannot be reached and no one seems to know his whereabouts.'

'Well, what a coincidence.' I was barely coherent. 'What about organising resistance here? You've got several hundred servicemen at your disposal. There's a couple of Navy boats in the harbour. Christ, man, you can't just sit on your fannies!'

'It's not my decision,' he snapped back. 'I've been *ordered* to offer no resistance. Avoiding loss of life is the main concern. After all, from what you say, Irazola doesn't represent Spain. His will be an act of rebellion, wholly illegal. It will be up to the legitimate government to deal with him.'

The man was unbelievable.

'Haven't you been listening? Unless somebody does something Irazola will very soon *be* the legitimate government. They're going to exile the King or worse, and install a dictatorship with Russian collusion. Think of what that will mean for all of Europe, let alone Gibraltar.'

'Don't talk to me as though I'm senile. How would defending Gibraltar prevent that?'

I smacked the palm of my hand to my forehead. 'By upsetting their timetable. Irazola needs Gibraltar and he needs it fast. It's his launching pad. If he fails, or he's simply delayed, the timing of his coup will be upset and may even be scrapped. It'll give Sanchez a breathing space to fly back from South America and muster support. Also, the removal of the King and Government is timed to happen *after* the announcement of the surrender of Gibraltar.'

Sir Gilbert flopped despondently into the nearest armchair. 'I've had my orders. I can't flout them. If I authorised a military response and it backfired – say hundreds were killed – it would be the end of me.'

'You fucking coward!' I stormed. 'Screw your career. You're the only one who can stop it. Just get –'

I broke off in mid-tirade. Was he the only one? What about Michael Vella and his militia. The home guard I had dismissed as primitive and ineffectual. Without another word I wheeled round and stamped out.

My chauffeuring doctor was long departed, so I set out to walk the half-kilometre to Vella's apartment, praying he would be home.

He was. Not only that but El Jefe and Peter were with him.

'A council of war?' I enquired, when he let me in.

'I never expected to see you again,' Vella confessed drawing me into the centre of the vast living room. Peter rose slowly, as if his joints were stiff.

'I think I owe you an apology,' he said and stuck out a hand. Though nonplussed, I accepted it and the apology, unmerited though it was.

'Why the change of heart?'

'Your telephone call from Madrid,' Vella explained. 'We owe you a great debt for that.'

Gratitude always embarrasses me.

'Not greater than the one I owe you.' A bout of dizziness came over me and I felt my legs buckling. I grabbed Vella for support. The room was changing shape, straight lines becoming wavy, the floor undulating like a fairground tilt-a-whirl.

'What's wrong?' Vella said, alarm in his voice.

'Nothing … an aeroplane accident. Just let me sit down.'

He and Peter all but carried me to the couch. I crashed down onto it. Vella laid hand on my forehead.

'You're running a temperature.'

'It's nothing,' I repeated, and gulped gratefully from the glass of water Peter handed me. The dizziness receded.

El Jefe said, 'We heard a Spanish aircraft crashed on the runway. Were you involved?'

'Not now, Eduardo,' Vella protested.

'Now's a good time. Yes, I was involved.' I ran briefly through the train of events that had led up to the destruction of the helicopter and Elena's death.

'Poor girl,' Vella said, concerned as always with the human aspect.

'Never mind the girl,' Peter said callously, which made me want to hit him, but I didn't have the energy to stand let alone get into a brawl. 'You haven't explained what made you so important the Spanish Air Force was prepared to risk an international incident to stop you.'

I set the now empty glass down on a nearby coffee table. All eyes were on me, as if sensing some momentous revelation.

'You won't like the news I've brought you,' I said, 'but Irazola's forces are going to march into Gib at five o' clock am. the day after tomorrow.'

The room went very quiet. So quiet I could hear the hum of the refrigerator in the kitchen.

Peter recovered fastest. He shrugged and looked at Vella.

'I warned you,' he said.

'They must be mad,' Vella said. 'Spain will lose all possible sympathy –'

'Who said anything about Spain?' My voice was harsh. 'This is a strictly one-man show, with Vladimir Putin waiting in the wings. And the man behind it all – Julio Irazola – claims to be the son of Franco.'

That really floored them.

'Franco's son?' El Jefe said, his voice an awed croak. 'My God, is it possible?'

'The bastard sired many bastards, I suspect,' Vella said bleakly. 'Be that as it may, a lot of Spaniards will flock to his banner for this reason alone.'

I gave them the rest of it, no frills. As a bonus, I also threw in the outcome of my recent interview with the Governor.

'So they won't offer even a token resistance?' Vella said, aghast.

'Not a single bayonet will be fixed in your defence.'

'We are grateful to you for coming here to warn us,' El Jefe said from the depths of his armchair. 'But I am a little surprised that the Governor should take you into his confidence to such an extent.'

Peter, quick to seize on any discrepancy, moved to confront me. 'Yes, André. How is it that the Governor spoke so freely in front of you?'

I gave a sigh. 'This is no time for in-fighting, Peter. Let's just say I'm not what I appear to be but that I'm on your side. Will that do?'

Peter took a step forward, jaw jutting. 'No, it fucking well won't!'

'Leave it, Peter!' Vella rapped out, in a sergeant-majorial tone. 'André has done more than enough to prove where his sympathies lie. I accept him as a friend and an ally, and so must you. We are going to need all the allies we can get. Especially …' Smiling lop-sidedly, '… one who has access to such high places.'

'He is right,' El Jefe said, giving Peter a direct look. 'But it is as well that we understand the manner of this man who would run such risks to help us. He had no need to come back to Gibraltar, after all.'

Peter succumbed with a scowl. 'Very well. I would like to know just who and what you are, André, but these things will wait. What we must do now is decide on how to defend our country.'

'Defend your country is right,' I agreed. 'Not because you can win but because you need to disrupt Irazola's schedule, throw grit in the works of his military machine, buy time for the legitimate government to arrest him and his buddies. Tell me, did you proceed with the plan to form a militia?'

'Indeed we did,' Vella replied. 'But we are only in the preliminary stages. Peter has been the driving force, which will be no surprise to you. It is thanks to him that we have a command structure and can call upon a thousand volunteers. What we lack most apart from weapons is military expertise. Almost no Gibraltarian has done military service.

Those who have, like Eduardo here, are too old to fight, though naturally we shall make use of them in an advisory capacity.'

'A man with knowledge of explosives would be an asset,' El Jefe remarked, his expression wily.

Peter glanced at him then across at me. 'Have you served in the forces, André?'

'In a manner of speaking. I was an officer with Military Intelligence. A long time ago.'

'Is that where you learned to handle bombs?'

I coughed. 'In part. I was given a refresher course here in Gib. '

Vella brushed this aside. 'Will you join us, André? Help us organise, help us prepare our defences. Will you?'

'It's too late, you know. Any defence can only be rudimentary.' I tugged absently at cotton strands on my shirt that had once attached a button. 'And how long do you think a thousand untrained men, poorly-armed, could hold off tanks and trained troops?'

'We would use guerrilla tactics,' El Jefe said, and his eyes blazed with the light of battle. If someone offered him a rifle I was sure he'd be mixing it with the rest. 'Fall back on the Rock. Use the tunnels and the casements. Let them try and drive a tank in there.' His cackle set Peter off; even Vella grinned, his teeth a white grid in his brown features. 'We might even get some of the old guns working.'

'Without shells, what use would they be?'

Vella was not deterred. 'Even so. Will you join us, André?'

The 'Yes' was formed, needing only articulation, when the door bell buzzed. Clucking in irritation, Vella stalked off to answer it.

The long couch, where I sat, was in a shallow recess, obscured from the hall door. Had I been almost anywhere else in the room Linda might have behaved with more restraint, might even have tried to deceive me. As it was, her first utterance on entering was, 'Hi, darling, surprise-surprise,' and for the reason already mentioned, the endearment wasn't directed at me.

'Linda …' was all Vella said. I got up, much too quickly for my concussed brain. Linda and Vella were framed in the doorway, kissing; she on tiptoe owing to his height.

'How touching,' I said, and Linda pulled away with an exclamation of dismay.

'Warner! You're back.' She remained stock still for some seconds, then came slowly towards me, arms out, appealing. She as lovely as ever, vital, radiating health and happiness, her rich brown hair bouncing on her shoulders. Her dress was oyster-pink and figure-hugging. And her figure was worthy of it, the post-natal flab almost gone. Vella followed her, plucking self-consciously at his nose, clearly flustered by the exposure of his intrigue with Linda.

She came up close, held my hands. I let them lie in hers, stiff, like pieces of wood.

'Nobody told me you were here. If I'd known …' She flapped her hands helplessly. 'I didn't want you to find out like this, honey.'

'You don't need to explain. We're not married. We're not anything at all.'

Her mouth turned down. Vella came to stand beside her, ill-at-ease, an intruder in his own home.

'It started when Linda was in hospital.'

I didn't say anything.

'Look,' Peter said, acting as conciliator for once, 'this can wait, can't it? We were discussing the invasion.'

'Invasion!' Linda's eyes darted from face to face, coming to rest on Vella's. 'He's joking, isn't he?'

'If only he was,' he said, awkward still.

Peter, growing irritated, dragged me around, separating me from Linda. 'There are things we must do! We need you. Are you with us?'

I looked from him to Vella and finally to Linda; to Linda the longest of all.

'No,' I said, and Peter recoiled from me, as if I'd announced my contraction of a highly contagious disease. 'I've finished with Gibraltar.'

It was petty to let my spite overrule the strong sense of obligation that had drawn me back to Gibraltar in the first place. Perhaps on account of my semi-concussed state, Linda's duplicity and my discovery of it with it was blown up in my mind into a massive betrayal. That the other guilty party should be Michael Vella, a man I liked and respected, was doubly destructive.

'You mean you're going to abandon us just because Michael has fallen in love with your girl?' Peter took hold of my sleeve again, tugging at it in his agitation.

'Put yourself in his place,' El Jefe said, calm and unflappable, a disinterested observer.

'What do they mean, Warner?' Linda demanded. 'What's all this talk about abandoning them?'

I couldn't bring myself to speak to her.

'But you helped us,' Peter fumed, then, in an appeal to Vella: 'He helped us.' Ironic that he of all people, who once tried to kill me, should now try to enlist me.

'Never,' I denied. 'I never helped you. I work for money, not causes.'

'Not so,' Vella said, stirred at last to respond. 'In the beginning, yes, but not now. You didn't come here today for money. You came because you can differentiate between right and wrong. You came to keep faith – don't deny it.'

I backed away, towards the door. All of them watching me: Linda ashen, Peter flushed with anger. Vella and El Jefe stoic, emotions under control.

'You're a fighter at heart,' El Jefe said mildly.

'I'm a spy, not a gunslinger.' I was seeking excuses, lying to them and to myself.

'Warner – don't go.' This from Linda. I closed my ears, closed my heart, closed my conscience.

I left them there. Left them to fight their battle without me. I was done with it all: with Gibraltar, with GIBESTÁ, with Vella and his raggle-taggle militia, and with Linda, the girl I didn't quite love but had certainly trusted. Let Irazola's divisions roll over them. Let them hoist their red and yellow standard on the Rock's highest point. Let them plunge Spain into rule by dictatorship. Let them even hook up with Russia and take control of the Strait of Gibraltar and with it the Mediterranean.

As I descended the stairs a thought hit me with the force of a heavyweight punch. What had I said up there? *I'm a spy, not a gunslinger.* But that wasn't true, was it? If anything, I was more gunslinger than spy. And as gunslinger maybe I had a lot more to contribute than Vella's militia. A man with a particular gun and a particular set of skills is in a position to achieve things beyond the scope and competence of a makeshift army, no matter how many strong.

* * * * *

I dined at the Caleta though it was eating for eating's sake. No reflection on the standard of the cuisine but the fish resembled cotton wool and the vegetables all tasted alike. Even the wine – a Chablis Premier Cru, glinting gold-green – might have been some cheap tourist muck.

As I finished off the bottle, I surveyed the dining room. The other diners were mostly visitors to the Rock. If they knew what I knew the exodus would be instantaneous. Not that rushing to the airport would save them; tomorrow's flight to the UK was destined to be the last for many a day. But had I climbed on a table and warned them with a megaphone they would take me for a madman. Shriek with hilarity probably, as if I were a comedy act.

In the evening this, the eastern side of the Rock would always be in shadow, winter and summer alike. Now, as I sat there with my forebodings, the darkening sea took on a sombre aspect, the turgid swell sinister and menacing as some fearsome creature was lurking in its depths, waiting to be unleashed. Eve-of-war tristesse? Perhaps others before me, in August 1914 and August 1939, possessed of similar foreknowledge of conflict, had been overcome with such heaviness of heart as now afflicted me.

As well as mental anguish I was suffering physically. The hospital's painkillers were wearing off. My head was pounding, and the burns on my leg throbbed with ever more intensity. Even when a stunner of a girl, alone and on the face of it unspoken for, was shown to a table opposite I viewed her with as much passion as a policeman surveying passing traffic.

A liqueur bucked me up enough to indulge in some idle speculation on Richard Kirkland, and whether he had recovered from that kick to the skull. His phoney ID was blown. He was finished as the Prime Minister's aide, finished in Britain, period.

What would London be making of his and my disappearance? Another black mark for Warner, of that you could be sure. And if war did break out, what would be the fate of my still unsold bar in Malaga? To conclude the sale meant returning to Spain – and a Spain under the boot of Presidente Generalissimo Julio Irazola was a place to be avoided. The only saving grace was that if my venture into the hospitality trade did go down the pan, it wouldn't leave me penniless.

* * * * *

The nasal tones of Keith Jupp were the audio double of Ringo Starr. He was Liverpool-born and proud of it to the point of decorating the living room walls of his house with 45rpm singles of all the Beatles' hits start to finish. Pride of place, in a silver frame, was the rare and valuable 78rpm pressing of the group's version, recorded when they were still the Quarrymen, of the Crickets' "That'll be the Day" hit. One of only fifty in circulation.

After the usual enquiries about health we got down to business.

'I want a sniper's rifle, the best you can lay your hands on at short notice.'

'Not a problem, not a problem. You want to take out a person or a tank?'

He wasn't being entirely flippant about the tank. The Barrett M96, best sniper rifle in the world, shoots a 0.5in cartridge and has a range not far short of a mile. Originally it was designed as an "anti-materiel" weapon.

'A mere human. Range up to fifteen hundred metres, say.'

'Delivery where?'

'Gibraltar.'

'Gibraltar! You don't want much, do you, mate? Crossing borders is expensive. I'll have to deliver by boat.'

'No, you won't. We'll use mine. Bring it to La Línea, and we'll do the transfer there. '

Terms were discussed and agreed. He would drive overnight from his home in the town of Berga, in the mountains north of Barcelona, and expected to be in La Línea by mid-day tomorrow. If he was on time that would leave just seventeen hours before Irazola's tanks were due to cross the border.

* * * * *

At the border it was business as usual. The Brits weren't interested in me. Even on the Spanish side I was waved through on a casual flourish of my British passport. The *laissez-faire* attitude had me suspecting the border police had been instructed to let me in for the express purpose of picking me up down the road. But no, I drove to the Alcaidesa Marina, a stone's throw from the border, and nobody paid me heed. *Seamist*, being one of the larger craft, was moored at a berth close to the harbour entrance. I parked the Aston twenty metres from it, and was on board a few minutes after mid-day.

The Levanter was blowing steadily from the east, agitating the sea, making it chuckle against the dark blue hull. The decks and superstructure were under a sheen of beige dust carried by the wind from the Sahara. The Rock loomed over the port from its best-known aspect, the sheer north face, in shadow even with the sun at its zenith.

Keith had called my cell to warn me he would be late. 'No more than an hour.' I used that hour to hose the away the dust and restore the boat to gleaming. It was a few minutes before one o'clock when his black Audi SUV chugged down the service road and drew in next to the Aston. He dismounted, did a quick sweep of the immediate surroundings for potential hostiles. The box he hauled from the Audi's cargo space was too short for the full length of the rifle I had ordered, meaning he had dismembered it.

We shook hands, I plied him with a bottle of Bavasienne Blond, my preferred beer. He was partial to it.

'All I came for,' he grinned, wiping his mouth with the back of his hand and burping his approval. He was about fifty, of medium height, with the kind of full lips that women inject with botox to achieve. Shoots of grey were making inroads into his lank brown hair, and while he had always been thickset of build he could now fairly be described as paunchy.

For form's sake I told him he was 'looking prosperous'.

Never a man to delude himself, he retorted 'You mean I'm getting fat.'

We laughed in harmony, then got down to business.

The gun was a Finnish-made Sako TRG42. Among the best snipers' rifles in the world. The sort of gun you couldn't miss with. It was the black and green version, made partly of aluminum, with folding stock and cheek pad for users' greater comfort. He had broken it down into seven pieces, and demonstrated how to reassemble them in less than two minutes, so that it looked like what it was – a lethal weapon. I practiced taking it apart and putting it back together, and by the third cycle was almost able to match his speed.

'You'll do,' he grunted.

The kit included two five-round magazines, both loaded, a carton of twenty-five cartridges, less the ten in the magazines, a Sako custom bipod, and a scope sight.

The cartridges were .338 calibre Lapua magnums, known as Dangerous Game Solid. Seemed appropriate. Game didn't come much more dangerous than General Julio Irazola.

'They'll give you the best range,' Jupp said.

His statements were always made poker-faced, as if he were rating the performance of a car tyre or a power drill. Although we never discussed the purpose of the weapons he supplied, he accepted that the intended target was human. Accepted it and didn't flinch from it. You don't supply illegal guns for a living if you have issues with their lethal intent.

The scope was a Leupold Mk 6, $2000-worth of optics, suitable for use in low-light conditions. The specification included a recticle magnifier with range estimation facility. If I couldn't hit a target with this beauty I was in the wrong game.

'I set it up for one thousand metres, like you said,' Jupp informed me. 'It'll be good for a one-inch grouping a hundred metres either side of that range.'

'Good man.' I tested the weight. The use of aluminum in the stock made it lighter than many rifles of its size, but at six kilos it was no featherweight.

'Is that right, you won't be able to test it?' he asked, lighting a long unfiltered cigarette.

'Nowhere in Gib is out of earshot, and I can't stay in Spain.' I gripped his shoulder, squeezed. 'I guess I'll have to trust you.' The grip represented a warning as well as confidence in his skills. In other words, I was content to accept his word on the accuracy and sight settings of the weapon. But if he had steered me wrong I would not be forgiving.

'You should,' he said, in deadly earnest. Trust was his stock-in-trade. Without it, he would be out of business.

No money changed hands. That part of the transaction would be by internet transfer from a numbered account to a numbered account. Anonymous, fast, secure.

'If you can hang on to it afterwards, I'll take it back at a twenty per cent discount,' he said over our parting handshake.

It was rare for me to be able to return a weapon. The offer was appreciated though.

A minute later he was manoeuvring out of the parking bay and setting out on his return drive to Barcelona. The next stage of my operation was to transport myself and the gun back to Gibraltar, where I had already booked mooring space at the Mid-Harbour Marina, through a contact at the Yacht Club introduced by Harry, the Caleta front desk manager. It cost me mega-euros, but I wasn't in a position to quibble.

Abandoning the Aston gave me a twinge or two. If all went well, I would recover it after the fuss had died down. If not ... Well, the stakes were a whole lot bigger than a set of wheels, even exalted ones.

For so short a distance I left the sails stowed, and used the engine. Several guys were fishing off the end of the mole. They watched me putter past; I flipped a hand and they responded in kind. Boats came and went here throughout the day, every day. I was nothing remarkable.

As a precaution against being under surveillance I sailed due south, beyond the Gibraltar town waterfront until the buildings hid me from La Línea, then doubled back to enter the harbour from the south. Even if Irazola's agents weren't letting me out of their sight, I was out of their reach for as long as Gib remained in British hands.

It was Linda who answered Vella's cell phone, another twist of the knife in the wound of my injured vanity.

'Let me speak to Vella,' I said, without announcing myself.

'Who ... oh, it's you, Warner. Listen –'

'Put him on,' I snapped at her.

Her 'Oh!' made me feel like a louse, but she didn't react in kind and the next voice I heard was Vella's.

'André? What's up?'

'You don't need to assemble your troops. It's all going to be taken care of.'

An audible gasp, then 'Are you serious? The Brits are going to help us after all?'

A gust of wind stirred up a dust devil on the building site where a block of luxury apartments was to be constructed. Emblematic of Gibraltar's booming prosperity.

'No, that's not going to happen. But there'll be no invasion. Trust me on this.'

In the silence that came after I could hear him breathing, could sense the uncertainty.

'I wouldn't mislead you on something so important,' I insisted. 'Just go about your lives, you and Eduardo and Peter and the rest of Gibraltar. There'll be no invasion.'

'All right.' Reluctantly, heavily. 'We'll lie low. You had just better be right.'

'You trusted me before, trust me now,' I said curtly, and killed the call.

Chapter Thirty-One

The range from the first embrasure in the Great Siege Tunnels to the border post on Spain's side was just under eleven hundred metres as the bullet flies. From here I had the same outlook as the gunners of 1783 who had warded off another siege by the Spanish. My firepower was weaker but my range greater and my accuracy twenty times better. I couldn't expect to hold off an army; but I could cut off the brain, the figurehead, the inspiration, and leave the body directionless.

It was 4.30am. when I took up my position. The cab driver who conveyed me as far as the Moorish Castle, about a half kilometre from the entrance to the tunnels, was openly curious, even to the point of asking me what I was doing here when the castle was locked up and the ticket office not open for hours.

'It's a practical joke,' I told him. 'You'll read about it in the papers tomorrow.'

It was enough to allay any suspicions he might have harboured. He would read about me in the papers, I could guarantee that. He might even recognise my contribution to peace and the salvation of his homeland.

The false dawn was away across the still waters of the Mediterranean. No birds cheeped, not that many lived this high up the Rock, there being few trees to perch on. Breaking in was easy. I shot the lock with the VP70 Ribble had donated. A silencer would have been useful but it's surprising how the noise of a pistol shot dissipates in the open air.

Inside the tunnel the lighting was off, so I used my flashlight. I had the tunnel to myself, if you didn't count the effigies of gunners and engineers from three centuries ago. If they'd been real they would have approved, that much was certain.

The first chamber was occupied by an artillery piece and two troopers, one in blue with sergeant's stripes, the other red and kilted. Being made from wood or alabaster, they took no interest in me as I straddled the metal fence that enclosed the chamber. Even so, it was their home, and I hailed them with a friendly 'Good morning' plus apologies for the intrusion.

By the light of a flashlight I joined up the pieces of the rifle – barrelled receiver, bolt, trigger unit, fore-end, base rail, steel-aluminum-polyurethane folding stock. Then the appendages – sight, bipod, loaded magazine, every .338 round examined for defects. Making sure the safety lever inside the trigger guard was on by gripping it between finger and thumb and thumb and tweaking it backwards.

As zero hour drew near I was ready with the gun propped on the lower lip of the embrasure, the border post in my sight. Missing was unthinkable. My aim would be true, the gun was an impeccably engineered piece of equipment and my confidence in it absolute. The embrasure, roughly semi-circular, was barred to discourage people who thought they could fly. Between the bars there was plenty of space for me to insert the barrel. I decided the bipod was unnecessary. Resting the fore-end of the gun on the bottom rim of the embrasure would give me adequate stability.

The false dawn became true as the hour finger of my watch moved towards five and the minute hand towards twelve. Down at the border all was calm and as normal. A small van, headlights still on, was pulling up there and a Spanish guard left his office to inspect the vehicle; the driver alighted to open the rear doors.

I swigged from the bottle of Evian water, one of a pack of three I had brought, along with some fruit and a bar of chocolate. The waiting game was part of the kill. I wasn't impatient, or on edge, or in a hurry to get it over with. This was routine stuff to me.

Thirty minutes later puzzlement was creeping in, displacing the equanimity. Dawn was well and truly here, the tip of the sun's disc diffusing a pink aura over the horizon, tinting the sea. More cars, some pedestrians were traversing the border, mostly Spanish workers employed in Gib. Just a morning like any other morning.

By 6.00am. I was pacing the floor, physically and mentally. Puzzlement had been superseded by perplexity. Military manoeuvres worked to strict timetables. Not only that, but the later an attack, the less the chance of achieving surprise.

The sun was slanting through the embrasure, lighting up my two uniformed co-habitants. I alternated pacing with checking out the border for tanks and thousands of Spanish infantrymen. If the invasion had been called off, so much the better. It saved me from the job of taking out General Irazola. Only problem was, I didn't believe it had been called off.

It was 8.25 and I was preparing to leave before the tunnels opened to the public, when an explanation hit me. Irazola had hoped to kill me when he authorised the shooting down of the helicopter. But he couldn't be sure he had succeeded. If he had undercover agents stationed in Gib, which was highly likely, they would have reported my survival. And if I survived, I would have relayed his invasion plans to the Governor.

Moving that premise forward, he wouldn't have called it off, merely delayed it while he prepared a new plan. His agents would have reported no defensive preparations had been taken. If that was still the situation, say, two or three days from now, he could safely assume that the British and Gibraltar governments were either supine or had simply dismissed the notion of an invasion as fantastical.

Which still left me with the means and the will to put a stop to it, but no knowledge of the date and hour. Breaking into the tunnels every night until Irazola made his move was not the most practical proposition.

Meanwhile, I took the rifle apart, stuffed it in my backpack. The few inches of barrel that protruded from the top, I camouflaged with a strip of bubble wrap bought for that purpose. With no means of getting back to the hotel by road I made for the cable car. The occasional vehicle passed me, but I kept my thumb retracted. I was just a backpacker out for a stroll.

Then my cell phone chirped. It was a short sweet call from the Governor's secretary, ordering me to report to his office right away. The reason my presence was required was easy to guess. A dressing down for my alarmism over an invasion-that-didn't happen.

I almost didn't go. My credibility had been trashed by Irazola's failure to turn up at the head of his divisions. They might even arrest me for disturbing the peace.

The larger of my two suitcases at the Caleta Hotel would just about accommodate the rifle barrel wedged diagonally from corner to corner. The rest of the weapon easily fitted in the smaller case. Both cases had combination locks, and that was about as secure as I could make them. I stowed them back in the closet. The room reminded me too much of Linda so I left as soon as I was done, without even bothering to change from my sniper's outfit of black jeans and T-shirt, with sneakers.

The reason for the summons turned out to be unconnected with my warnings, but very connected with the invasion threat. Sir Gilbert was in his usual office, in the company of several people in civilian clothes and a high-ranking British army officer, introduced as Brigadier Hemingway-Towns. Oh, and Toby, looking severe. They were seated around an oval conference table. As I entered they looked me up and down sniffily, not impressed by my mode of attire.

I was presented as 'Mr Warner'. No first name.

'Sit down, Warner,' the Governor said.

The only empty chair was between Toby, my only possible ally, and a pinstriped clone. I sat in it.

'About the invasion –' I began.

'Hold on, André.' This from Toby, a restraining hand on my arm. 'There's been a new development. A certain Comandante Navarro contacted us last night, on behalf of your General Irazola. The big man himself has asked to meet up with the Governor, here on the Rock.'

Although stunned by this piece of news, my mind immediately started sifting through the opportunities this would create.

'Great. Arrest him.'

All present goggled in varying degrees.

'Arrest him?' the Brigadier boomed. He was a big man all over, and his uniform jacket a shade too small. 'On what grounds, pray?'

'On the grounds of plotting to invade Gibraltar.'

Now all present groaned.

'He is coming here,' the Governor said, in slow and measured tones, 'precisely to refute the rumours of an invasion that have been circulating. And to give us his absolute guarantee that no invasion is being planned or will take place.'

'What a relief,' I said without attempting to mask the sarcasm. 'Now we can all sleep peacefully at night.'

'André …' Toby's unspoken warning made no impression. In any case, I was done with the Governor, the British government, and the British army. My solution was the only solution and I now knew how to apply it.

'Goodbye, gentlemen,' I said, getting up. 'In a manner of speaking, you are all absolutely right – there will be no invasion. But it won't be for the reasons you think.'

My piece thus said, I took my leave and went to retrieve the rifle from my hotel room.

* * * * *

Because of the gun, I couldn't cross the border by car or on foot. I took a cab to the marina, complete with suitcases. On board I transferred the rifle parts back to my backpack, disguising the barrel as before. Then I retraced my wake to the marina at La Línea. A wad of euros changed hands and secured me a berth for twenty-four hours. More euros, from the cache of cash I kept on board, went into my pocket. The Aston was where I had left it, unmarked and unbroken into. I loaded the rifle in its box as supplied by Keith Jupp into the trunk and drove into town in search of a book store, where I bought a map and a child's ruler. Next I drove to the edge of town, where a motorcycle dealer called Motomocion was based. I parked the Aston a couple of streets away. Shouldered my backpack and went to visit the dealer.

It was only a small outfit and I found myself negotiating with the owner, a Señor Ramirez. From his selection of used bikes I went for a five-year old Kawasaki that was overpriced but in good shape. Reliability being more valuable to me than euros, I took it for a spin around the block, leaving the Aston keys as security.

We agreed a price. So far, so satisfactory. Then I discovered that buying the machine was the easy part. To be able to drive it away I needed to go through the new owner registration process.

'*Muy bien*,' I said. 'Let's get on with it.'

'*Lo siento, Señor, no es posible hasta mañana*.'

Why it wasn't possible until tomorrow didn't interest me. I spread ten hundred-euro bills on the laminated top of his counter.

'Is it still not possible?'

Apparently even money couldn't buy the necessary re-registration, but it could buy the turning of a blind eye. For a thousand euros he would stick trade plates on the bike, and I could ride off to my destiny. That old talking money thing again.

At 1.20pm. I set off for the hills and the encampment of General Irazola and his thirty thousand men.

* * * * *

Scrub and bushes screened me from the bustling encampment below. From my elevated position I could make out the details of tanks, trucks, and field guns. There were many comings and goings, vehicles kicking up dust, and general hubbub. No airborne patrols, for which I was grateful, though several helicopters stood around.

The map and the ruler enabled me to calculate my approximate distance from the camp. Over eight hundred and less than nine hundred meters. For the purpose of setting the optics of the telescopic sight it was accurate enough.

Close to the lake a long, low dais, like a stage had been set up since my last viewing. A microphone on a stand stood in the centre; a soldier was tinkering with it, a toolbox at his feet. Aside from the mike and the soldier, the dais was bare.

The sun was high in the heavens and the air was motionless. The gorse bush in whose shadow I lay didn't create much shade, so I roasted gently and sipped sparingly from my water supply. Two jeeps were parked on the trail at opposite ends of the camp, each occupied by two troopers. They would be on patrol duty, keeping the camp and its approaches clear of intruders. My bike was a few feet behind me, as good as invisible in the undergrowth.

At some point during the afternoon, despite my best efforts, I dozed off, eventually coming awake to a bugle's refrain. My watch told me it was five minutes before five o'clock. Twelve hours that seemed like twelve days since the invasion that never was. The back of my neck was sunburned and sore. Down in the camp all was hustle and bustle, with troops assembling *en masse* in front of the dais. Seeing them all together like that brought home to me the sheer numbers under Irazola's command. They would steamroller over any opposition Gibraltar could drum up. The outcome was not in doubt.

Through a gap in the ranks a line of men in single file approached the dias, like a boxer and his seconds on their way to the ring. Through the rifle scope I counted eleven, with the erect figure of Irazola in the lead. All but one of the other ten wore the braided peaked caps of general rank. My guess, given the numbers of troops, was a major-general for each of the three divisions, six brigade-generals for the six brigades, and a lesser rank, bringing up the rear. I focused on him and brought the face of Comandante Navarro, the General's *aide de camp*, up close and personal.

The eleven mounted the dais by a short flight of wooden steps and took up position, side by side, Irazola centre stage behind the mike. The men had fallen silent amid an air of expectation of an announcement that was going to change lives. Movement in the undergrowth behind me, hopefully not a snake. A small bird with blue and gold feathers landed on a branch of my bush, only to rebound into the air immediately, tweeting alarm or annoyance at my presence, or maybe just happy to be alive and on the wing.

If Irazola was intent on being assassinated he couldn't have made it easier for me. He stood there, fists on hips, back straight as a plank, and at exactly five o'clock began to address his men.

'Soldiers of the Republic,' was his opening line, his voice clearly audible to me, reverberating across the valley. 'Tomorrow will be a day to remember for Spain and for the memory of General Francisco Franco, our great leader to whom I dedicate the action that will follow.

'You will all have been wondering why we are here, in this place, training for what is obviously a seize and hold operation. You will have heard different rumours. Always there are rumours. Sometime they are even right.' He laughed into the mike and taking their cue from him the congregated troopers laughed too. 'Well, I am here to dispel those rumours and turn them into facts.' He paused, his head swivelling from left to right as he surveyed his forces. 'Tomorrow morning, fellow soldiers, at zero five hundred we will cross the border into Gibraltar and annex the peninsula to Spain.'

The collective gasp suggested that the rumours, if they were accurate, had been discounted, that few of the thirty thousand had believed them. Then a single cheer broke the thrall, was joined by a second, then a third, then the whole vast body of men was cheering, flinging their berets in the air, many of them jumping up and down in delight.

The General let them off the leash for a minute or two before restoring order. I was impressed by the display of emotion. Returning Gib to Spain was a popular decision.

'We do not expect any resistance,' the General asserted with conviction. 'The British were warned but we persuaded them that the warnings were false, and they have made no preparations to defend themselves. However, if there should be resistance, it will be dealt with according to the rules of war and the Geneva convention.'

Big of him. A largely unarmed population was going to get fair treatment. I clipped the loaded magazine in place. I worked the bolt and shunted a round into the breech. With the lake behind him and the blue skies up above, it was a dramatic setting for the General's last rites.

* * * * *

Two rings was all it had taken to get her to the phone.

'Hello … André?' Husky, breathless.

'Who else?' Actually it could have been lots of people probably, particularly guys. She didn't encourage male admirers, just attracted them by her classy good looks, her character, and her subtle sexy aura.

'I love you,' she said, her usual opening gambit.

'I love you too, sweetheart,' I said, my usual comeback.

'What are you doing?'

'Right now? Talking to my sweetheart, wishing she was here or I was there. How's my other sweetheart?'

My other sweetheart was Maura's daughter, Lindy, ten years old, a gorgeous blonde version of her mother and bright with it.

'At school. She's due home soon so if we talk long enough you'll be able to chat with her. She still goes on about you all the time.'

That touched the sentimental side of me. While I was absorbing it, Maura went on, 'I didn't mean what are you doing right now, darling, I meant with your life.'

Our conversations always led back to that. My life. The taking of other lives, worthless though they generally were. Stop the killing and Maura would be mine again. If only they would let me, had been my constant refrain. Now, finally, they had let me, for a whole year.

On this occasion it wasn't them at all. It was me, just me, and me alone. The imminent decision to kill would be on my head alone. It might avert conflict, even full scale war, and if Maura didn't exist, I would have no qualms about going through with it. Certainly it wouldn't trouble my conscience. Irazola was a soldier, he was about to invade another country. People, including innocent people, could die. If I could prevent it, it was my duty to do so.

Three choices were open to me. Let him invade Gib, leaving me to get on with my life, of which Maura would hopefully become a part. Or kill him and keep it to myself, which would mean lying to Maura. Or kill him and tell her, which would likely mean the final end of us as a couple.

The dot recticle was positioned on Irazola's forehead, though I hadn't yet decided where to hit him: head or chest. A chest shot would be more certain but somehow less satisfying. It was a choice that faced all assassins when shooting at long range. The head was smaller but more instantaneous. The chest was easier to hit, but two shots would be needed to ensure a fatal outcome.

The midday sun was giving the back of my neck a beating. Visions of Maura and memories of that phone call from a week ago were receding into the background, crowded out by more immediate challenges. I was once more the consummate pro, the human killing machine that could be relied on to deliver.

As Irazola wound up his address with a rousing '*Viva* España! *Viva la republica*!' the massed ranks responded by chanting 'Ir-a-zo-la, Ir-a-zo-la …' over and over. Irazola, the new Franco, saluted them, true Fascist style. The revered leader of thirty thousand men, sworn to restore Gibraltar to its rightful owners. And if blood must be shed to make it happen, he was the man to shed it. The cause was just, the methods a necessary evil.

As I stroked the trigger Maura's image returned to superimpose itself over that of General Irazola. I hesitated for a couple of beats only. This thing was bigger than the thing between Maura and me.

I squeezed the trigger, an act so natural to me it required neither thought nor effort.

The stab of flame from the muzzle and the sharp report as the small calibre bullet sped on its way, were unseen and unheard by the uniformed mass who witnessed the result. A red bubble popped up in the centre of Irazola's forehead. For an extended moment he remained standing, his face set like a stone carving, his eyes still open. Then his legs buckled and he toppled in slow motion off the front of the dais onto the steps, where he came to rest, his right arm still flung out in a salute to his own demise.

That's from Elena, General. A goodbye kiss to her *padrastro*.

A great stillness descended on the gathering. Every man in the basin of the valley froze, became an army of waxworks. First to react was Navarro. He took an uncertain step towards his dead master. It was his last step on earth. I had made him a promise when he presided over that humiliating striptease the day Irazola's lackeys hauled me off the street. *I'll get you for this*. I let him have it in the chest. One-two and down he went. Easy. Satisfying.

Reaction was belatedly setting in among the throng. The brass on the dais converged on Irazola, the troopers began to surge backwards, instinctively distancing themselves from the target zone. Two of the generals stooped over their Commander-in-Chief. I worked the bolt, took out one, then the other, emptying the magazine. Changing magazines was a two-second job. The other generals, belatedly coming aware that they too were targets, leapt off the dais on the lake side. One of them stumbled and I finished him. Even when the surviving generals mingled with the troopers they were easy to identify by the gold braid on the peaks of their caps and their red lapel tabs. They went down, one after another, as they milled about in panic, like chickens with a fox in the coop. The second magazine emptied. I reminded myself that the men down there were a disciplined force, who would be quick to recover and organise a counter-attack. Already troopers to the rear, closest to me, were fanning out into the scrub, preparing to hunt me down. Any delay in quitting the scene would give them

I abandoned the rifle and its accessories, keeping only the Ribble-supplied VP-70 for self-defence. The line of bushes formed a screen between me and the troops as I scuttled to where the bike lay under its concealing foliage. I dragged the foliage off, and mounted up. Prayed the engine wouldn't let me down. My prayers were answered.

It wasn't until I emerged from the scrub, already travelling at fifty kph, that I was spotted. A great roar went up, followed by a ragged fusillade of shots. But the range was extreme and I was bent low over the bike's tank, making a small target, weaving frantically over the rough ground.

The dirt track came up and I hit it at a forty-five degree angle. I opened the throttle and the bike responded, thrusting me from fifty to a hundred in seconds and almost dumping me in the road. One of the patrolling jeeps was on the track ahead of me, seemingly oblivious of the furore down at the lake. I veered away from the track and the jeep carried on with no change of course.

The gunfire dwindled to nothing. I reckoned they would need a minimum of ten minutes to get a chopper in the air and another five for the chopper to catch up with me. By then I would be back in La Línea, the bike abandoned in a side street, and me just another visiting tourist among hundreds of the species.

Chapter Thirty-Two

The morning after I stopped an invasion single-handed I breakfasted on the terrace with Toby. It was in the nature of a farewell meal, as he was due on the daily flight to Gatwick later in the day. No news had seeped through about the events at the lake. The Spanish papers were mute on the subject.

We chatted about nothing of substance while we ate – bacon, scrambled eggs, sausages et al. Only when the coffees had been served did he venture to talk "shop".

'It's been a frustrating business,' he said, tapping the rim of his cup with a teaspoon. 'You did some excellent work, but ultimately results are what count.'

Knowing what I knew that he didn't know, it rankled that my efforts were so readily written off.

'You had Vella on toast, after I planted the nitro in his fridge,' I reminded him. 'The police let him go.'

He bridled. 'They could hardly do otherwise when that Pilchard chap confessed.'

'If you and they were going to respect the rules of habeas corpus and the rest you should never have hired me in the first place.'

A cloud moved aside for the sun, which flooded onto the terrace in full force. Toby shielded his eyes and switched from tapping his cup to drumming on the table.

'You won't be paid, you know. Unless ...' He nibbled at his underlip.

'What's the unless? Technically, you don't owe me anything outside my expenses. I didn't deliver on my brief.'

'The unless is, you could still earn it if you're interested.'

A waitress with an exceptionally large bottom passed by. Toby caught my eye, and we exchanged grins, as guys do.

'Yes,' he said, when I didn't respond. 'You could still collect your million if you've a mind to.'

I exaggerated a yawn. 'Get to the point, Toby. I'm kind of tired of working for the British Government, but I wouldn't say no to the million, if you don't expect too much in return.'

He crossed his legs, fastidiously arranging his pants so that the crease lay dead centre of his knee.

'First, let me ask you a question. Why do you think we especially selected you for the job?'

'You told me. Independent, available, previous track record…' I was checking them off finger by finger when a mocking gleam in his eyes pulled me up.

'Well, of course these were useful attributes for the job in hand,' he said with a vague smirk, 'but hardly unique to you. What we really needed above all was insurance.'

I blinked. 'Insurance?'

'In case you failed in your primary objective of bringing GIBESTÁ crashing down, dear boy. As a last resort we needed someone who could – how do you chaps say it? – burn Michael Vella.'

Burn Michael Vella.

The meaning was clear but slow to infiltrate. I had accepted the job on the understanding that they weren't asking me to kill anybody though, come to think of it, Toby had never said as much. It seemed like I had been kidding myself all along.

'Is that what you're now asking me to do?' I said at last.

He nodded. 'Right up your street, I would have thought. Easier than trying to stop a revolution, at any rate.'

Toby's analysis couldn't be faulted. As he put it, GIBESTÁ, even if the invasion was off, was still active, still a threat to Gibraltar and the British connection. Chop off the head and the body would wither. No different from my *casus belli* to justify my private declaration of war against Irazola.

'I've no quarrel with your reasoning,' I said, after I had gotten used to the effrontery of his proposition. 'It's your being so reticent about what you really expected from me that bugs me just a little.'

He went to work on me then with all guns blazing. All the reasons why GIBESTÁ had to be crushed, including the danger that independence would weaken the Rock and Britain's stake in it, tempt Spain to renew its efforts to establish overlordship, and put the Mediterranean at risk of Russian naval incursions. It was inevitable that the postponed talks on the future of the territory would be revived and their outcome was as uncertain as ever.

As he talked in his forceful yet beguiling style, the arguments in favour of eliminating Michael Vella were bolstered by my new-found personal hostility towards him. Yes, Michael Vella, was the man who had saved my life, but also the man who had stolen Linda from me and not even had the moral courage to own up until he was caught out. The loss of Linda I could bear. If Vella had been a stranger I would have let it go. It was the betrayal by him more than the cheating by her that really hurt.

So why not accept the contract? Avenge myself, do right by Gibraltar, and earn a million pounds in the doing. A win-win-win situation.

Whether he talked me into it, or I talked myself into it, I agreed to do it. Maybe, in my confused state, my loyalties torn between Vella and the British Government, torn anew by the Vella's betrayal of me with Linda, I was incapable of making an objective decision. Nor of considering how I could bring myself to kill Michael Vella in breach of my private code that forbade me from killing the innocent.

'Tell Ribble I need a sound suppressor for an H and K VP-70,' I said.

* * * * *

He was home. When he answered my phone call I cut him off without announcing myself. I collected the Aston from the Caleta parking lot and made it to his apartment in twenty minutes. It was sunny, with a balmy breeze from the east to take the edge off the heat.

Vella answered the door in person. Even beamed at me, as if I were a long-lost brother back from adventures in darkest Africa.

'Come in, André, come in.' He shook my hand as I entered, his grip firm and oh, so sincere. 'It seems you were right, they didn't invade after all. What went wrong?'

He led me across the entrance hall to the living room with its gloomy wallcovering, low seating, and extensive mahogany carpentry. The sliding French window that extended the length of a wall was half open, admitting the coos of pigeons and the cheery chatter of children at play in the park opposite.

I glanced around for Linda. Thankfully she was absent.

'Linda's in the shower,' he told me. 'Let me get you a drink. We can celebrate.'

Better to get it over with right away, before she joined us and became a witness. Better too she didn't know it was me who did it.

Too late. I was in the act reaching behind me for the VP-70 when the door to the bathroom opened and she emerged, wrapped in a blue bath towel, her hair damp and spiky.

'Hi, Warner,' she said cheerfully, not at all self-conscious over her state of undress. But then I had seen all it all before.

She came up to me, planted a kiss on my cheek. Her hair smelled of shampoo. It was a familiar smell, too readily recalled.

'Still sore at me?'

I grinned obliquely. 'I'm getting over it.'

Vella cleared his throat, looking flustered. 'What about that drink?'

'Sure. Too early for hard stuff. Tonic water will be fine, with ice if you have it.'

Linda dragged me to the nearest couch and pressed me down onto it. With the VP-70, over a foot long with the sound suppressor fitted, down the back of my pants, sitting in a low seat was bordering on painful.

'It's good to see you, you know. Even as a friend.' Her face clouded. 'We are friends, aren't we?'

'Best of.'

Vella looked pleased and crossed the room to the drinks cabinet.

'The invasion didn't happen,' Linda said, sitting beside me, hugging the damp towel to her.

'Correct. It's off for good.'

We chatted on about inconsequential stuff until Vella returned with my tonic and a juice of some kind for Linda.

'Tell us what happened. You called me and predicted it wouldn't happen. Did you manage to prevent it somehow? You personally, I mean.'

I nodded. 'Somehow.'

His brows converged. 'Don't you want to tell us about it?'

'Best you don't know. Just be happy about the outcome.'

As I sat there in some discomfort in his living room, with its views across the bay to Algeciras and the hills beyond, it dawned on me that to kill him meant killing Linda too. Even with the protection of Toby's crowd, if I left her alive as a witness I would never get out Gib. It even crossed my mind that Linda's removal might well be part of Toby's grand scheme. Devious thinking, but then it was a devious business I had gotten myself mixed up in.

Vella had served himself a glass of water. He came and stood facing Linda and me, fingering the wart that punctuated the end of his moustache.

'Will you go on with your independence movement?' I asked him.

'Certainly. You've bought us a reprieve, we need to make use of it. The British government has proved it can't be relied on any more.'

Toby was not being alarmist with his predications about GIBESTÁ after all. The quest for independence would continue. It was driven by emotion, like Brexit. It was easy to imagine it precipitating a Spanish takeover, especially if the Brits did a Pilate and opted out.

It was all down to me then. The man who saved the Rock. I groped behind for the VP-70, jerked it free of my waistband and out into the open, sound suppressor and all.

Vella stiffened; Linda expelled a cry of fear, sliding along the couch, away from me.

'They just hired me to kill you, Michael. You're a nuisance, an embarrassment, an obstacle to peace and goodwill in Gibraltar. They want you out of the way.'

His jaw dropped.

'They've ordered you to *assassinate* me?'

'Happens all the time. Even in so-called civilised countries.' I pointed the gun at him. He flinched, but his jaw jutted in defiance. He wasn't about to beg for his life.

The safety was on. I stroked it with my thumb.

'You're a good man, Michael Vella. But you've made enemies in high places and they're not going to give you carte blanche to do your revolutionary thing.'

'If you kill him, you'll have to kill me,' Linda said, stumbling a little over the words. 'Won't you?'

My shrug spoke louder than an admission.

Without getting up, Linda reached for Vella's hand. It hurt to watch that demonstration of solidarity. Hurt, but not badly enough for me to put a bullet in him, and especially not in Linda.

'Bang,' I said, with a sardonic chuckle deep in my throat. 'You're dead.'

They stared at me, nonplussed, disbelief written in their expressions.

I reversed my grip on the gun, proffered it to Vella. 'Better take this. You might need it one dark night.'

With patent reluctance he accepted the gun from me, holding it gingerly as if he expected it to explode in his face.

'You mean …'

'I mean assassins are plentiful if the price is right. Dead, you're worth a million sterling to them –'

Linda's reaction was a shocked 'A million!'.

Vella sat down abruptly on the couch behind him.

'They're prepared to pay you a million pounds to kill me?' His voice was unsteady.

'That's right.'

'And you're prepared to give up that much money and let me live.'

'That's right too.'

I gulped down my tonic and vacated the couch. Vella and I clasped hands without speaking. Linda was gazing up at me, her lips slightly parted, her eyes wide and slightly moist. I mimed a kissing motion at her with my mouth.

'Some causes matter more than money.'

No goodbyes were said. None were needed. Outside, the sky was end-to- end blue, the breeze still balmy, and the smell of ozone elusive in the nostrils. It was almost a good day to be alive. For a decade and a half I had trodden a dirty trail through a dirty underworld, but on this day at least I felt clean again.

END

Also by

Lex Lander

and available from Amazon

Don't miss the next instalment of the André Warner saga

CONTRACT IMPOSSIBLE

André Warner, Manhunter Vol VI

Publishing early 2020 in eBook and paperback format

Printed in Great Britain
by Amazon

82713550R00208